A VIOLENT MAN

Copyright © first published 28th March 2013

Text copyright © Michael J Siddall 2013

Cover Art copyright © Elijah Siddall 2025

Proofreaders: Elijah Siddall.

All rights reserved

The moral right of the author and illustrator have been asserted.

ISBN 9781463705756

PUBLISHED 2013 BY M&E&B BOOKS LTD

<u>Condition of sale</u>

No part of this book may be reproduced, or stored in a retrieval system, or transmitted in any form or by any means, electronic, mechanical, photocopying, recording or otherwise, without express written permission of the publisher.

This book is sold subject to the condition that it shall not, by way of trade or otherwise, be lent, resold, *hired out or otherwise circulated without the author's prior written consent in any form of binding or cover other than that in which it is published and without a similar condition including this condition being imposed on the subsequent purchaser.*

This book is a work of fiction. Names, characters, places and incidents are either products of the author's imagination or are used fictitiously. Any resemblance to actual events or locations or persons living or dead is entirely coincidental.

CHAPTER 1 … *DUEL TO THE DEATH*
CHAPTER 2 … *ROADTRIP*
CHAPTER 3 … *HOT GYPSY BLOOD*
CHAPTER 4 …. *AS GOOD AS DEAD*
CHAPTER 5 … *THE DEBT*
CHAPTER 6 … *DESOLATION AND DESTRUCTION*
CHAPTER 7 … *BEG FOR YOUR LIFE*
CHAPTER 8 … *NO IDLE BOAST*
CHAPTER 9 … *A MURDERED FRIEND*
CHAPTER 10 … *THE VISITOR*
CHAPTER 11 … *THE WARRIOR RETURNS*
CHAPTER 12 … *TOUGH AS AN IRON NAIL*
CHAPTER 13 … *THE HUNTER*
CHAPTER 14 … *NO PAST LIFE*
CHAPTER 15 … *DEATH OF A GOOD MAN*
CHAPTER 16 … *THE TRAP*

CHAPTER 17 ... *AWEFUL VISIONS*

CHAPTER 18 ... *A CURSE OR A GODSEND*

CHAPTER 19 ... *PURE INNOCENCE*

CHAPTER 20 ... *FORCE OF NATURE*

CHAPTER 21 ... *KILLER ON THE LOOSE*

CHAPTER 22 ... *SEEDS OF DESTRUCTION*

CHAPTER ONE

Duel to the death

It was midnight when the rain of boiling oil and arrows ceased. Horrific screams of the dying rang in the air, and broken bodies littered the battlefield, many cut in half, others mutilated beyond recognition. There was blood everywhere, staining the earth crimson. Thomas Flynn sat astride his white stallion waiting. His steed looked ominous. Ghostly even, draped from head to hoof in black cloth, studded with silver and surrounded by murky trailers of mist. With a writhing stare, he waited, his dark eyes scanning the battlements of Alnwick Castle, searching for his deranged brother Malcolm.

In his early days, Thomas was a common street fighter, rough and ready. A man always on the edge. Now he was a seasoned swordsman with style and nimbleness of foot. This he thought was because of his hot gipsy blood.

He had, he believed, inherited his handsome features from his beautiful mother, a capable, outspoken woman, though she turned to prostitution to keep food on the table when his father went off to sea. He also said his short temper came from his drunken father, whose death by hanging at an early age shocked no one. His parents were less than affectionate and strict. Even as a tiny child, they made him sit upright at the table and he must not touch the back of his chair. If he did, his father, a man of wilful and forceful character, thrashed him with a leather belt.

He didn't remember him; save for the single memory of his mother's final beating. She had died screaming, bloodied and battered by his father. And even now as a young man, the screams rang in his ears, filling his dreams at night, torturing him. Eighteen years of his life passed in the blink of an eye. Now he was older, wiser, and ready to take back what was his from his evil brother.

A cold wind whispered across the land as Thomas stepped down from the saddle, tethering his horse to a post. He climbed the stone steps of the south wall up to where Malcolm was waiting for him. An eye-patch covered Malcolm's scarred left eye, his dark hair looked ragged, and he wore the same clothes as Thomas, a black and gold tunic, matching leggings and calf-length boots.

Alnwick Castle stood out like a sore thumb on the plains of Northumberland with its sky-towering parapets, but it was a castle of ghosts. "I've no experience of sieges, only of battles and killing," said Thomas in a husky whisper.

Bright moonlight flooded the walls in slanting shafts and Malcolm smiled. "Today you will have a new experience, death. For I am deadly beyond your imaginings and will slice you in half with a single cut."

Outside the castle walls, ten thousand battle-hardened warriors waited, armed with every imaginable siege-engine of destruction. Dark, powerful horses pulled catapults along, ready to smash the walls, battering rams to breach the gates, and trebuchets to fire flaming coal oil over the enemy, killing many. Dust drifted high into the night air.

Behind the army, another force of five thousand reserves stood ready, camped in tents with flags flying and banners bright and polished. They longed for the cry of battle and the chance to settle their differences with a single duel to the death between the two brothers.

Thomas wiped the sweat from his face. He drew both short-swords, striding forward. "The devil and hell's dark abyss comes for you Malcolm, and both are filled with a terrifying blackness."

His brother smiled, unblinking and unafraid, a steely glint in his eyes. "I think not. Not this day." He drew his serrated broadsword.

"It's the best time of day for a duel. It's quiet and our warriors will hear your screams," said Thomas.

Malcolm shook his head in a slow controlled fashion, fixing his brother's gaze. "I remember the joy of fighting you when we were adolescents, with fists, feet or weapons and treasure the memories that I never once lost a fight because of my many more hours of training."

Thomas leapt forward, one of his swords slashing from left to right, aiming for Malcolm's neck. "An artist may spend years fashioning a work of greatness, but a single mistake will ruin the whole thing."

Malcolm dropped to one knee, his brother's blade slicing air above him. "I don't make mistakes," he whispered, his own sword licking out to nick the bicep of the other.

A flash of crimson bloomed on sweaty skin. Off-balance Thomas stumbled, falling, tearing the shoulder of his tunic. He climbed back to his feet.

Malcolm rose from his knee, leaning forward, thrusting his blade at the other's chest who parried it, tumbling again to the cobbled stone, hitting his head hard. Malcolm smiled, recalling their first-ever fight with blades. *A massacre at the least,* he thought, *but then Thomas was always a slow learner.*

Thomas rolled to his knees, rose and advanced again. He leapt forward, one of his swords slicing from right to left, aiming at Malcolm's exposed stomach. His brother arched backwards, his own sword shooting out to nick Thomas' other bicep. Another flash of crimson bloomed on his skin beneath the tunic.

Malcolm hawked and spat. He grinned, holding to Thomas' incensed gaze. "You're not doing too well, are you, brother?"

Thomas touched the deep wound. "Son-of-a-whore."

Malcolm nodded. "You should know. We had the same mother. Father said she was a devil-possessed and thrashed the demon from her often."

Their mother had been a whore and beaten to death by their father while in a drunken stupor. An angry mob dragged him screaming to the gallows, hanging him without trial afterwards. Thomas and Malcolm, aged five, watched both events wide-eyed in horror, unable to look away. Then the local sheriff hauled them off into the freezing night, taking them to Alnwick Castle, where they stayed for the next twelve years under the watchful eye of baron Sedgwick and milady Ann, both of whom thrashed them daily after abusing them in front of each other. That was when their living nightmare began.

Incensed by the remarks, Thomas launched a sudden attack, catching Malcolm by surprise. Before he could react, Thomas' right hand lifted, a sword slashing downwards. Terrible pain exploded in his brother's body and his sword fell from his hand. Malcolm stared at the blade embedded in his chest and an agonised groan burst from his lips as acid fire filled him. He fell to his knees, but the sword held him upright.

"You thought me an easy kill brother, but heart and determination can conquer any obstacle," said Thomas, driving the blade deeper. The body toppled to his left. He dragged the blade clear, sheathing both swords, lifting his brother's still body to his chest. No emotion showed on his face. He turned to Malcolm's stunned, silent men. "It's over," he shouted with madness in his fever-bright eyes. "Take the body, burn it and tomorrow at sunrise there'll be a reckoning."

A soldier bowed, rose, and swirled his red cloak around his shoulders. He took the body from Thomas, hefting it over his shoulder, marching down the steps of the south wall towards an awaiting carriage, crafted in mahogany and gold. Another soldier moved to the carriage door, wrenching it open, pulling on the three steps. Taking hold of the door frame the soldier carrying Malcolm's body pulled hard on it and climbed into the carriage, closing the door behind him. He rapped on the hatch and the carriage took off, travelling up the street away from the castle. Thomas watched from the battlements, listening to the clip-clop of hooves and the iron-shod wheels rattling over the cobbles. An icy wind whispered over the great walls, lifting his long braided hair from his shoulders and he shivered, his eyes following the carriage until it was out of sight.

At sunrise the next morning, there was a public gathering in Gallows Square. Thomas offered Malcolm's soldiers the choice of joining his forces or a hanging. Skilled, intelligent men of great bravery, they hailed their new commander and chanted his name except for ten men.

Thomas' men grabbed their arms, tied their hands behind their backs and hauled them towards the scaffold, and as each man reached the steps and struggled, the hangman leaned forward and smote them hard on the back of their heads with a wooden cudgel. Then, one by one, his men dragged them up the ten steps and placed a noose over their heads, tightening them around their necks. They sobbed and soiled their hose awaiting execution. The trapdoor gave way beneath them. They dropped into the darkness of the shadows, kicking and thrashing. Thomas watched them die as one of his soldiers approached him.

"I don't understand why they chose death instead of following you, milord," said the soldier.

Thomas turned, staring hard at the man. "They died because they understood what loyalty is, even unto death."

***

Over the next ten years, Thomas' world shrank to a grimy, fireless room above a noisy tavern in London, where he mourned his brother's death. And with no more problems to solve or battles to win he had become a wandering drunkard, leaving his old life behind, but if he were honest and told the truth he missed it, even though his childhood nightmares of abuse still haunted him. So he drank gin when alone to numb his senses.

Summer had ended now and a harsh wind whispered across England. Henry III sat on the throne holding the reins of power at the tender age of nineteen in 1226 A.D., and Thomas was a handsome man with strength and size who looked bigger and more powerful than he was, primitive maybe? Aged twenty-eight, he was a good-natured man of modest means who bore many, many scars that sent his body into painful spasms on cold winter nights.

There was a knock at Thomas' door. He ambled across the bare room and opened it, staring at a small, balding fat man who looked like an overstuffed chair. He scanned the rosy face, fixing the man's gaze. "What can I do for you?"

"Have you plans for this evening?" Forin asked.

Thomas shrugged, laughing, "Only the same plans I had for last evening, to stay in my room and get stinking drunk. But I'm a tad short in the coin department."

"Would you consider working for me as my doorman?" asked Forin passing him a goblet of mulled wine. "I'll pay you two silver coins each evening or three if you need to throw someone out."

"Can you wait while I check my almanack to see if they've invited me to court?" Thomas chuckled in his husky, light-hearted voice. He picked up his old, worn, black and gold doublet from the end of his pallet bed, putting it on, and picked up his double sword belt from the chair next to the door, looping it around his waist, fastening it. "Might as well get drunk downstairs then, instead of being alone upstairs." He closed the door behind him, following the innkeeper down the stairs into the tavern.

Golden lantern light glowed at the windows and a rush of welcome heat enveloped them both as Forin pushed the door open. There were log fires burning at either end of the long, oak-beamed, whitewashed bar and drunken rowdy customers cajoled each other with dirty jokes and fanciful stories. Thomas scanned the room, spotting a silver-bearded giant of a man in a corner with a young serving wench upon his knee. He eased his way through the mixed crowd of privateers and noblemen, smugglers, slavers, swindlers and cut-throats, smiling at a young whore who stared at him with open hostility because he passed her by without a second glance. He sat at a corner table, his back to the wall, and ordered meat and potato pie from Forin.

When the food arrived, the meat was tender, the gravy thick and rich. A musician appeared from a back room playing light and lilting dance music on a flute and then he sang. The atmosphere in the Lazy Rat was less than delightful, but fine wine flowed and the guests behaved themselves. An easy night's work for two silver pieces thought Thomas.

But as the evening wore on and wine flowed, the atmosphere became tense and customers argued and bickered amongst themselves. Thomas quelled two or three small incidents and ejected one raucous, rude lad. Then a group of noblemen rounded on the innkeeper, claiming his food tasted like horse dung. They demanded a refund. Thomas moved to the men, speaking to them, saying they were often funny but superficial and very pompous; settling them back down without incident. The night ended without trouble. And from that day forward, Thomas Flynn worked as a doorman at the Lazy Rat with his reputation growing like wine seeping from a cracked jug.

***

One hundred and sixty miles to the north, Cyrano, a tall man of sixty years with iron-grey locks of hair was opening the Dog and Duck; a black and grey building that reared up from the Nottinghamshire land like rotting teeth. Inside the inn, his grey-green eyes scanned the carnage. Among the broken cups, mugs, plates, tables and chairs were at least three dead bodies, the men killed in vicious knife fights. Tired of the bloodshed and hungry to move on he decided he needed help. But the only local man with a reputation for suppressing extreme violence, his friend, Vodas, was now too old.

"What shall I do?" he asked the serving wench cleaning the mess, his voice a quiver. "I love it here, but the customers are animals."

"It's sickening," she said, mopping the bloody floor.

He swore, dragging three corpses out into the courtyard one at a time. One man had died without a sound, but his bowels had opened. The stench had filled the inn. He looked upon the bloated corpses and thought how ugly death was, and with a surge of willpower shouted, "I won't quit. I won't give up, my livelihood is at stake." He swore an oath to find someone like his friend, Vodas, with a reputation for quelling violence: a soldier, a mercenary and a killer of men without a conscience. He left the corpses for the undertaker to collect.

After a further night of brawling and extreme brutality at the inn, he walked through stands of birch and oak the next morning in a lighter mood. Flowers were no longer in bloom, but he rested on a hillside while his men searched for someone with a reputation bold enough to discourage his violent customers. His men came to him that evening carrying the same name on their lips, but the man they spoke of was living and working in London.

He went to bed that night, waking early the next morning in the faint light of pre-dawn as bruise-purple thunderheads stacked up in the south-east. He drew a deep breath, feeling a cool breeze upon his skin. "Thank you, Lord, my men have keen ears and sharp eyes and I now know the name of my benefactor." He swung his legs from his bed and dressed, pulling on his dark grey leggings and a doublet of grey silk that matched his calf-length boots. He ran his fingers over his hair, shaved to the scalp to prevent lice, and a draught chilled him, so he threw his heavy grey coat over his shoulders.

Outside rain sheeted down and the distant rumble of thunder drummed out in the heavens. The sun was clearing the eastern hills, and the storm passed in seconds. He waited until the rain had stopped and strode from the inn to his grey bay gelding tethered nearby. Saddling the horse, he hooked a rucksack full of food over the pommel and stood for a moment before climbing into the saddle. Then he heeled the horse, riding out onto the open ground, giving the gelding his head and it thundered across the plains in a mile-eating gallop.

***

That night the London streets were quiet and deserted, except for prostitutes plying their trade, and tramps and down-and-outs slouched in the recesses of doorways. A bitter wind was blowing from the north as Thomas, hooded and cloaked walked through the winding alleyways and passages towards the Lazy Rat, coming into Gallows Square just as the moon hid behind a screen of clouds. Pausing, he shook his head, gazing at the single corpse hanging from the gibbet there. "A sign of the times," he said with a tone of sadness.

There was a crack like a whiplash. He jumped at the sound. Laughter echoed from the shadows as a man stepped forward, punching him hard in the face with a clenched fist. He dropped to his knees, bright lights shining before his eyes, a great buzzing in his ears.

The attacker hauled Thomas up the gallows steps by his collar with his right hand. The fingers of his left hand reached into the pocket of his old coat producing a small leather pouch. He shook it. "Hell's teeth man I thought you were tough. Not tough enough to stop me hanging you for the princely sum of twenty silver pieces."

Thomas choked. "Have we met before?" he asked, trying to rid himself of his dizziness.

The stranger shook his head. "No, sir."

Thomas rolled to his knees, his gaze unblinking, fastened on the man's hooded face. "May I enquire then as to our quarrel, sir?"

"You have made enemies these last months. Powerful men willing to pay for you to disappear." said the broad-shouldered young man lowering his hood, revealing his wild blond hair, green eyes and pockmarked features. "I'm Dardo, the one who will take your job and reputation at the Lazy Rat."

Thomas surged upright, a sword flashing into his hand, the point pricking the man's belly. "You're lucky not to be dead. Never say what you'll do. Just do it." His throat was dry, his heart hammering in his chest.

The young man's strong face trembled, and he blinked hard. "I'm not a killer and have no wish to take your life. I was trying to scare you off. That's what my employer told me to do."

Thomas looked into the man's eyes, seeing no hatred there. "Do you always do what you're told?"

Dardo nodded. "Yes, if I'm paid."

"What were you before you became an unsuccessful assassin?"

"A farm worker, working the fields caring for sheep and cattle. Not the most interesting or exciting job."

Thomas sheathed his sword. "Hence the broad shoulders. Okay, I'll let you live and keep your twenty silver pieces, but it will cost you."

"Cost me?" said Dardo looking confused.

Thomas rubbed his aching jaw. "You can buy me a meal and fine wine at my favourite inn on my only night off duty. I mean to enjoy it after our little skirmish. That's one hell of a punch you threw. It was like being hit with a brick wall."

Dardo smiled. "I floored you with a left hook. Works every time! And your offer is agreeable."

"Tell me, lad, are you any good with a sword or bow?"

"No, just my fists."

Thomas strode off with Dardo following. "Well then, I'll make it my task to teach you both."

***

Three days later, after an uneventful tiring journey, Cyrano dismounted his horse, tethering it to a hitching post. He entered the inn known as the Lazy Rat, making his way past a raucous crowd of revellers. His face pale and gaunt from his long ride, his eyes darted from side to side as he strode through the crowded room.

Through a great confusion of noise, he heard the smashing of crockery coming from a back room, and as drunken eyes rounded on the loud clatter, an iron hand gripped his throat, dragging him into a shadowed corner.

"Give me money you old bastard," whispered the filthy, gap-toothed robber, pushing his meaty face nose to nose. "You look too rich for your own good." He thrust a needle-sharp dagger up under Cyrano's chin, pricking the skin, drawing blood.

Cyrano coughed; eyes wide. "How... how much do you want?"

"My affections are not expensive to buy, so hand over your purse and we'll see how much you can afford," sneered the thief, hawking and spitting on the sawdust-covered floor.

Our world is full of robbers and murderers, and the one thing they have in common is a small imagination, thought Cyrano. He gasped, breathless with fear. "Just name your price."

"Hand over your purse old man or I'll slit your throat from ear to ear. Come on, I'll leave you with change."

Cyrano reached into his coat pocket, pulling out his purse and the robber snatched it.

A third man stepped forward from out of the shadows, grabbing the robbers knife hand, punching him hard in the face with a clenched fist that smashed his nose to a pulp. He dropped like a stone. "Earn an honest crust with hard work, perseverance and discipline, because you show no talent what-so-ever for thieving," snapped Thomas. His sarcasm escaped the thief; he was unconscious.

Cyrano dropped to his knees, hands steepled in front of his face, whimpering. "Oh, thank you for saving me, young man."

Thomas held out his hand to him, hauling him to his feet, leaving the robber where he lay. "You're my guest tonight, and I bid you a warm welcome. Come and join my friend and me and we'll enjoy my only night of freedom."

Cyrano followed him through the crowded bar to a corner table where his friend sat smiling. "You're good, Thomas. The best. That was impressive," said Dardo.

"You're easy to impress, lad, but I'd say it's a fair estimate of my talents. I'm as highly strung as a thoroughbred horse, faster than the wind, stronger than a bull and fearless," snorted the warrior.

Cyrano's eyes widened. He smiled.

Dardo laughed. "Modest too."

"Sit you down," offered Thomas, "and have a goblet of the finest wine in the land."

Dardo was drunk, light-hearted and loose-tongued, but liked for his unmistakable comic company. He sat staring at the newcomer. "Meet... meet my good friend, Thomas Flynn, he adopted me tonight," he slurred, stripping off his shirt, throwing it across the room at a welcoming looking whore. She smiled at him with obvious intent. "Umm, er, well, will you excuse me, friends," he said, rising from his stool. He ambled over to the girl and sat beside her, wrapping his long arms around her. They kissed and cuddled.

Thomas fixed Cyrano's gaze. "You must excuse my new friend; he uses the English language as appropriately as a wooden cudgel. In fact, for someone who has no stammer, he does it well. So, what brings you to the Lazy Rat?"

"You," said Cyrano, his voice low and deep.

Thomas shrugged. "Why?"

"I need help to clean out the thugs and thieves from my inn. And I need the best."

"The mercenary, Vodas, is the best and his reputation precedes him."

"He's old, his sight failing."

Thomas had a steely glint in his eyes. "He's still the best. I've seen no one faster with a blade or better with a longbow."

"I want you to work at my inn," said Cyrano, "and I'm willing to pay whatever it takes to get you there."

Thomas cocked his head to one side, raising an arm to catch the innkeeper's gaze. Forin strolled over to their table after collecting empty goblets on a tray. He stared at the pair, tapping his foot. Thomas ordered food for himself and Cyrano, flipping the Innkeeper a silver coin, who in return reached into his pocket, producing three copper coins in change. He strode off into the kitchen, closing the door behind him.

Thomas spun his head to Cyrano, meeting his gaze again. "I *will* come and solve your problems. But I want twenty silver shillings in my hand now as a retainer and a wage of two shillings per day. Three if I have to fight someone."

The other sighed. "I can live with that. It's costing me a fortune in damages each week at the moment." They shook hands and sat back smiling at each other. Forin came back with two meat and potato pies. They ate in silence.

After an hour Dardo had had his fill of the young wench and was on his way back to Thomas' table when a small stocky villager stood up, colliding with him. "Mind where you're going. You're a clumsy dolt," the villager shouted.

"Sorry," said Dardo, moving past the man, "but you bumped into me." As he walked on the villager's foot struck him on the behind, launching him from his feet. He fell against a chair, striking his temple, almost knocking him unconscious. He shook his head and rolled to his knees, hauling himself upright. "You… you are an arrogant individual, my friend, for a man with a haircut like a badly thatched cottage. Are you sure you have that wig on the right way?" he stammered aloud, rolling his hands in front of his face, boxing fashion.

The villager pulled a knife from inside his boot. "I'll gut you like a fish. You're a son-of-a-whore," he said lunging forward.

Dardo sidestepped the man, grabbing the knife wrist with his right hand, jerking him forward. His own momentum sent him crashing into the tables.

The villager rolled to one knee, slamming tables aside. Climbing to his feet, he flashed the blade from side to side. "I *will* kill you."

Dardo laughed, his eyes glazed. "You tire me, brother, and I'm drunk and can see two of you, but I have a fist for you both."

Thomas and Cyrano watched with great interest but took no part in the fight. Thomas wanted to know how good Dardo was with his fists because the lad had stunned him earlier with a stiff left hook, nothing more. And the farm boy didn't carry a blade. Either he's confident and capable of defending himself or just a fool asking for trouble, thought Thomas.

The villager lunged again. Dardo sidestepped in the opposite direction, throwing a vicious right uppercut. It landed on the man's jaw and lifted him from the floor, knocking him senseless. He dropped like a stone to the floorboards with a heavy thud.

Another stranger stepped forward with a stern stare that would reduce a rabid wolf to foaming jelly. Shaking his head, he hefted the unconscious villager over his shoulder and carried him from the inn, muttering colourful profanity as he left. Forin calmed his customers.

Thomas vaulted over his table. "You did well, unarmed against a man with a blade," he congratulated.

Dardo smiled. "I told you I was a good fighter. Shall I fetch you more ale?"

Thomas nodded. "Aye and one more for our guest. I think it's been a long time since he's tasted ale this good. Although he tells me he's had more than enough of our entertainment in his tavern." He strode back to where Cyrano was and sitting. "The lad's outstanding, he reminds me of me when..."

"How soon can I expect you at the Dog and Duck?" interrupted Cyrano.

Thomas leaned back in his chair, stretching. "I'll be with you no later than sunset, three days hence."

Cyrano smiled, nodding, taking out his purse. "Your retainer, twenty shillings you said, yes?"

Thomas nodded.

Dardo returned with more ale and saw him counting out the money, "What will you do with so much money?" he asked.

Heads turned, ears pricked up and eyes shifted to the three friends.

"Maybe you should let the whole tavern know of my good fortune," said Thomas, "I don't think everyone heard what you said the first time."

Dardo swung around with his fists up and tripped but stayed upright. "Why do you want everyone to know?" he slurred, dribbling spit.

"I was being sarcastic my friend, making the point it's not a good idea to speak of money in a place such as this. Robbers and cut-throats may spy on us and be listening," said Thomas.

Dardo swung around again, putting his clenched fists up in front of his face. "Where are they? I'll batter them to death!"

"No, my friend, I said robbers might be in here listening, not that they are."

"Oh, okay. You… you needn't tell me twice," Dardo stammered, tapping his nose.

Cyrano finished counting out the money, drank his ale and gave directions to his inn. He bid his hosts farewell. And as he made his way back through the crowded room towards the door, he stopped and turned, gazing back at Thomas with a sobering stare, "You know, with your reputation, I thought you would be much bigger," he said walking out into the cold, misty night air.

CHAPTER TWO

Road trip

One hundred and sixty miles to the north in Nottinghamshire, a slender, dark-haired young man stood shadowed in a doorway. He fought to hold down a rising tide of desolation and despair, his hard but handsome face, and even harder eyes reflecting the pain and sorrow he felt. His hand was bleeding, the flesh stripped to the bone. He knocked on the door. Within moments an elegant young woman answered it. Her eyes were blue and her long hair shone like spun gold.

"Who are you and what can I do for you?" she enquired noticing the man's bloodied hand. She had a gentle smile.

"Can I come in?" he asked. "It's been a long night, and I'd appreciate your medical attention."

"Yes," she said, stepping aside. When he had entered she closed the door, leading him up three flights of stairs and through a corridor to a long narrow room with several pallet beds, bidding him to lie on one. He lay on a bed and she examined his injury. "How did you come by this wound?"

He gazed up at her. "Ozhan did it for not paying a wager, and then he set fire to my house, killing my servants without a conscious thought. The man is evil, with a diseased mind and soul so black they would obscure the darkness of hell if it exists. He's the devil himself, I'm sure."

The young doctor took a sharp intake of breath at hearing the baron's name.

"Thank you for your hospitality. I wouldn't have survived if I hadn't fled my home two days ago. The baron rewards those who fulfil his desires, while those who fail, die. He is the bringer of death and destruction."

"He has become death itself. What's your name?"

"Vant. What's yours?"

"Lira. Lay back on the bed and I'll dress your wound."

***

Tired and hungry, Thomas and Dardo moved on for the next three days without saying a word to each other. Now they rested their horses at the edge of a village, the houses abandoned and a fifty-foot wide river beside them.

They sheltered for a while in a deserted barn then moved on again, passing a log cabin built on the open ground, bordering the tree line of the hills. And for most of the daylight hours they rode, angling their journey ever northward, sleeping beneath the stars at night.

The sun had set fiery red as they paused at the crest of a rise bordering Nottinghamshire to the south. Shrouded in mist, there were oaks, elms and birch growing everywhere, so they pushed on, and by dark could see Nottingham shining like a beacon in the moonlight. A whispering wind flowed over the whole landscape and the smell of grass wet from the recent rain made Thomas feel at home. His dark eyes scanned the city before leaving the hillside on the forest road, moving under the overhanging branches, watching the moonlight dapple their trail. There were no bird songs to fill the air, but the forest intoxicated him.

Dardo groaned and spoke. "How much further must we ride? My backside is on fire and I'm considering eating my horse, I'm so hungry."

"According to Cyrano's directions, we're almost there," said Thomas.

Dardo stared at his friend, "Why do you do what you do?"

Thomas shrugged. "To eat."

"Are you ever afraid?"

"I'd be a liar if I said I wasn't. Everyone's afraid sometimes, but I don't dwell upon it. It's hard enough trying to stay alive."

"Have you ever lost a fight?"

Thomas shrugged again. "Nobody ever wins, there's always pain and bloodshed on both sides of an argument."

A young boy with a slingshot darted from the shadows of the trees and let fly with a stone. It struck Dardo high on the head, staggering him. He fell from his horse in an unconscious state, pounding the floor.

Thomas gasped. "What the hell?"

The boy reloaded in the blink of an eye, methodical in his every action. "Your money or your life?"

Thomas laughed without humour. "How old are you, lad?"

"Old enough to take your money."

"That's what I love about the young," countered Thomas, "their ability to go on flights of fancy."

The boy was angry. "Your money or your life?"

Thomas' grin faded. "Aren't you too young to be a highwayman, and if not, shouldn't you be aiming an arrow at me, not a stone in a slingshot?"

"You're too old to be dressing up in warriors clothes, aren't you? I'll take whatever coin you and your friend have and then be on my way."

"My friend and I are poor and have no coin."

"You look too well fed to be poor," the boy observed.

"Only because the forest feeds us," said Thomas.

Dardo groaned, coming back to his senses. Sitting up, he rolled to his knees. "The boy hit me with something," he complained, holding his aching head.

"A stone, and a rather large one at that according to the red lump swelling on your forehead," said Thomas, his voice deep and harsh. "I can't believe I'm being held to ransom by a boy of twelve years old or less, with nothing more than a slingshot."

Dardo came to his feet, rubbing the wound. "And a bloody good aim."

The boy hefted the slingshot as if to throw. "Be silent and give up your coin so I may be on my way. I've much to do."

Thomas reached for his purse. "Ok, ok, you win; I don't fancy a bump the size of an egg upon my forehead. I'd not live such a thing down in my new job as the doorman at the Dog and Duck."

The boy's strong face trembled, his eyes haunted. He lowered the slingshot. "You're the new doorman at the Dog and Duck?"

"Aye," said Thomas. And before he uttered another word, the boy turned and fled back into the shadows of the tangled forest whence he came.

Thomas scratched his head, staring at his friend. "What just happened? The boy had me cold and I would have paid!"

Dardo rubbed his throbbing forehead and climbed back into his saddle. "Maybe your reputation precedes you."

***

Cyrano had lit wood in an iron stove in the dining room and a fire was burning. Warming his hands he gazed out of the leaded window overlooking the courtyard. It was dark, raining and lightning forked. He shuffled through the swinging doors into the kitchen. Sunset had come but Thomas Flynn hadn't. With a heavy heart, he questioned whether the swordsman would ever arrive, and he could do nothing but hope. "It will be one of those nights, I feel it in my water," he said to himself.

A white-robed cook with brown eyes and a gentle smile flittered around the kitchen cooking soup and making bread-rolls, whistling as she worked. Everything smelt delicious. The aroma drifted out into a dining room full of customers. Cyrano took turns serving in the bar and taproom which was no easy task.

An hour passed and there was no sign of Thomas. Two hours. Then as the wine flowed, the revellers became boisterous and fights broke out. Drunken customers overturned tables and threw chairs around the room. Goblets flew in the air and there was the odd terrifying scream as something hard collided with a face. It was a typical savage night except nobody had died yet.

Outside the tavern came the sound of heavy hoof beats. Moments later, the doors burst open. Thomas and Dardo entered, shaking the rain from their coats. For a moment they were still and silent, their expressions thoughtful.

"I'm not a vain man," said Dardo at last, "but the weather's ruined my hair."

Thomas smiled. "Then the next time you visit a barber, have it shaved close to the scalp."

Dardo shook his head. "My hair's strong and wild, like me, and shall stay that way."

Thomas' nostrils flared at the delicious aroma wafting his way like a warm breeze. Both men stepped into the bar.

"I'm so hungry," said Thomas closing the door, and they stood scanning the crowded room. The ceiling was white and low, supported by thick oak beams and there was a stone fireplace with a marble hearth set against the south wall, roaring with a blazing fire, the windows shuttered and the floor sawdust-covered.

"You have a contract here with Cyrano, not I," said Dardo. "What makes you think he'll need me too?"

Thomas turned his head, fixing his friends gaze. "If this inn is half as violent as Cyrano says, it's always wise to have a contingency plan."

Dardo shook his head looking puzzled. "What's that?"

"Another plan of action and I'll pay you with my money. You're my responsibility, not his," said Thomas, noticing the upturned tables, chairs and unconscious customers scattered around the room. He knelt to check the hidden dagger sheathed in his left boot, then standing back to his feet he tightened the sword-belt around his waist.

They spoke no more, walking on through the bar, stopping at a table by a window. Thomas sat, gesturing for Dardo to sit opposite him as a tall, wiry, young man with a wide moustache approached them.

"What's your pleasure?" he asked.

Thomas took a deep breath, focusing on the man's face. "What's the food like here?"

"It's good. The innkeeper's daughter cooks it."

"And the ale?" asked Dardo.

"That's good too."

"Then we'll have two of whatever's hot and available," said Thomas, "accompanied by a jug of your finest ale."

The man nodded, swinging around, heading for the kitchen and within moments returned with two meat pies and fresh vegetables, served in separate dishes.

Thomas licked his lips, tucking into the meal. Dardo did too. The young man disappeared again, returning moments later with a large pitcher of ale.

"We thank you, keep the change," said Thomas, hefting the young man a silver coin. He went back to the kitchen with a smile on his face.

A blind harp player appeared from a back room, playing dance music.

Thomas smiled. "It's a small world."

"You know the harpist?" asked Dardo.

"Aye, he's good, but I hope he doesn't sing. His voice is past the range of human tolerance. In fact, it's so annoying that deaf people refuse to watch his lips move. And I hope he dies before me because I don't want him singing at my funeral," snorted Thomas.

Dardo laughed, picked up the pitcher of ale and poured, filling their goblets. Both drank, draining them in one large swallow. He filled the goblets again, ate his pie and sat back stretching his arms above his head.

Thomas sat quietly listening to the music.

Dardo looked thoughtful. "Doesn't seem such a violent place, maybe Cyrano exaggerated just to get you here."

Thomas finished the last of the pie, stretched and leaned back as two broad-shouldered young men with hard features approached, walking as if they had fouled their hose and could smell it.

One of them pushed back on his chair, almost tipping him onto the floor. "You've made a mistake."

"You're sitting in my friend's chair," said the other with the looks and charm of a warthog.

Thomas rose to his feet, picking up the chair, looking around it. "Do you see a name anywhere, because I don't?"

The young men glared at him. "I sit here every evening," said the first.

"And I sit there," said the other pointing to Dardo's chair.

Dardo fixed Thomas' gaze. "I spoke too soon."

Thomas frowned, "You want these two specific chairs out of the many chairs in here?"

Dardo stared at the two posturing bullies who achieved the unusual feat of being sinister and ridiculous at the same time.

"That's my chair," said the first, clenching his big, hard hands.

"And that's mine," warned his friend, clenching his fists.

Thomas let out a deep sigh. "Then you shall have them," he shouted, smashing his chair over the first man's head and shoulders.

Dardo rose and vaulted the table, reaching the second man just as he was unleashing a snaking left hook at Thomas' jaw. An uppercut slammed into the man's chin like an iron hammer, dropping him like a stone. He didn't rise. The first man rolled to his knees, hauling himself upright, just in time for Thomas' booted foot to cannon against his face, catapulting him into the gawping crowd. He fell, banging his head on a stool and didn't rise. Dardo moved alongside Thomas and stared into the awed faces of the crowd. "Let me introduce my friend. This is the legendary swordsman…"

The crowd parted and Cyrano stepped forward carrying two goblets of ale. "Thomas Flynn and his good friend Dardo who are now in my employment," he interrupted.

A customer whispered to Cyrano. "What's the story behind this Thomas Flynn?"

"You mess with him and he'll seal your fate forever," said Cyrano, his voice icy.

***

The young man's face trembled, blinking hard as an iron fist struck him full in the face, sending him sprawling to the dirt. Dizziness swamped him. His attacker hauled him upright. Another fist hit him full in the face, smashing his nose.

A tall, thin man with long hair and beady eyes hauled him upright again and grabbed his arms, pinning them behind his back. Then a big man with a flat, brutal face pummelled and hammered his belly until he couldn't breathe. The young man slid to the ground gasping for air and then rolled to his knees, groaning, struggling to fill his lungs.

An iron hand gripped his throat. "This is my city, you little bastard, and never forget it. Sign the papers now or I swear I'll cut your fingers off, one by one," said the big man.

The young man nodded and begged in a whisper. "No more. Please don't hit me again. I'll sign the papers and you can have the farm."

Ozhan dragged him to his feet, thrusting the deed in front of him. Trembling, the young man blinked back tears, taking a quill pen from the hand of one of his attackers, who turned his back for him to rest the document on his shirt. He fought to focus on the brown parchment, signing it as the big man's scarred face lingered inches away from his own, watching him.

In his days, baron Ozhan had lived to enjoy a single talent, to terrorise the souls of lesser men. He drew a dagger from his belt and placed it under the young man's chin, who felt a trickle of blood as the needle-sharp blade pricked his skin.

The young man rubbed the sweat from his eyes and focused on Ozhan's face as the dagger lifted him to his toes.

"You could have saved yourself this beating, you little bastard if you had signed last month. Now pack your belongings and take your pleasant little life and wife elsewhere and don't come back," warned the baron.

The young man spun on his heel, staggering back to his log cabin, closing the door behind him. The baron and his men climbed into their saddles and rode off laughing with the signed documents.

***

As the sun rose in the east the next morning, Thomas and Dardo sat by a vast lake exchanging thoughts. The sky was blue; the air warm, green and long was the grass and birds of every kind and colour chirped in the oaks behind them.

"I admire Cyrano's courage," said Thomas, "but the helpless are leading the hopeless at the Dog and Duck and that's why every bullyboy and thug entertains there. We'll change that. We'll throw the scumbags out on their ears."

Dardo's eyes wandered out over the shimmering lake. He rolled to his knees, pushing himself upright. "I've killed no one, ever, in a fight, but I will if I must."

Thomas came to his feet, remembering his father's bloated face, his tongue protruding; the hangman's noose tight around his neck after he had killed his mother. "Death is an ugly thing brother, but sometimes it has a bitter-sweet taste and is necessary."

They walked around the lake, across a narrow valley full of oak, alder and birch and the sun shone in a blue sky. The snow of distant hills glistened like white fire and the sculptured beauty of the land amid forest and streams awed them.

"If we stick to three simple rules," said Thomas, "we needn't kill anyone. Number one: never underestimate your opponent and always expect the unexpected. Number two: take the fight outside; never tackle trouble inside the inn unless it's necessary. And Number three: be nice until it's time not to be."

Dardo looked confused. "How will I know when it's that time?"

"I'll tell you," said Thomas, "but if someone gets in your face and calls you a whoreson or gutter-scum, I want you to be pleasant. Ask him to leave the inn, but be polite. If he won't leave, we'll help him leave, but we'll both be polite. Remember, it's not personal; it's a job."

"Calling me a whoreson isn't personal?"

"No, it's name-calling to prompt a reaction, so sticks and stones may break your bones, but calling names won't hurt you."

"What if somebody calls someone I love a whore?"

"If they're not, you've nothing to worry about, have you?" said Thomas with a smile. "I want you to be pleasant until it's time not to be pleasant. Then we'll take out the trash before it makes the place stink, so-to-speak."

Dardo winked, tapping his nose. "Know what you mean, Thomas."

Both men nodded, heading back to their horses.

Then, much later that day, back at the inn, Thomas fell into a deep sleep and awoke with a start, his heart beating like a drum. Dardo was shaking him. "Bad dream my friend?"

Thomas rolled to his feet from the pallet bed. "I never have a good one."

The fire was almost out, so he added kindling and quickly blew the dying embers back to life. "I dreamt I was a bird soaring high above the hills, riding the warm air, weaving through clouds in a far-off land, watching elk and deer migrate, then I turned back into a man and fell." A log rolled from the fire, onto the hearth and stopped at his feet, jolting him back from remembering his dream. He picked up a set of long iron tongs, lifting it back onto the fire. He stretched and yawned.

"They say every dream means something," said Dardo. "I wonder what that one means."

Thomas shrugged, yawning again, rubbing his eyes, ignoring the comment. He moved to the window. The sun had set behind the hills. "I never sleep in the day; it must be the effects of this Nottinghamshire air."

"Would you like a cup of nettle tea?" asked Dardo hanging a kettle over the fire.

Thomas nodded. "Aye, and then we had better get downstairs. The inn will be open and Cyrano will wonder where we are."

Within moments the kettle had boiled. Dardo moved to the hearth, wrapping a cloth around the handle of the kettle. He lifted it from its iron bracket and returned to the table, filling two slender cups with boiling water, adding a small muslin bag to each. A sweet, delicious aroma filled the bedroom. He stirred the contents of each cup, hooking out the bags, passing one cup to Thomas, who tasted the brew and smiled. "I've not had nettle tea for years, cheers and here's to our first night on the job, may it go without a hitch and any violent consequences."

The tea lifted their spirits, warming their insides, and within minutes both men dressed and walked downstairs, armed and ready for action.

***

The young woman slid from the red-haired, silver-eyed giant man's lap, moving away into the crowd as he drained his tankard of ale. He drew his dagger, slamming it point first into an oak table. "I'll fight both of you or either of you," said the skull-faced colossus, his voice thick with contempt. "And when you are dead, I will eat your livers."

"My friend and I work here, and all we ask is that you leave the inn peacefully," said Thomas. Dardo nodded. Cyrano hid.

The giant man stood up, drawing his long broadsword. "If I leave, I'll leave in pieces. Not in peace. And if you can kill me, you can have my possessions, including the whore-wench I brought with me."

Thomas looked hard at the man. He was barrel-chested and powerful. But he swung to Dardo nodding his acceptance. "I think he looks old, fat and lazy. Death might be an improvement and a good career move for him."

The giant man glared back at Thomas twice as hard. "If I don't swallow you whole, little one, I'll still feast on your liver after I've torn off your aggravating head, I promise."

Thomas turned to face his friend. "A stupid person's idea of clever rhetoric. I bet he's so conceited he raises his hat every time he speaks of himself."

"Can you take him?" asked Dardo looking worried, his voice a whispering whimper.

Thomas nodded, drawing both swords. Stepping up to meet the giant man he took up his fighting stance, and the crowd parted, backing away in silence as he darted sideways, dodging a ferocious cut to his belly. Then he leapt back, swaying away from a slashing cut to his chest, which he parried, but such was the power of the blow that Thomas went spinning to the floor. However, he made it to his knees as his adversary leapt towards him with his sword raised, then rolled away as it slammed into the floor hitting an iron nail. Bright sparks lit the air like a flash of gunpowder.

The giant's anger swelled and he staggered back under the sheer weight of his sword. Thomas changed to an opposite stance and waited. The other leapt forward, his broadsword slashing from right to left aiming at Thomas' head. Thomas dropped to one knee, the blade slicing air above him. A short sword flashed out nicking the giant's ear and blood trickled down his neck. Thomas smiled, rising as the man lunged again. He parried the thrust and spun on his heel, hammering his fist into the man's face and he tumbled to the floor, slicing a deep cut several inches long to Thomas' bicep. Crimson bloomed on his skin, blood dripping down his arm, but he realised it wasn't a bad cut. "Before I've finished with you, you'll wish you hadn't caused trouble tonight big man and will wish you'd left when asked," said Thomas examining the wound.

The giant man shook his head in defiance and came to his feet. "Die," he shouted, lunging forward.

One of Thomas' needle-sharp blades met him, slicing through his neck, half decapitating him and blood sprayed out as he fell, freckling the faces of the crowd of horrified onlookers. Thomas' eyes were fever bright and his hands trembled as he sheathed both swords. The panic gone, he relieved the giant warrior of his bulging purse. "A jug of ale if you please Cyrano, and someone to dispose of this self-appointed King of Nobodies," he said remembering his days practising swordplay with his brother Malcolm in the old courtyard at Alnwick Castle.

"Why is Malcolm so much faster than me?" he had asked Master Gallus their trainer. "We're twins with the same musculature, the same drive, and the same ability."

Gallus had answered with one word: practice, and from that day forward, Thomas spent every spare hour of the day doing just that. Hours turned into days, days into weeks and weeks into months until ten long years passed and he was unbeatable with a hundred victories behind him and a vast reputation in front of him. The lips of many spoke his name with pride. Only those who feared him whispered it.

***

Patients filled the young healer's hallway, and the bright morning sunlight filtered through the high-arched windows in a constant stream. Moans and groans filled the air as Lira walked the long corridor, trying to judge who needed her attention the most. Thomas' handsome features drew her attention with his dark eyes. He sat at the end of the line of injured, holding his bandaged arm; his black and gold tunic stained and a mess. Dressed in a loose-fitting white gown, the ties undone, she approached him and sat by his side.

"Hello, I'm Lira, how did this injury happen?" she asked, unwrapping the bandage to inspect the seeping wound.

"In an argument," said Thomas.

Lira screwed up her face. "It's a big ugly cut."

"Not surprised, it was a big ugly man who did it."

"What do you do for a living?"

"I work at the Dog and Duck."

"Doing what?"

"Doorman. I take out the filth when it makes the place stink."

Lira frowned. "It's not a nice place. They send me everything, except what the undertaker collects."

"I'll change that," said Thomas with an air of confidence.

Stunned she stared into his eyes. "On your own?"

"No, I have a friend."

"I think you'll need several more," Lira insisted.

She stood and beckoned for him to follow her to a long, narrow room full of pallet beds and bid him lie on one, which he did. She cleaned the wound with a secret recipe of herbs and mosses, stitched it up and dressed it again. Thomas never flinched once which surprised and impressed her.

"Doesn't the pain bother you?"

"Pain is necessary."

She stared at him. "I have many patients waiting out there who would disagree."

"Pain keeps us alive. The instant the giant man cut my arm, I knew my predicament was serious and let my subconscious mind take control. Subconscious reactions are faster than conscious actions."

Lira finished bandaging the wound. "That's true."

"Do you like music?"

She fixed his gaze. "Yes, but not noisy taverns and rowdy customers."

Thomas shrugged. "I neither, but I have to eat and it's just a job."

"Where do you hail from, your dialect isn't local?"

"Northumberland, but I've travelled far and wide."

"Are you staying in Nottingham long?"

He smiled at her again with soul-searching eyes like those of a lost puppy-dog, "I might if I can get to know you better."

Her face blossomed crimson with embarrassment at his awkwardness and she avoided his gaze. He leaned closer to her, so close he could smell the rose-scented perfume of her hair and he sighed. The effect was disconcerting but somehow pleasant to her. She looked into his eyes and saw the fear of rejection there. Quickly she said, "A picnic would be pleasant and I'll bring the food."

His face lit up, beaming like a puppy with a new home. "I must go before you change your mind. When shall our picnic take place?"

"Call upon me at your own discretion."

Climbing to his feet he strode over to the doorway and turned, glancing back at her. She's a delight, he thought, beautiful, kind and caring, lacking nothing in the eyes of a suitor. He opened the door, stepping out into the street and the freshness of the nearby fields greeted him. It was almost as delicious as Lira's intoxicating perfume. He took a deep breath of fresh air and sighed. "I'm in love."

Outside, screams filled the air bringing him to his senses. His eyes darted to the left, and he saw a group of hard, rangy men, hungry-looking like vultures, laughing and creating a disturbance. There was a loud neigh and a large black horse at least eighteen hands high reared up in front of him, and it was so close that its forelegs struck him in the ribs sending him sprawling. He fell to his knees gasping from the kick, the huge animal towering over him, the rider hooded and cloaked in black with a gold-crest embellished on the front of his tunic.

Thomas rose, clutching his bruised ribs as the group of laughing men formed a ring around him. Behind the men, a building was burning with sickening screams filling the air. A strong wind was blowing the flames, turning the house fire into a raging inferno that hissed and crackled.

The rider dismounted, lowering his hood. "Leave well alone, Flynn. The house burns and everyone in it because they owe me a debt they cannot repay. I'm baron Ozhan and I own this city and almost everything in it," he said coming nose to nose, his blunt face covered in grotesque scars. Both of his eyes seemed to glow in different colours. His left eye was blue like a swordfish. The right eye was red like a hot burning coal and his odd gaze and incredible ugliness hypnotised Thomas. Only a mother could love this King of the Gutter, he thought.

"What I don't yet own will soon be mine, including the woman Lira," snapped Ozhan.

CHAPTER THREE
Hot gypsy blood

At last, the horrific screaming stopped and the blazing house collapsed into showers of sparks. Rubble tumbled into the cobbled street and Ozhan's men laughed again as thick, black smoke swirled, drifting away in long trailers like the morning mist. The smell of soot lingered in the air and even having killed their terrified victims, the men's bloodlust was still running high. Now they fixed their eyes on Thomas.

A man with an unpleasant tattooed face, chin-beard and a crown of straw-coloured hair pushed his way forward. His eyebrows climbed his forehead. "We've heard of you. They say you're lightning fast with your blades, but I know I can take you in a fair fight."

Ozhan scowled at his man. "Watch what you say to him. Mr Thomas Flynn is more than a handful at the best of times, so I'm told."

"Codswallop, kill him and let's be off," said another man.

Ozhan regarded his men in silence as Thomas fixed his gaze on the first man with the straw mop who stood two heads taller than he did. "I'm not only lightning-fast, but I spit thunderbolts too," he countered.

"What are you waitin' for, kill him and let..." the second man began again.

Thomas' dagger struck the man in the throat, then both swords flashed into his hands. "Is that fast enough?" he asked, his eyes challenging his opponents.

"Bloody hell," gasped two of the men in unison. "That *was* quick."

"Who wants to die next," said Thomas, "you Ozhan?"

After a survey of his men's terrified faces, the baron shook his head. "Back to the farm," he ordered, mounting his stallion, staring down at Thomas. "You are a dangerous man, my friend," he admitted.

Thomas nodded, staring him in the eyes. "Take the corpse as a reminder of that, and keep your pets on a leash, otherwise I'll come looking for *you*."

***

The brightness of the eastern sky behind the Dog and Duck faded as Cyrano glanced out of his bedroom window at the coming twilight. Daylight didn't dispel his fear of what was to come with the fall of darkness because as frightening as the ruffians acted by day, they were worse at night. Animals behaved better.

So, to distract himself from his misery, he had taken to drink. He shed his fears when the demon took hold of him, and it warmed his insides better than the morning sun, besides making him forget his troubles. In fact, when he was drunk, he had a childlike face, with a big boyish smile, even though there was no mistaking the hard set, grey-green eyes.

The sun had set and faded behind Nottingham's tallest buildings, leaving an orangey hue in the sky, when a knock on the bedroom door startled Cyrano. A soft female voice called out, informing him that customers had arrived and the dining room tables needed setting.

He swallowed hard and drained a full tankard of ale in a single gulp. Taking a deep breath, he turned toward the door. There was dread in his eyes. It showed. "I'll be downstairs in a moment."

He wiped his sweating brow. *I'm a fool keeping this place open and I know it*, he thought. Opening the door, he stepped out into the corridor and trudged down the stairs in his half-drunk state and went into the bar. It surprised him to see Thomas and Dardo sitting at their regular table, and no one wanted to dispute it was their table.

Relieved and bolstered by their presence, he staggered the full length of the bar, grinning. The crowd stopped whatever they were doing and laughed at him with his drunken boyish smile, which looked ridiculous.

"What... what are you laughing at?" he slurred; his blunt, honest, rosy face a picture. Turning, he tried to pull a tankard of ale from an oak cask, slipped and fell, hitting his head hard on the bar top, almost knocking him unconscious. Thomas and Dardo rose from their seats and leapt over the bar just as he rolled to his knees and shook his head. "Boy, come here!" he shouted.

The dining-room door burst open. A young lad of twelve years stormed into the room. He stopped short, staring up into Thomas' face, where recognition dawned. He stared at Dardo. Both men's eyes widened. They stared back at the boy.

"We've met before," said Thomas.

Dardo rubbed his forehead. "The lad with the slingshot."

The boy looked horrified.

Thomas gripped the lad's ear. "I'll have a word with you if you don't mind."

The boy took a deep breath and exhaled. He looked mortified. "So much anger."

Thomas and Dardo chastised him for his sinful deed in the forest, but then Cyrano explained it was his son and that he had become lost in a world of his own hatred after the death of his two brothers under the wheels of a runaway wagon, driven at the time by one of Ozhan's men. The boy seemed sad and tormented.

The boy's heart sank at the thought of his lost brothers, a year to the day, and his dark eyes misted and filled. He stood weeping.

Thomas cuddled him. "You think of them still?"

The boy nodded; the question cutting through his thoughts like a knife. "I think of bygone days, sunshine and meadows and of laughter with my brothers."

"I'm sorry," said Thomas, "but you must not let the loss cloud your future."

The boy half smiled, shaking his head, wiping the tears from his face. His hair was dark and his skin ivory white. "I have no future without my brothers."

Thomas shook his head. "You're wrong. Now you have three futures to fulfil. Yours and theirs. Wouldn't it be better to make them proud rather than give up? If you succeed, they won't have died in vain."

"I'm sorry for the misunderstanding in the forest," said the lad. "You're right and I'm wrong. After the death of my brothers, I hated everyone and everything because I prayed so hard for their souls."

"Sometimes God seems to be deaf, dumb and blind," said Thomas, "but we humans are no better."

"Is it true you're a great swordsman?" asked the boy, a glint of hope in his eyes.

"That's what they say, but I wouldn't believe most of the stories. Only the ones where I've battled giants, dragons, goblins, trolls and dwarfs, killing them all," Thomas said with a wink.

"And saved fair maidens?" said the boy.

"Some maidens were less fair than others, but a hero does what a hero should. He saves the maiden even if she has the face of a goat."

The boy laughed, wiping the tears from his eyes. "You're hilarious and I'll be strong. I'll grow up to be three warriors rolled into one."

Dardo slapped his forehead, chuckled and rolled his eyes like loose marbles. "Then I hope to God I don't meet the one with the slingshot again."

The tavern broke out into laughter.

Thomas smiled, "Anything's possible."

Just then, the doors of the tavern burst open and four of Ozhan's men entered. One had straw-coloured hair and was two heads taller than Thomas. He was a huge, barrel-chested man and his chin beard was like an old sweeping brush, sawdust included. Cyrano slumped to a chair, his drunkenness overcoming him. Thomas stared hard at the four men. "Come in and sit you down friends, you look weary."

"Our ride has been murderous," said the golden-haired man, his voice slurred with tiredness, his hard smoke-grey eyes showing no emotion. The four men pushed and bullied the crowd, making their way towards the bar.

"What's the matter with him?" asked one man called Aris, pointing a finger at Cyrano slumped in the chair snoring.

Dardo half-smiled. "He's a little worse for the drink. I think he likes his own ale too much."

Aris, a small, bald, stout man with a scarred face turned and drew his dagger, slamming it point first into the bar-top. "Then who serves tonight?" he asked in a bullying voice.

Dardo and Thomas shrugged.

"I'll serve," said Dody. "I've done it before and know all the prices."

"What's your name, whelp?" said Aris in a threatening voice.

"My name's Dody and I am no whelp, you ugly son-of-a…"

"Now, now," interrupted Thomas with a cough, "spare us the blasphemy and do your job."

The boy stared at Thomas, wishing to grow as tall, dark and handsome as his newfound hero, for as much as he loved his father he did not wish to be the image of the man who sired him. He gave a shy grin and tugged the curls of his long hair as the men lapsed into silence, brushing the mud from their black leggings. Clearing his throat, Thomas asked the men what they wanted to drink. They looked like they'd cut their mother's throat for a silver penny.

"We want your best ale," said the golden-haired man.

Dody nodded, pulling four tankards of ale from an oak cask, passing them to the men.

"Do I frighten you, boy," asked Aris, noticing Dody was staring at him.

Dody shook his head, "No, but the man who gave you those ugly scars would."

The huge man laughed. "A wise boy. I gave them to him." He drew a large hunting knife from a deep pocket, produced a whetstone from another and sharpened the blade with long smooth strokes. He glanced at the boy, then at Thomas. "Do I frighten *you*?" he asked.

Thomas smiled mirthlessly. "My friend, your face would frighten anybody, including the devil, and I have bad dreams already. Why do you try to intimidate the boy?"

For a heartbeat, the man stood stock still then his laughter boomed out. "By heaven, you're a cocky mongrel. I take it then my face displeases you?"

Thomas shook his head. "No, but I'm glad it's your face and not mine," he countered with an air of arrogance. "But, I find you to be a brutal, witless, big-mouthed, scoundrel."

The man scowled. "By God, you think highly of yourself, little man."

Thomas nodded. "I think I would prove a handful even for the four of you."

Dardo nodded too. "He has hot gypsy blood I'm sure, for he moves faster and more often than they."

The huge man tensed, closing a hand around his sword hilt.

Thomas stared hard at the man and laughed. "I could cut you all to shreds without blowing my breath or breaking out into a sweat."

The man stilled, taking a deep breath, staring into Thomas' dark eyes. He remembered their confrontation the day before in the street outside Lira's surgery, visualising the warrior's lightning-fast delivery of the knife to his friend's throat, and the speed at which he had drawn swords.

"Well, you ugly son-of-a-whore, are you going to unsheathe your blade or not?" asked Thomas.

The front doors swung open, the rusted iron hinges grinding. Ozhan entered, and the whole tavern fell silent as he crossed the room towards the bar, eyes narrowing, knowing his men had forced Thomas into a confrontation. "Cold like ice that man is and harder than an iron nail," he announced.

The golden-haired man smiled, showing his broken teeth and he spat on Thomas' boot. "That I am."

Ozhan stared at his man. "Not you, you great oaf… him… Thomas… you're just big and ugly. He'd cut you down before your blade cleared its scabbard. Look at the steely glint in his eyes. He's waiting for you to try something."

A young man's face floated before the baron. "Now I remember you. Ten years ago, you fought your brother, Malcolm, on the battlements of Alnwick Castle in Northumberland, slicing and dicing him without a conscious thought. Do you remember me? I was the soldier who took his body from you and carried it down to the awaiting carriage. But afterwards, why did you not take up the stewardship of the castle? Why did you disappear?"

"Those times are a drunken blur," said Thomas. "I went to claim what was mine, but when I had it within my grasp I realised it wasn't what I wanted, so I'd killed my brother for nothing. I grieved and became a drunkard to forget, but even the demon drink doesn't wash away the nightmares of those days."

All eyes were on his haunted face.

"You fascinate me," said Ozhan in awe of the man. "You return from the wars a hero, claim what's yours, fight and kill your brother, gutting him like a fish and then disappear for ten long years, only to reappear in another city as a tavern brawler. What logic lies behind your thinking, man? You had it all and threw it away."

Thomas shook his head in a slow controlled fashion. "If a happy man gains riches and power it might make him even happier, but riches and power don't make a miserable man happy and I was miserable."

"Hmmm," said Ozhan at a loss for words. He sat down on a bench, cupping his chin. "What's your point?"

"A dying man doesn't dwell on whether he is or isn't rich and powerful, he concentrates on every breath he takes and hopes it's not his last. He fights to survive. And that's what I do. *Survive*."

"You're a scholar with a fool's thinking," said Ozhan.

"It doesn't matter what you think of me, but it matters what I know about you. I've seen your kind in every backstreet," said Thomas with a fierce stare on his face. "You are scum. All you ever do is take what isn't yours, from the poor and defenceless, because they're terrified of you. And when they have no more to give, you inflict great pain and suffering upon them, ending in death. The world is full of your kind and would be better rid of you."

The baron looked into Thomas' eyes and was silent for a moment. He rose from the bench. "We're the same, you and I. Come and join me for a jug."

Thomas shook his head. "*No*."

"You're a wilful man," said Ozhan, and with a great effort he held back the angry retort that swam in his mind, but there was a truth here and he knew it. A person rarely acknowledges what means the most to them until they've lost it, and Thomas had been in that position ten years ago and lost everything with a single stab of his sword.

Again silence hung upon the air.

Ozhan stared into the warrior's eyes, holding to his insane gaze and he shrugged. "Maybe another time then," he said wanting to retreat, knowing neither he nor any of his men were in the same league as Thomas with swordplay. "Come," he called to his men, and they ambled behind him through the hushed crowd like a flock of sheep.

Thomas watched them leave. "One day I'll kill them all," he said with a hard edge to his voice.

***

Two days later, Thomas and Dardo were out on the Nottinghamshire grasslands behind the Dog and Duck practising swordplay and archery. "No, no, no, you hold a sword like a girl with a limp wrist and you're no better with a bow, so it's better if you use your speed, strength and fists, for I cannot teach you what you want to learn," insisted Thomas.

"But it's my dream," said Dardo.

Thomas stepped forward, sheathing his swords. He laid his hands on his friend's shoulders. "Yes, but it's a nightmare for me. You have no talent with either weapon, so let's get back to the inn, I've work to do."

"You judge me unworthy?"

"No, incapable. You have a limited ability with weapons and would be a danger to yourself."

The bright morning sunlight flared in Thomas' eyes as his gaze roamed across the vast grasslands. Three riders headed their way on horses taller than any he had seen before and the three men looked like large, powerful warriors as they galloped towards them with increasing speed.

Thomas stared at the distant riders, his hand shielding his eyes from the sun. "This looks interesting."

Within moments the three men rounded on the two friends, tugging their reins, coming to a halt, sitting their horses, staring at the pair.

"Do you know of a baron Ozhan and his whereabouts?" asked one man.

"You wish to find Ozhan?" said Thomas.

"Are you deaf? Why do you answer a question with a question?" asked the second rider, dismounting.

Dardo frowned. "Is it his employment you seek?"

The dismounted rider swaggered over to Thomas. He was broad-shouldered, barrel-chested and seven feet tall with silver hair and sunken brown eyes, his face bearing many deep scars. He wore the black leather tunic of a mercenary as did the others. Towering over the pair he stood for a moment. "Yes, he sent for us. Where can we find him?" he snapped, drawing his sword, his voice deep and harsh.

"Are you asking me or forcing a fight?" said Thomas.

The leader considered the question. "Fight him!"

Thomas drew both swords.

The huge warrior, holding his blade double-handed lunged forward, sending a wicked scything cut. But Thomas parried it, his own blades slicing out, slamming into the warrior's upper arm, plunging through muscle and tissue, causing him to scream. He stumbled, falling to his knees, groaning, the fiery pain exploding in his mind.

"Get up and fight through the pain," the leader shouted.

The warrior climbed back to his feet, making another double-handed lunge, but again Thomas parried it, plunging his other blade into the attacker's belly, levering it up, and up again. Blood sprayed from the wound, covering his arm and the man screamed, falling to his knees again, more fiery pain swamping his mind. He pitched forward from his knees, his face striking the grassy knoll. Thomas hacked at his neck twice and the head rolled clear.

Thomas fixed his gaze on the leader's dead eyes and a red beard. "Is that enough killing or is there someone else?" he shouted with bloodlust. "Is there someone else?"

"You fight like a demon, my brother," said the leader, his face crisscrossed with scars. "Are you a mercenary?"

Thomas sheathed his swords. "Aye and I can *kill* anything that lives and breathes."

The leader dismounted, hefting the corpse over his shoulder, placing it belly down in the fallen warrior's saddle with no reverence or ceremony. He picked up the head and placed it in a large saddlebag and remounted his own stallion in silence, gripping both sets of reins with trembling hands. "After what I've just witnessed, I'll give you the benefit of any doubt I have. That's enough killing for today. Now, will you point the way to Master Ozhan's abode and we'll take our fallen brother and ride?"

Thomas and Dardo stood stock-still, their gaze unblinking, fastened on the two mercenaries. Thomas' arm swung out, his forefinger pointing to the south-east. The leader nodded and the two mercenaries led the corpse-laden horse towards lower pastures, heading in the pointed direction. Both friends watched until the riders disappeared from view over a rise on the faraway hillside.

***

The following morning, a loud knock on Lira's door startled her. She opened it to see Thomas standing there wearing forest greens and calf-length boots. He had a smile on his face and a picnic basket in his hand. She wore a white shawl and russet dress.

Minutes later they walked across a narrow valley full of alder, birch and pine, and even though it was a winter's day the weather was beautiful, the sun shining in a clear blue sky, with the peaks of distant snow-capped hills glistening. And as they walked, climbing to a high hillside overlooking the City of Nottingham, his mind wandered and was far from the trials and tribulations of recent days. Today there were no swords slung around his waist as they came to rest and sat by a trickling stream.

Lira's golden hair glinted in the sunlight. "You seem lost in thought. What are you thinking?"

Thomas smiled, shrugging. He reached out to stroke her cheek. "Just how full of surprises life is."

She smiled, gentleness radiating from her in complete contrast to his strong aura. "Why do you say that?"

He shrugged again. "Because it's true. I fight a giant man, get hurt and meet an angel."

She laughed. "I'm not an angel."

"You look like one."

She blushed. He took her hand, lifting it to his lips, kissing it. "You're exquisite."

"How many others have you complimented so?"

He stared at her quizzically. "I'm not a rogue or a two-timer."

"Good," she said, wagging her finger at him. She opened the picnic basket producing two knives, two wooden plates, cornbread, ham and two small earthenware jars containing butter and pickles.

He lay on the grass, looking up at the sky. "What do you wish for in life?"

She leaned in close to him. "Pleasant memories in my old age."

He sighed, inhaling her perfume. Drawing her down to the grass he kissed her lips.

She pulled away from him. "Please don't fall in love with me, my life uncomplicated and I want to keep it that way."

He looked puzzled. "Are you not happy here with me?"

She ran her fingers through his hair, "I wish for many things, but love is the last thing on my mind right now."

"You can't ask someone not to fall in love with you. Love is uncontrolled and for the moment."

"I agree, but not this moment. I have problems right now."

He looked hurt. "What problems? Problems are better spoken of, not kept locked away."

She shook her head. "You're a strong man, but my problem is my problem."

He looked saddened with a heavy heart.

She saw rejection in his eyes.

"Shame about the wonderful woman I fell in love with, she needs no man."

***

Later that night in the crowded, smoky bar at the Dog and Duck, Dardo inquired, "How was the picnic?"

Thomas looked miserable, his spirits low. "Don't ask."

"You're usually good company my friend, what's wrong?"

"Not sure. I know Lira likes me, but I suspect there's someone else."

"If she's interested in someone else why would she go on a picnic with you?" Dardo reasoned. "It makes little sense."

Thomas sighed. "I know, but I have this feeling. Every time I gaze into her eyes it's as if she sees someone else."

"Someone might have hurt her. It's not always easy to forget a bad experience."

Thomas nodded. "Maybe."

"Give it time, my friend; she may come around to your way of thinking."

Thomas nodded, "If nothing else, time is a great healer."

Before they could say another word, a tall, thin man wearing a long, grey robe entered the tavern and approached the bar. He was bald, his face angular, and he stood for a moment, then ordered a tankard of ale from Cyrano. In the lantern light, the newcomers face looked ancient. The innkeeper served him and he made his way through the crowd with clumsy movements, his twisted right leg several inches shorter than the left. The crowd laughed, and he didn't seem to mind, but the sound cut through Thomas. "What's so funny?" he shouted to the roomful of revellers.

"My walk," said the old man, "but that's my misfortune."

"I don't understand where the humour lies," shouted Thomas.

The crowd fell silent as the man limped on and sat in a far corner alone.

Thomas stood up, making his way over to the old man, "You would honour us if you come and join my friend and me," he said for all to hear.

The old man rose from his chair, following the warrior back through the crowd to their table. Thomas sat down, pulled up another chair and motioned for him to sit. "You're a kind soul, my brother, a little hospitality and conversation would be pleasant."

Dardo moved over to accommodate the old man, who shuffled around until he seemed comfortable. "What's your name?"

"Gorl," was the reply.

"Well, what brings you to the Inn this evening? We've not seen you in here before," said Thomas.

"I came looking for protection," said Gorl looking weary, his voice distraught.

"Protection from whom or what?" asked Thomas raising an eyebrow.

"Those who want to take what is mine," said Gorl. "They're coming."

Thomas looked at Dardo. "He's too old to take up the sword."

The old man wiped the sweat from his brow. "I'm willing to pay for my protection. Are you the one named Thomas Flynn with the fierce reputation?"

Dardo nodded. "Aye, he is."

"Will you honour me with your help? I'll pay you well," said Gorl, producing a purse from a deep coat pocket. He opened it, gold dust glinting in the dim light.

"Put that away, old man!" snapped Thomas. "Many here would see you dead for such an amount of gold."

"Most here would kill you for a lot less," added Dardo, "and you still haven't mentioned who is coming for you?"

The old man's face trembled, his eyes haunted. Fear ripped through him and he shivered. His eyes misted over and a glazed expression replaced the look of fear. "Ozhan and his thugs are coming for me," he whispered. "He's found out there's gold on my land and wants it. Three days he gave me to clear off my property and tomorrow is the third day."

Thomas shook his head and swore. "I'm a swordsman, and without being modest, the best, and even though I have no quarrel with Ozhan, I will make your quarrel mine, because he deserves to get what's coming to him."

Gorl broke out into tears and sobbed, he was so relieved, and a vestige of hope shone in his green eyes. "How can I thank you?" he said, drying them. "I'll pay you any sum you ask."

Thomas glanced at Dardo. "We have enough funds to sit out the cold season, but an extra purse of gold dust would do us no harm if that's agreeable?"

Gorl nodded. "Let's make it two purses. I put a high value on my life."

"Just how much gold did you find on your land?" asked Dardo, eyes wide.

"A hill full," said Gorl with an uneasy smile that echoed in his close-set eyes.

"Then two purses is agreeable," said Thomas.

Dardo nodded his approval, "Did Ozhan say when he would arrive on the third day?"

"Aye, he did," said Gorl. "He said if I was still on my farm by sunset, I wouldn't see another sunrise. I would be dead, my body burned, my ashes scattered to the wind."

"Then we shall arrive at your farm well before sunset and await them coming. Go home, rest and I assure you we'll solve your problem," said Thomas.

Gorl gave them directions to his farm, paying Thomas half in advance, and as he stood up to leave, he swayed almost falling. Dardo caught him and half carried him through the crowded room to the door. Outside he helped Gorl mount his gelding and waved goodbye before returning to Thomas.

"Why were you born a hero?" Dardo asked.

Thomas shrugged. "Just lucky I guess."

CHAPTER FOUR

As good as dead

The farmers' huts and cottages were ill-kept and their owners no longer took pride in them. Lira's father, Tobin, was one of those farmers, besides being the local blacksmith. Ozhan had threatened him with great violence, giving him an ultimatum to leave his land, but he was a big and strong and a proud man so he ignored it. Still, he was no match for the bully baron.

Lira's face screwed up in a knot. "Sorry about the supper, father, it's been a disaster," she said, looking tired. She was wearing a white flowing dress and sandals, and had made a stew with lamb and vegetables, which had smelt delicious while cooking, but lost its flavour in the eating after her father mentioned Ozhan's name.

Tobin ranted on about Ozhan's violent behaviour towards the farmers and his plans to take over the whole city by force. "What are we to do? There's no one brave enough or skilled enough to help us."

"The common people of Nottingham don't compare favourably when stacked up against the might of the men who stand with the baron," Lira observed.

Thunder sounded overhead. Tobin shook his head. "What are we to do?"

Lira stood up, clearing the plates and dishes, removing the tablecloth and she walked over to the small leaded window by the fire, watching rain sheet down as a web of lightning forked in the night sky. Thunder sounded again, louder this time and not so distant with a deep sustained rumble that echoed throughout the farmhouse. Tobin's Red Setter barked and shivered by the fire, its ears flattening back against its head, looking around, growling. Tobin climbed to his feet and ambled over to the dog, stroking it as it leaned into him. "Shh, it'll pass soon," he whispered.

Outside the wind howled like a banshee and rain lashed the farmhouse. Lira peered through the watery curtain on the windowpane and could just make out two shadowy figures crossing a nearby bridge as more lightning forked, illuminating the sky. "Someone's coming this way, are you expecting company, father?"

He took a deep breath, his face twisted, and he said something, stopped, tried again and shook his head. He was damp with sweat, fear flashing in his eyes and his heart was pounding. "The baron's coming for me."

Moments later, they huddled together seeing two dark shadows slide past their window and then there was a loud knock on the door, startling them. "W-who's there?" stammered Tobin.

Someone outside muttered something, but he and Lira couldn't make out what it was. In a panic, she cried, "Oh my God, who's out there?"

There was another loud knock at the door, frightening them even more and their blood froze. Then everything went quiet.

Lira's pupils grew large, staring at the door. "I don't like this."

Tobin trembled, a poker at the ready in his hand. "I don't like this either."

A voice outside startled them again. They jumped. Thomas opened the door, grinning around it. The rain was dripping from his hair. "Sorry, didn't mean to scare you both, but the storm caught us out on our way home, can we stay here until the weather clears?"

More thunder drummed out overhead and the heavens opened in an even greater deluge of rain. Lira bid them come in as she glanced out at the rainwater bouncing off the inky surface of the nearby lake. Thomas shucked off his heavy, grey coat and moved to the fire to warm his hands. Dardo followed him, removing his lighter coat of blue. A small log fell from the flames, rolling onto the granite hearth at their feet and Thomas picked it up with his bare fingers, jerking it back onto the fire without using the iron tongs.

Dardo looked surprised. "Are you fireproof too, besides all of your other extraordinary talents?"

Thomas smiled, staring into the flames, remembering their first meeting on the gibbet in Gallows Square and wished his chin had been fist-proof, not fireproof that night. Turning to look at Lira, his gaze moved on and he fixed his eyes on Tobin instead, who was wearing a doublet of grey silk, embroidered with gold and silver thread and leggings of a lighter grey. He was a tall man, a proud man, slender yet powerfully built with a thin clean-shaven face, his hair dark and curly, his eyes blue, standing statue-still with a haunted stare on his pale face.

"I apologise for startling you," said Thomas, "but on the way back to our lodgings at the Inn the weather turned in an instant." His keen brown eyes stared hard at the older man.

Tobin smiled, shaking his head. "It's of no consequence, and you're welcome to stay for the night if you so wish. There are two spare rooms upstairs."

Lira nodded her approval while Thomas' eyes wandered around the room. Two lit lanterns were hanging in their iron brackets on the south wall, a fire burning in the hearth on the north wall, the whole place tidy and the farmhouse filled with the aroma of herbs, spices, stew and vegetables. It was an inviting scene, save for the strained atmosphere.

Has Tobin and Lira been arguing before our arrival? Thomas wondered. "Are you sure it's convenient for us to stay?" he asked.

Dardo noticed the tense atmosphere too.

"It's convenient," said Tobin, his spirits lifted by their presence, but Lira's dog backed away from the two men into a corner, growling.

"Blood's not used to company," said Lira.

The name surprised Thomas. "Blood?"

"He's a Red Setter, hence the strange name," she enlightened with a smile. "It's father's idea of humour, but I'd say it's his age."

Tobin stretched, yawned and sat on a stool by the fire. "Age makes fools of us all," he whispered to himself, thinking of the times the baron and his men humiliated him with Lira present. If I were younger, he thought, I would challenge him to a duel and cut off both his ears and nose before dealing the final death stroke.

Another smouldering log fell from the fire and rolled onto the granite hearth, jerking Tobin from his thoughts. Thomas reached down and picked it up with his bare fingers again, throwing it back onto the fire. As he did so, he saw a blistering mark around the blacksmith's neck, which looked like the mark a gallows noose would make. It was healing but looked to be only a few days old. Tobin noticed him staring at the mark and covered it up with his collar. Poking the fire he hung a kettle over the blaze. "Lira will make us a cup of nettle tea."

"Have you any rose-hip tea instead?" asked Dardo. "It's my favourite."

"Aye," said Lira. "It's made to a secret recipe of mine."

Tobin's ancestors had dwelt in the hills for centuries, keeping themselves to themselves, but now Ozhan threatened to take everything away from them because they appeared to be rich in the eyes of the local city dwellers. Greed began the whole land grabbing affair, and decisive action by a hero would be the only thing to end it. Thomas might be that hero, Tobin thought. His awesome reputation and credentials preceded him.

Within moments the kettle was boiling. Lira wrapped a cloth around her hand, lifted it from its bracket and walked over to the table, filling four slender cups with boiling water, adding a small muslin bag to each, and she made sure that Dardo's cup had the rose-hip tea instead of nettle. A sweet delicious aroma filled the room as she stirred the contents of each cup and hooked out the bags, passing one to each of her guests, then one to her father.

Thomas tasted the brew and smiled. "Thanks, it's appreciated."

Dardo nodded, smiling his appreciation too.

Tobin stood up quickly. "I'm off to bed now. Lira will show you to your rooms when you're ready. Goodnight gentlemen, I'll see you in the morning." He kissed her on the cheek, turned and headed for the door glancing back at the warrior. He cocked his head, took a deep breath and shrugged. "You know, Thomas, with your reputation I imagined you would be much bigger!"

Thomas burst out laughing, almost choking on his tea. "Wow, how many times has that been said before," he replied as Tobin stepped through the doorway and climbed the stairs to bed with his tea.

***

The following morning, miles distant at Gorl's farm, a fist struck the man full in the face sending him sprawling to the dirt. The baron grinned, his eyes narrowing. He glanced around at his men and cursed. "You said you had put the fear of God into the old man, and that he'd gone a week ago, but the old bastard is still here. He hauled the injured man upright with iron fingers gripping his throat.

There was a great buzzing in the man's ears and dizziness swamped him as he fought to focus on Ozhan's brutal face. The baron smashed the man back to the floor, "You disgust me! And do you know why you disgust me?" he said, hauling the almost unconscious man upright again. "Because you're a liar and a bleeder!" He punched the man's face again. Bright lights shone before his eyes and he tried to rise, but the baron kicked his face, smashing his nose, knocking him unconscious.

"He's a loser. Dispose of him," the baron gestured to his men. "Now who else needs to apologise for not getting the job done?

The six men stared at each other. Stard, a wiry, dark-haired man with silver teeth knew his life was over and nothing could prevent Ozhan from killing him unless he apologised and made good his promise to get rid of Gorl from his farm. The baron wanted the old man's gold and nobody would stand in his way.

Stard stepped forward, humbled, his soul scaled and pitted from a life of crime and killing. "I apologise, Oz," he said, staring into the baron's bloodshot eyes. "I am sorry and will make good my promise to you. Gorl is as good as dead now."

Ozhan drew his dagger, pricking the blade under the skin of Stard's chin. "I couldn't quite hear you." The point was needle-sharp and Stard felt a trickle of blood on his neck. In his moment of terror, he looked into the face of his tormentor, cursing his soul, knowing his life was over unless a guardian angel fell from the sky or a miracle happened.

Ozhan pricked the skin a little more, lifting Stard to his toes. "I told you to get the old bastard off this land and now he's barricaded himself in the farmhouse. Do I have to do everything myself?"

"We… we apologise Oz," the others stammered together, "but we can still burn the old bastard out!"

"Oz, there's someone coming on foot," another man called out.

The baron removed his dagger from Stard's throat and he fell to his knees. Stard blinked and strained to focus on the two newcomers.

"Good day to you gentlemen," said Thomas, laying his heavy coat over a tethering post.

Dardo nodded, acknowledging his friend's sentiment.

"Leave well alone, the pair of you," warned Ozhan. "This matter is nothing to do with either of you."

Thomas fixed the brutal man's hard gaze with an even harder stare. He drew his swords. "Wrong, the old man paid us to protect him and his property, so here's my advice, leave now, all of you, while I'm not in a killing mood."

Two men in black leather tunics stepped forward, drawing their swords.

"Ah, the two young mercenaries from yesterday," said Thomas. "You found who you were looking for I see. I thought we might meet again, sooner rather than later."

Dardo drew his sword, standing beside Thomas. "I'm not much good with this, but maybe they aren't either," he whispered.

Thomas frowned, pushing him aside. "They're mercenaries. Killing is their trade, and it's no time for heroics my friend. I can take them both," he whispered back.

Thomas' words gave Dardo relief, and he leaned against the tethering post, but he didn't sheath his sword. "I know it's difficult being my friend sometimes, but I'm here if you need me," he said with a weak smile.

Thomas patted him on the shoulder. "You are a good and loyal friend."

"Kill him," snapped Ozhan. "Kill the whoreson."

Both men nodded, storming forward with their two-handed swords slashing towards Thomas' head.

His swords flashed up to block the stroke. He spun to his right, a blade licking out, cutting deep into the flesh and muscle of one man's shoulder.

The man screamed. "You're a scum-sucking bastard."

Thomas ducked under a slashing cut, ramming his other blade into the man's belly, wrenching it up into his heart. Blood sprayed and air hissed from the man's lungs. He fell to the earth dead.

Never had the baron's men seen anyone dispatched with such ease. Thomas seemed devil-possessed; his eyes feverish.

The second mercenary stood for a moment, staring at his dead friend in disbelief. "Yesterday morning the sun rose over me and my comrades, now two are dead, so there's much here to think on," he said, sheathing his sword. "I'm no coward, but I am outclassed brother. You have a talent for killing and a swiftness like no other I've ever seen. Your mastery of the short-sword is amazing and I do not wish to die today."

"Do you serve me or not?" shouted the baron, his voice deep and menacing.

The mercenary shook his head, mounting his black stallion. "Serve you? No! Keep your money! What use is gold or silver to a dead man?" He thrashed his reins. The horse bolted, galloping off into the distance.

The baron called to one of his own men, who dismounted and approached Thomas.

"I don't care what the mercenary said, you're still just a man and will bleed if cut," he announced.

Ozhan drew his sword and tossed it to the man, who caught it by the hilt. "Use my blade, you'll find it lighter and easier to handle than your own."

The man was tall, broad and handsome with a shock of black hair like a lion's mane, his eyes dark and slit like that of a panther too. He attacked, his sword slashing towards Thomas' face.

Two short-swords flashed up to block the stroke, but the man was ready for the move and spun to his right, his fist slamming against Thomas' cheek. Thomas staggered backwards as the man aimed a slashing cut at his neck. He dropped to one knee, surging upright, his other blade snaking out, stabbing the man's shoulder, ripping his vest and penetrating his muscle right to the bone.

Dreadful pain exploded in the man's shoulder and his face twisted as if someone had squeezed his genitals, but he only whimpered. The man attacked again and Thomas ducked under another slashing cut, ramming his own blade deep into the man's chest. His sword dropped from his hand and an agonised groan burst from his lips as acid fire filled his whole body. His knees buckled, and he fell to the ground, face first, dead.

Thomas relaxed and in that single moment, a great weariness descended upon him. His hands trembling with the aftershock of the fight, his keen eyes stared at the dead man who was younger than he was.

"Whoever trained you trained you well," said Ozhan, "but why do you defend the weak and stupid? Join me and I'll make you rich. Join the winning side."

Thomas shook his head, his eyes filled with hatred. "You don't understand do you?"

The baron looked confused. "Understand what?"

"Ten years ago, I was on the winning side, driven by something I didn't understand or try to explain because I had everything a man could wish for: a kingdom, power and riches. But the one thing I didn't have was happiness. I left that kingdom for two years to fight in the wars and then travelled far and wide in search of happiness. When I couldn't find it I returned and fought my brother, killing him to reclaim what was mine. In doing so, I lost my soul and became a drunkard, but found a vocation that brings me joy. To defend the weak and needy. I love being able to beat back the fire that burns in evil men's hearts knowing I can save the day."

Ozhan ground his teeth. "You're a fool for refusing my offer."

Thomas shook his head. "No! You're the fool and when you least expect it life will deal with you most unkindly. Now take your thugs and go. And leave the old man alone!"

The baron's anger swelled, but he moved on rather than force another confrontation with the warrior who barred his way to Gorl's gold. His men mounted their horses and his brutal face trembled with fury as he mounted his. He stared at Thomas and then spun his horse and they all took off like a pack of hounds. He glanced back fleetingly, and the image of Dardo and Thomas laughing burned into his mind just as if branded by a hot iron.

***

Later that night, Thomas and Dardo were listening to the blind harpist in the Dog and Duck when Lira came by, wanting to talk, to explain her confused feelings. As she stepped inside, the music ceased. Thomas shifted his gaze to her, fidgeting in his chair. "What are you doing here?" he asked.

She looked embarrassed, staring at the floor as she made her way over to their table. "I need to talk to you. I heard what you did for Gorl today and it's brave of you both."

Dardo smiled at her and laughed, "Umm, the baron thought better of his venture and went away without a smug look on his face."

"But he'll be back with more thugs," said Thomas. "A hill full of gold is a hell of a temptation and he won't stop now I assure you."

She pulled up a chair and sat down quickly. "That's what I want to talk to you about Thomas."

There was silence for a moment. Then the harpist played as the crowded room buzzed with conversation again, but eyes watched and ears listened to every word they said. The eyes and ears belonged to four cutthroats sitting across from Thomas, wearing ill-fitting sack-cloth clothes.

The main eavesdropper, a bald man with a fully tattooed face answered to the name of Yorden, and to Thomas he stood out like a sore thumb. "Be careful what you say, the baron has spies everywhere," he whispered, nodding at the four men drinking across from him.

They smiled, turning back around, pretending to talk to each other.

"That was convincing," said Lira in a sarcastic tone.

Thomas shook his head. "I could spot them at ten miles distance, even without the lighthouse on each of their heads." He chuckled good-humouredly, elbowing Dardo who returned fire.

"This isn't the perfect place for our conversation, but it's private enough if we keep our voices low," whispered Lira. She relaxed, a hesitant smile blooming on her face. "What do you know of Ozhan?"

Thomas raised his eyebrows. "He's a violent man with a diseased mind and soul who wants to rule over all of Nottinghamshire."

"Do you want to know the awful truth?" she asked, taking a moment to pull herself together before speaking again. "He's doing this because of me. I rejected him three years ago, and he beat me so violently I almost died. Now he believes in his own twisted mind that if he gives me what no one else can, I'll love him."

Thomas' mouth responded before his brain could even register what Lira was saying. "Have you ever loved him?" His common sense told him it was inappropriate, but curiosity got the better of him.

Lira looked shocked by the question. "No, never. He's ugly on the inside, besides being ugly on the outside too. He's a vicious, twisted thug. A madman."

Thomas cursed himself for even asking the question.

"Well, uh, what gave him the idea you loved him in the first place?" asked Dardo.

"Because I showed him kindness when I tended to his wounds after the fight that could have killed him," she said. "He mistook kindness for love in his own twisted way, and he's hounded me ever since that day. He even threatened to kill my father, to change my mind, but father stood up to him and his men and they hung him in Gallows Square. Fortunately for my father, the rope snapped, and a fight broke out distracting Ozhan."

Thomas nodded. "I saw the rope burn on his neck the other night."

She hesitated for a moment, taking a deep breath. "Now you know the truth and why I fear him."

"Fear is natural in such circumstances," said Thomas, "it causes a fight-or-flight response in animals and humans, but we'll make sure no harm befalls you or your father."

"You can't be everywhere and protect everyone, it's not possible," Lira told him.

"We can have a town meeting and keep track of the baron."

"But how do we meet the other landowners without the baron finding out?" asked Dardo.

"We'll invite them to Lira's surgery as if it's for a talk about the healing power of herbs and mosses," said Thomas tapping his nose. "We'll only message those the baron has threatened or who have suffered violence and had their homes burned. They can keep an eye out for the baron and if something happens, we can be there in no time."

"Ozhan has more men than the two of you can handle alone," advised Lira.

"That's true but I'll figure that out later."

"What a Godsend you've proved to be," she said, climbing to her feet, kissing his cheek. "My father has recovered from his ordeal, but I fear more encounters with the baron might prove fatal."

Thomas marvelled at her extraordinary beauty as she turned to leave without saying another word.

She walked out into the cold night air.

He straightened up in his chair and stretched with a grunt.

Dardo was silent for a moment, staring at the formidable figure sat in front of him. "You know Thomas; you never cease to amaze me. You have the mental strength of a giant and the courage of ten men, reminding me of my childhood hero."

Thomas smiled. "And who was that?"

"Robin of the Hood. The only difference is he used a bow and arrow to good effect while you need only your brains and tongue."

Thomas laughed. "Brains beat brawn every time with a little help from cold hard steel."

***

A large map of Nottinghamshire and hundreds of drawings littered the walls of the baron's ostentatious den, with its polished wooden floors and elegant fixtures and fittings. On the map, he had coloured lands to the north purple, hills and valleys to the south brown, forested areas to the east green, and black dots showed worthless land. Red dots peppered the hills to the west. These were the homesteads and farms he wished to gain by whatever means necessary. Land rich with gold.

Ozhan lay on a couch studying the map with utter concentration when a servant tapped on his door disturbing his focused mind. The man entered, bowing.

"There's someone wishing to speak to you, sir. The person is waiting in the library and claims to be the only soul ever to win the warrior, Thomas Flynn in a fair fight."

The baron jumped to his feet. "Interesting! Has the fool got a name?"

"The name given was Nelan, sir."

Ozhan chuckled. "Sounds like a girl's name."

"It is a young woman, sir."

"Even more interesting," said Ozhan. "Well, don't just stand there, send her in man."

The servant did as ordered.

The baron smiled as the wiry woman entered. She was tall, dark-haired and slim, her blue eyes vibrant and alive with youth, and a long thin scar ran the length of her left cheek. It didn't spoil her great beauty. Dressed in a doublet of scarlet and black hose, she threw back her matching cloak, straightening her high collar before adjusting her sword-belt. He motioned for her to sit. She slumped to a chair, closing her eyes. "It's been a monstrous journey," she said, her voice slurring with weariness.

"Where do you hail from?" he asked.

"Northumberland," she replied.

He slumped to his chair, leaning back, staring at the warrior woman with the golden hawk's head emblazoned across the front of her doublet. "You make a bold claim, and after seeing Thomas fight with my own eyes, it's hard to believe by any stretch of the imagination."

Nelan frowned. "Why, because I'm a woman?" Her voice was light, her eyes showing no emotion.

His head sank back into the cushioned chair and his breathing deepened. "No, not because you're a woman, because I've seen hard mercenaries humbled in seconds by this man. His speed is beyond belief, his skill unmatched."

The door opened and a cool draft touched her neck, making her shiver as the servant entered, carrying a silver tray containing two goblets of red wine, which they both drained in a single swallow. There was also bread and cheese in thick chunks, which they ate, leaning back once more.

"You need rest," said Ozhan. "We'll talk more tomorrow."

Helping her to her feet, the servant led her to a bedchamber with a four-poster bed and she undressed, covering herself with thick blankets and she fell fast asleep and she dreamt of her days under the command of Master Gallus, her mentor, fifteen years earlier. She was ten years old at the time and Gallus was an old man even then, and long dead now, but in his prime, he was the greatest swordsman the world had ever known. "Time is not on our side and old age can be unkind," he himself had said in a moment of wisdom.

In his darkest hour, he had accepted a rare challenge from one of his own students and come to grief. Thomas Flynn was the student's name, and he showed inspired brilliance in his own swordplay, but to Gallus' dismay, he preferred to fight with twin short-swords and not a broadsword. To prove his point, Thomas in a moment of complete madness challenged Master Gallus to a duel using real weapons, rather than the blunted training weapons. Gallus had accepted, hoping to prove his own point by outwitting and disarming Thomas, but the duel went wrong when Gallus tripped and stared down in disbelief at the blade embedded in his chest. With a dreadful groan, he had fallen to the dirt, dead.

The accident mortified Thomas. He had great love and respect for his teacher and no intention of harming him, but Nelan swore an oath of vengeance for the death of her mentor because he had been a father to her since the day her own parents died of a plague. Five years later, Thomas and Nelan duelled for an hour and she was a single cut away from killing him when the other students stopped the fight.

Now as always the dream was the same, she was crying and Gallus was trying to find her, to protect her from an ugly, shadowy shape with a corpse grey face and yellow eyes. She screamed and then screamed again. "I don't want to die!"

"But you are dead and so is Master Gallus," whispered the opal-eyed thing. "And the one responsible is

Thomas Flynn." She awoke with a start, her heart pounding, her skin damp with sweat. She threw back the blankets and climbed from the bed. It was morning, so she dressed. There was a knock at the door. She answered it and a spidery stick-like figure with sunken eyes loomed over her. She glanced up at the man. "Yes?"

"The Master requires your presence downstairs, milady," said the servant.

"Tell Master Ozhan I'll be with him in a moment," she instructed, closing the door in his face. Turning, she picked up her sword belt from the back of a chair, looping it around her slender waist, fastening it, and then reached down placing a dagger into the hidden scabbard in her boot. This was something Thomas had taught her to do, and it had saved her life when her assailants had knocked the swords from her hands. She swirled her cloak around her shoulders, opening the door. There was no sign of the servant as she walked along the narrow corridor towards the staircase and descended, listening to the clattering sounds of swordplay.

As she walked, she noticed the echoing murmur of voices and the cushioned sound of panting. Screwing up her nose, she squirmed, choking, her breath freezing in her throat because of the stink of stale sweat and rancid breath in the air. And as she rounded the bottom of the stairs, she came face to face with several warriors who crowded around her, butting her shoulders, grinning and whining their greetings. She pushed her way through them, whispering gruff threats that offered great violence if they didn't allow her to pass. They drew back as the baron's harsh voice ordered them to and he offered his greeting to her. She feared none of the men.

Ozhan approached her, hooking his arm around her neck, leaning against her slender frame, pushing her off balance.

Nelan edged away and sat by a large open fireplace with a tiled hearth, closing her grip around the leather-bound hilt of her sword. She drew the blade from her sheath, polished iron sliding on oiled cow's hide as the dawn sun burst through a high-arched window over her shoulder, dowsing her hair in a fiery light. She raised her weapon in a salute to the Master. "I offer my help to tame the warrior, Thomas Flynn if you so ask it."

Ozhan grinned. "If you can do the deed and kill Thomas, you shall have as much gold as you can carry."

CHAPTER FIVE
The debt

Thomas stood on the hillside overlooking Nottingham for a long time in silence. He was rigid; a vertical frown line etched on his brow, his body shivering in the cold rain. He wrapped an arm around Lira's shoulder, folding her into him. The sun shone from behind, throwing long shadows that pooled at their feet, and the wind whipped around their bodies lifting their cloaks of black wool.

"The waters good around here, the soil fertile, the grass rich and green, but Ozhan is destroying this community, bit by bit, piece by piece," Lira whispered.

Thomas nodded in agreement. "We must stop him, and soon."

"But how?"

"Not sure yet, but I will kill him if I have to," he assured her.

"You look dreadful," she told him. "How long is it since you last slept?"

He nodded. "Days," he said. Then for a moment, he was silent, his expression thoughtful. He gave a tired smile, his face thin and drawn; his cheeks covered in black stubble, eyes dark-rimmed and weary. He shivered, memories flaring of his dead mother, father and brother. "You are alone. You will always be alone," they whispered in his mind.

***

Over the next seven days there followed a scatter of activity and several secret meetings in and around Lira's surgery. Many, many people came. Worried, frightened farmers and landowners besides city folk who Ozhan and his thugs had threatened or assaulted. They turned up in their droves to listen to Thomas' plans for their future safety and knowing his fierce reputation they felt more at ease.

But there were those who wouldn't take his advice and wanted to leave their homesteads, to move on to new pastures rather than risk their lives under Thomas and Dardo's protection, despite their promise to keep them safe. This troubled Thomas because it sent a clear message to the other farmers and homesteaders to do the same thing.

"It's wrong," Thomas said at the meetings, "to leave everything you have worked hard for all of your lives, just because of one man, and if you run now, you will never stop running."

Lira and Dardo watched and listened, mesmerised by his show of conviction for their plans, but dozens of farmers remained unconvinced.

"It's a complete waste of a lifetime's work if you pack up and leave when threatened. I have the skills to defeat Ozhan and his thugs, but you must put your trust in my abilities," Thomas told them.

Thomas' upbringing in Northumberland was hard, but it taught him never to worry about what people thought, said or did, as his focus was the key to unlock any door. At the tender age of seventeen, he had met Master Gallus in a forest in Northumberland, where together they sat beneath a single giant oak talking of many things, including the power of the mind. Gallus, an expert in the art of sword and bow explained that the skills of a swordsman came a poor second to the heart of a swordsman. "Without the heart, the skills are useless," he had said.

Thomas had shrugged, asking why?

"When you can tell me that, you will have grown to be the legendary swordsman I know you can be," the Master answered.

Now, in the present day, the lack of support the city folk gave Thomas troubled him, but it didn't surprise him. Terror filled their hearts.

***

An hour after the meetings, Thomas tugged on his reins, halting his stallion at a crossroads. Anger flared as recent memories flooded his mind again. If he had known a week ago what he knew now, he might have left well alone, left the landowners and farmers to their own fates instead of getting involved. But he was in love with Lira even if she wasn't in love with him. The perils are great but the rewards should be greater, he thought.

He heeled his horse forward, cantering along a tree-lined avenue, the road ahead almost deserted as he trotted towards the Dog and Duck, and everywhere he looked he saw the signs of the baron's oppressive rule: innocent people hung in Gallows Square; a poor wretch dying of thirst in the stocks and women and children starving on the streets.

He entered the courtyard gate to the stables. Tugging on the reins he halted, dismounting, and the great white's head nuzzled him as he rubbed his hand over the broad brow, leading it into a stall. A wide-eyed groom appeared from out of the shadows, making the horse a bed of straw and Thomas hefted the boy a copper coin.

"Thanks for your help," he said, winking at the boy. "Will you take good care of my horse? His name is Battle."

The boy blinked. "That's a strange name for a horse."

Thomas smiled. "He's a strange horse, but a faithful one."

The boy nodded. "I'll fill a small sack of grain." He ran off to the far end of the stable, returning with the feed sack a moment later.

Thomas ruffled the boy's hair as he fed the horse. "What's your name, boy?"

"Godwin, son of Berwyn, from the House of Longmire," the boy answered with a smile.

"Then I'll say good day to you, Godwin, son of Berwyn, from the House of Longmire." Thomas marched from the stall and out of the stable door. A cold wind whispered into the courtyard. He raised the collar of his heavy grey coat as it rained and he lifted his eyes to the heavens, holding his face to the downpour. For a moment he stood stock-still, then he opened the back door of the inn, stepping through, entering the dining room. It was dark inside and he could hear a deep, rumbling growl and see two eyes that shone like silver. A set of ivory white teeth bared at him.

Something crashed into his chest, hurling him to the ground. One moment he was on his feet and the next he was on the floor gasping for breath with the air punched from his lungs. A man's voice sounded. The creature backed away into a corner. In the dim light, Thomas could make out the shape of a huge dog. "You... you must be a stranger in these parts," he whispered, "for I live and work here and would remember if we had met before today."

A shaft of moonlight shone through the arched window and the dog's coat seemed to glint with flecks of steel. Tired and hungry, Thomas rolled to one knee and climbed to his feet. "You might have warned me about your hairy friend," he snapped, noticing the innkeeper.

"Only bought the mutt this morning, and I was just opening the place up," said Cyrano, stepping into the dim light. "You're lucky I was here, otherwise my hunter-killer friend might have mistaken you for an intruder and chewed your rosy arse." His laughter boomed out as he lit a nearby wall-lantern, then another and another, until a golden light radiated throughout the room, bathing the walls. In moments, the atmosphere of the whole place seemed warm and inviting and even the dust motes in the air gleamed.

Now Thomas saw the dog. It was enormous. A wolfhound of extraordinary size. "The bloody thing's bigger than a donkey," he said. The hound continued to growl, baring teeth, but Thomas laid a hand upon the fierce animals head and stroked it until it whimpered with delight.

Cyrano watched through astonished eyes, looking like a man carved from a turnip, "Have you no end to your extraordinary talents?"

Thomas shook his head. "Have you not noticed that I have a knack for taming fierce creatures," he said, climbing to his feet. He turned and marched upstairs, making his way to the back bedroom and went inside, closing the door behind him. There was a pitcher of half-drunk ale on a table by the pallet beds and Dardo was fast asleep, snoring in his slumber.

Downstairs the bar and dining room was tidy once again, the broken shelves mended, and there was no evidence of the day's savagery. There had only been one fight and Cyrano had quelled it using the wolfhound. Now two maids sang a song in the dining room and both worked hard setting places for the evening meals. The blind harpist came through the open back door and played in readiness to entertain while Cyrano milled around, filling the wall lanterns with more coal oil. He drew the heavy red curtains and shut the back door to keep out the cold night air, then washed and polished every pewter goblet, until they shone like silver.

At last, he wrapped his white linen apron around his waist and opened the outer double doors, changing the closed sign to open. Then he stepped behind the bar ready for service. He didn't have to wait long. A tall, thin man wearing long robes of grey velvet entered and approached the bar. His hair was long and dark, his eyes blue and he glanced around the room fixing his gaze upon Cyrano's tired face, and then stood for a moment. "It's been a long time since I visited Nottinghamshire," he said at last.

Cyrano scratched his head. "Good evening and welcome. What can I get you?"

The newcomer smiled. "A goblet of your best ale innkeeper. Someone told me you serve the finest ales and wines here."

Cyrano nodded. "Oh, good. Would I know the man?"

The stranger laughed, turning around, his eyes focussing on Ozhan's scarred face in the doorway.

Cyrano couldn't hide his emotions, his fear was obvious. His face trembled, and he sat on a stool behind the bar.

"I'd like a word," said the baron, his tone harsh.

Cyrano looked terrified.

"You're not a wise man, for you don't heed warnings and don't pay your debts when you need to," Ozhan said.

"I'm not sure I know what you mean," said Cyrano wiping the sheen of sweat from his furrowed brow. "Can you explain?"

A golden-haired man entered the bar and stepped in front of him. "I'll explain it to you," he snapped.

"Shut up while I'm talking," the baron scolded, holding him back with an outstretched arm.

The warrior stepped away. "Sorry, Oz!"

"Last week my merchant, Stard, came to collect a debt you didn't pay, and that makes me furious. Everyone else in Nottingham has paid except you. Well, I supply the ale you serve, but you haven't paid for it so you're out of business until you pay the debt in full." The baron fell silent, walking around the bar, coming face to face and nose to nose with Cyrano, who was shaking like a leaf, terror etched on his face.

"Now I understand," said Cyrano in a husky whisper.

Ozhan's iron hand shot out, gripping his throat, hauling him up into the air. "You better understand you old bastard. You have seven days to pay what you owe or your lights go out forever, and I'm not talking about the ones around your walls!"

Cyrano whimpered. "I... I guarantee payment," he stammered.

"There are cheaper wines and ales, old man, but the best doesn't come cheap. You have seven days to come up with the money. Don't waste them," said Ozhan releasing his grip.

Cyrano fell to his knees, gasping for air as the baron marched towards the double doors, pitching along as if his next step might bring him to his nose. His men followed behind, slamming the doors shut, changing the Open sign to Closed, and they disappeared into the night laughing, cheering and jeering.

Cyrano was breathless with fear and remained on his knees considering the threat. Ozhan didn't make idle threats that much he knew. "I'm a dead man," he whispered.

Thomas and Dardo entered the barroom by the stairwell door, looking confused because he was still on his knees, clasping his throat, "What's going on?" they asked, looking around the empty room.

Cyrano rubbed his hand across his mouth as if trying to wipe a bad taste from his lips. He shook his head, fear shining in his eyes. "Nothing."

Thomas stared at him, his dark eyes raking the innkeeper's face.

Cyrano scrambled to his feet, fear causing his heart to pound. He stood up and shivered, jaw agape, realising the enormity of the baron's threat. "What am I to do?" he asked, his eyes haunted. "We need law and order and we have neither."

Dardo shook his head. "The man talks in riddles."

Thomas approached Cyrano, hooking an arm around his neck, letting him feel his strength. "You look troubled my friend. What's your problem?"

"I will die soon," Cyrano said. "The demon, Ozhan, is coming for me in seven days. This place has never made much money and I owe him a debt I can never repay. He will kill me for sure, I know it."

Thomas shook his head. "Over my dead body, he will."

"And mine," agreed Dardo, running his fingers through his mop of curly hair.

"Taverns with reputations for violence lose money rather than make it," said Thomas, "and that's why we have to get rid of the filth that makes this place stink, speaking figuratively I mean."

A glint of doubt shone in Dardo's eyes. "But how do we do that with the baron breathing down our necks?"

"Look on the bright side," Thomas said. "We have seven days to find out before he comes back."

Dardo nodded.

Thomas ambled over to the double doors, opening them, turning the Closed sign around, changing it back to Open. "Might as well make the best of the time we have." He walked over to Cyrano, patting him on the back and slumped into his usual chair at his usual table with his back to the wall and bid Dardo sit with him. Cyrano served them ale, watching them playing Push Penny, just for something to do.

Within an hour the tavern was heaving with regulars and everyone was behaving themselves, mindful of Thomas' awesome presence. The blind harpist appeared from a back room playing his usual mixture of light and lilting dance music, and the delicious smell of beef stew, liver and onions wafted into the bar-room as if blown by a butterfly's wings.

Cyrano served his customers but was in a world of his own, mindful of the fact he could think of no one who would advance him a single silver piece, never mind the sum of five hundred silver pieces he owed the baron. They'll torture me and I'll die with my fingers cut off one by one and my throat slit, he thought. He had heard many rumours about Ozhan, and what he did to those who owed him money and didn't pay. It had not mattered that they couldn't pay, because he took great delight in torturing the innocent, besides the guilty.

Such a rumour had reached his ears about the baron's so-called Choir, whereby he would kidnap ten people at a time, strap them into chairs in his dark cellar, forming a circle and place a cloth bag over each of their heads, tying it around their necks. Then he would smash each one in the face with his big hard fists, making them scream, and beat their bare feet with an iron hammer, smashing their toes, causing them to scream in even higher tones. This, he called his Choir. Then he would silence them by driving a long nail into their foreheads with an even bigger hammer when their screams didn't amuse him anymore.

Cyrano came back from his daydreaming revery with a start when Thomas tapped him on the shoulder. "Stop looking so worried. Evil carries the seeds of its own destruction, and the baron will come to a sticky end well before you do."

His panic faded, but a quiet longing to be young again by at least thirty years and fearless like Thomas replaced it. "There are those who walk through life never knowing fear, how lucky they are," he said, his heart heavy.

"Cheer up," Thomas scolded, "we will let nothing happen to you, or your son."

"That's easy for you to say, you're not frail with wasted muscles and arthritis. I'm a self-confessed coward too," said Cyrano.

"Stop enjoying your despair. Feeling sorry for yourself is a waste of your energy," said Thomas in a disdainful whispering voice. "You're not alone; you have many friends, most in the same situation. I'll stop Ozhan. Do you understand what I'm saying? Well, do you?"

Cyrano looked up into the earnest young man's glittering eyes and shrugged.

Thomas looked shocked. "You don't believe me, do you? But then why should you, no one else has stood up to the Baron before have they?"

"No, never," said the other trying to quell his mixed emotions of hatred and fear.

Thomas' swords flashed into his hands.

The innkeeper reeled from the shock, but there was no doubting what he saw. It awed him. "I'm... I'm sorry for doubting you. Please don't cut me," he said on the verge of panic.

Thomas looked stunned. "Calm yourself. Did you imagine I would hurt you? I was trying to prove the point I'm fast, skilful and capable of bringing Ozhan's murderous reign to an end." He slammed both swords back into their sheaths in the blink of an eye.

"Don't know what to think anymore," whispered Cyrano, his eyes wide.

Thomas shook his head. "I am not surprised, but I am not a murderer for hire. My Master told me I have the seeds of greatness within me, and I offer you my esteemed friendship and protection. Do we understand one another now?"

Cyrano nodded.

***

As the night wore on, Thomas and Dardo were getting drunk, singing and swaying as if on a ship's deck. Thomas insisted upon doing tricks with his dagger and swords and by midnight they were dancing and fooling around, making fun of Cyrano, when the doors of the inn swung open with a bang. Thomas jerked as if slapped in the face, "W-what in God's name?" he said, his eyes blurred and unable to focus.

A man and a woman entered, shaking the rain from their hair and heavy black coats. They stood glancing around; then approached the bar.

Cyrano sipped at his brandy and then wiped his lips. "What can I do for you?"

"Have you rooms for the night?" inquired the man, his face scarred from many knife fights.

"With soft beds?" said the woman, her blue eyes holding to Cyrano's gaze.

How beautiful she is, he thought. Large eyes like a child's, a small pert nose and full red kissable lips.

"You are beautiful milady," he said without thinking. "Umm… that is… if you'll pardon me for saying so."

She smiled, her expression cat-like and took the crystal globe from his hand, sipping the brandy. "I'll be rich soon too, and I'm not offended by your observation. I'm flattered."

Cyrano's face coloured bright red, his eyes dwelling on her tantalising full breasts and something stirred his blood as no other woman ever had regardless of the scar across her face.

"You're handsome, do you have a mistress?"

Her companion looked stunned. "Can you not cavort with every man you meet?" he scolded, his face twisted in anger. "We have urgent business to attend to soon!"

"Pleasure before business," she said. "He's sweet and I find him intoxicating."

Rising from his chair Cyrano smiled, taking the glass from her hand, refilling it. "He's young, strong and has fallen in love with you. His jealousy shows."

She shrugged and giggled. "Older men are more interesting. They use words with fantastic timing and are never in a hurry."

"Stop your prattling woman," her companion told her.

She sidled forward, closer to Cyrano, taking the filled globe from him again. "Are you happy with your life?" she whispered.

"Yes, well, happy enough," he coughed, the words almost choking him.

"I could make you happier, even if only for tonight."

"What... what do you mean?"

"You know what I mean."

Cyrano's eyes narrowed. "You misread me, milady. I'm flattered by your proposal, but sins of the flesh no longer interest me. I'm sixty years old and no longer potent."

Her companion roared, "Enough of this foolishness! Have you two beds for the night?"

The innkeeper smiled, nodded and shouted for Dody, who came running. He stood gawping at the beautiful female as Cyrano took a silver piece in payment for a one-night stay, asked them to sign the register and bid the boy to take them to their rooms. He breathed a sigh of relief as they walked towards the stairwell door.

Thomas and Dardo had listened to the conversation and heard every word. Both men laughed.

"The black widow would have eaten you whole Cyrano," Thomas cautioned. He climbed to his feet, making his way over to the bar, spinning the register to look at the two signatures. The male warrior had signed first. His name was Talon. Thomas' eyes widened, then widened further still. The female had signed Nelan, but he had not recognised her.

***

Gorl stood at his high balcony window, gazing out towards the west with his eyes fixed on the dozen riders galloping towards his farmhouse. He watched as they surged through a gap in the hillside onto open ground, angling their way up the slopes, and heat flared inside his head. There was the onset of a terrible fear as his enemies mounts galloped his way. He was alone with no way of getting word to Thomas of his hopeless plight.

At the top of the hill, Ozhan pulled up, signalling for his men to surround the farmhouse which they did. He sat stroking his fingers through his stallion's black mane and his odd eyes searched the run-down property.

Gorl watched from behind his bedroom curtains. His trembling had stopped but the terrible fear remained. At first, he had felt an overpowering sense that this was all just a bad dream, born of his torment, but as the morning wore on the awful truth became clear, the baron was back, knew he was alone and would kill him.

"Come out, come out, wherever you are," Ozhan's deep voice tormented. "Two wrongs don't make a right so I'll try three."

Gorl froze, hiding behind his curtains. "Go away and leave me alone!"

Ozhan ran his fingers through his hair. "Old man, if you're not out here by the time I count to three, we will burn you out, so it's your choice."

Gorl bit his lower lip and trembled. What shall I do? I'm alone and desperate, he thought.

Ozhan counted. "ONE!"

"I'll give you five bags of gold dust if you go away!" Gorl shouted.

"TWO!"

"Ten bags," shouted Gorl at the top of his voice.

Ozhan laughed. "Old man, why would I accept your offer when I can burn you alive and take it all? Your time's up now. THREE! Burn the old bastard out!" he told his men.

A dozen men were milling around on their horses, shouting and laughing, making torches from branches and rags doused in coal oil. They lit them, tossing them onto the roof and through the windows and within seconds a great roaring blaze engulfed the farmhouse. Ozhan watched the old man running back and forth on his short twisted leg in the burning building, desperate to save his belongings and his last sight of Gorl was of a screaming human torch, his clothes aflame, staggering past the bedroom windows.

To anyone else, the sight would have been gut-wrenchingly awful, but the baron laughed, enjoying the spectacle. "The silly old bastard should have quit and given up, but he didn't, so rot in hell!"

***

It poured with rain in the night, putting out the fire, but Gorl was dead and the farmhouse a burnt-out, smouldering shell. The next morning, Thomas and Dardo stared down into the ashes and saw Gorl's twisted body there, his features bloated and charred. They couldn't imagine the sheer terror he must have felt, knowing no one could save him, no matter how loud he screamed.

Thomas stood stock-still, his face pale, his misted eyes haunted. Dropping to his knees he raised his face to the heavens, letting out a blood-curdling cry. It was part anger, part pain. He punched the ground hard almost breaking his knuckles. "I should have been here. The old man trusted me with his life and I let him down," he said; his voice thick with emotion. "He was such a frail old man and I can hear his screams in my head, gut-wrenching, awful screams."

Dardo placed his hand on Thomas' shoulder, "The old man is no more, my friend, and there's nothing you can do about it now."

Thomas came to his feet, blinking the misted sheen away. He swung around and climbed up into his saddle as the dawn sun crept into view over the snow-covered hills, making them shine like diamonds. "No, I can't, but I can save the other farmers. Soon, I will show the baron and his thugs the entrance to hell."

Dardo climbed into his saddle and both men shook their reins and moved on, heading back towards Nottingham.

***

Two black stallions drew master Ozhan's beautiful walnut and silver carriage along with its seats of red leather and velvet, but he sat uncomfortably not enjoying the ride. The sound of iron-shod wheels rattling over the cobbled street irritated him and his sturdy frame sitting astride a saddle suited him more. But he enjoyed the grandeur of his great wealth and loved the poor folk seeing his carriage.

The driver called to the horses, and they slowed to a halt. Ozhan's journey had been much slower than expected and caused even greater irritation. Bad-tempered he rose from his seat, flung open the carriage door and stepped down into the main street beside the treasury door. He swirled his cloak around his broad shoulders, muttering profanity to himself, carrying two large black sacks filled with gold.

There was a mass clattering and scraping of chairs and stools as he entered the Treasury, and everyone stood up as a quiet young woman welcomed him. She had the longest eyelashes, the brightest eyes, the most beautiful smile and the whitest teeth. He fumbled with the heavy, gold dust-laden bags as he walked, and gold glittered around the edges as the bright morning sunlight filtered down in slanting rainbow-hues from the narrow windows. Dust motes danced in the air and sparkled like tiny jewels as his feet scraped across the stone floor.

Another young woman greeted him. "Good morning Master Ozhan."

"Morning," he mumbled, fidgeting with the bags.

All eyes were on the fat, flatulent, old windbag, his ugly face like an ill-kept grave. With an air of dignity, he handed the bags to the woman's accompanying colleague, a tall man with greying hair and sunken eyes, who gripped them and shuffled off into a back room, closing the door behind him.

In the Great Hall of the Treasury, the candles burned in their sconces and there was the nervous buzz of whispered conversations between the clerks as they scurried about their business avoiding the baron's evil, scowling gaze. But, his wild-eyed, stern expression softened as the young woman hooked her arm through his. He wiped the perspiration from his brow with his free hand and smiled at her, showing his crooked teeth. "Does your husband suspect what you are doing?" he whispered.

"No," she whispered, walking him back to his waiting carriage.

He chuckled. "Good!"

CHAPTER SIX

Desolation and destruction

The old cart rolled on down the long, dusty, road approaching the city gatehouse, pulled along by a single grey gelding. It was almost high noon. Lira tugged on the reins and stopped by the Iron Gate, smiling and nodding at Methuselah, the ancient Gatekeeper of Nottingham as he opened the iron grille, gazing up at her. He nodded back, his leathered face pale and drawn. Shaking the reins, the old cart rolled on again towards the ruined Church of Saint Matthias, where she could hear the wash of a nearby stream blending in with the clatter of iron-shod wheels and the clip-clop of the horse's hooves.

As she rode, turning recent events over in her mind, she thought of Gorl's terrible murder. She had treated him at her surgery for bumps and bruises when he had tripped and fallen over his twisted leg and had liked the old man. He was a gentle soul, very fatherly, and less than a week ago she saw him playing Ring of Roses with his grandchildren in the garden on her last visit. Gorl hated the game with a passion but was always willing to take part even though he felt foolish because of his impediment. He was a loving grandfather and a kind soul to all people.

Without warning the thunder of hooves roused her from her daydreaming, and at first, she couldn't decide which direction the sound was coming from because it filled the air around her as it gathered momentum. The ground trembled with the rumbling noise and a strange sense of danger warned her to pull over to the side of the road and take cover. She shook the reins hard and the powerful sweating horse gave a mighty heave, propelling the cart through a gap in the hawthorn hedge. She jumped down and wedged the wheels with stones.

Then she gasped with shock as a dozen horses galloped past, their manes streaming out and eyes rolling in panic. Ozhan was leading the group. He was laughing and cracking a long whip, followed by a band of mercenaries, bigger than any she had ever seen and their tattooed arms waved a variety of weapons. Pikes, staffs, spears, knives and long broadswords. They swayed back and forth in their saddles as their horses clattered off down the road, disappearing around a bend.

***

Scornful laughter and derisive snorts broke the silence. Dardo was instructing Dody in the manly art of boxing. "No, no, no. You hold your fists too low. Keep your guard up at all times and protect your face with your fists and your stomach with your elbows. If you were shadow boxing, the shadow would win!" said Dardo.

Thomas watched from the sidelines, awed by his friend's passion for his brutal art. Why anyone would want to fight with their fists is beyond me, he thought, clutching the twin hilts of his swords. The loud toll of a church bell ended Dody's first lesson, and both master and pupil wiped the sweat from their brows, shaking hands. It was getting late and through a high slitted window, Thomas could see the glaring red and gold fingers of dusk stealing down into the courtyard of the Dog and Duck. Soon it would be time for the inn to open, and he had mixed feelings about his chaotic job as a doorman, stirred throughout many months, but this was a time of change for the warrior. A great upheaval had begun. The catalyst to this event was the murder of Gorl. He felt a great responsibility for the old man's death and it weighed heavily upon his broad shoulders.

Strange echoing noises filled the boundless silence in his head throughout the long hours of the night, almost driving him mad, and out of the chaotic mess a purer thought rose within him and became so heavy it seemed to hang over him like a great dark storm cloud. Part of him was uncertain about what to do to Ozhan and his band of thieves and thugs, but another part of him screamed like a wailing banshee through the halls of his mind… kill them all. As time passed, everything seemed in confusion. He contemplated long and hard, consulting those he trusted, but none could give his thoughts order. "We can talk until our strength drains from us, but we are powerless to change what has happened in past months. You must see beyond Gorl's death and not blame yourself. Look to the future," Lira had said.

Then, almost in answer to his anxious wonderings, a new thought entered his head like a divine revelation. He knelt down, raising his eyes to the heavens, begging God to bless his endeavours, and he swore an oath to create order where there was none. All agreed that there was no one more suited to the task, as he was the bravest and fairest of all warriors, while Ozhan was spineless, floating in his own endless sea of evil darkness, despair and misery.

"In place of chaos and anarchy, let there be laws for growth and development," said Thomas to his friends and neighbours at one gathering after another. It would be an immense task, even though he was tall and strong as an oak tree, but he knew he was the only man capable of overpowering Ozhan and his paid assassins to restore order.

***

The farmers dashed off, bumping into each other in panic as they tried to get through the farmhouse gates together. They had seen Ozhan and his men coming along the hillside at lightning speed, armed with bows, pikes, swords and flaming torches, greedy for plunder and hungry for blood. We're doomed, they thought as arrows filled the air like rain and screams of the dying echoed along the hillside.

Ozhan and his mercenaries rushed to form a barrier around the trapped farmers and he laughed. "Defend yourselves if you can," he shouted as each of the farmers tried to hide behind the other. Then he and his thugs charged headlong into the hapless men, baring teeth, eyes wide, lashing out with long swords, their huge horses bowling the farmers left, right and centre, until they fell back and scattered in disorder.

Everything seemed shrouded in a red mist as the cries of the victims rang out and barns blazed. Cattle and horses bellowed and whinnied in pain and Ozhan thrashed around killing and laying waste to everything in front of him like a phantom figure until all the men, women, children and animals were dead.

Ozhan glanced at the scenes of desolation and destruction wreaked by him, and he laughed, his odd coloured eyes glinting in the bright morning sunlight. As he rode away from the dreadful scene, glancing back, he saw the bloodshed, misery and death he had caused. His eyes were cold and grim, filled with hatred for his victims, his long hooded robe drenched in sweat and blood. He laughed again and rode on with his thugs trailing after him.

***

One hour later, Thomas, Dardo and Lira were amongst the many mourners at Gorl's funeral when the news came in of the farmers' massacre. A timid hand tapping Thomas on the shoulder had snapped him from his respectful reverie and then a strangely garbed figure with a deep icy voice had informed him of the terrible news. Sweat dripped from his clenched fists like stinging acid and he stumbled forward in shock, the news hitting him like an earthquake. The newcomer placed his hands on Thomas' shoulders, holding him upright, but his lungs felt as if they were bursting. Now he floated through the red mists of anger and saw himself wielding two dazzling short-swords.

They were weapons of terror with battle-scarred blades that had a single word etched on each. *Justice!*

Cursing, his leaden limbs disobeyed him and he dropped to his knees in the icy mud. Now he understood fear and panic. He shivered, wiping the cold sweat from his brow with his shaking hand as the loud toll of the church bell brought him whirling back from the realms of his living nightmare to reality. He stood up, his eyes misted and haunted. "What in God's name is happening around here?" he asked.

Lira shook her head. "I don't know." She hooked her arms through his and Dardo's, and they walked on through the graveyard together deep in thought. Had they voiced their thoughts, it would have been what to do next? All of them had heard the report of the massacre. There were forty men dead, thirty-two women and fifteen children, the farmhouses and barns burnt to the ground and livestock slaughtered. They walked on in a daze, wondering who would be next.

Down the ages, diligent monks planting fragrant flowerbeds with many varieties of summer blooms had tended the beautiful old church grounds, but now it was getting overgrown and weed-covered. The three friends wandered past the river, past the berry hedges, a strawberry patch and into the old orchard. This had been Lira's favourite spot when she was a child where the aroma of ripening fruit: apples, oranges, pears and plums mixed, blending in with the subtle fragrance of the rose and the lily in the summer months. Now it was all gone and a depressing sight.

The early morning sunlight glinted off the ripples of the water as they sat beneath a big old chestnut tree. A single birdsong filled the air, but it seemed tinged with sorrow. Once there had been a pleasant and peaceful existence in Nottingham, but it passed with the baron's arrival.

Lira sensed Thomas' distress and patted him on the shoulder. "Somehow things will be fine and we'll all get through this terrible time together," she said, trying to lift his flagging spirit, but the deaths of the farmers and their wives and children unnerved him. His eyes wandered out across the floor of the valley, watching the homesteads smoulder. A huge swath of green once dominated the central part of the valley, but now a black swirling haze smelling of soot hung over it all.

Thomas stared at the aftermath of the Holocaust. "Oh Lord, what a mess."

"Should the other farmers pack up and move now?" asked Lira.

"Don't know what to think."

"Maybe Ozhan will leave the rest of them alone," said Dardo.

"Oh dear, what shall we do?" sighed Lira.

Thomas stood up brandishing his swords. "We'll be ready for the baron next time. I'll find high calibre mercenaries to gather intelligence of future incidents and be waiting."

Dardo couldn't help shaking his head in admiration. His friend had hidden depths of courage and endless reserves of stamina. "Yes, that's what we'll do. We'll be ready next time!" he said tapping his nose as if he had come up with the idea.

***

Ozhan admitted his visitor into a large, low-roofed, comfortable hall paved with flags, warmed by a bright open fire and furnished with costly cabinets of mahogany.

"I don't like Thomas any more than you do," Nelan said, trying not to incur her master's wrath, "but I don't like your methods either. The farmers were defenceless and had no chance of survival."

Ozhan's baleful eyes scanned her face and a sickly smile wandered over his countenance.

With a sigh of relief, she stared back at him. He's in a good mood and willing to listen, she thought. Then at lightning speed, his hand shot out and grabbed her by the throat. Lifted from the floor and hauled into the air, she howled.

In a fit of rage, he shook her like a rag doll and hurled her, half-senseless towards an open doorway. "Get out! Get out!" he shouted. "And the next time you come, tell me what I want to hear or I'll spit roast you in your own juices and eat your liver! Is that clear?"

His angry words rang in her ears. She nodded in agreement, climbed to her feet and staggered away clutching her throat, gasping for breath.

***

Thomas rapped the table with his calloused knuckles. He leaned forward and paused, staring into the crowd. "Hmm, can we have order, please? Order! Tell me brothers, who amongst you will join the cause and fight Ozhan?"

A gap-toothed old man wrinkled his nose. "I would if I wasn't so old and stiff," he shouted.

The crowd laughed.

Thomas chuckled and paused, staring at the old man and his voice dropped to a secretive whisper. "Hmm, see me later and we'll work something out."

The crowd laughed again. Then, each one stood listening to him, their ears pricked up, each one armed with a staff, pitchfork, sword or bow.

"One day the baron and his thugs will come down your road. You'll see them and shake with fright. You'll be alone with your families, the birds will stop singing and the grasshoppers will be silent too. It will be a summer or winters day like any other, except fear will grip you, watching the pale riders coming closer. Their horses will trample your picket fences, knock down the posts and the riders will burn your barns, and when their bloodlust is high, they will come looking for you… your wife… and your children. They will torture and kill you," said Thomas with an icy stare.

The young men gripped their weapons tighter, listening to the graphic details of their demise and they could feel the hackles prickle on the back of their necks. They shivered.

"Listen to Thomas!" shouted Lira. "He knows Ozhan's kind and his methods better than most. We need you all to join us to defend this city because three hundred armed men is a formidable deterrent against most threats!"

Thomas nodded. "All we need do is stay together in a show of force, using the element of surprise against them. If Ozhan has an armed mob, we'll have a bigger one!" he said. "The baron knows the value of fear as a weapon, so if we show him we're not ordinary, panic-stricken individuals, he will think twice about attacking us. And yes, he's a fearsome figure with his scarred face and odd glowing eyes, but remember... someone else gave him those ugly scars!"

A crippled old man stepped forward. "It's easy for you to talk; you're a swordsman with a fearsome reputation. He isn't coming looking for you."

"Then think yourself lucky that I'm on your side and not his," countered Thomas, and the crowd cheered.

"Thomas is right, Ozhan is a bully. When he realises that you're not afraid of him, he'll leave you all alone," said Lira.

Sharp and clear, another voice rang out in the crowd. "Can we beat him and his thugs? Can we?"

Dardo swaggered forward, answering in his friend's stead. His reply was harsh and unafraid. "If Thomas says it shall be so, it shall be so. But, if you're a doubter, go home and take your chances on your own."

***

Later that night, Lira's legs locked around Thomas' hips, her nails raking his back as she rose towards orgasm. He kissed her lips gently, then repeatedly with increasing ardour. His hands fondled and caressed her breasts and they made love slowly, increasing the rhythm. There were moans and sharp gasps of breath as he too moved with increasing urgency, and she sighed as they climaxed together. Satisfied, Lira kissed his lips, cuddling into him.

"You're beautiful Lira," he said. "I think I've loved you from the first moment I saw you."

"Likewise," she admitted, cuddling him tighter.

His arm circled her waist, and he hugged her, kissing her full red lips. He was a good lover and Lira appreciated the tenderness of his skills.

"I'm a lucky man," he whispered.

"And I'm a lucky woman," she whispered back, and she relaxed her mind for the first time since the whole Ozhan affair began. They fell asleep in each other's arms and dreamt of brighter days.

***

Very early the next morning, silence hung upon the air as Thomas, Lira and Dardo held a whispered conference in a clearing at the edge of Nottingham forest. They conferred awhile as Thomas strode out among the crowd, laying his hands on the shoulders of many, trying to stiffen their resolve. It worked. Then he noticed movement in the nearby bushes and he summoned Dardo, pointing to where he had seen the undergrowth stir, "Over there, to the left of that oak. Look, they're moving again."

"We've got to do something, it might be a trap," said Dardo.

Thomas dispersed the crowd of willing followers and hurried to the tree line, drawing his swords in readiness for action. Dardo chased after him, carrying a long pike, and on reaching the spot where the bushes moved Thomas parted the branches, thrusting a sword into them. A breathless boy huddled down on his knees stared up at him, his face red from running. "Dody, what are you doing here?" he spat.

The lad coughed. Caught red-handed, it embarrassed him. "Sentry duty. I heard a whisper about the meeting and thought I'd keep watch for you in case of trouble." Mud covered the boy's long, sinewy body.

"What have you been doing? You're filthy!" said Thomas.

Two bright eyes shone from beneath a crust of mud, blinking. "Tripped while running."

Thomas laughed. "You look like someone's shadow!"

Dardo laughed too.

Dody remained motionless, except for his blinking eyes. In his hands was a bag of smooth pebbles and a slingshot which he had proved to use with great force and accuracy.

Dardo's eyes rounded on the weapon and he rubbed his forehead looking pale. "Bad memories."

***

One hour later, Thomas, dressed in forest greens, darted through the early morning mist covering the woodland floor. The air was thick with the odour of pine and cedar and the forest track covered in tiny russet needles. He was chasing a stag of huge proportions. It was a twenty-four pointer, weighing six or seven hundred pounds and he had never seen one that big in his entire life. Thomas spotted it while out testing his fitness, skill and agility in the forest, awaiting intelligence of Ozhan's plans from his embedded spies.

Now, he ran like the North Wind, chasing it, and with every stride he took he ran faster and faster. But, after fifteen-minutes, he lost sight of it and dropped to his knees from pure exhaustion.

Then Dardo arrived, breathless and red-faced from running too. "There's been another mass killing," he announced with a chill in his voice.

The words jolted Thomas.

Dardo beckoned his friend to follow him and led the way to a large clearing beside a river. Evil hung in the air as surely as they breathed. Bodies of men, women and children lay sprawled everywhere, burned and mutilated, their throats slit from ear to ear in a ritualistic murder. Someone had hacked the farm animals to death too. No one had survived the massacre. Thomas looked at Dardo and gasped in disbelief. "What in God's name happened here?"

Dardo looked sick to his stomach. "Ozhan!"

Thomas turned, heading back to his tethered his horse. "It's time to end this slaughter. There is a need for Ozhan to die!" he snapped.

***

Thirty minutes later, through high slitted windows, Thomas watched the rose pink and gold fingers of the sun's rays stealing down the walls of the meeting hall. Farmers, stockmen and traders filled the room, everyone and anyone who could handle a weapon. Even Tobin, Lira's father, stood at the back of the hall with his huge blacksmith's arms folded and his ears pinned back.

Thomas dressed in his black and gold leather tunic and matching leggings was standing at the head of the noisy crowd. He stared at their angry expressions, and even as the morning sun shone brighter, thunder rumbled overhead and rain lashed the windows.

"Silence! silence!" shouted Dardo, raising his hands in the air, trying to bring the chattering crowd to order.

Thomas nodded to him and Lira moved alongside them both, sitting behind a large trestle table. She was wearing a loose-fitting white gown. The swordsman hammered his fist on the table to get everyone's attention and then paused, looking at them ponderously. The crowd fell silent. "What has happened to you people? You are not the people I knew. Has the heart and soul gone out of you? Ozhan wants you to rot and die and you don't even put up a fight," he said with despair in his heart, "I know you don't want to fight, but life here could be so much better if you do."

A farmer stood up looking around the hall. "It's easy for you to talk, you're skilled in the art of war, but we're not."

"That isn't the point. If I'm willing to stay here to save your hides, why aren't you willing to fight alongside me? Should I give my life for yours if you're not willing to do the same in return?" scolded Thomas.

In anger Lira jumped to her feet. "Listen to this man. He's trying to save you from a fate worse than death. Would you rather live as slaves to Ozhan and die of old age, or would you rather fight him and risk dying as free men and women with pride in your hearts?"

Thomas looked at her in wonderment as she scolded the crowd on his behalf. She was even more beautiful when angry. "Thank you, Lira," he said. "Need I say more? You know what we must do. The baron will not go away of his own accord or let you live peaceful, productive lives. He's a murdering thug, who will see you all dead to carry out his grandiose schemes. Many are dead now, tortured with their throats slit and burned. How many more of you will suffer such fates in the hours of the night? Think of your children if no one else because they deserve better."

Hushed murmurings filled the meeting hall and then the clapping of hands. Two mercenaries stared at each other. "Fine speech," announced the female, wearing two short swords, "but useless."

Thomas shivered as old memories flared. Dressed in black with a cloak, Nelan looked more like a demon from a shadow-haunted wood.

Outside the rain was heavy, and it cascaded down the walls. His gaze wandered across the room to her glittering eyes. "I assume you are in Ozhan's employment?"

Laughter greeted Thomas' words and the hairs on the back of his neck bristled. He shot an angry stare, gripping the hilts of his swords, his shoulders hunched; "Now you listen and take heed of what I say. You and your kind are not welcome hereabouts, so I want you to deliver a message to Ozhan. Tell him law and order is coming to this city. Law and order! Tell him he's asked for what he will get because he's finished here. After this day, if we catch him, you or any of his hired thugs, we'll kill you all without blinking an eye. Tell him I'm coming for him. Tell him the devil's coming with me to show him the gateway to Hell."

Nelan's companion, Talon, smiled. "Hmm, Thomas Flynn, I've heard of you. Law won't work around here," he countered.

Thomas drew his swords, "I've no more to say on this, but I see you need convincing."

Nelan stepped forward, drawing her swords, but Talon threw out his arm stopping her advance. "Many times these past months travellers whispered your name, afraid to speak it aloud, awed by the folk legend that surrounds you but I know I can kill you."

Dardo and Lira looked at each other, shaking their heads, watching Thomas push his way through the crowd towards the two mercenaries. A deathly hush fell upon the whole gathering as elbows nudged ribs, but Thomas' scornful snorts and derisive laughter broke the silence. "Ahem, er, why my good fellow," he said clearing his throat, "while I respect your bravery, I recommend that you look to Nelan for guidance, for she is the only one who has ever beaten me in a fair fight, and that was many years ago. I guarantee she couldn't do it now."

Feeling abashed, Talon drew his sword. Thomas smiled at him. Dardo couldn't help but shake his head in admiration as usual because it always seemed like his friend had hidden depths of courage well beyond what any man should have.

Without warning, Talon charged headlong towards him, lashing out with his weapon, but Thomas' swords shot up at lightning speed, crossing in front of his face, stopping the blade of the other. Bright sparks lit the air as Talon's superior strength bowled Thomas over and he fell to the floor. Talon threw back his head roaring with laughter. "I have no chance against you, eh? Is that what you said?"

Thomas rolled to one knee and climbed to his feet. "You may win a battle, but you have no chance of winning the war, even though you're fast for a big man," he said, throwing himself forward, slicing air above the other as he ducked out of harm's way.

Thunder rumbled overhead as the clattering of swordplay echoed around the meeting hall, and lightning flashed through the high windows, illuminating even the darkest shadows. All eyes rounded on Thomas as one of his swords licked out to nick Talon's shoulder, causing a flash of crimson to bloom on his silk shirt. Thomas found it impossible to keep the smile from his face as he resumed control of the fight, parrying Talon's next thrust, and the next, and the next. Then he spun on his heel, hammering his fist against Talon's jaw. He tumbled to the wooden floor with a clatter, but rose again and advanced, fighting long and hard.

"There is a need for you to die now!" announced Thomas finally, his voice cold. Slamming one of his blades into Talon's chest he drove it in up to the hilt. He staggered back, falling to his knees. A long groan burst from his lips as his barrel-chested upper body slumped forward, thudding against the floor.

The crowd of onlookers gasped.

"Have you ever seen anyone move that fast?" whispered one man.

His friend whispered back, "Hell, no!"

Thomas knelt beside the corpse, pushing Talon to his back. He dragged his blade clear and wiped it on the body. He rose and turned to face Nelan. Her eyes pulsed with living colour and he could feel the hate emanating from them. "How many times must I prove I'm the best?" he asked.

"Do you think so?" she countered, her voice faintly mocking.

He moved alongside her, laying his hand on her shoulder. He whispered, "I do and we can prove it here and now if you wish, but I want you to deliver a message to the baron. Tell him I'm coming for him. Tell him revenge is not what I want; it's a reckoning for Gorl's death, the slaughtered farmers, homesteaders and their wives and children."

Nelan swung around to meet his gaze. "I will give him your message Thomas, but we will meet again soon to see whose blades are swifter and sharper, yours or mine." She walked along the hallway towards the street and pushed open the double doors of the meeting hall, marching out into the morning rain, disappearing around a corner.

CHAPTER SEVEN

Beg for your life

Two days later, Thomas' armed men halted to the sound of a horse's hooves thundering towards them. Dardo looked to the warrior for reassurance, his eyes resting on the scout who was heading their way in a mile-eating gallop. Within moments, the scout was back among his own men giving his report. "The element of surprise is ours," he said, wiping the sweat from his forehead. "Ozhan's men have camped two miles from here in a small glade and they're still sleeping!"

"Good," said Thomas. "The baron understands the value of fear as a weapon, but we'll show him how valuable surprise can be." He barked his orders, whereupon his men closed ranks. Then they made their way through a forest of oak and birch on horseback towards the glade and Ozhan's drunken, sleeping men. And even though the afternoon sun shone through the filigree of overhanging branches, the birds had ceased to sing and a deathly silence prevailed.

On approaching the camp, Thomas gestured to his men to surround it and then barked for them to strike. They closed in on the enemy. Taken by surprise, drunk and half-asleep, the baron's men tried to grab their weapons, but the circle of horsemen hemmed them in and they died screaming. Thomas' men killed them within mere heartbeats, the bare earth stained crimson with their blood. Afterwards, his men searched the camp but Ozhan had escaped.

Thomas sat astride his stallion, eyes staring at the carnage. "This will happen to the baron's men, any who wear his gold crest, but when we find the man himself, I will hang him from the nearest tree for his crimes."

"What makes him do what he does? He's already rich and powerful," asked Dardo.

"Ozhan has an empty soul and no heart. He can never steal enough, kill enough or inflict enough pain."

"Then, what does he want?"

"Retribution."

Dardo looked stunned. "For what?"

"His mother giving him life."

Thomas swung his horse to the west toward another of the baron's encampments, forty men following his lead. "Keep together men," he ordered, and they bunched in a tight group. They galloped down the slopes of the hillside onto the level ground in pursuit of more of their enemy with unmatchable speed. The sounds of yelling and screaming filled the air.

As they approached the second camp, Thomas saw twenty men running to their horses, vaulting into their saddles at the foot of a hill, and to his right was a mound of burnt, mutilated bodies. Farmhouses and barns were blazing and the smell of soot lingered in the air. Thomas beckoned his men to follow him down the hill in pursuit of the raiders and when he reached the foot of the hill; he dismounted. In the bright sunlight, he stared into the distance, scanning the vast grasslands. He patted the long, sleek neck of his horse. A wolf howled, and the horse swung its head towards the sound.

The torn bodies of the baron's victims lay everywhere and there was a pile of severed heads left as a warning to the other farmers. Thomas kicked them into the ashes and swung back into his saddle. He heeled his mount forward. "Let's find them and kill them all!"

His men followed without question, and the sound of screaming horses filled the air as he swung his mount towards the west again, following the raiders down the slopes to level ground. "How many in the raiding party?" he asked his scout.

Dardo edged his mount alongside Thomas' as the scout noted every single hoof print.

"Twenty," the scout reported, "and they're heading for the Northern Quarter of Nottingham."

Thomas' face hardened. "That's strange; Ozhan's farm is in the Southern Quarter."

Dardo scratched his head. "The Northern Quarter has a feel of evil to it and is a vista of bare rock and dry earth, why would they be heading there instead of to the safety of the baron's homestead where the grass is green and rich?"

Thomas gripped the reigns of his mount even tighter. "Ozhan's trying to trap us!"

Dardo peered into the distance, heeling his horse harder and every rider twitched with anxiety at the thought of a trap.

"But where would he spring the trap?" asked Thomas.

The scout pointed north. "A narrow pass two miles thus."

Thomas winked at his men. "Then we'll set a trap of our own."

He swung his horse to the north-west and galloped off with the whole group following him to the thunder of hooves. Above him, heavy grey skies and steady rain prevailed over the whole miserable landscape, but Thomas' eyes never veered away from the far horizon until the top of a narrow pass came into view. Then he slowed his horse to a trot, holding up his hand bringing his men to a halt. He dismounted, striding to the edge of a high ridge and could just see Ozhan's men breaking the cover of trees on the rim of the rocks below him. The warrior smiled to himself. Ozhan and his men had gained the high ground, but he had gained the higher ground and the element of surprise.

Within moments Thomas assembled his band of recruits around the top of the escarpment at the edge of the steep plateau, overlooking the whole pass, and signalled for his men to load their longbows. They did it and shuffled forward as he raised an arm. "It's our lucky day.

Each man took a careful aim at his target, pulling back on the grey goose-shaft betwixt his fingers and awaited Thomas' command. Some could see their target but others couldn't and made their best guess where their target was. Ozhan may have won a few battles in his time, but I'll win this war, Thomas thought.

Even Dardo sported a longbow, peering down the long shaft of his arrow at the nearest target he could find. A warrior sat clinging to a branch, high up a tall pine tree. Fleetingly, he shifted his gaze, looking across at Thomas' arm held high. Clad in his favourite black and gold tunic, he was a heroic-looking figure with a fearless stare on his face, leaning forward, peering down with his eyes fixed on the baron's men.

Dardo watched in admiration, wonderment in his eyes, waiting for his arm to drop, signalling the release of a hail of arrows that would no doubt decimate their enemy. If only I was like Thomas, he's the bravest and most courageous man I've ever known, he thought.

Thomas' arm dropped and the longbows sang. Forty grey goose-shafts spun, whistling through the air, and three smashed through the skull of one man, pitching him forward from his cover in a tree onto the rocky ground. Another man in an elm jerked as if stung, rose to his feet on the branch and then his legs gave way beneath him. He fell to his death with an arrow embedded in his throat and the canyon echoed to the high-pitched screams of the wounded and dying. Dardo's arrow found its mark too, much to his surprise, slamming home, tearing into a man's skull right between the eyes.

There was no response from the enemy as Thomas' men reloaded their bows, firing a second volley, then a third and even a fourth. Their trap was working much better than he had hoped, his surprise attack winning the day as arrows smashed through armour, flesh and bone. Ozhan's men were dropping from the trees like autumn leaves in a strong wind. Thomas watched the enemy fall, one after another and listened to their dying screams. "I warned you I was coming and hell was coming with me," he whispered as the longbows sang again.

One of the baron's men lurched forward from his cover in a tree. Three arrows stuck him in his chest and one tore away his nose, but he stumbled forward, hurling a spear before dropping dead. It took one of Thomas' Bowmen through the chest, knocking him back into the others, smashing them from their feet. Then, Thomas saw another bowman's face swept away in a crimson blur as an axe whizzed past him, spraying shards of bone everywhere. He picked up the dead man's quiver, placing it over his shoulder and picked up the longbow, notching an arrow to the bowstring in the blink of an eye. His face was expressionless. He let fly, sending volley after volley into the axe man's chest, arms and legs, pinning him to a tree with a final shot to the forehead. "Did you enjoy that you bastard?" he shouted, punching the air. Thomas' men ran left and right, letting fly with another murderous hail of arrows that slammed into the rest of the baron's men, who now ran for their lives, but still, there was no sign of the man himself.

***

Every mercenary standing in the low-roofed hall twitched with fright as Ozhan's loud voice rang out. They could feel their hackles prickle and shivered despite the heat from the blazing fire. A huge warrior nudged his friend and whispered, "Listen to him. He thinks he's a god!"

The warrior's friend pricked up his ears and whispered back. "They say his presence stops the birds singing; wilts the leaves of trees and he has the power of life and death. I'd say he comes close to being a god.

The huge warrior wrinkled his nose. "Codswallop and old wives tales. He doesn't scare me and I'll only do as I'm told for so long. So if he wants to shout and stare at me with those odd eyes of his, he had better prepare for a sharp shock!"

The baron rapped his calloused knuckles on a trestle table. "Give me your advice, brother," he said, pointing a finger at the warrior. Then he paused and stared at him, "Hmm, do you know, something about you annoys me... so what should I do about it?"

The warrior laughed; his face hardening. He fixed Ozhan's steely gaze.

"Did you ever hear the story of how I came to power in Nottingham?" the baron asked with an air of menace in his voice. He paused, waiting for a reply.

The warrior shook his head, surprised by the question.

Ozhan rounded on the man and stood by his side. His voice dropped to a secretive whisper. The warrior leaned forward listening. "One day someone will write in the Chronicles of Nottingham that I was too young to be a great warrior at the time of my rise to power, and like you, I was impulsive and felt invincible. They will also write that in times of trouble I had the gift of being a natural leader because trouble is my middle name, so when I'm speaking, no one else should!" Ozhan paused, waiting for a reaction, saying nothing more.

The warrior was fearful as he stared into the baron's eyes, for they glowed as he spun on his heel and turned back, slamming a dagger into the man's chest, driving the blade up to the hilt. He gasped, staggering back in shock, falling to his knees, his barrel chest slumping forward until his brow thudded against the wooden floor.

Ozhan waved his hand dismissing the corpse, and he sneered, "I will write that I killed everyone and destroyed everything standing in my way because nothing and no one will stop me from fulfilling my true destiny. You can't have heard how I came to power otherwise you wouldn't be dead now." He put his arm around the shoulders of the dead warrior's friend. "Come with me," he said, his voice low and deep. He pushed open a pair of double doors and they entered a large, circular room ablaze with the light of fifty lanterns. "You seem to be a sensible man, m'dear," he said, his voice faintly mocking. "What price would you put on a man's life... fifty pieces of gold... one hundred... two hundred?"

"I suppose it would depend on the man," replied the other, and together they walked the long corridors of Ozhan's mansion and descended a circular stone staircase to the lower levels where many flaming torches shone on the bare walls. The air carried the smell of coal oil.

A thin, malnourished rat ran across their path as they moved towards two locked iron gates, and then a small, fat man wearing long robes of black appeared, darting out from a room off to the left, bowing. He was bald, the skin of his face stretched tight around an angular skull. "What can I do for you, Master?" he inquired, bowing for the second time.

Ozhan waved his hand, dismissing the man. "I want my friend here to witness something.

After the gatekeeper had gone, the baron unlocked the iron grill and entered, followed by the mercenary who looked worried. Just beyond the gates but out of sight, laid on an altar was a naked young girl, strapped by her arms and legs. Her great beauty stunned the man, and he seemed seized by a qualm of faintness.

The young girl shook her head and wept. "Oh, please my Lord, set me free!"

Ozhan swung to look at her. She was sixteen. He smiled, stroking her hair.

"Don't hurt me," she begged.

He stared at her. "Child, be silent," he said, plucking a large curved dagger from inside his waistband, and he plunged it into her heart. Her slender body arched up, and a strangled cry tore from her lips as he dragged the blade clear. "She was innocent of any crime, but to gain control over my fellow men, I must show extreme violence."

The warrior listened, fearing Ozhan's menacing manner, and he thought before speaking, "No disrespect intended, my Lord, but killing a mercenary or an innocent child doesn't guarantee that."

The baron shook his head. "No, but murdering my daughter for no good reason should if my men have brains."

The warrior's eyes widened with alarm, his head hanging in despair. "Your daughter? Yes, yes my Lord that would prove your point to anyone."

Swinging away from the man, Ozhan bid him follow. He locked the iron grill, leading him back to the upper levels of the mansion and back into the Great Hall, where the other mercenaries were sitting around the floor, sharpening their weapons. As soon as he entered, their strong faces showed signs of fear.

For a moment the baron was silent, his expression thoughtful but hard. He stroked the scars of his face. "Now do you understand why I have their complete attention whenever I enter a room? They live to please me and die painfully if they displease me. I've always yearned for the unattainable and when I'm disappointed, which I always am, I kill the people who let me down, that's fair isn't it?"

The warrior's face was thin and drawn, his eyes dark-rimmed and haunted, having watched his friend die and then the girl. "Yes, my Lord," said the man, not knowing what else to say, "but why did you sacrifice your own daughter? Had she displeased you somehow?"

"Not at all, I wanted to prove my point. My warriors must fear me above everything; otherwise, when facing the enemy they would take off like startled pigeons. Death can be quick and painless, but you'll fight twice as hard for me if I tell you I will make your murder long and painful. Now you know this for sure, don't you?" said Ozhan, his voice icy. He hawked and spat on the toe of the man's boot, pushing him back among the other warriors. "You may be new here, but remember what you've seen today and you will live longer than most."

The man pushed his way back among the ranks with the baron's unblinking stare fastened on him.

"A man needs to know his limitations, but I have none," said Ozhan

**

After two successful campaigns against the baron's men, many came forward, pledging their service and allegiance to Thomas. Most were farmers and their workers, but there were whole families who had fought in many wars for generations. Even noblemen who could trace their bloodlines back centuries came forward to help rid Nottingham of Ozhan and his thugs.

Now it was midnight and armed men and women shuffled into the Dog and Duck and sat listening to Thomas' every word. "The map has many red dots, lots, showing where Ozhan has murdered, burned, pillaged and raped without a conscious thought and he won't stop until he's killed all of you and stolen your land." He pointed to several destroyed homesteads on the map, folding his arms into his chest. "I've started something I will finish, with or without your help, but your help will make the task much easier!"

Dardo and Lira took a seat to his right with Tobin, Lira's father, sat on his left.

"The baron consumed a good part of the land around Nottingham before King John died and has gained more in his 'cat-and-mouse' games since then, using the most brutal tactics. But no longer is it a game, for the cat is now the mouse and the mouse has become a demon with bloodied eyes and fiery breath!" Thomas looked to his friends and stiffened, shaking his head. Even as he spoke, a sharp, frightening hiss seemed to rip through the stillness of the night, lingering and dying into silence, though it was only part of the crowd's imagination.

"We're with you," a man shouted.

"We're all with you!" chorused the whole gathering.

"Nothing will compensate Ozhan for the losses he will suffer. We'll hit him hard and keep hitting him until nothing of his still stands!" said Thomas.

There was nothing more to discuss. The whole gathering had nominated Thomas as their leader with a full vote of confidence and all that remained to do was to prepare for the coming hostilities. No doubt many will die on either side, thought Thomas, but the good and innocent people of Nottingham will suffer and die if they don't take up arms and make a stand against the baron's tyrannical rule. He dismissed his would-be army to the sounds of cheers and they dispersed, out through the main doors, disappearing into the night looking happier and much more determined than when they arrived.

Will their resolve change in the light of day? he wondered as he watched them leave. His volunteer army had swelled from forty men to over three hundred. They prepared for the hardship to come.

***

Early the next morning, the high, warm sun shone on Thomas, Dardo and Lira as they galloped past the milestone lodged in the earth by the side of the road. Nottingham Abbey 20 miles.

Abbot Alfred, a good friend of Lira's father was expecting them. He was to bless them and their dangerous venture, seeing Ozhan as the devil in human form. But he saw a future full of hope since Thomas arrived in Nottingham. It seemed to him to be yet another manifestation of the playing out of the eternal struggle between good and evil with Thomas as their guardian angel.

Leaving the main Nottingham road they took the old forest road, riding towards the distant hills under a spreading filigree of hanging branches, watching sunlight dapple their trail while listening to the endless rhythm of stream and river. Bird songs filled the air. And once again the smell of the forest intoxicated them.

For most of the morning they rode, angling their journey to the north-east, and by mid-day, they could see the outline of the Abbey, with its towering lead-capped spires rearing up like the jagged peaks of mountains on an elegant backdrop of blue sky and white cloud. It stood flanked on one side by woodland shade while the other side overlooked undulating sweeps of hillside and meadowland with its ancient gates facing the long winding road to the western perimeter. They reached the Abbey as dozens of terrified families hurried from all over Nottingham to gain safety before the scourge of Ozhan broke upon them in the impending bloodbath.

Up the dusty road they came, mothers protecting and herding their children as fathers and older relatives provided a rear-guard. The Abbot stood by the gates with his sandals peeping out from beneath the baggy folds of his brown habit. He stood stock-still, gazing up at the sky and then shifted his gaze in wonderment to the oncoming horde of homeless people with their eyes fixed on him. He blinked and sighed. "Oh, good heavens, I need the strength of the Lord." He looked weary and sat on the stone floor, resting his back against the gates.

Thomas, Lira and Dardo entered the gates of the Abbey to a chorus of loud cheers. Dismounting, they strolled over to a tethering post and tied up their horses, bidding the Abbot a good afternoon as he climbed back to his feet. He studied the look in Thomas' eyes. "You are all welcome," he said, laying a wrinkled old hand on the warrior's shoulder.

Thomas shook the other hand. "I respect you and I am honoured to be in your presence, Father, and it's nice to know even a tyrannical predator like the baron will keep the faith and leave these poor people alone while they are within these walls. Will you bless us and keep us under the protection and the watchful eye of the Lord?"

The Abbot's weary expression softened and his mood lightened as he bobbed a quick bow to his friends. "Come children and eat," he said, leading them through the gates into the Great Hall. Inside sunlight flooded down in slanting shafts from the high-arched windows, and a million dust-motes danced and swirled in the light breeze wafting through as they trod the stone floor. The Abbot marched straight forward, halting in front of a giant picture hung on the grey stone wall, painted centuries earlier by a founding father of the old Abbey. He gestured, bidding them sit at a long trestle table beneath it. "It's beautiful isn't it?" he said.

The three friends studied the chronicle of earlier times in Nottingham while Abbot Alfred sat beside them on a stool. A humble Friar entered, and the Abbot beckoned him to his side, whispering in his ear. He left the way he came, returning moments later with two wooden trays full of bread and cheese. "How are the cellar stocks, John?" he asked the Friar.

The Friar smiled. "We've enough food and drink to fill the bellies of an army," came the reply, and again he left, returning moments later with another wooden tray with four goblets and a jug of wine on it. He placed them down onto the table, bowed and left for a final time, closing the door behind him.

Now the Abbey bell tolled out twelve times, and all activity ceased as everyone walked to their allotted place to eat and drink. Thomas and the others sat with their heads bowed as the Abbot said grace, and then they ate and talked for an hour until the Abbey bell tolled again. Then the Abbot took them into the Chapel, blessing them and their brave venture before they left.

***

Back on the Nottingham road, they trotted, chatting, until they galloped their separate ways. Lira headed home. Dardo wanted another drink of wine and made a beeline towards the Dog and Duck, while Thomas went sightseeing, making the best of the afternoon sun.

It was dark when he returned to the tavern. There were no signs of life. The double doors at the front had the closed sign on it and there were no lights in the windows.

As he dismounted his horse, a cloaked figure approached him from out of the shadows, the newcomer offering him a sealed parchment. Curiously he took it, breaking the seal as the mysterious stranger disappeared back into the shadows without saying a word. Thomas unrolled the scroll, holding it up to the moonlight.

It said: "I've taken two of your friend's captive and give you notice and guarantee that one of them will die tonight by my hand. I shall toss a coin to make the choice of who lives and who dies. It's a pity you won't know which one until it's too late." Ozhan's signature concluded the message.

Thomas sucked in a deep breath and gasped. "No! No! Oh, God no, this cannot be!" he shouted with a strangled cry. His limbs became flaccid, his eyes shrouded by a red mist. He swung his stallion around, remounted and whipped the reins, disappearing into the cold night.

CHAPTER EIGHT

No idle boast

Out near the lake, the rain sheeted down and thunder drummed out overhead. Thomas swore. If the lightning struck strike him now, he would be a happy man even though fried alive. He swore again as a web of lightning flashed nearby illuminating the inky lake, and he bared his teeth at the heavens, but the storm passed as soon as it had come and the moon shone bright and clear.

Angling his horse towards Tobin's homestead through the darkness of night, under the cover of trees he switched direction now and then to make sure no one was following him. He travelled in haste, keeping a watchful eye on his back-trail. Then for twenty minutes, he galloped onward.

Now, high above the point at which he had last switched direction he climbed the hill towards Tobin and Lira's homestead, and like at the Dog and Duck, it too was in darkness. The ground beneath the horse's hooves was muddy from the recent rain and squelched as it paced beneath the familiar spreading oak towards the farmhouse. Thomas leapt from the horse and ran to the door, pounding on it.

There was no answer. Blood their dog didn't bark either. Panicking, he rapped on the door again. Still, there was no answer. Now his heart pounded like a blacksmith's hammer on an iron anvil and he was hyperventilating, almost passing out from breathing so hard.

The door flew open. A dark figure, backlit by a single lantern, lunged forward in the doorway startling him.

"Have you lost your senses, man? Or are you worse for the drink?" a voice shouted. "Do you know what the time is? Only thieves and cutthroats are abroad at this hour!"

Thomas' eyes widened. "No! No! Lira, where's Lira, I must see her?" Tobin tried to close the door. "Go home man and sleep it off for God's sake!"

Thomas forced the door open. "No. No! You don't understand!"

Tobin pushed him away. "There's nothing to understand, I can smell the ale on your breath!"

"Please let me explain, you don't understand!"

"Understand what?" a silky voice asked. Lira pushed past her father, rubbing her sleepy eyes.

"He's drunk! The man's full of ale!" Tobin blustered.

Thomas threw his arms around her. He kissed her forehead, a great relief washing over him like a tidal wave as he smelt her rosewater perfume. "Lira, thank God you're safe."

She gazed up into his dark eyes. "What is it, Thomas? What's the matter?"

He passed her the parchment. She unrolled it and read the message, her eyes widening in horror. "Good Lord!" she gasped, swinging back to meet her father's gaze. She handed him the parchment. He read it, looking stunned and embarrassed realising the implications.

Now Thomas' eyes widened and the swell of relief he felt knowing Lira was in safe hands disappeared. "Then if you're safe, Dardo must be the one in deadly danger!"

"Do you think so?" she asked. "Maybe it's just an idle boast to scare us?"

Thomas shook his head, his expression as hard as nails. "The one thing Ozhan never does is make idle threats. He tried to hang your father for no good reason and almost managed it."

Tobin nodded. "You're right, but how did you know he tried to hang me?"

Thomas pointed to Tobin's throat. "I saw the rope burn around your neck a few days ago. Now get back inside, barricade the doors and windows and arm yourselves. I'll be back as soon as I can, and no matter what happens, don't open the door to anyone but me!"

Lira stepped back, and the door slammed shut in his face, the draft blowing back his hair. He swung around, ran and vaulted the tethering post onto his horse. Grabbing the reins he angled the stallion back towards the Dog and Duck, taking off like a bolt of lightning in a mile-eating gallop.

Passing under the spreading oak he rode back along the muddy trail, heading for the main Nottingham road and the only thing he hoped was that he would find his friend alive.

When he reached the main highway, he heeled the horse harder, following the wide tree-lined road. The weather was clear, the moon shining through the low-hanging branches dappling his trail. And as he rode his mind was razor-sharp, recalling better days, wishing for his friend's sake he had more lives than one to give for him as he remembered his own tortured history and years of abuse.

The last leg of his journey was up past the lake and he shivered, confused and uncertain, his mind racing as he heeled his horse harder still. He had read stories of heroes in the castle library when he was a child and they spurred him on, but no hero felt as he did now, helpless. He could even hear the baron's mocking laughter in his mind.

Fifteen miles and thirty minutes later, his horse slid to an abrupt halt outside the Dog and Duck and the lights were on and the doors open. Thomas' veins seemed to be full of stimulants to violent activity and he was ready for anything, but his mouth was dry and his heart beating fast. Memories of Dardo's friendship flared, lifting his spirits as he jumped from his stallion and entered full of hope.

Inside the inn a golden light radiated throughout the room, bathing the walls and ceiling. He scanned the room he could just make out the shape of Cyrano's hound in a corner beside the bar, and as he approached, it growled baring teeth. He laid a hand on the fierce animals head and stroked it until it quieted.

Then he noticed a strange bundle curled up in a corner beneath the bar. Dardo stank of drink; was out cold and Thomas couldn't rouse him. "Oh, God," he whispered, noticing another crumpled bundle at the far end of the room. He leaned forward, hunching his shoulders, trying to get a better look at the bundle.

He moved closer. It smelt of a mixture of soot and coal oil. The wolfhound growled, baring teeth at him again protecting whatever was lying on the floor. He stroked the dog. "What's the matter? What are you growling for, boy?"

He froze for a moment, his other hand hovering over a blanket covering the bundle. Something wild and frightening burgeoned in his stomach just from looking at it, and his heart came up and darkened his eyes. He touched it and it was cold. Thomas stared at his bloodstained hand, his eyes bleak and haunted, despair washing the colour from his face as he realised it was a dead man. He pushed the corpse to its back. Cyrano had half his face burnt away, and someone had buried a dagger deep in his chest with a piece of parchment attached to it.

Thomas took a sharp intake of breath. "Oh, my God."

Someone had tortured Cyrano before stabbing him to death. Thomas' face was grey, his hands covered in sweat and blood, and for the first time since he was a child, he cried.

The dining-room door burst open. Cyrano's son, Dody, was standing in the doorway staring down at the corpse and his eyes sank deep into his skull, recognising his father's torn body and he screamed.

Thomas reached out, grabbing the boy, cuddling him, but he struggled and screamed again. "Get off me! Go away and get out of here! That's not my father, I know it's not! He's asleep in bed and he'll be getting up soon. Get off me!" He wriggled free and beat on Thomas' chest.

Thomas held him off until he calmed and then his arms encircled the boy's shoulders, drawing him close. Dody was murmuring in a shocked voice and whispering that God wouldn't let anyone take the life of his father. Deep, rasping sobs tore from his throat as he broke free of Thomas' grasp and ran back upstairs to his bedroom, slamming the door shut.

Now Thomas knew it was real. His friend was dead. Drawing the knife blade clear of Cyrano's chest he removed the parchment and held it up to the lantern light. It said, "Tails."

Thomas ran outside, ran from the things that tore at his heart and made him ache worse than any physical pain he had ever experienced. He ran to the tethering post, beating his fists on it, startling his horse. He beat the post until his knuckles ached and bled from the many small cuts. Screaming in pain and anger, he lashed out at the empty night in search of his imagined adversary; then dropped to his knees, his eyes swollen and red from the rubbing. He looked up at the crescent moon and the millions of stars and swore an oath to those who had died under Ozhan's blades. He swore it again to almighty God that not another soul would perish if he could do something about it.

***

It was past midnight. Ozhan chatted to Nelan in his ostentatious den, considering his next move. "When Thomas comes, and he will come I assure you, don't disarm him, just kill the bastard and have done with it!"

She shrugged. "Whatever you say, Master."

"Are you sure you can take him in a fight?"

She nodded, "I did once and can do it again. I should have killed him years ago while I had the chance."

"It's a relief to hear you say that, after seeing the man in action."

"I'm in a killing mood."

His unblinking leering eyes stared at her more than ample breasts. "It would be a shame to spoil your mood. Will you allow me to soften it after you do the deed."

She shook her head, disgusted by the thought. "I never mix business with pleasure!"

His demeanour became sullen and a sickly smile wandered over his evil countenance. He pushed his face, nose to nose with hers, his eyes aglow. His hand shot out at lightning speed, grabbing her throat. He pulled her closer, his tongue flicking out, licking the scar on her cheek. "Who do you think you are? Do you imagine you're too good for me? We have things in common, you and me."

She howled as he lifted her from the floor, hauling her into the air. He shook her as he would a rag doll, madness in his eyes. "I could rape you here and now if I wanted to, you whore-bitch!"

On the verge of passing out, she shook her head. "You won't do that!"

He bared his teeth. "Why not?"

She gasped for air. "Because you need me to kill Thomas, and that means more to you than anything else, including raping me."

In his fit of rage, he hurled her towards an open doorway. "Get out! Get out! And consider yourself lucky I need you for now!" His angry words rang in her ears for the second time in a month, but this time she didn't nod in agreement. She climbed to her feet and staggered away, clutching her throat, gasping for breath, regretting the day she had fallen in with Ozhan, the deranged cut-throat. His maniacal laughter echoed along the hallway as she left his mansion by a back door, knowing how lucky she was not to have incurred his full wrath.

***

The morning of the following day, Nelan paced around a spreading chestnut tree she had slept in, as the faint light of dawn appeared. She looked up at the cloudless sky. *I'm crazy to get involved with the baron,* she thought as the icy hand of fear gripped her, remembering his last words. *Yes, I hate Thomas Flynn with a passion but now hate and despise Ozhan even more. He is the most brutal, cold-hearted man I have ever had the misfortune to meet. In fact, he's insane and evil.*

Now she saw Thomas in a different light and believed the death of their trainer, Master Gallus, was nothing more than a tragic accident, which Thomas had said many times. A cold wind whispered across the land, chilling her and she shivered, lifting the collar of her heavy grey coat. *What is wrong with me? I wouldn't usually work for a scum-sucking bastard like the baron, even though I am alone and friendless. He's an arrogant, ugly son-of-a-bitch.*

Within the halls of her subconscious, she felt disappointed with herself and surged back into control. She blinked, taking a deep breath. I won't be his lackey, she assured herself. I won't.

With the dawn came pangs of hunger and she spent an hour trying to catch a trout in a nearby stream, but each time she scooped it up, it wriggled free and returned to the depths. She decided enough was enough and ate leaves and berries just to suppress her hunger. The air cold against her face, she knew winter was closing in fast. Within a few weeks, snow would come down from the hills and blanket the ground.

The new day began in a haze of soft sunlight that crept across the countryside, expanding and bursting forth over woods and meadows. Birdsongs rang in the air and the dewdrops on plants, flowers and spiders' webs sparkled like tiny jewels. It is a beautiful day, she thought, trying to forget the baron and her problems.

She sat beneath the chestnut tree, listening to the birds while watching nature's extravaganza. She marvelled at its glory, but there was a bittersweet to it. Death is ugly. Life is beautiful. Yet the two are inseparable. You can't have one without having the other. And as she sat, her mind was far from the ways of a warrior. Far from battles, war and killing, and far from her own tortured history, for like Thomas and his brother Malcolm, there was abuse in her past too. Her scars, mental and physical were as deep as theirs, if not deeper. That's why she found solace in killing evil people.

She daydreamed how good life would be if Ozhan didn't spoil it, and even as the notion came to her, she could hear his mocking laughter in her mind. She looked across the elegant backdrop to the City of Nottingham with its sculptured beauty, amid forests, rivers and verdant meadows. One day, nothing will be here if he has his way, for he will rape, pillage, kill and destroy everything.

Nelan took a deep breath. The smell of grass, wet from the recent rain made her feel at ease and at one with the land. She had loved the countryside, even as a small child. Swinging her gaze to the left, she noticed the baron's mansion high on the hillside, shrouded in mist and it looked evil, as evil as the man himself, she thought.

She leaned her back against the bole of the chestnut tree and relaxed. Then a voice sounded, startling her. "You must be a stranger in these parts, milady," said the man, and a powerful hand gripped her arm, hauling her upright. She blinked, coming to her feet and spun on her heel.

She shrugged his hand away. "Who might you be, sir?"

The newcomer smiled a gap-toothed smile. He laid his coat over a nearby tree stump. "Good morning milady, sorry I startled you. Berwyn's my name, poaching's my game, and it's not wise to be sitting here. Master Ozhan doesn't take kindly to us trespassers."

The man smiled again, holding up two plump pheasants. He was tall and muscular, dressed in forest greens and soft black leather boots that curled up at the toes. A hawk-like nose dominated his face, and he spoke with a lisp.

"The baron doesn't take kindly to anyone, on or off his land," she countered. Then the surrounding woodland burst with the sound of birds fluttering and rodents scurrying into hiding.

Berwyn picked up his coat, throwing it over his shoulder. He swung around and headed towards the forest to their rear. "Someone approaches. Best go, we had. Follow me, milady, and I'll show you the way out of here."

She didn't like his look but followed, wanting nothing more to do with Ozhan.

Berwyn slipped through the forest with stealth. Nelan struggled to keep up, but he seemed to know every square inch of the dark wood. He paused and stood stock-still. Cautious he waited for several seconds, melting into the shadow of an oak, watching and listening for movement, no matter how small. There was none. He walked on saying nothing, preferring to cloak himself in silence, but when he spoke it was to give directions. And so, for thirty minutes they made their way across the forest track. It hissed like the fall of rain as their feet passed over the dried leaves and pine needles. Now they left the cover of trees at a crossroad and he pointed out the direction she should go, bidding her farewell.

"Good luck to you, milady. I hope good fortune favours you," he said with a wide grin and he disappeared back into the forest on the far side of the road.

She stood for a moment. A steep hillside greeted her eyes and a glistening stream rippled by the roadside with sheep feeding on a patch of grassland. She ran up the hill and along a deer trail. At the top of the ridge, she ran down into Nottingham main street and her sullen mood vanished and all thought of the baron disappeared with it.

Now she needed new employment and a place to stay, only having three copper coins to her name. Not knowing where she was, she angled her journey north, hoping to find the Dog and Duck and the swordsman Thomas Flynn.

CHAPTER NINE

A murdered friend

Thomas stood at his high balcony window, looking across Nottingham. The anger was still with him, but the trembling had stopped, even though Cyrano's memory nagged and tugged at his thoughts. The last time he had seen him alive he was laughing, joking and playing with Dody without a care in the world, but now the sensitive, caring, funny man was dead, and for no good reason.

At first, he felt an overpowering sense of grief but it grew into something else as the morning passed on into the late afternoon. Hate, rage and the wish to kill filled him. He stood on the balcony, wondering how he could get to his enemy. Ozhan had paid a fortune to build his home on the hillside with its tall spires, buttresses and bulwarks, and it was more like a fortress than a mansion. So whenever he encountered any resistance he fled for the sanctuary of his protective walls, knowing it would take a small army to rout his forces.

Thomas remembered the old stories. Years earlier, the people of Nottingham welcomed the baron into their flock with open arms, giving him a huge tract of land in the south, so he could grow crops and build a herd of cattle. But he had demanded ever more land, and as the years passed and his group grew in numbers he dammed the rivers, bringing drought to the rest of the community. Then when representatives tried to mediate, urging him to reconsider, he tortured them, skinning them alive or he beat them to death with a hammer. Then, Ozhan's mercenaries sacked the city, annihilating it. Thomas remembered the last line of a chilling poem: "Ozhan is coming while you sleep in your bed, slaughtering everyone until all are dead."

He ran his fingers through his hair and sighed. Twice now he had encountered Ozhan's forces, vanquishing them, but fortune smiled on the man himself. Both times he was not on the killing fields.

Most times Thomas needed nothing more than a good horse, supplies and a handful of silver coins to make his way through life, but everything changed with the strike of a single knife blade to his friend's heart. Now he needed to get inside the baron's mansion. But he would have to breach his gates first.

Anger flared once more, causing his hands to tremble. In the old days, he would have paid Ozhan a visit and smashed his door in, but times change and so had he. Now he was more careful, considering his options before using rash actions. Now he needed a key to open a door rather than a hammer to knock it down with brute force.

Leaving the balcony he strode to the kitchen, filled a goblet full of water and drank. A loud knock came at the back door, startling him, causing him to jump; spilling water. He made his way to the observation hole and slid it open. Whoever was outside had their back to him. He opened the door. "Good afternoon to you, friend how may I be of service to you?"

The caller swung around close to the observation hole.

Thomas' eyes widened. "What are you doing here, Nelan?"

"I'm here to settle a score."

Thomas flashed a sarcastic smile. "It's always a displeasure to see you, milady."

Dressed in a long black coat, a stylish black tunic of oiled leather, dark leggings and calf-length boots she looked like a demon from a dark forest. Two short swords hung at her sides beneath the folds of her coat. "Good to see you too, Thomas," she said in a mocking tone, "but I'm not here for a fight."

In his young life, he had summoned strengths that seemed joyous and raucous in battle and in peace, but now he had the urge to attack without mercy. Ozhan had killed his friend, and she was his ally. He unbolted the door and opened it.

"Are you frightened, Nelan?"

She gave a weak smile. "Should I be?"

"You take a great chance coming here, milady. God's teeth, my instincts are to strike you down after what has happened here."

"And I wouldn't blame you for it," she said trying to defuse the situation, "but it would be folly to fight each other for the wrong reasons. Besides, we have bigger fish to fry. Fish with sharp bones that stick in your craw too."

He gave her a questioning look, swinging away from the door.

She stepped inside and could sense his utter contempt for her. She laid a hand on his shoulder, drawing him back. "I didn't come here to fight. I came to offer my help against the tyrant Ozhan. But I will fight if I must, just to prove my sincerity."

He turned his head and stared at her. "Why switch sides in the middle of a war?"

"Because I now know the baron is an insane tyrannical brute!"

"Oh, how stupid of me to forget that tiny thing," said Thomas. "I suppose you overlooked that fact too when he offered you gold to terrorise and murder innocent people."

She shook her head. "No. I offered my services as a means to an end because I knew he wanted you dead and I thought I did. But I've been following your progress and have seen you help this community and its people without hesitation or payment. Now I've realised you are a good man and would not have killed Master Gallus on purpose. So I renounce my oath to kill you."

The stairwell door swung open. Dardo was standing there holding his head, back-lit by a single lantern. "The baron hit me with a lump of wood," he complained, "so how did I get to bed?"

"I carried you," said Thomas. "I thought you were drunk."

Dardo rubbed the back of his head. "I was getting drunk with Cyrano when Ozhan and his men came bursting through the back door. Then the lights went out for me."

Thomas shook his head in dismay. "You're not the sharpest arrow in the quiver sometimes, are you?"

Dardo sulked. "Where is Cyrano? Did they knock him senseless too?"

Thomas could feel the blood-lust growing within him again. He seethed with anger. "No, they butchered him and burnt his face off," he whispered in an icy guttural tone. "I've laid him on his bed and covered him, ready for burial."

Dardo rubbed the back of his head again and his fingers came away bloody. Dizziness swamped him and he stumbled, falling to the floor with a great buzzing in his ears.

Thomas and Nelan helped him back to his feet and sat him in a chair. He looked bewildered.

"I wish it was only his head that hurt like mine," he said.

Nelan laid a hand on his shoulder. "The blow to your head has blurred your senses, my friend."

"You're the warrior, Nelan. I saw you fight in London two years ago."

She nodded. "I tried to disarm the fool, but he attacked, slashing my face, and I had to defend myself. It was a shame. He was drunk and out of order, but I didn't want to kill him.

"Are you here to help us?" Dardo asked.

"If you think you need my help, I will give it."

Thomas shrugged. "Why not? I would say no, but a fool falls before his pride."

"Age and pride make fools of us all," she said.

"That's just what I'd expect a woman to say," countered Thomas looking superior.

Nelan shot him an angry stare. "Don't be so smug. I'm trying to be of service. I've no reputation, but every acorn has the makings of a great oak."

"No one wants to hear about the acorn."

"You pompous, self-indulgent, self-righteous…"

Thomas interrupted her. "Enough! I was joking! We will be proud to have you help us."

The loud toll of the Nottingham Abbey bell brought their bickering to a halt. They stood stock-still, in thought, listening to its resounding tones. Down long ages, the old Abbey had stood for harmony and peace, bringing goodwill and refuge to all people. They shook hands.

"I'm hungry, anybody else want something to eat?" asked Thomas with the best grace he could muster under the circumstances.

***

Much later that evening, after Thomas had been back to Tobin's farm and told Lira and her father the terrible news of Cyrano's murder, he opened the Dog and Duck in honour of their late friend's memory. He sat at his usual table with his back to the wall and the blind harpist played a more serious, sombre music than usual. Dardo picked up a pitcher of ale and poured, filling three goblets, and Nelan made a toast to their departed friend, but the tavern was full and she could hardly hear herself speak over the hubbub. Thomas remained silent, his expression thoughtful. *What am I doing? A good friend is dead, murdered, and I'm sitting drinking,* a voice whispered in his head.

"What now?" asked Nelan.

The question cut through Thomas' thoughts.

"Do you have a plan?" asked Dardo.

Thomas shook his head looking as grim as a corpse hanging from the gibbet in gallows square. His face was thin and drawn; his cheeks covered in black stubble, eyes dark-rimmed and weary. He looked into her bright eyes and gave a tired smile. "No. We need to get inside Ozhan's mansion, but it's built like a fortress. He'd see us coming whichever way we approach."

Dardo sat beside Thomas, "Do you realise the impossibility of what you're planning?"

"That depends on the manner in which we approach the problem," said Nelan. "Nothing's impossible and subtlety is a better approach than brute force. Being invited in rather than having to break down Ozhan's door is the better choice. What if I went back to the baron and told him you will join forces with him? I think he would grab the chance to fight alongside you rather than having to kill you."

Thomas smiled at her and then stared at Dardo with a look of revelation in his eyes. "You're right! I was looking for a key to unlock Ozhan's door and you are the key, he trusts you."

Dardo tapped his temple. "Good thinking."

The reality struck Thomas. He sprang to his feet. "If we approach the baron's mansion from the woodland side together, he will send out an armed guard to see who's coming. He may even ride out himself as he's a curious man, and just three incoming riders won't cause him too much alarm."

As the hour grew late, they made plans for Ozhan's demise. Dardo was drunk and stared at his empty goblet. "What drives you, Thomas?" he asked, forcing himself upright in his chair. He hiccupped, burping in his friend's face.

Thomas wafted the air in front of him. "Hell's teeth man, how many drinks have you had tonight?"

Dardo's eyes crossed for a moment and he hiccupped again. "Just enough to dull my senses and rid myself of the thought of dying soon."

Thomas turned his head, fixing his friend's gaze. "I was five years old when a monster came and ate my world, swallowing my mother and father whole, leaving my brother and me alone. Now it's here again in a different guise, but now I'm older, wiser, skilled and stronger. I won't let it happen again. I will kill the baron before he kills all of us, I promise."

Dardo hauled himself upright and staggered over to a couch. He fell onto it and turned, opening a window. Cold air struck him in the face as he leaned out, staring into the courtyard. He leaned further and further out of the window. "I feel sick!"

Thomas grabbed him, dragging him back into the room. "I think it's time for you to go to bed, my friend, before you fall on your head."

Dardo's eyes rolled in their sockets and the ceiling spun as something horrible happened in his stomach.

Moaning and groaning he retched and passed out. Thomas caught him before he hit the floor and carried him off to bed, bidding Nelan goodnight.

***

As the sun's first rays flung wide the gates of dawn, Ozhan girded himself for another day of battle. His mercenaries sharpened their weapons under his critical eyes and they scuttled around his hall collecting ropes to make torches, ready to light. He had press-ganged most into his service by giving each one of them a savage beating and they lived in fear of their lives.

Dozens of candles burned low in their sconces around the hall and the distinct smell of coal oil filled the air. Without warning, the baron stormed into his new recruits, lashing out with his big fists, bowling them left, right and centre using his great strength. Baring his teeth, his eyes glowed. "I want Thomas Flynn dead, his friends dead, his horse dead, everyone and everything to do with the swordsman dead and his memory erased forever and then I never want to hear his name mentioned again."

At lightning speed, the big man's sword flashed clear of its scabbard. Enraged, he sliced off a man's ear and the tip of another man's nose. "You're greedy for plunder and booty and can have whatever you want, provided I get Thomas Flynn's head," he snapped, his voice echoing throughout the mansion.

The group of men fell back, scattering in disorder. Ozhan threw back his head roaring with laughter. "No guts, eh? Well, you better get guts, because soon you'll be in a real fight."

The two injured men scurried away backwards, bleeding, with his angry words ringing in their ears. They dashed off, bumping into each other in panic, trying to get out through a door together.

The baron had enlisted one hundred new recruits, mainly gutter-scum, but with a good scattering of seasoned mercenaries, and those press-ganged by his savage beatings, coupled with threats of a painful death were always the ones he made an example of in front others. It was his way of keeping them all in line. Fear shone in their eyes and none doubted he would spit-roast them in their own juices if they crossed him.

"Read them the articles of allegiance," the baron snapped to a silver-eyed giant as he himself swaggered back and forth reciting them from memory under his breath.

The man did as instructed. "You're in the service of Master Ozhan now. So, if you do not do your sworn duty you'll join the Master's Choir!" the man blustered after reading the articles. "I take orders from Oz, and you lot take orders from me. Remember that and we'll all get along just fine. Disobey and die!"

The baron nodded his approval. Sheathing his sword, silence hung upon the air while he and the giant man had a whispered conversation. Dressed in black oilskins, matching boots and a hooded cloak that flitted in the light breeze sweeping through the hall, Ozhan looked fearsome with his powerful broad shoulders, scarred face and savage manner. And the one thing his men now knew for sure was that he had no natural sense of fairness, no perception of wrong-doing and he never felt guilty about his rude manner or brutality, in fact, now they knew he had no conscience at all. The world to him was full of men with little or no imagination, men who couldn't recognise his genuine genius, but in reality, the one thing they recognised was his megalomania, which produced his delusions of grandeur and fits of rage.

He once asked his father, "Why are there so many fools and weaklings in the world?"

"Boy, they rule the world so we may prosper," his father answered.

How true that one simple fact turned out to be in the baron's eyes. He thought he had no equal and so trusted no one, not even the silver-eyed giant. He had climbed the ladder of power alone until he stood on the top rung looking down upon lesser men and considered himself a god, having to make no excuses about anything or answer to anyone as he thought there was no higher being.

Ozhan spun to face his men. "Do you understand the rules, you gutter-scum? You work for me and if I say jump, you jump. If I say bleed, you bleed. If I say die, you die for me! That's it, no questions asked! Are we understood?"

The whole group nodded, slinking back into ranks because he looked so fierce, all except for one man. The baron swaggered forward, taking on a threatening posture and his eyes searched the man's face. "Do you want to dispute my authority?" he asked, tapping his fingers on the hilt of his sword.

The man's eyes glinted. He kicked a chair over and swore. "Listen, you don't scare me. I'll do your dirty work and even die for you because I'm a paid mercenary, but don't think you can treat me like this other gutter-scum, because you can't!"

Ozhan drew his sword, laughing, and as the echoes died around the room, his face went grim.

The other men backed away, watching him shaking with fury.

"You're young and headstrong, my friend, are you ambitious too?" Ozhan said, launching himself at the man with a snarl. He was in mid-air when his fist knocked the renegade flat.

The man groaned and shook his head. He lay stunned, staring at Ozhan standing over him.

"Think yourself lucky it was my fist and not my blade that took you from your feet! Maybe you thought a big strong warrior like you could deal with an older man like me? Well, you were wrong! As a child, I lacked love and attention, so I beat people up just for the hell of it!"

Turning on his heel he stamped his way out of the Great Hall, followed by the silver-eyed giant. He stopped and turned. His icy voice echoed down the long hallway. "Don't make the mistake of not taking me seriously just because I let you live. I'll need you all tomorrow, and you'll beg on your knees for a quick death if you don't fight well. Plus, I'll make your torture long, lingering and loud before you die if you betray my articles of allegiance!"

***

It was now noon, and the sun shone overhead as the forests and meadowlands stirred to the bold voice of the Abbey bell bringing farmers and their families hurrying to their place of sanctuary. It was a time of great danger, Thomas and Dardo told them. Both men had ridden to the farmers' homesteads to give warning, and all carried what little belongings they needed to out-wait the holocaust to come.

Up the long, dusty road they came, not stopping or resting until they reached the Abbey, where Brother Mathias stood by the gates with the Abbot, welcoming them all. Grateful thanks shone in their eyes as each one smiled, nodding, knowing they would owe their existence to the Abbot and his high walls, and all who entered received food, shelter and sound advice.

Tobin and Lira were the last to arrive, tired, hungry and breathless from their long walk. The Abbot and Mathias closed the great gates when Lira spun around looking back down the road through the bars. She could hear the distinct beat of horses' hooves in the distance. "Two riders are coming, but I can't tell who they are," she said.

Brother Mathias gripped his walking staff tighter, thinking it might be Ozhan's scouts, and he felt the hair prickle on the back of his neck as the horses drew nearer. Now they stood still, peering down the road with their hearts beating fast and their mouths dry. Closer and closer the riders came and Lira could just make out a black cloak flitting in the breeze. Then, a voice rang out sharp and clear from a high parapet. "It's Thomas and Dardo!"

Lira breathed a sigh of relief. "Oh, thank God."

The Abbot and Mathias pushed open the gates, allowing them to enter the entrance overhung with laurels. "Good to see you," said the Abbot.

Both warriors dismounted. "Can we rest here a while, Father?" asked Dardo, his face pale. "We've ridden far, through the night, and we're exhausted."

The Abbot nodded, his solemn expression softening. He put his arm around the young man's shoulders, shuffling his sandals in the dust. "Dardo, my son, if threatened less we could take life a little easier, then we would live with dignity and humility. But the cruel baron with his pitiless heart and Godforsaken black soul will not allow it to be so. Rest while you can. Both of you are welcome within these hallowed walls so, come and follow me."

Thomas and Dardo followed the Abbot and Mathias at a sedate pace to the Great Hall, strolling past its cloistered walls towards a room filled with pallet beds. Sunlight filtered down in slanting shafts from a high, stained glass window and dust motes danced and swirled as they all walked the stone floor.

The Abbot halted in front of a door and bid them enter the Room of Silence, the pride and joy of the Abbey. Here the Fathers studied before bedtime. Thomas and Dardo entered, sitting on the cool sheets of two beds, resting their backs on the wall, and the Abbot studied the wonderment in both men's eyes as they gazed, around the simplistic looking room.

"Are you surprised by our lack of possessions and comfortable beds in the Abbey?" asked the Abbot, his hands tucked inside the baggy sleeves of his old, grey habit.

Both men nodded.

The Abbot peered into Thomas' eyes and tripped over his loose sandals. "Goodness gracious, I must get a new pair of these," he said, pointing at his feet. "Rest now and we will speak later." He turned and wobbled his way back along the cloisters with Mathias, his sandals flip-flopping beneath the folds of his habit.

Thomas smiled, watching him, thinking what a comical figure he cut as he once again tripped over his sandals, saving himself from falling just in time. Every picture tells a story, he thought.

Just then the whole building echoed to the sound of the Abbey bell, and moments later another Brother in a brown novice's habit entered the room carrying a large wooden tray with a mixture of cheeses, oatcakes and a jug of mead on it. Without uttering a word he placed the tray onto a small table and left. Thomas and Dardo looked at each other and ate, drank and conversed in low tones for over an hour, fixing their plans for the baron's demise in their minds before falling fast asleep.

***

That night inside the Great Hall the Abbot sat on the stone floor, resting his back to the wall. "Come and sit with me a while, my children," he offered, addressing his congregation and his flock gathered around him looking bewildered. "We are men and women of peace, but we need strength of character. I vowed a long time ago to heal the sick, care for the injured and give shelter and aid to the impoverished, but today a great evil overshadows us and Ozhan is its name. But, fortune smiles on us because we have a legendary swordsman to aid us!"

As the Abbot spoke, his tone increased in volume and intensity. "Thomas Flynn is a fierce, fearless fighter who has faced the enemy many times in single combat with a sword, bow or his fists and feet, and I know even against overwhelming odds he will drive the merciless monster and his bunch of murderous cutthroats from this land to emerge the victor. But, he needs your help. Even the thunder of the heavens has lightning's support. Thunder rolls and lightning forks, felling huge trees, and then raindrops spear the ground as they stretch into silver rods in the same fashion a hail of arrows from fifty bowmen will spear Ozhan's henchmen. So, who will volunteer to deliver a winged message to our sworn enemy?" the Abbot asked, knowing Thomas had recruited a good number of men himself.

The crowd looked horrified, shaking their heads at the Abbot's suggestion, and they wittered amongst themselves in hushed tones until one man stood up and called out. "Father, we're farmers, not warriors! We know nothing of bows and fighting!"

The Abbot scratched his chin. "Hmm, I know my son, but sometimes we have to be bigger and braver than we are, and I would rather live one minute as a free man, than a whole lifetime as a slave to the baron."

A small boy of six years approached and tugged the Abbots habit. "I will fight, I'm not afraid," he said, a child's faith and courage shining in his eyes.

"Yes, I believe you will fight," said the Abbot smiling, searching the faces of the congregation. His heart couldn't help soften towards their awful plight, but Ozhan was coming and death was coming with him.

CHAPTER TEN

The visitor

Hearty cheers interrupted the Abbot's speech, one hour later, as Thomas and Dardo entered the Great Hall.

"Couldn't sleep," said Thomas.

"Me neither," agreed Dardo.

Oohs and ahs greeted their arrival and the crowd patted their backs as they pushed their way through the poor but proud people towards the Abbot, who was still sitting with his back to the wall.

Thomas silenced the hubbub by raising his hand. "Cock your ears and listen. Men and women of Nottingham, I see those amongst you who are far too old and infirm to take up arms against the baron and his followers, but also those amongst you who are strong and should fight. Death will come to you sooner rather than later if you don't take up arms against those with murder in their hearts. I realised this a long time ago when I sought to escape my problems by fuddling my wits with gin and strong wine. Drunk or sober, you have no escape. So, it would be better to die at a time and place of your own choosing, rather than having it forced upon you. No one wants to die, but if I must, I will face it as a free man. Will you?"

One member of the congregation stood up, applauding Thomas' oration. Then another stood up and clapped. And another, until the whole gathering was on their feet clapping. Now they cheered louder and louder.

One tall, young man shouted, "I will fight."

Another broad-shouldered youth yelled, "Me too!"

"I will fight," said another, and another until Dardo lost count.

"You are an eloquent speaker, Thomas, and have a way with words," said the Abbot. "I spent an hour trying to do what you did in less than a minute."

Dardo smiled too, patting Thomas' back, "Maybe it's your solid-looking sensible manner that appeals to them?"

Thomas laughed. "It's more likely to be my solid-looking, sensible short-swords that have convinced them, my good and faithful friend."

The Abbot smiled at their lighthearted banter and he couldn't help shaking his head in admiration at their stiff resolve, which seemed to have hidden depths.

***

Meanwhile, Ozhan the tyrant was having a bad dream. He had lain down on his four-poster bed for a well-earned rest, while his men were going about their allotted tasks and weariness overcame him.

In his dream, a dark mist-shrouded everything and cries of panic and torment rang out as homesteads and barns burned and cattle bellowed in pain. He thrashed about, killing and laying waste to all in his path; then a ghostlike figure appeared. At first, it looked like a bat that kept growing bigger and the closer it came the bigger it got. He didn't relish meeting it, so he turned to run, but the faster he ran, the faster the bat flew.

Glancing back, he saw the carnage the thing had caused in its life and it reminded him of himself. He ran faster still through the dark mist, sweat oozing from his hands and brow like acid and he stumbled, catching himself. He ran on again, looking back once more, the strange creature hard on his heels, growing larger and larger with its eyes cold and grim, but now it looked like a dragon that had grown into a giant wielding bright claws.

Although his lungs were bursting, he put on more speed. But his heavy leaden limbs let him down, forcing him to run slower and slower until he stopped. Now he understood mindless fear and raw panic for the first time. He stumbled, falling into the icy water and turned, realising his fate. The creature was upon him, raising its claws high, ready to strike, it changed into the swordsman Thomas Flynn and his deadly twin blades struck.

The loud toll of the Abbey bell brought him back from the realms of his dream to stark reality and he shivered, wiping the sweat from his brow with a shaking hand. What did the dream mean? Is it a bad omen, he wondered? It was so vivid he trembled. A knock on his bedroom door snapped him from his dream.

A servant entered, "Someone is here to see you, sir. The lady is waiting in the library."

The baron nodded. "Oh, well, tell her I will be down directly."

Moments later, he pushed open his library door. A woman was standing, cloaked and hooded in front of a blazing fire.

"Well, did Flynn fall for our ploy?"

The visitor turned, revealing her bright blue eyes and dark hair. "I was convincing. Thomas believed my story."

The baron smiled, nodding his approval. He walked towards her, his eyes scanning her face and he put his arm around her shoulders. "Nelan, you're a fascinating woman and you intrigue me."

She shrugged his arm off, backing away. "This is business, Ozhan. I don't want you to get any funny ideas about me and you. I'm not a woman to hurl myself on my back and open my legs just because you're a powerful, wealthy man." Her point was plain as daylight.

He tensed for a moment, the light of madness in his eyes and for a heartbeat, he stood still and then his laughter boomed out. "By heaven, you exalt yourself, woman. I said you intrigued me, nothing more!"

She looked embarrassed but sighed with relief.

"I may be ugly, scarred and have the face of a demon, but one woman has captured my heart. She is a beauty to behold and works in the treasury. Her husband works there too. But he knows nothing about our affair or the fact we are robbing him of his fortune. Nor will he know. His ignorance is the only thing keeping him alive!"

She stared at him. "Do you enjoy killing?"

"What I enjoy is none of your damn business," he snapped, his irritation rising, "but the answer to your question is yes. Sometimes the longing for blood grows within me like a rampaging herd of wild pigs."

She slumped down into a chair by the fire with her legs crossed. He's as mad as a March Hare, utterly insane, she thought.

He strode to the library shelves and plucked his diary from a bookcase that covered the whole wall. Sitting opposite her, he opened the book and stared at pages marked Saturday and Sunday. Red ink circled Sunday. "Tell me of your plans for Thomas Flynn's murder," he said with no emotion in his voice.

She was chilled and trembled, able to feel the evil emanating from the monster sitting opposite her, but during their meeting, there was much useful information exchanged. She told him of her meeting with Thomas, and that they planned to get rid of the baron by making him think the swordsman wanted to change sides. Thomas would come to his mansion under a white flag of truce, thus gaining easy access. Once inside, he would kill the baron, and so she had baited the trap.

"Once inside the mansion, he will be the dead one," said Ozhan smirking.

He interrupted her thoughts by pounding on a table. "That's good, my dear. Bring him here tomorrow and when he's dead, I'll give you what you deserve!" His words echoed around the library walls, sounding more like a threat than a promise.

She reflected she had used desperate measures to secure his promise of reward, but justified it because the baron was as uncompromising as he was murderous, and she knew if her double-edged plan failed she wouldn't live to see another sunrise. So she went back to her lodgings to get a good night's rest, knowing she would need her senses sharp and her mind clear for her plan to succeed.

***

The following morning, high on a hillside overlooking Nottingham as dawn appeared, it ushered in a bright new day. The sky was blue and filled with clouds, looking like the sails of ships billowing in a light breeze, but Dardo with exhaustion and anxiety gnawing at his heart didn't feel good. Darkness swept over his soul and his spirit pitched, plunged and seemed in shreds and tatters because he had practised for weeks with a longbow up in the hills alone and he was no better now than when he had started. And he needed to be accurate with the weapon now, more than ever, if he was to be of any use to Thomas because

Ozhan the ruthless monster with his pitiless heart would kill them, taking great pleasure in doing so if given half a chance.

He also knew his fearless friend needed every ounce of support he could muster, because the baron's mind was full of plans for their destruction, and Thomas' loyal band of followers would suffer a similar fate if they failed their mission.

Dardo looked down the shaft of his arrow, aiming at the dark braided hair of a child's doll, pinned to a tree trunk at fifty paces, and he waited, his hands trembling. He closed one eye, adjusting his aim. "Help me find my mark, Lord," he whispered, and compensating for the strong crosswind he released the arrow betwixt his fingers and it took flight. It flew straight, piercing the doll's hair, cutting it in half. He couldn't believe his eyes or his luck and he almost fainted from the shock.

A cheer rang out from behind him and he spun on his heel. Thomas smiled, clapping his hands. "Well done. Never thought I'd see this day."

Dardo smiled back scratching his head. "Me neither!"

Thomas tapped the hilts of his swords. "Today is the day of reckoning my friend. And tonight the baron will be dead when a blood moon rises."

Dardo shivered as memories of Cyrano's terrible murder flared within him. His killers had attacked, without warning, and they had burned his face with coal oil so bad his bone shone through his skin, and then stabbed him to death. He could even hear the baron's mad laughter echoing in his head. Thomas was a killer of men too, but one he admired for his lethal skills because he was an honourable man and amiable if left alone. He had no anger or hatred, not even for Ozhan, but there was a score to settle and neither of them would eat, nor sleep now until they had settled that score.

High on the hillside, Thomas and Dardo took a deep breath of fresh air, focusing their eyes on the lone rider heading their way. It was Nelan, riding at a gallop, and as she approached, she gestured for them to follow her towards the Southern Quarter of the City.

Thomas nodded. "We may not need an armed mob to vanquish Ozhan and his paid assassins if our plan works today," he told Dardo, a tone of hope in his voice.

Both men mounted their horses. Then for the next fifteen minutes, the three friends galloped across roads, alleys and avenues, lines of shops, stalls and workplaces, passing the lion statues on the Nottingham Bridge until they hit the Great North Road, leading to Ozhan's mansion. Nelan swung her horse, angling it southward and Thomas and Dardo followed, remembering landmarks as they passed several horses being exercised by a farmer in a nearby field. Neither of them had ever seen the baron's palatial mansion up close, but they knew it was a fortress in its own right.

After crossing several barren fields, his home with its white walls and spires, buttresses and bulwarks came into view. Thomas scanned the layout. The stories are true, he thought, the mansion is a fortress! They stopped, catching sight of several riders heading their way. Thomas turned his head, staring at the neighbouring checkerboard of meadows and fields, dissected by a meandering river and he noticed more riders coming. "The baron's taking no chances today," he said.

An odd haze hung over the whole hillside, obscuring their vision, but they could see the baron's mansion. Swathed in mist and shadows and backed by a forest a mile distant from where they were sitting astride their horses it loomed large and sinister. They squinted against the light of the morning sun to see it.

More riders headed their way from the courtyard and stables, and within moments had closed on Thomas and his associates, surrounding them. "What are you doing, wandering around in this meadow?" snapped their leader, a tall man with a sudden glint of suspicion in his grey eyes. He wore a mercenary's attire. "This is the baron's land!"

Nelan stared at the man. "Master Ozhan is expecting us."

The guard stared back. "Are you Nelan and Thomas Flynn?"

Not caring for the look of the man Thomas interrupted, "Yes, and my friend Dardo."

"The baron said there would be two of you."

"Well, now you see we are three," Thomas countered.

The guard hesitated; then shook his reins, heeling his horse forward, angling it back towards the mansion. "Follow me," he snapped.

Thomas, Nelan and Dardo swung their horses round, following the guard. The troop did the same, cantering in unison at the rear. They rode back through the fields and within a few minutes were beneath the walls of the mansion. Baron Ozhan stood at his high balcony window, gazing out towards the North, but he switched his gaze, waving his men into the courtyard and then disappeared from the window.

The troop swung their horses to the left, riding onto the high ground of the courtyard, through open iron gates and stopped. The leader dismounted. Thomas and his friends did too, as the guard beckoned them to follow him towards a high entrance overhung with ivy, where another guard came to fetch them. He took Nelan by the arm. "The Master is waiting for you in the Great Hall," he said, leading her up a flight of spiral stone steps. The troop of riders lead their horses into the stables to feed.

Thomas took a deep breath to steady his nerves; then he relaxed and climbed the stairs, followed by Dardo, whose eyes were shifting from side to side, expecting attackers to leap out at any moment. At the top of the steps, the guard opened a door and Nelan entered first, unhooked her black sable cloak and draped it over a chair. She stared at the fine artwork decorating the silent and serene room. Thomas and Dardo entered, striding across to an arched window, staring out. Their eyes wandered across the floor of the valley and the view was breath-taking. It looked like a magical kingdom. Another door at the far end of the room opened, and a voice boomed out. "Well, here you are at last. Come on through please!"

Dardo was so startled by the voice he jumped and then froze on the spot. Thomas ambled across the room as Nelan entered the Great Hall. It was bright inside with whitewashed walls and many oak beams supporting a low ceiling. Sunlight flooded through the windows, and as Thomas stepped into view, he realised the situation was every bit as bad as he feared it would be. There were already forty men present, and they were the largest and strongest in Nottingham.

The baron seated himself at the back of the room. Standing beside him to his left was the grey-haired giant, his second in command and to his right was a tall slender swordsman in a forester's garb of fringed buckskin. Thomas strode across the room to a chair and sat calmly, facing the baron. Nelan and Dardo did likewise. None spoke.

"Welcome friends, good to see you've finally come to your senses," said Ozhan, his face devoid of expression. "Would you like something to drink?"

Thomas shook his head. "No!"

"Something to eat perhaps?"

The trio shook their heads.

"Well, suit yourselves," said the baron.

Thomas scanned the room, fixing his gaze on a portrait hanging on a far wall.

"My father," said Ozhan.

"Looks like an important man," said Thomas.

"He was a whore and a bastard!" the baron snapped. "But you're a smart man, aren't you? Although you haven't been too realistic of late. God, I'm just like you, brought up the hard way in the backstreets, and when I came to this city, it was not even on a map until I made it something. God-damn-it, King John visited here once because of me. You ask anybody and they'll tell you!"

Thomas' blood boiled and his anger flared. "You've gotten rich off the poor people of this city," he admonished with an icy stare.

The baron laughed. "Yes, and I'll get a lot richer. I believe we all have a purpose in life, a destiny, and I have faith in that destiny. It tells me to gather unto me what is mine. For God's sake man, you're a killer. Tell me you don't love it and I'll call you a liar because I know you do. You wouldn't be the man you are if you didn't. You've killed many men, saying it was in self-defence, but you and I know that isn't so, don't we? So, tell me, how much it will cost now you're working for me?"

Thomas shifted from his seat to a nearby window, watching Ozhan's men edge towards the door, blocking their only exit. It's a trap, he thought, I should have known.

The baron watched them too.

Thomas drew his swords and vaulted a table, unleashing a kick against the grey-haired giant's head, knocking him senseless. "There is no amount of money that could persuade me to work for you!"

The baron threw himself from his chair, rolling to safety.

Dardo reacted, pulling a heavy wooden cudgel from his tunic. Taken unawares, he felled several men where they stood. Then he held his hand up in front of a man's face and shouted, "Stop! Look Ozhan, I thought you liked a fair fight? Well, I count at least forty of you and three of us. That isn't fair!"

The baron smiled, shaking his head.

Dardo pounded heads again. "But we don't mind waiting if you want to fetch another forty."

Thomas was too busy to laugh. And Nelan vanished in the ensuing melee.

Dardo struck heads with lightning speed, throwing in the odd uppercut for good measure, while Thomas' swords flashed from left to right and back again, thrusting, cutting and slicing as his friend pummelled and pounded the enemy. Bodies fell everywhere, moaning and groaning, covered in blood.

The baron disappeared too, and it was a scene from hell, death lingering in the air. Outnumbered but not outclassed, Thomas and Dardo retreated, but as they ran for the door, Thomas ran one way down the corridor and Dardo went the other.

Four swordsmen rounded a bend, and with a blood-curdling scream Thomas charged them. His sword sliced through the skull of the first, the throat of the second decapitating him and the ribs of the third. He stumbled fleetingly and then leapt upon the forth, using one of his swords as a dagger, driving it through the man's chest into his lungs.

Thomas fell on top of him but staggered upright. A spear flashed past him and he spun around on the spot, staying away from a wild slashing cut from another swordsman. His riposte passed through his attacker's wrist, sending his hand spinning through the air. More of Ozhan's men rounded the bend.

Thomas rushed them, his sword hilts clubbing left and right knocking them senseless. Then he plunged both swords into the last man's chest. "Die, son-of-a-bitch!" he snapped.

The sound of more pounding boots came echoing along the corridor. Thomas slunk into the shadows, waiting for the men to pass. He grabbed the last man in a headlock, inching further back into the darkness, pricking a blade under his chin. "Where is the baron?"

The man choked. "He'll kill me if I tell you."

Thomas cut the man. "I'll kill you if you don't."

A crossbow bolt slammed into the man's forehead and he slumped to his knees. Thomas let go of him and he crumpled to the floor. The baron's laughter echoed along the corridor. Thomas leapt over the corpse and charged. Another crossbow bolt sang and tore into his left knee. He darted back into the shadows, the pain intense, blood pooling in his boot. In agony, he scrambled up the corridor searching for cover.

Another crossbow bolt flashed past him. He spun on the spot, swaying away from it. Reaching down, he pulled the bolt from his knee.

Ozhan appeared in front of him, blood spattered on his face, eyes glowing. Thomas hesitated, his face pale, eyes haunted; his mind empty of emotion except one, the burning wish to wreak revenge for Cyrano's death. His brown eyes held to the baron's insane gaze for a moment. He was silent, but then Ozhan's fist struck him full in the face, sending him sprawling down the corridor.

Bright lights shone before his eyes, dizziness swamping him. He slumped back onto the floor. Through a great buzzing in his ears he heard Ozhan's laughter, and then an iron hand gripped his throat, hauling him upright.

"I told you to leave well alone, Flynn," the baron whispered. "Now I will cut out your eyes and eat your liver!"

The swords knocked from his hands, Cyrano's face swam before his eyes, his life torn from him, and Thomas faltered, filled with panic, his resolve failing.

The baron seized the moment, drawing a dagger from his belt and it flashed for Thomas' chest. Thomas' left hand shot out, his fingers closing around the baron's wrist and the blade stopped short by an inch. "Faster than a thunderbolt," he said, his eyes gleaming once more.

Ozhan struggled to pull away from his grip.

Thomas' right hand came up, sunlight gleaming on the blade of his own dagger, but before he had time to use it an arrow hit the baron's knife-hand, knocking his blade clear. He looked stunned, staring at the shaft through his palm.

Pain seared up his arm as he cried out in agony, and his fat face, bloated from rich living jerked as if slapped, a vein throbbing at his temple. "Are you mad? I own this city!" he snapped, swinging around to see Nelan notching another arrow to her bowstring.

"I've never been saner!" she countered, firing for a second time. This time the arrow took him in the belly, lifting him from his feet, slamming him against the wall.

Fear welled up in him and in a blind bottomless rage he let out an animalistic cry and yelled, "No, you can't do this! I own this city and you swore my allegiance!"

Dardo appeared from out of the shadows, bow in hand. "We own this city and don't you forget it!" he yelled back. Levelling his bow, he let fly.

There was a hideous shriek when the arrow hit the baron's chest, the bloody point emerging from his back. He stared down at the arrow in disbelief and an acid fire filled him. He slumped to his knees but stayed upright. "I – I own this city. It's mine," he groaned.

Dody stepped forward from the shadows too with his sling cocked. He'd followed his three friends to the mansion. "No, we will always own this city and you can go to hell!" he screamed. Something had died within him with the death of his father, and a terrible coldness had settled on his soul. Darkly exultant he extended his arm and let fly.

The others watched in awe-struck silence as the black pebble thudded into Ozhan's forehead with such force that the top of his head exploded, sending blood and shards of bone spraying through the air. He pitched backwards, falling face upwards onto the floor where he lay with his neck twisted to one side. He vomited and died there and then in a pool of his own blood.

The four of them gazed upon the corpse which moments earlier had been a terrible threat, but there were no cheers or congratulations, just relief. Thomas said nothing, his wounded body rigid, but Dardo placed a hand on Dody's shoulder. "It's over, the baron's dead," he said.

Tears streamed down the boy's face.

Nelan pulled a scarf from her belt and gave it to him. "Wipe your face, boy," she said, giving a weak and weary smile. "It is over now!"

He wiped away the tears. "I miss my father."

"We all miss your father," said Thomas. "He was a good man."

"He was generous and gentle too," added Nelan.

"And funny," said Dardo brushing his hand through the boy's hair.

Thomas reached out and held the boy, and in that instant, Dody heard his father's voice echoing in the halls of his mind. "I love you Dody, my boy! You will be handsome, tall and strong one day, just like Thomas, and I will be even prouder than I am now."

CHAPTER ELEVEN

THE warrior returns

<u>FOUR LONG YEARS PASS.</u>

Thomas Flynn cut a heroic figure dressed in his black and gold tunic and matching leggings. He rode his white stallion along the dusty road back towards Nottingham with his good friend Dody, a young man of sixteen years now. Pausing they squinted up at the cloudless sky and their sable cloaks fluttered in the light summer breeze blowing southward. Dody's tunic, leggings and boots matched Thomas' attire, right down to the twin short-swords strapped to his waist. He was a perfect replica of the swordsman, even to the finest detail of his long, dark braided hair. His grey-green eyes glittered in the same fashion too.

Thomas had moulded him, shaping his persona and skills for four years, ever since his father's death. He was big now, strong and ready to take up the warriors' mantle, wielding a sword and bow, but to Thomas' dismay, his favourite weapon was still his slingshot because he could knock out the eye of a toad at fifty paces. Both men feared no living thing.

Now they rode past the milestone lodged in the earth by the roadside, heeding the letters graven in the stone: *Nottingham – 25 miles*. Thomas spat over the milestone as three young boys playing in a field waved as they passed. He smiled, waved and bid his friend to do the same. Dody waved, squinting as the high warm sun shone upon them. "Do you think you're the greatest and bravest swordsman who has ever lived?" asked Dody.

Thomas had a smile on his face. "If I said yes it would make me seem rather conceited, wouldn't it?" he replied in his husky tone, studying the wonderment in the young man's eyes.

Dody stared in admiration and looked at Thomas as if he was a priceless treasure. "I suppose."

"Listen, you've been my son since Ozhan made you an orphan and I love you like a son, but have you not learned anything over the years? We are men of peace, and peaceful men find strength when needed. I can, and do when required to, but doubt whether that qualifies me as the greatest and bravest warrior who has ever lived."

Dody smiled. "You're a wise man, I know that, and that's why I've found my true vocation. I vow to help the sick, care for the injured and give aid to the wretched and impoverished wherever we travel, I so swear it!"

Thomas nodded to Dody with a stern stare. "And that's why we're honoured and respected wherever we go. Keep those standards and people will treat you with kindness and courtesy."

The young man was humbled and enlightened.

They rode past the old Abbey where Brothers Alf and Mathias busied themselves weeding the graveyard and noticed fat Friar Hugo busying himself rebuilding the stone walls. He cut a comical figure wobbling his way from one part of the wall to another breathing hard, his large sandals flip-flopping beneath the baggy folds of his habit. Sweat beaded on his forehead and ran into his eyes, stinging them.

They rode past a farmyard full of hay wagons until they came to a river where a man was playing and fighting with a fully grown grayling. They watched him wade into the shallows to secure his catch, dragging it up the bankside gasping for air. Then they rode for the next hour, always angling their journey down the long road until the great city walls came into view.

Thomas scanned the horizon towards the Dog and Duck. "Hmm, nice to be home again. Not much longer now and we'll be resting and eating a meat pie and vegetables smothered in rich gravy."

Dody sighed. "Good, I'm so hungry and was thinking of eating my boots!"

Thomas scratched his chin whiskers. He clapped his friend on the back, "Wonder if Dardo will be at the inn? I've missed him!"

Dody was glad to be back in Nottingham. His young head was in a whirl. While Thomas wondered if anyone would have kept the cellar stocked up as it had been his responsibility before they left Nottingham. His thoughts turned to Lira, his wife, and he couldn't wait to see her and his four-year-old child.

A chorus of ooh's and ah's from a gathering crowd greeted their arrival as they entered the city gates under Methuselah's ever watchful gaze. The old man had been the gatekeeper for what seemed an eternity. Aptly named he was. Now all eyes were on the two swordsmen as their white stallions cantered side-by-side along the roadway with both men sitting bolt upright, looking rather regal. Thomas waved his welcome to the onlookers and Dody doffed his cap and feather, smiling like a Cheshire cat.

Thomas grinned too. "I always feel like a celebrity whenever I come home."

Dody nodded, waving his arms like a windmill to the people until they ached, and then the thunder of hooves roused them both. The loud noise seemed to fill the air around them as it increased in volume and the ground trembled and rumbled. Thomas' sixth sense warned him to get off the road, so both men heeled their horses through a gap in a hawthorn hedge and waited.

Dody gasped with shock moments later as a giant horse galloped past, its mane streaming out, eyes rolling in panic, and then another horse shot past and another. There must have been twenty, and the riders were huge men, bigger than most with tattooed arms waving a variety of weapons - pikes, knives, longbows and spears.

The leader was the fiercest, most evil-looking man Dody had ever seen. He was wielding an axe and carrying a decapitated head. "Did you see that?" Dody gasped.

Thomas nodded. "I did but I'm not sure I believe what I saw. The leader looked like a demon!"

Both men wheeled their horses around, heeling them back through the gap in the hedge. Stunned by what they had seen, Thomas and Dody headed for Tobin's farm hoping to find out what had been going on while they were away, and there was no one better to ask than Lira's father. He was the local blacksmith and Recorder of the Nottingham Archives and would know all the gossip.

    The sun was clearing the eastern hills, bathing the forest in golden light as they angled their journey towards the Old Nottingham Road. Once there, they cut across several homesteads using well-known shortcuts to get to Tobin's estate, and as they rode through stands of birch and alder, passing under a spreading oak Thomas' mood lightened. He loved trees. They seemed timeless, unlike humans, and as a child he had spent many an hour climbing them, swinging from the branches like a monkey, way above the ground.

    As the warmth of the sun dispelled the creeping waist-high mist gathering around the trees, Thomas and Dody looked ghostly and their horses seemed to float through the mist like swans on a lake. So, after their fast, racy ride, they arrived at Tobin's homestead and their horses came to a halt, giving a long pealing whinny. Both men slipped from their saddles, tying their mounts to a hitching post, and Tobin's red setter barked announcing their arrival. He came out to greet them, followed by the dog. It looked around sharply, growling at them with its ears flattened against its head.

Tobin ambled over and shook their hands. "Shh, they're friends, you remember them don't you?"

Thomas winced. "That's one hell of a grip you've got there, blacksmith! I think you're stronger than the last time we met, and it's so good to see you again. You look well."

Dody nodded his acknowledgment and smiled, stroking the dog as it leaned into him. Tobin bid them enter and they followed him into the farmhouse with the dog growling at Thomas, but wagging its tail at Dody.

"That damn dog of yours has never liked me," said Thomas.

Dody grinned, "The dog has taste and is a good judge of character. He likes me."

Thomas laughed. "That doesn't mean the dog has good taste. It means the dog follows a follower, rather than a leader, and I am a leader!"

Inside the farmhouse, both men fixed their eyes on Tobin. He was still a tall, powerful proud man with a clean-shaven face, but his dark curly hair was now greying, giving away his age.

Thomas stared at Tobin's hands. They trembled. "Why are you shaking and why is the dog skittish? What's happened while we've been away?"

A look of abject terror and despair succeeded Tobin's expression of friendliness. The blacksmith's blood froze. "More gutter-scum have arrived in Nottingham and they've been threatening homesteaders and farmers. They threatened me too."

Thomas felt the irritation rise within him and anger flared. "What did they threaten to do?"

"They threatened to break our bones with axes and hammers if we didn't give them what they wanted."

Dody winced. "And what is it they want?"

Tobin sighed. "Our farms and our life's savings."

"Did you give them anything?" asked Thomas.

Tobin nodded. "I had no choice, believe me; they would kill me for a lot less."

Thomas fixed the blacksmith's gaze. "They would. I think they passed us on the Nottingham road, twenty big men, meaner and moodier looking than most and their leader looked more like a devil than a man."

"That sounds like them," said Tobin wiping sweat from his face as he marched into the kitchen. "I'll make a cup of nettle tea for us all."

"Have you any rosehip-tea instead?" asked Dody. "That's my favourite."

"Aye," replied Tobin, "and it's made to Lira's own recipe."

Within moments the water was boiling. Tobin wrapped a cloth around his hand, lifted the kettle from its bracket and went over to the table, filling three cups with water, adding a muslin bag to each. A sweet aroma filled the room. He stirred the contents of each cup, hooking out the bags, passing one cup to each of his guests.

Thomas sipped the brew and smiled. "Thanks, it's much appreciated."

Dody nodded, smiling his appreciation too.

Tobin groaned, hanging his head in despair. "It doesn't matter how much time passes, death or slavery is all we wretched humans can look forward to in life."

The leader's blunt, scarred face floated before Thomas' eyes nagging and tugging at his thoughts. *Was the man the baron's relation, his son perhaps? There was a distinct resemblance.* "The man I saw, the leader of the group, bore an uncanny resemblance to Ozhan, and for a single moment, I thought it was him. I'd have sworn it was, even the man's eyes shone in the same fashion."

"Don't worry Tobin, we got rid of Ozhan and can do it again, even if he is back in the form of a ghost," said Dody.

***

Ten miles to the north, high on a treacherous hillside, all the fires of *Hell* were being unleashed; raining down upon the small settlement of Tor's Deep, inducing an overwhelming choking fear. Men, women and children were screaming, moaning and praying to God. It made little difference. No one could stop the huge fireballs from rolling down from the hillside and setting fire to their village. The land and buildings burned and screaming warriors hacked and slashed the villagers to pieces.

At the end of this dreadful event, a burst of unearthly haunting laughter resounded throughout the hillside as more warriors arrived to wipe out the rest of the settlement. Now nothing remained, not even hope. The raiders had stripped the land to the bare earth, and no one survived the horrifying onslaught.

High on the hillside overlooking the settlement was a beautiful raven-haired woman and a warrior watching the destruction and carnage and they laughed. Their swords glinted in the sunlight. "What do you think about, Ozhobar, when you're in a killing mood?" asked the young woman, her brown eyes holding to his insane stare.

He laughed again. "I'm always in a killing mood because I see visions of the devil and get jealous wishing for the power he possesses. What about you, Kira?"

She shivered. "I'm a courtesan. A whore for the nobility and love and admire wealthy, powerful men, but you're one of a kind Ozhobar. So, pleasuring you always is my only concern!"

***

Later that evening Thomas opened the bar at the Dog and Duck. Golden lantern light glowed at the windows and there were log fires burning at either end of the long, oak beamed room. Rowdy revellers crammed into the bar, and as always, Thomas eased his way through the mixture of noblemen, privateers and farmers, chatting and making conversation. Then he sat at his favourite table, his back to the wall and ordered meat pie from a beautiful blonde serving wench.

When his meal arrived a musician appeared playing light and lilting dance music, and with fine wine flowing and good food served hot and steaming everyone was behaving and having a good time. The inn was different now Ozhan and his band of cutthroats, thugs and thieves had disappeared from the clientele.

Thomas was eating his meal when Dody came through the dining-room door with a big smile on his face. Dardo was following him. "Look who I've found!" he announced looking pleased with himself. Both men ambled over and sat down beside Thomas.

Dardo was already drunk. He stared at Thomas and placed his hand on his shoulder. "My… my friend, it's so good to see you and Dody here. Please don't leave me again, I don't like it," he slurred with a stammer.

Thomas laughed, turning his head. He stared hard into his friend's shining green eyes. "I won't leave you again, because you drink all the profits while I'm away."

Dardo stripped off his shirt, showing his rippling muscles. He threw it across the room at a friendly looking whore. She smiled, beckoning for him to join her. He hiccupped. "You must excuse me, my friends, I've business with yonder wench and she awaits my coming."

Thomas watched him weave his way through the crowd clumsily towards the girl. "Nothings changed here then?"

Dardo collapsed onto the woman's lap and she stroked his curly blond hair. "My hair is strong and wild like me," he said, kissing the girl full on the lips.

Thomas smiled, shaking his head. "No, nothing ever changes."

Dody laughed. "You wouldn't want him to change, would you?"

Thomas shook his head. "No, he's big, broad and clumsy, but I wouldn't want him any other way."

Just then the door of the tavern burst open and four men entered, including one a full head taller than anyone else. He was a huge man with dark, curly hair, a chin beard and it was obvious he was the leader. Thomas stared hard at the men. Dressed in the forester's garb of fringed buckskin they looked like they would cut their own mother's throat without a second thought. The big man scanned the room, spotting Thomas, and he pushed his way through the crowd with his men following him. He stared mad-eyed at the warrior. Stopping in front of Thomas he folded his arms across his barrel chest.

"You *are* Thomas Flynn, aren't you?" said the man.

A hush fell over the room as Thomas' eyes roamed from face to face then back to the big man. "Yes, yes, I am. Have we met before, sir?"

The man drew his sword. "We've not met before, because if we had, you would be dead!"

Thomas chuckled. "What's our quarrel?"

The man slammed Thomas' table aside, knocking him to the ground. "I want you *dead!*"

Dody and Dardo were on their feet, rounding on the other men.

Thomas' anger flared. He pushed the table aside and rolled to his knees, hauling himself upright. His swords flashed into his hands. "My friend, you will wish this day had never happened because if you want a fight, I'll give you one! How many pieces do you want carrying to your grave in, sir?"

The man backed off, slamming more tables aside, giving himself room to move and the tavern's clientele edged away from both men to a safer distance, giving them more room.

"I'd like to know the name of the man I'm about to kill," said Thomas.

"Stard!" snapped the man, launching a sudden attack, sword raised high.

Thomas leapt back and then launched himself forward, catching the man by surprise, and his right-hand sword hilt lashed down onto his adversary's head, stunning him. Stard staggered back, vision blurring, but he aimed a wild cut at Thomas' head. The blade slashed high as Thomas dropped to one knee and then rose again, his left-hand blade snaking out, pricking the shoulder, tearing the man's skin. Stard fell back with a gasp.

Thomas grinned. "You're good, lucky too, but I'm better!"

Stard launched another sudden attack, aiming for the belly, hoping to catch Thomas off guard.

Thomas blocked it and one of his blades slashed down onto the man's hand, chopping it away, his sword falling clear. "You overestimate your talent."

Stard screamed, charging forward, plucking a dagger from his belt. "You whoreson bastard!" Then a terrible pain exploded in his body as he stared down at Thomas' blade embedded in his chest. Stard dropped the knife, his knees buckled, and an agonised groan burst from his lips as a searing pain filled his whole body.

Thomas drove the blade deeper, holding the man upright, staring into his disbelieving eyes. "I've changed my mind; you are neither skilled nor lucky today." He pushed the man back with his booted foot and dragged his blade clear. The body toppled to the ground. He stared at the other three men. "I found no joy in killing your friend, so take his body with you and leave before I kill you all!"

One man backed away, fear shining in his eyes. "I don't want to die today."

"Then leave before I change my mind," Thomas told him.

Together the three men lifted their dead comrade over the shoulder of one and they pushed their way through the crowd and left the way they came. Thomas walked to a window and watched them heave the body over the saddle of a black stallion. Then they mounted their horses and rode away. He swung around to his friends. "I'm glad you did as I asked and left well alone because if you two had helped, the others would have joined in and it could have been a bloodbath with innocent people getting hurt."

"Never thought for one moment you couldn't handle the four of them!" said Dardo.

Dody nodded. "Me neither."

They rearranged the tables and chairs back to how they were before the fight and the music began again, changing from light and lilting to the powerful rippling chords of dance. The crowd reformed and the buzz of conversation was in the air again as the smell of cooking filtered into the bar, rich and heady, and normal service resumed with serving wenches leading customers from the bar into the dining room for their prepared meal. Thomas looked around him, scanning the customers' faces and it was as if nothing had happened. A sign of the violent times. A man's life didn't count for much and if you lived beyond twenty-five years, you were lucky. He was lucky, but then he was skilled in the art of killing men.

A slim young man with dark, close-cropped hair approached Thomas. Around his waist was a sword-belt from which hung two short-swords like his own. Thomas also noticed the hilt of a throwing knife in the top of the man's knee-length boot. The newcomer smiled. "It was impressive the way you dispatched

Thomas shrugged. "I'm always interested in a wager."

The newcomer stepped in closer, whispering in Thomas' ear.

Thomas smiled. "You don't say. Really? When and where would such an event take place?"

The man leaned in closer, whispering again. Thomas' face lit up like a candle. "So, how much is such a wager going to cost me?"

The young man held up five fingers of one hand, making a zero with the forefinger and thumb of his other hand. "Fifty silver pieces."

Thomas smiled again imagining the winning of a wager at ten-to-one-odds. "We can start any time you like, but tell no one else about this matter. What's your name, friend?"

"My name's Hobar and I'm at your service."

***

Striding through Nottingham later that day, Thomas stopped at a tavern for a meal and then he walked the two miles to his destination where he met Hobar and another man who was thin-faced and stick-like, almost spidery with a hunchback. His clothes were only rags. Thomas nodded his welcome. "Right, well, I'm all ears, friends. We can make a lot of money between us if you can set up that piece of action you mentioned earlier. Can you?"

"I can set it up today. But what's in it for me?" asked the hunchback.

"I'm in it for you and I'm the one risking my life. We've all been down the long hard road and I for one would like it a little easier." said Thomas.

"Have you fought in the dungeons before Thomas?" asked Hobar.

Thomas looked uneasy. "No, but I'll take my chances."

The hunchback ran his fingers along Thomas' scarred arms. "You look a little past your prime and I already have a fighter willing to risk the dungeons."

Thomas nodded. "Hobar spoke of your fighter. I've come across him before and he laid down for me when I threatened to cut off his ugly head."

"Friend, every town has a tavern, and every tavern has a bar with someone in it who thinks he's as tough as an iron nail, but they all come to Hobar or me when they need the stake money for a fight. But if my fighter is a loser, I end up a loser, understand?" said the hunchback.

Thomas' eyes sparkled with anticipation. "I don't want your money. I have fifty silver pieces. You bet it all on me and if I lose, you lose nothing. But if I win we all win!"

The hunchback wiped the sweat from his brow looking worried. "I hope this works. Otherwise, we're all going to be dead if you lose. And my life's a wager I'm not willing to pay!"

CHAPTER TWELVE

Tough as an iron nail

"Well, well, my old friend the hunchback with another potential winner!" sneered the Ringmaster. "Who is it this time? Your wife? We've had your brother, mother and everyone else!"

The gathering crowd laughed and jeered at the three men.

Hobar laughed with a sneer looking confident. "We'll wipe the smiles off your faces this time!"

Thomas stepped forward, taking off his old, black leather tunic, revealing his amazing physique with the many deep scars. The crowd stilled. Dressed only in black hose and leather boots, Thomas' dark eyes scanned the full length of the dungeons. Around the walls flaming torches lit the great catacombs and skeletons in chains hung everywhere. The dungeons were now obsolete, but the stench of death lingered in the still air.

An iron door at the far end of the main chamber flung open with a loud crash and a silver-haired warrior answering to the name of Eldar entered wearing black leggings and boots, nothing more. He ambled over to the hunchback laughing, pointing a finger at Thomas, "Your warrior is a little old for fighting, isn't he?"

"Their man is a mighty warrior and fierce," whispered Hobar, looking at Thomas.

Four men covered the entrance to the dungeons, making sure that no one else came in and no one got out without paying their wager. Spectators barked their bets back and forth as both swordsmen circled each other. It was now midnight and pitch-black outside, "You sure you want to do this, old man?" snapped Eldar.

Thomas nodded. "The Lord makes me fast and skilled always," he whispered crossing his heart. He stared at his sweaty hands. "Yes, I do. See how my hands tremble with anticipation. My blood is up and you are about to die today."

The crowd fell silent, hypnotised by Eldar's clumsy movements, and he was so big that he seemed to struggle to stay upright. The Ringmaster, dressed in black velvet robes explained that there were no rules to the fight. Both men could use a weapon if they wanted, be it a sword or knife, or they could use their fists, feet, bite; stamp or knee the other anywhere, and their only aim was to survive and defeat the other. The contest would only end when one of them was dead. Hobar and the hunchback were backing Thomas all the way with every silver penny they had and hoped and prayed that he'd become the Ultimate Fighter.

Both warriors turned to the crowd, bowing to their peers, and in that single moment, both men's humour vanished. Thomas drew his swords. Eldar drew his serrated broadsword, and both looked at each other with rabid stares that would kill an elephant.

Thomas attacked first, but the big man blocked the blow, sending a two-handed sweep that almost hammered home against his head. Thomas attacked again, ramming his own blade towards Eldar's belly who then ducked under a second slashing cut.

Eldar laughed. "I'm the strongest!"

Thomas nodded, his left-hand blade licking out, catching the lobe of the other's ear.

Eldar groaned, straightening up, cupping his hand over the wound and warm red blood trickled through his fingers.

"But I'm the *fastest!*" said Thomas.

Elgar groaned.

Thomas fixed his foe's insane gaze. "Oh, come on, it's a tiny cut. It doesn't need stitches."

"You bastard!" snapped Eldar, fear replacing anger.

Thomas stepped back; then leapt high, his booted foot cannoning against Eldar's face, catapulting him back into the crowd where he fell and impaled his head on an iron spike protruding from the dungeon floor. He didn't rise. Thomas hawked and spat on Eldar's boot as a sign of disrespect. Then someone drew back the iron bolts on the entrance door and it groaned inward as the hunchback stepped into the fighting arena, raising Thomas' arm. "The winner in quick time!" he announced, looking more than pleased. Hobar joined him, lifting Thomas' other arm as the Ringmaster stepped from the shadows, placing his thick fingers into the pocket of his coat, drawing out an ancient gold chain, priceless and handsomely crafted. He draped it around Thomas' neck.

Thomas looked confused. "What's this? What are you doing?"

The Ringmaster approached Thomas looking shocked by the speed at which he had dispatched his opponent. "Eldar died with honour, but this chain is yours now. You've saved him from his own madness and despair. Hell's teeth, you're the winner and the man all others must defeat now. Survive ten contests and we'll crown you the Ultimate Warrior and give you all the gold you can carry!"

The words stunned Thomas. He didn't know whether to laugh or cry when the Ringmaster handed him a purse of gold and silver coins to do with as he wanted. "What does the chain mean?" he asked.

The hunchback smiled. "It means you're on your way to becoming the greatest fighter who has ever lived."

***

Two days later as the sun's rays flung wide the gates of dawn, Thomas, Dardo and Dody were high on a hillside overlooking Nottingham, and they had removed their silk shirts to allow the sun's summer warmth to their skin.

Dardo slid off a dry stone wall to sit beside the warrior. "What are you thinking, Thomas?"

Thomas smiled and pointed. "I want to climb that tree and have fun."

Dody laughed. "Wow, that's strange, I was thinking the same thing!"

Dardo shook his head. "You two never cease to amaze…" he said, but before he finished the sentence, both men were on their feet running. And with breath-taking speed and skill, they raced to the oak and up its trunk where they swung out onto a thick branch, ran across it and sat smiling at each other.

Breathless, Dody smiled. "I win."

Thomas laughed. "Like hell you do. I win!"

Dardo rolled to his knees, hauling himself upright, and he strode over to the spreading oak. He cupped his hands around his mouth. "Hello, are you coming back down now?"

There was no reply.

Dardo shook his head in dismay. "Is anyone going to answer me?" he asked, unable to see either man. The next moment, Thomas and Dody lifted him from the ground with breath-taking speed, up into the branches with his legs flailing, and they bounced him from branch to branch until he came to rest on the highest one. He shook his head trying to catch his breath. Parting the branches, both men smiled at him and laughed. But before they decided what else to do a noise nearby caused them all to freeze.

The friends ducked down amongst the branches and crept toward the sounds. Then with great skill, they bounced from tree to tree like squirrels, using the branches as springboards, until, high in another spreading oak,

Thomas parted the leaves again and stared down at a sleeping man, but before Thomas could decide what to do, a stranger appeared on the scene. The friends remained motionless, watching the newcomer who seemed in a cheerful mood. He hummed and prodded the sleeping man with his booted-foot.

"Chaney, wake up, man! It's me, Ozhobar! You remember me don't you?"

Chaney's eyes opened, and he groaned.

Ozhobar cocked a mocking, sympathetic ear. "What, you don't remember me? Well, let me remind you who I am and what I want, my old friend," he said, placing his foot on Chaney's throat.

Chaney struggled, fighting for breath, helpless to stop his tormentor, while Ozhobar took great pleasure in hurting him by leaning his full weight upon his throat. "I'm the new baron and I want my money! Where is it?"

There was no reply so Ozhobar leaned harder and Chaney sucked fiercely for breath.

Thomas and friends couldn't stand to watch Chaney suffer any longer. They swung down from the tree like three monkeys, landing in the grassy clearing. It surprised Ozhobar. Chaney made a final gurgling whimper and lay still.

Thomas fixed Ozhobar's odd gaze. "I'm here, there and everywhere like an old, bad penny! So, take your big clumsy booted foot off the man's throat before I show you my blades!"

Ozhobar stared at Thomas, grinding his teeth. "Stay out of this, whoever you are. You're on my land and have no business here!"

Thomas let go of the long, whippy branch he was clinging to, and it sprang forward, crashing into Ozhobar's head, poleaxing him.

Dardo smiled. "Didn't think you could hold on to that branch any longer."

Dody ran back to where they had tethered their horses, returning moments later with a rope.

Thomas bound Ozhobar, hand and foot, to the tree, waiting for Chaney to regain consciousness, and then they pressed on home leaving their senseless enemy bound and gagged. And as they walked their horses it rained, but within minutes the hot summer sun shone upon them again and clouds of mist arose from the woodland floor, mingling with the golden shafts of light filtering through the trees.

They walked on, listening to the birds singing, bees humming and watched frogs jumping, and each flower and blade of grass sparkled with raindrops.

Now Thomas' mood lightened, and he hummed a tune, cheering them onward towards the Dog and Duck. "I think you better come home with us, Chaney, and you can tell us what happened back there in the woods."

Too weak to talk, Chaney nodded.

Ahead of them lay a vast pasture of meadow on common land that had once belonged to the old Abbey, and even though here, no tree, path or landmark looked familiar, Thomas knew where he was.

The brilliant summer morning hummed to the bustle of diligent farmers and homesteaders working the fields, milking their cows and tending the orchards, while Thomas licked his lips dreaming of nut-brown ale, strong wine and aged mulberry brandy. These were his bestselling products at their inn. No wonder Dardo drinks the profits, he thought.

***

Much later that evening at the inn, Chaney groaned, hanging his head in despair. "What am I to do? Ozhobar will kill me for sure the next time we meet."

Dody shook his head. "That depends on the company you keep, and right now you're in the best company."

Thomas and Dardo nodded, seating themselves for an early supper of honey-cornbread, cheese and goat's milk. The other two men joined them and they ate and talked of the day's events about the baron. Ozhobar had let Chaney hunt on his land for the princely sum of five hundred silver coins per year but he never paid it and Ozhobar wanted what was his and would kill for it.

After supper they leaned back on their chairs, listening to the light rippling notes of the flute and then the harpist appeared from a back room and played too.

Thomas yawned, stretched and relaxed. He stroked the huge wolfhound that fidgeted and scratched for fleas beside his booted foot. It's been a funny old day, he thought.

Chaney shivered, itching and scratching. "That dog makes my skin crawl."

Thomas pretended not to hear because the dog had been his good friend Cyrano's faithful mutt.

***

When Thomas awoke the next morning it was a beautiful summer's day again. Where's Lira? he wondered, rolling to his feet from the pallet bed, the other side empty. He strode over to the window, overlooking the courtyard, and could see her hanging out the washing by the picket fence that framed a square of their garden at the centre of which two squirrels played. He stood looking at her. She looked like a princess in her white cotton and lace dress. "God blessed me when our paths crossed," he said to himself.

Somewhere outside a cock crowed, shrill and hollow like a trumpet, disturbing his thoughts. Lira turned around knowing he was watching her. She smiled, waved and blew a kiss, her eyes twinkling. He pretended to catch the kiss and put it to his lips. There was a gleam in his eyes. I was so lucky to meet and marry such a beautiful woman, he thought. She is a delight!

The sun shone through the bedroom windows, making pools of bright gold on the bare floorboards. Bees hummed and droned in the herb garden and flowerbeds outside and the steady click of the old windmill sounded sleepy.

Thomas turned away from the window and dressed, fussing with his clothes, pulling on his leggings and tunic, straightening and smoothing them with hard hands. Then he braided his long hair and felt an excitement that made him stop and go back to the window to behold the one he loved so dear. He stood watching Lira's graceful movements as she hung out the washing and then proceeded up the path towards the back door of the inn, smiling and waving. They had run the old place after Cyrano's murder, to keep his memory alive, and people were safer now in Thomas' steely presence. The community owed him so much.

Lira swept their little girl indoors and her soft voice receded, leaving only the sound of squeaking toys and the jingle bells. Thomas finished dressing and went downstairs. Homemade toys, rattles and straw dolls cluttered the floors, and he strode over them, picking up an old, worn, stuffed dog, placing it on top of a pile of toys in a space under the stairs.

She watched and smiled. "That's my favourite; I treasured it when I was a child and still do to this day."

Thomas smiled back at her, "Olivia's favourite too!"

Walking over to the child he stood a moment, his brown eyes holding to the child's innocent gaze and the words that followed were always the same. "I will love and keep you for all the days of my life and will sacrifice anything for you both, so help me God," he whispered to the child, crossing his heart. Now the tempest that raged within him as a warrior and swordsman had simmered down, so he was a good father without hatred or prejudice, unlike his own parents. He wanted to duplicate Lira's gentle style if he could but a long history of violence isn't easy to overcome.

Thomas dressed the four-year-old girl in a yellow dress and black leggings.

She smiled. "I will always love you too, daddy and mummy."

He leaned over her, kissing her forehead. "I am blessed," he said, and then a loud rap on the back door startled them, making them all jump.

Lira looked surprised. "It's a little early for callers."

He strode to the door, swinging it open. His eyes widened. It was Hobar and the hunchback. "May we speak to you in private?" whispered the latter.

Thomas gathered his thoughts. He coughed. "Umm, it's a little early in the morning for peddlers to be calling at my door," he said, stepping outside into the courtyard. Lira craned her neck, trying to catch the conversation, but he slammed the door shut behind him.

Furious and grinding his teeth, Thomas snapped. "Hell's teeth, what are you two doing here? I told you not to let anyone know of our acquaintance!"

"We had to come. We've arranged a duel for tomorrow night and we had to tell you," said Hobar.

Thomas calmed. "Who do I fight?"

The hunchback put a hand on Thomas' shoulder, "A man named Farris."

"Ever see him fight?" asked Thomas.

Hobar shook his head. "No, but they didn't bring him all the way from London to lose, and they say he sliced and diced the last swordsman, humiliating him, toying with him, cutting him several times before he gave the death stroke. Then he took the warrior's ears and nose as trophies."

Thomas was silent for a moment, looking steely eyed, "Then the man has a great big hole in his armour.

"How so?" asked the hunchback.

"When I fight, it's for a quick, clean kill. Farris' weakness is his vanity. He has to make himself look good."

The hunchback groaned. "Oh, I hope you're right."

Thomas nodded. "I am right, without a doubt, and know my craft. I'm the best swordsman and people will remember me for my skill, so what time does the match take place?"

"Midnight," whispered Hobar.

"How much is the purse worth?" asked Thomas.

The hunchback rubbed his hands together, a greedy twinkle in his eyes. "Five hundred silver coins, with an extra one hundred if you kill Farris within the first ten strokes."

Thomas looked into the hunchback's glittering eyes. "Okay, I'll see you both tomorrow, before midnight, now be off with you and next time find a different way of contacting me. Do *not* come back here."

For a heartbeat, the hunchback and Hobar stood stock-still and then they spun around and disappeared from the courtyard. Thomas relaxed, turned around and opened the back door, stepping inside again.

Lira tapped her foot looking impatient. "Who were those men?"

"Just peddlers trying to sell their wares," said Thomas dismissing the question.

Lira looked surprised. "Strange!"

Thomas coughed. "Umm, yes." He disappeared back upstairs to avoid her pursuing the issue.

Later that day, Thomas walked through stands of oak, alder and birch alone and his mood lightened because trees were his favourite things. The ground beneath his feet was muddy from the recent heavy rain and his booted feet squelched as he trod the wide pathway, scaring the birds from the branches above him. But, as he walked his thoughts turned to the coming fight, and he felt alone and friendless because he daren't tell anyone what he was doing. The Dog and Duck had lost money at an extraordinary rate and the only way of saving their livelihood, and their home was to fight for money, something he would never have considered a year ago. And even though he was a mercenary and a killer of men, he still considered himself honourable, even though his recent exploits seemed less so. But now his choices were few.

Thomas walked on past the old Abbey, waving to the friars working the fields and it made him feel even guiltier. Brothers Alf and Mathias were weeding the graveyard as usual, and the enormously fat Friar Hugo was busy rebuilding the dry stone walls, wobbling his way from one section of the wall to the next, breathing hard with his large sandals flip-flopping beneath the folds of his habit. What a simple life, Thomas thought.

Then his thoughts turned to his mentor, the late Master Gallus, and regret and sadness tinged them. During training sessions, he had told Thomas to use his great skill for truth and justice, and he was now no better than a common street fighter even though the means seemed to justify the end. Would Gallus have understood my predicament? he wondered. Maybe not! He could hear his exact words ringing through the halls of his mind. What is wrong Thomas? What do you think you're doing? You're no better than an assassin is now! He could even picture Gallus' angry red face with those hard-set, expressionless, grey eyes and he was ashamed for the first time in his life.

***

One day later, at midnight, Farris whirled upon the baying crowd, leaping into the air snarling with his sword drawn. Everybody scattered in panic. The Ringmaster stopped the proceedings with a loud angry bark. "Here now, enough of that. You're here to fight the swordsman, Thomas Flynn, not scare the crowd to death. Go back to your corner."

With reluctance, Faris did as instructed.

It was cold in the dungeons and Thomas felt a chill creeping into his bones as a heavy iron gate inched open and more spectators passed through a bristling forest of men and women, emerging from a tunnel with walls of immense thickness. The noisy crowd of thugs, thieves and murderers were all now baying for blood, calling out Farris' name. Thomas climbed a broad flight of steps, moved across a great square and stood at its centre. Faris followed him, grunting and snarling.

Thomas fixed Faris' bloodthirsty stare. "So glad you could come, and I don't mean to be insensitive but, who's got the purse money?"

The Ringmaster stepped into the square. "I have the purse and you'll see it when one of you is dead!"

"Well, I'd like to see it before my man kills your man," said the hunchback.

The Ringmaster laughed. "Your man won't kill my man; just remember Faris is undefeated in eight contests. Come, have a drink and watch my man work, he's good!"

"You won't have time for a drink," said the hunchback, "good he may be but our man is better!"

It was past midnight and Thomas was already impatient. His face was grim, and he gave a cursory bow to his opponent. Eyes unblinking he strode towards the huge barrel-chested man with sandy hair and a chin beard like an old brush and he moved with great energy. Drawing his swords both blades flashed towards Faris' belly.

Farris backed away, parrying the blows, holding his blade two-handed, elbows protecting his sides. He ran forward, sending a wicked sweeping cut that Thomas parried, but such was the power of the blow he spun to the floor. Thomas gasped for air and rolled to his knees, switching his grip on one sword, holding it dagger-like and he waited then surged upright as Faris danced towards him. He slammed the blade into the big man's ribs under the armpit, through muscle and bone, and a hideous croaking scream ripped from his lips. Faris stumbled, falling to his knees. Thomas plunged the other blade into his belly, levering it up, and up again until the blade hit the man's breastbone and lodged there. Blood sprayed from the wound, drenching Thomas. Dragging both swords clear he delivered a final sweeping cut to the neck that removed Faris' head from his shoulders, and the blow was so swift it echoed with a hissing sound throughout the whole dungeon.

Thomas stood for a moment, but no cheers chorused. "Just as I thought, big, old, fat and out of condition," he said, wiping his bloody face with the back of his hand. The hunchback stepped forward from the shadows, handing Thomas a towel and he cleaned himself.

The ringmaster handed over the promised purse of five hundred silver pieces. "You've entertained us today warrior, but could you make it last a little longer next time?"

Thomas sheathed both swords. "I don't think I can." He made his way towards the gatehouse door, an arm around the hunchback's twisted shoulders. Both men smiled as they left the dungeons, slamming the iron door behind them.

***

Not far away, Lira was furious. Thomas had disappeared again, leaving her alone with their child. She paced the bedroom floor, estimating the time at well past midnight. Where is he?

Thomas had disappeared from the inn with the last two customers, a spidery-looking hunchback and a tall slender young man with close-cropped hair, and they looked like ruffians but she knew Thomas could handle anyone.

The bedroom door opened, and she felt the touch of a cool breeze as he entered. He looked dreadful. His face was thin and drawn; his cheeks covered in stubble, eyes dark-rimmed and weary.

There was a glint of madness in Lira's eyes. "Where have you been until this hour?"

Thomas looked like Lira had caught him red-handed in another woman's bedroom. His face coloured red, and he coughed, "Oh, um… er, well, you see I had a little business to attend to tonight."

Lira stared at Thomas. "Drinking business?"

A long sigh escaped from his throat and he nodded. Lira drew nearer, and Thomas backed away in a panic, knowing there was no smell of alcohol on his breath. "I'm sorry for coming home late, but you know how Dardo rambles on when he's drunk. Can't get a word in edgewise!"

Lira laughed and snapped, "Yes, I know what Dardo's like and what you're like too. I saw you leave the inn with that hunchback and another man. What are you up to Thomas?"

He shook his head, screwing up his face not knowing what to say and then he saw the future before his eyes. One day I will have to explain to her and my friends what I have been doing to earn enough money to keep the inn open. Lira, in particular, won't understand.
Thomas could hear Lira's words ringing through the halls of his mind. "You used to be an honourable man, the people's guardian, their hero, but you cannot justify what you've been doing behind my back and I cannot live with a man no better than a murderer!"

Thomas felt ashamed and decided never again to engage in the hunchback's activities, even if they were short of money. Shaking his head, he returned to the present, "My love I have not been up to anything."

Still tapping her foot Lira remained silent, watching Thomas, studying his face, and he convinced her he was telling the truth.

"Promise me," Lira said.

Thomas nodded. "I promise." He clasped her hand and within five minutes they were in bed fast asleep.

***

It was the morning after Lira's confrontation with Thomas and he was to visit the Abbot for his advice. Now he rode unarmed, up the long dusty road towards the Abbey, dressed in forest greens, and he noticed brothers Alf and Mathias still weeding the graveyard. As usual, Friar Hugo was also still rebuilding the dry stone walls higher and higher, wobbling his way from one section of the wall to the next, breathing hard and sweating. Nothing ever seems to change around here, Thomas thought as he waved. The friars waved back and then carried on doing their allotted chores.

On entering the Abbey gates Thomas stopped to make way for a party of friars bearing baskets of fruit and bread and he nodded to them, heeling his horse aside to allow them to pass. They smiled, nodding their thanks and went on their way to distribute the food amongst the needy. The Abbot appeared from a doorway to Thomas' left. He folded his arms into the wide sleeves of his habit, staring at the swordsman. "Can I be of service to you, my son?" he asked, pointing to two wooden chairs by the doorway.

Thomas climbed down from his horse and they sat staring at each other. "I'm in desperate need of your council Father Abbot."

The Abbot smiled. "Ah, how many times a day do I hear those same words?"

Thomas nodded. "I dare say you do, Father, but when I tell you my problem, I don't think you will have encountered it often, if at all."

"Then I shall sit here listening intently my son. You have my full attention."

"Father, I'm a warrior by nature and I have a history of violence. I was also a mercenary as you well know, until the birth of my first child; my beautiful Olivia, and although the last few years have been the best of my life, they are the hardest I've endured. Money is scarce, even though our inn is full most nights, and Lira yearns for a second child, but we seem incapable of making a happy event happen. And worst of all, I miss the action and adventure of my past life."

The ancient-looking Abbot unfolded his arms from his sleeves, placing a firm hand on Thomas' shoulder, holding to his gaze. "Money is always scarce. God's will is unknown to us all. And change is inevitable and not always easy to swallow my son. That's why life is so unpredictable! But the unpredictability makes it all worthwhile. At least, that's what I believe. If we each knew our destinies, living wouldn't be worthwhile."

"You make it sound so simple, Father Abbot, but life at the moment is anything but simple. Lira and I are surviving, not living," said Thomas, but deep inside of him he was screaming for help.

The Abbot smiled. "You make your life complicated, my son. A wise fish travels with the flow of water and swims downstream to spawn, not upstream. But you're a very complicated and special man, born no doubt under the stars and a quarter-horned moon, always ready to fulfil a warrior's destiny. And that's why you will always be able to shoulder the burden placed upon you, even when you think you cannot." The Abbot gazed into Thomas' eyes. He could somehow see and recognise the nightmare that was shadowing his days. "You will never live to be a ripe old age, but you will die trying to do what is best for all concerned. Besides, early death is not as bad as we imagine. You will not grow old and infirm like me. People will always remember you for the way you are now... young, handsome and strong."

"I suppose that's true, Father," said Thomas in a tight voice, "maybe there's a reason for everything and a solution to every problem. I am trying hard to do what's best for all concerned."

The Abbot smiled again. "Has our little talk helped?"

Thomas nodded. "I think so, Father," he said, unaware that his life would transform in the next few hours.

***

The time for dinner came and went as Thomas made his way back along the dusty Nottingham road towards the Dog and Duck, and he found great solace in the bright sunshine, but then without warning, the thunder of hooves startled him. It filled the air around him as it gathered momentum and the ground trembled with a rumbling noise. His sixth sense warned him to get off the road, but he gasped as a great black horse galloped past, towing a covered wagon that bounced from side to side with no driver. The cart side-swiped his stallion, and it reared up on hind legs unseating him, and he fell onto the hard ground hitting his head, knocking him unconscious.

Blood dripped and seeped into the ground from a small wound to his temple as he lay in the road.

CHAPTER THIRTEEN
The hunter

Thomas lay unconscious for a time. Then he stirred and felt something nuzzling his face. He opened his eyes. It was a horse. Then a man's voice sounded, and the horse backed away as a powerful hand gripped his arm, hauling him upright. Thomas touched the deep cut on his temple. "Ouch!"

In the sunlight, the hunter's hair seemed to glint like flecks of steel and his grey-green eyes shone like quicksilver. "You must have taken a hard fall, my friend," he said, holding the swordsman upright, but Thomas had no memory of the fall. He groaned, holding his head with trembling hands.

"Are you a stranger in these parts?" asked the tall, slender hunter, dressed in a forester's attire.

Thomas looked quizzically at the man, staring straight through him. "I am… am…" he stammered. "I don't know who I am."

"It must have been quite a fall to knock you that senseless! Come. You can stay in my cabin until your memory returns. It's well built, warm and dry and I've food enough for two."

Thomas nodded his acceptance, looking bewildered. "Is it far?"

"No, only about a mile. Do you have a horse?"

Thomas shrugged, his dark eyes scanning the road. "If I had, it's gone now."

The hunter nodded, leading his horse with one hand. He hooked his other arm around Thomas' back, holding him upright.

Leaving the Nottingham Road both men took to the Old Forest Road, heading towards the distant plains, striding under the overhanging branches, watching the sun drifting across the sky while listening to the ceaseless melody of river and birdsong filling the air.

Within a quarter of an hour, the hunter was striding through his vegetable patch with Thomas following him. He tied his bay gelding to a tethering post, unhooked a leather rucksack from over the pommel and unsaddled it. Both men entered his log cabin together. It was airy inside with dried animal hides and meat curing everywhere, and the smell was raw and stifling, but somehow comforting to Thomas.

Now the last rays of the sun radiated through the windows and doorway, bathing the walls in golden light, with shadows dancing on the low ceiling. Thomas walked to a window and took in the sunset, a glorious sight.

Thomas spun around to face the hunter.
"What's your name?"

"Mathis. I live here alone. My wife died two years ago."

Thomas shuffled from one foot to the other. "Sorry to hear that."

"Welcome to my cabin, friend. Do you remember your name yet?"

Thomas looked bewildered. "It's so strange; I can't remember anything before the moment we met."

"Well then, I shall call you Thomas after my father until your memory returns," said Mathis in an ironic twist.

Thomas smiled, not recognising his own name. "Was your father a hunter too?"

Mathis nodded. "The best. Take a seat and I'll feed you." He moved around his table, took up a wooden plate and cut beef and flatbread with his hunting knife. He cut himself the same, and both men sat eating in silence. When they had eaten their fill, Thomas took Mathis' plate from him, cleaned both in a bucket of water and wiped them dry with a cloth. He sat back down studying the hunter, a thin-faced man with an awkward smile and close-set pale eyes shining like quicksilver, and his fringed buckskin clothing was old, worn and had seen better days, but the hunter was old, worn and had seen better days.

"Do you remember anything at all?" asked Mathis.

Thomas yawned. "My memory is a blank canvas. It's as if I've just been born." He was enjoying the emotional solitude because there was no sense of panic or fear, just a peaceful feeling. His injury removed the weight of the world from his shoulders and for once in his life; he didn't have a care in the world. "Oh, well, it will come back in due course I imagine," said the hunter in a gentle reassuring voice, his eyes calm and bright. He'd no earlier experience on which to base such an assumption but didn't think it was a mistake to set his guest's mind at rest. Mathis did the same for his long-time companion, the only woman he had ever loved when she was dying. He had even tried to deny the fact, scolding himself for being a morbid old fool, right until the inevitable end, but consoled himself that he had made her short life better and her lingering death slightly easier. His eyes misted at the thought.

"What is it, Mathis, you look sad?"

The hunter wiped his eyes. "Old memories."

Both men retired for the night. Mathis showed Thomas to a room at the rear of the cabin. It was light and clean, and before getting into his pallet bed he stared out of the bedroom window. The night sky looked beautiful and clear and he found his eyes drawn to a group of stars twinkling brighter than the rest. They hypnotised him and he couldn't stop staring at them, but the distant shimmering lights made him feel ill at ease, lonely and sad as if he were missing something but didn't know what it was.

Not far away, Lira was looking through her bedroom window at the same group of twinkling stars, wondering what had happened to Thomas and why he hadn't come home.

***

The next morning, Thomas and Mathis were up at dawn, poaching rabbits. They were out at the back of the cabin and Mathis seemed tense, walking just ahead, picking his feet up high and putting them down on the moist ground. Spinning his head from side to side, he moved with his eyes sweeping the undergrowth, searching for his quarry while keeping an eye out for danger, "A man can get hung for doing this but we have to eat!"

Thomas' eyes darted from side to side and he imagined the landowner's gamekeeper behind every tree, but the place was stiff with rabbits. There must have been at least a hundred of them bobbing and bouncing around in the ferns and among the tree-stumps, and it was an amazing sight. A poacher's dream. And how close they were, most of them only twenty paces from where he stood.

It was dark inside the forest with little sunlight coming in, and both men had skirted the edge for two hundred yards until they approached a clearing where a large patch of the sky appeared ahead of them. Mathis told Thomas that the clearing was the perfect place for young rabbits to be in the woods in late June because the gamekeeper guarded them and now they were ripe for the picking.

Both men advanced in a series of quick crouching spurts, running from one tree to the next, and then they stopped, waited and listened before running on again, grinning and nudging each other in the ribs, pointing through branches at the rabbits.

Thomas gasped for breath, "How the hell are we going to catch any of these critters?"

Mathis smiled. "With good sized pieces of apple."

"What?"

"They love apple."

"I don't believe it."

Mathis paused, a gleam of pride in his eyes. "It's amazing, but I discovered that rabbit's love apple, even though they have trouble swallowing it. And they spend so much time trying to swallow it you can walk up to them calmly from your hiding place and pluck them from the ground."

"So that's how it's done," said Thomas, and even though he moved with caution through the undergrowth, the noise of his footsteps seemed to echo around the forest as though he were walking in a cathedral.

"Shush!" said Mathis. "I'm trying to revolutionise poaching and you're announcing our presence."

"Sorry," whispered Thomas looking embarrassed, and before either of them could bag a single rabbit, a gamekeeper came treading up the forest path with his dog, padding quick and soft-footed at his heels. They spied him through a hedge as he went by them.

"Don't worry, he won't come back today," said Mathis.

"How do you know that?"

"Because the gamekeeper knows where I live and hides outside my cabin waiting for me to come home."

"Smart man."

Mathis shook his head. "Not as smart as me. I dump what I steal elsewhere, before going home. He can't touch me then."

They watched the gamekeeper and his dog disappear up the path before Mathis came out of hiding, spreading the apple around, and then they both stood watching and listening. Within seconds, the rabbits were eating nature's bait, and both men were loading them into sacks. They were soft, floppy and warm.

Mathis finished loading his sack first. "The Abbot is partial to roast or braised rabbit. He'll bless me for this lot!"

"They're for an Abbot?" said Thomas, having no recollection of ever meeting the man.

"Aye and he'll bless me this time for sure. It helps feed the needy at the old Abbey."

"Does he know they're poached?"

Mathis shook his head and smiled. "Don't be silly, he wouldn't bless a common thief. I tell him I raise 'em myself!"

Thomas finished loading the rabbits and humped the bulging sack onto his shoulder. It had eight inside and weighed more than he thought he could carry because he struggled to lift it. Thomas groaned. "I don't think I can carry this."

"Drag it," said Mathis.

The duo started back through the forest, pulling the sacks behind them until they reached the boundary of the wood and peered through a hedge into a long lane. Sliding through the hedge they dragged the sacks after them, along the dusty ground, and then it rained, the drops spearing the ground and within seconds the lane was awash, and both men looked like drowned rats.

Far away down the lane, Thomas saw a dark shadow approaching, and as it got closer, he realised it was a horse-drawn cart driven by a small woman, her clothes only rags. Thomas stared hard at the approaching cart and driver and then it stopped, and the woman jumped from the driving seat and put the hood up in haste. Thomas heard a baby crying in the old cart and it seemed hysterical, the shrill voice growing louder, but as soon as the hood was up, the crying stopped and so did the rain. The woman climbed back up onto the cart, whipping the horse, and the faint muffled sound of clip-clopping hooves and the rattle of iron-shod wheels began again.

The cart drew alongside both men and the woman slowed it to a halt, staring at them. She was lean and brown with sharp features and two long sulphur-coloured teeth protruded from her upper jaw, overlapping her lower lip. Her eyes were black as night and moved over the pair, studying them. She stared at them with a fascination. "You up to yer old tricks again, Mathis, poaching the Master's land?" she said, nodding her repulsive head. "You're no clever'n a dog, you are!"

Mathis shook his head. "Get away with you, you hag," he said with a hiss. "Be on your way and mind yer own business if you want to stay healthy."

The woman held her head high, sniffing the air with a nose twitching from side to side like a rat. "Now listen here you," she hissed back, speaking all her words with an immense relish as though they tasted good on her tongue. "One day, I'll go to a fancy hanging, and there'll be a man with a bag over his 'ead and a noose tied good an' tight about his neck, and I'll cheer because it'll be you!" The hag whipped her horse and shot off laughing, "So put that in yer pipe and smoke it, old man!"

Thomas looked dumbstruck. "Who the hell was that?"

"A crazy woman," said Mathis. "My mother."

***

The morning after Thomas' disappearance, Lira and Olivia were sitting in the sandbox in the backyard of the Dog and Duck, playing with small shovels and pails. Olivia sobbed, asking where her daddy was and Lira had become a gibbering wreck with no answer to give her. Over and over they transferred sand from one pail to another, and the time for dinner came and went unnoticed.

Lira's heart beat fast and her hands trembled. Thomas had stayed away from home before without telling her where he was and what he was doing, but not for this long, so she was fretful and panicking for all the right reasons.

Olivia threw down her sand pail, screaming, "Someone's taken my daddy away!"

Lira looked stunned and didn't know what to say. She knew there was a reason for everything and a solution to every problem, but she was stumbling around in the shattered pieces of her own grief and loss. "Sometimes," she began in a tight voice, "God takes the ones we love, and not at a time of our choosing, but I don't think he would take daddy yet, because he's far too young, handsome and strong, so cry no more my darling." She wiped the tears from Olivia's eyes, kissing her forehead. "But if he has taken him," she continued in a whisper so low that Olivia couldn't hear, "I won't hate him but I'll never forgive him."

***

Two more weeks passed and Thomas' disappearance was on everyone's lips. Dardo and Dody opened the bar at the Dog and Duck each night, praying for him to come strolling home, while Lira raised Olivia with the help of a local nurse. In hushed conversations between revellers at the inn, they spoke of Thomas dying under mysterious circumstances, stabbed to death in a drunken brawl or something similar, but his friends didn't believe it. There was no way someone would catch him off guard. Such was his prowess that his friends couldn't even imagine a situation he wouldn't handle, which left them with the question, where was he?

Minutes turned into hours, hours into days and days into weeks, and the whole community prayed each night for his safekeeping and swift return, but it did not happen. Then, one month to the day after his disappearance, Lira found out she was pregnant again. Now more than ever she needed support and guidance, so she sought the Abbots advice.

Now the forest and meadowlands stirred to the bold voice of the Abbey bell as Lira and Olivia travelled up the dusty road in their horse-drawn cart, and as usual, Lira could see the familiar sight of brothers Alf and Mathias weeding the graveyard and Friar Hugo rebuilding the dry stone walls. Lira waved, and the Friars waved back; then carried on doing their chores, and as the cart entered the Abbey gates the Abbot appeared from out of an arched doorway and bid her stop. As usual, the Abbot folded his hands into the wide sleeves of his habit, staring at her. "Can I be of service my child?"

Olivia was fast asleep in the back of the old cart, so Lira climbed down from the driving seat without disturbing her. She fixed the Abbot's judicious gaze. "Yes, Father, I need your counsel."

The Abbot pointed to the two wooden chairs by the doorway. "Then sit and tell me what ails you, my child."

They sat in silence, staring at each other. Lira looked sad. "Father, one month ago my husband, Thomas, left home and didn't return, we argued the night before and I was angry and said things that inflamed the conflict. Now I don't know where he is and I'm worried. Everyone is worried. He wouldn't leave without saying why and not come back, even though we argued."

The Abbot unfolded his arms from his sleeves, placing a firm hand on Lira's shoulder, fixing her saddened eyes. "Thomas came here a month ago seeking my advice, but he had a money problem. Are you saying no one has seen him since then?"

Lira sobbed, and somewhere inside she was screaming for the Abbot's help. "Yes, Father he's missing!

The Abbot stood up and placed his arm around her shoulders, trying to comfort her. He was strong for an old man. "Come, come, child, calm yourself. I've no idea what has happened to your husband, but I know he's not dead. This I feel in my bones. The nightmare that is shadowing your days will end soon, I am sure, so wipe away your tears, go home and have faith."

She wiped the tears away with the back of her hand, "Oh, Father, I have faith, but do you think so?"

"I do! Thomas is an exceptional man, and extraordinary things happen to exceptional people, but the whys and wherefores are unknown to us. Have faith in the Lord and your husband will return home to you and your child."

Lira stood up, wiping more tears away, grief shadowing her eyes making them darker. "My children, I'm pregnant again!" she corrected

The Abbot pushed himself to his feet. "God bless you and your children, Lira," he said, helping her back up into the driver's seat of the cart.

Lira looked back at Olivia who was still asleep, pausing, she sighed, still on the verge of tears.

Olivia's eyes opened, "Mommy is everything all right?"

Lira tried to smile and sighed. "Yes my darling, but I have to confess, I'm not looking forward to a future without your father." Then her mind wandered. We lived way beyond our means and spent money before we had it, but it wasn't our fault, the inn has drained our resources and kept us in poverty. Maybe that's why Thomas left, he's working somewhere else to earn money for us, she thought.

Olivia's delicate brows screwed up into an anxious frown. "When will daddy come home?"

Lira's expression of hope collapsed into one of forlorn reminiscence as many weird thoughts and images flooded into her mind before she continued. "Soon, my darling, soon." She spun her head around, waving goodbye to the Abbot in silence, and then set off back through the

Abbey gates, down the long road to the sound of the horse's hooves and the rattle of iron wheels. Her whole life was different now without Thomas. Even the surrounding air seemed heavy, and the shadows that scarred her soul grew deeper and more menacing with each passing day.

***

Later that night, Lira sat alone in her bedroom on the end of her pallet bed, crying. Then she stood up, walked to the window and stared out at the night sky. It looked beautiful, crisp and clear and once again she found her eyes drawn to the same group of stars, she had noticed nights earlier. Again they twinkled brighter than the rest, and this time they reminded her of a warrior stranded in the heavens.

***

Not far away, Thomas was gazing out of the hunter's cabin window again at the same group of stars, and once again they hypnotised him and he couldn't stop staring at them twinkling in the night sky. Somehow they reminded him of a golden-haired goddess, fixed in the firmament, and once again he felt sad as if someone had taken something away from him. It was as if his mind was wandering through a pitch-black wood.

"Would you like a drink or something to eat?" asked Mathis jolting him back from his thoughts.

Thomas looked miserable. "No, I'm not hungry or thirsty, but thanks anyway."

Mathis looked into Thomas' face. "Do you know, I'm glad you came into my life the other day? I was considering ending my life because I've been so lonely since my wife died."

Thomas looked stunned. "You mustn't talk like that. It's against God's laws to take your own life, no matter what the reason."

A loud banging came on the hunter's door, "Mathis come and look what I've found!"

Both men jumped. Mathis groaned and climbed to his feet from his rocking chair by the fire and ambled across the room, lifting the iron bar to open the door. "Who's that at this hour?"

An old, fat man dressed in rags was standing there with a torch burning in his hand. "Come and see what I've found!"

Mathis stood in the doorway, mad-eyed, silhouetted by the firelight. "What are you doing, creeping around at this hour of the night; knocking on doors?"

Sanson gasped for breath. "I was poaching and found something! Come and see!"

Mathis, his temper flaring, swung his head around to fix Thomas' tired gaze. "I better go with the crazy old fool and find out what he's found; otherwise neither of us will get any sleep tonight."

"I'll come too," said Thomas climbing to his feet, and within five minutes they were ambling down a craggy hillside, cut in half by torrential flood waters. Both men were following Sanson, guided by bright moonlight when the hillside shook and the earth trembled.

"What the hell caused that? I thought the earth would open and swallow us!" said Mathis.

Thomas shrugged. "Don't know, but it's stopped now so let's keep going!"

Both men followed Sanson to where the hillside came to an abrupt halt, exposing a pair of ivy-covered marble pillars and a cracked lintel stone.

Thomas, scrambling up and over the mud, half-covering the entrance. "Is it an ancient tomb?"

Sliding over the mud into the entrance, the other two men followed him, and all three men halted before a huge statue that seemed to stand guard over the broken stone doorway. Moonlight shone down on the marble statue and Mathis gazed at the carving, trying to figure out who it was. He stared at the plinth. The date read: 1194 AD and mentioned Richard the Lionheart and the Third Great Crusade, but nothing more of the engraving was legible. The invasive floodwaters of the nearby river had eroded it.

Mathis stared. Is this the Lionheart's resting place, he wondered?

The statue was of a man ten feet tall with a sword and shield. It had large eyes, an angular face and a snarling mouth.

Sanson touched the statue. "He looks fierce!"

"A mighty warrior," said Mathis.

Thomas stared at the cruel scarred face and chuckled. "Hell's teeth! Who'd dare fight someone that ugly? I dread to think what his wife looked like, don't you?"

The three men laughed, the sound echoing around the tomb.

Thomas pushed his way into the burial chamber, "Why would anyone want a statue that ugly guarding their grave?"

Mathis' torch flared over a coffin. They edged towards it, lifting the cracked lid. A dismal screech as of animal terror rang from the coffin and bats spiralled out, startling Thomas and friends. They sprang back.

Sanson took a deep breath, laying a hand to his heart. His face was ashen and the others could hear his teeth chatter. "Mother of God. Scared the daylights out of me that did."

Thomas and Mathis sighed, laughing with relief. "Me too!" they said in unison.

The ground trembled and shook, and Thomas swore as the tremor died away. All three men stood for a moment and a second quake hit, hurling them from their feet. The coffin slid sideways from its plinth, struck the wall and shattered into pieces. Mathis and Sanson lay hugging the earth for several moments as the rumbling continued, then silence settled on the land. Rolling to their knees the men, climbed to their feet and stood wide-eyed, staring at the contents of the coffin scattered around the floor of the tomb. Hundreds of gold and silver coins, diamonds, emeralds and sapphires lay before them.

Mathis gasped. "It's a fortune!"

Speechless, Thomas nodded and stared with a backward glance into the darkness of the tomb to make sure no one followed them.

Sanson threw himself onto the ground amidst the treasure, grabbing handfuls, his eyes fever bright. "We're rich!" he yelled, and so lively was his excitement he stood up, laying a hand on Thomas' arm, shaking him again, crying out they were wealthy men.

"Pull yourself together, man!" snapped Thomas.

Sanson's eyes widened, but his face slackened. He stared at Thomas saying nothing more.

Thomas turned. "Where do you think this treasure came from Mathis?"

"The Turks. It must be Saracen loot," said Mathis. "In 1194 King Richard plundered the Turkish empire in the Great Crusade so I assume it was their treasure.

Thomas looked at Mathis. "Is this Lionheart dead?" he asked, having no recollection of the man or his crusade.

Mathis laughed. "He better be, he's buried under the earth!"

"Then we've found ourselves a fortune," said Sanson shaking Mathis' hand.

Thomas thought for a moment, and then his hand rose covering his mouth. He sighed. "I'm rich, but I don't even know who I am!"

***

Ozhobar rode like a phantom across the moonlit landscape with his cape flapping behind him. Cracking a bull-whip above his head he galloped on through the night, digging his spurs into his horse's sweaty flanks with forty warriors followed his lead.

He was the biggest, most savage warrior who ever crossed Nottingham's countryside, save for his father, Ozhan. Now he was on a mission. Word of Thomas' disappearance had spread like wildfire and he would take full advantage of the fact. Everyone would fear him and follow him or die. Beresford, his second in command, rode beside him carrying a long pike with a head fixed at the top. He had killed the man only an hour earlier, toying with him before beheading him.

Wild-eyed with the smell of blood in their nostrils they plunged ahead without conscious thought, and straight on their panicked horses galloped past the milestone at the roadside as they hit the Old Nottingham Road, heedless of the letters graven in stone: *Ferret's Farm, 15 miles.*

Ozhobar needed no instruction where the farm was or how far. He knew it well. As a child, he had spent many an unhappy hour there until the age of fifteen, when he had run away to sea. Four years later, after crossing the wide oceans and treading the jungles of the world, he jumped from ship to shore after learning of his father's sudden violent death. Now he wanted what was his by birth: every inch of land that his father terrorised and murdered for, and he intended to get it back by inflicting as much pain and suffering as possible on the terrified population of Nottingham. Thomas, their great protector had disappeared, and that's all he needed to know.

The shadowy outline of the farm stood before Ozhobar shrouded in mist, and the night wind howled, carrying the reek of brimstone. His sombre eyes surveyed the house, watching wooden shutters swing open and shut in the gale. It was an eerie scene, set in midnight black.

He rode forward with the bloodied parchment and nailed it to the door, nodding grimly. Then his men burned the place with everyone in it. Thick smoke rose from the blaze, billowing towards a barn, and soot stained the whitewashed walls. Acrid fumes seeped from the narrow windows. Inside it was an inferno.

Horrific screams came from the farmhouse as it collapsed in showers of sparks and rubble tumbled to the ground. Ozhobar's men laughed. More smoke swirled, drifting away from the house in long trailers; the smell of burning flesh lingering in the air and even after they had killed their terrified victims, their blood lust was high.

Spooked by the terrifying scene, Ozhobar's stallion whinnied in fear, trembling beneath him, the man himself consumed by hate, greed and bloodlust. Laughing, he gripped his reins with one hand and rode the skittish horse up to the collapsed building. He reached into the ashes, snatching a scrap of parchment from the smouldering door. "Now it's over and done!"

Nearby, a swinging door on a barn squeaked, the shrill sound cutting through the darkness. Ozhobar spun his head, eyes rounding on the sound and his horse reared up on hind legs with front hooves pawing the empty air. Steam jetted from flaring nostrils and its eyes rolled in their sockets. "There's someone in the barn, drag him out here now and we'll have a hanging!"

There was the sound of someone dropping a metal bucket and running footsteps. Ozhobar's startled stallion snorted, shaking its head. "Easy boy." He tightened his grip on the reins, fighting to control the horse.

One man threw a noose over an oak beam protruding from the barn wall. It hung and swung back and forth in the howling wind that wailed like an army of damned souls. Then Ozhobar's gaze locked on a solitary figure limping towards him. A nine-year-old boy. He was sobbing and wiping his runny nose.

"Why won't someone help me?" he said. His breathing was shallow and his throat rattled from inhaling the smoke. Glassy-eyed, he stared into eternity.

Thunder rumbled on the horizon and the wind whipped up the dust at the boy's feet, enveloping him, forcing him to close his eyes. The dust devil disappeared, and the boy opened them again. He fixed Ozhobar's gaze. "You son of a whore. You've murdered my whole family."

Ozhobar smiled. "I lead a wild, sinful life, filled with drugs and liquor, and have far too many women to pleasure me, but the shocking truth is I get more pleasure from killings than anything else. What's your name, whelp?"

The boy stood in tearful silence a moment. "Godwin, son of Berwyn, from the House of Longmire." He began to pray. "Please, Lord, don't let this evil monster claim my soul. Rescue me and I promise to go to church every day and never utter another sinful word." His haunted eyes stared up into his tormentor's face, searching for any spark of humanity. He found none. Then he stared up at the starry night sky, knowing God wouldn't answer his prayer. Godwin knew he would die.

Ozhobar's eyes seemed to glow and burst into flame. Godwin's teeth chattered and the more he trembled, the more the baron's eyes gleamed as though they were soaking up every ounce of terror. "You will die now, and it will feel worse than you can imagine!"

Sheer, unrelenting panic washed over the boy like a tidal wave. He sobbed. "Please don't kill me!"

Ozhobar nodded to his men, and they grabbed Godwin, dragging him screaming to the noose. Tying his hands behind his back, they looped the noose over his head, tightening it around his neck and he sobbed and screamed awaiting his execution. They hauled him into the air, kicking and thrashing. The baron watched the boy choke and die for what seemed an eternity, then he swung his horse around and rode off into the night without a backward glance.

CHAPTER FOURTEEN
No past life

Lira stood at the top of Nottingham Hill amid fragrant flowers with a bright blue sky overhead. Golden sunlight warmed her face. She stared at her inscription carved into the bark of an oak, "Lira loves Thomas forever"

Lira carved those words four years earlier and experienced a bitter-sweet pang inside her heart as she contemplated life without Thomas. She sighed. "This whole nightmare started when I lost my temper and said awful words to you a month ago. Now I'm so sorry and miss you more than you will ever know. Where are you? Are you dead or alive? Are you hurt and helpless? Not knowing is the worst of all." Lira took a moment to mourn Thomas' loss once more and would always regret her harsh words had cost her so dearly.

Hours later, at the Dog and Duck, Lira's eyes glistened. She had been crying all afternoon and was beside herself with grief. Olivia was crying too, making the situation worse. Memories flooded into Lira's mind of Thomas and her kissing and making love beneath the spreading branches of a majestic oak tree. Lira had conceived Olivia that day, and it was a beautiful, romantic, unforgettable day. Now she was alone with Olivia.

Lira still couldn't believe what had happened, wouldn't come to terms with the fact it might have been her fault, didn't want to exist without the love of her life because one argument had gotten out of hand. There was no bitterness or anger in her thoughts only regret.

***

Nearby, Thomas didn't know of his past life, fame, or of his deeds, but what he had was a new destiny to fulfil.

A year flew by like fast-moving clouds on a windy day and over time, the legend of Thomas Flynn faded, even though the memory of his exploits lingered on and would never die. He stood gazing out of Mathis' cabin window at a beautiful morning with the sun shining and birds chirping in the trees. Thomas took a deep breath and wondered what his mission in life was? Then his friend the hunter crashed through the heavy oak door like a bolt from a crossbow, knocking it off its hinges. He hit the stone floor and skidded beneath his table. Mathis shook his head trying to clear his dizziness, and bells rang in his ears as he pushed the table over, slamming it out of his way. It crashed against the far wall. Mathis climbed to his feet, hauling himself upright. "Come on, you son-of-a-whore!" he shouted.

A scarred, tough-looking man with ragged hair and crooked teeth loomed in the doorway, back-lit by the sun. He wore a black patch over his missing left eye. The gamekeeper lost his eye, torn out in a fight with a poacher. The poacher lost his life.

Thomas watched the gamekeeper hunch his broad shoulders, bending his head to enter the cabin doorway. Wild-eyed with the smell of blood in his nostrils he hawked and spat. "You never learn, do you, Mathis?" he sneered. "I think I'll spit-roast you now!"

The gamekeeper never looked more menacing. His eye glowed with the fervour of his profession as he threw back his head, relishing this long-awaited confrontation, and his black teeth showed as he gave a broad grin. "Knew I'd catch you one day. It was only a matter of time!"

The gamekeeper's voice echoed with the timbre of a raving lunatic and a fist struck Mathis full in the face, sending him sprawling again. Mathis lay, battered and bruised, looking like a rotting carcass but rolled over, crawling towards the shadowy corner where Thomas was standing, watching. The gamekeeper growled like a wild animal. Eager for the kill he gazed at his victim with sadistic glee. He drew his sword. "Your hide belongs to me now, and if I don't spit-roast you and eat your liver, Master Ozhobar will hang, draw and quarter you!"

Thomas lurched in front of Mathis, protecting him. "What the hell's the matter, man?" he shouted, and before the gamekeeper could strike, he spun around, grabbing a brass poker and shovel from the hearth, holding them like swords.

The gamekeeper laughed, stalking towards him with a hideous smile on his face. He paused as though unsure whether it was worth the effort of killing Thomas first. "What use are those?"

Thomas looked down at the poker and shovel in his hands and scowled. The gamekeeper lunged at him with his sword. Incredibly, Thomas parried the blow with the shovel and lunged with the poker, and it caught the other by surprise, striking him high on the temple. Reeling backwards, clutching the wound, he stared at Thomas with murder in his eye. Blood seeped through his fingers from the cut.

Thomas backed away, but the gamekeeper took an enormous leap, punching him hard on the jaw, sending him spinning to the floor. He shook his head to lose the dizziness clouding his mind and rolled to his knees, hammering the toes of the other's left foot with the poker.

There was a terrible animalistic shriek as pain shot up the gamekeeper's leg and through his whole body. He hopped around the room clasping his toes. Thomas rose to his feet casting him a venomous look, again getting ready to defend himself with the shovel and poker.

Mathis groaned, rolling onto his back, gazing up at Thomas with a vengeful stare. "Kill the bastard!" he said with a gasp.

Thomas swiped with the poker at dizzying speed, knocking the gamekeeper's other leg from under him. He hit the ground hard, falling onto his neck, breaking it and didn't rise again. Thomas kicked him with his booted foot to make sure he was dead. And stone-cold dead he was!

Mathis, holding his jaw, stared at the corpse with incredulity, "How the hell did you do that with just a shovel and a poker?"

Thomas stared at the two household items in his hands, "Not sure how I did it. Something came over me, an irresistible urge as if I knew what to do!"

Astonishment gleamed in the hunter's eyes. He hauled himself upright. "Your speed was frightening!

Faster than a spreading forest fire. Do you think you were a swordsman before you lost your memory?" Thomas shrugged, shaking his head, "I still have no recollection of my past life what-so-ever," he said. Then he found himself trapped at the centre of a nightmarish vision.

He was raping a woman.

He beat her to death with bloodied fists.

A man appeared in a doorway.

A brutal fist knocked his teeth out.

Whips cruelly lashed his back in the street.

Callous stares ignored his pleas as he begged a gathering mob not to hang him.

He screamed while approaching the gallows, watched by two young boys from the upstairs window of a tavern.

The crazed mob tied a noose around his neck, chanting for a hanging.

Then everything went black and the pageant of suffering stopped. Thomas dropped to the floor, curling into a quivering ball, covering his eyes and his face contorted into a mask of horror. He had relived his mother's brutal murder and his father's hanging but wasn't sure what he'd seen, having no conscious memory of either act.

***

In the bar at the Dog and Duck, the early morning sunlight filtered through the stained glass windows. Dardo was fast asleep, collapsed over a table, his head resting on his arms and Dody was snoring beneath the table, comatose with the drink.

Since Thomas' disappearance, drinking was all they did besides fight. Lira did her best to control them and the patrons in the tavern, but she was fighting a losing battle. With Thomas' steadfast influence gone, an icy chill descended on the place each night. Tempers flared, scuffles erupted and then all *Hell* would break loose. It seemed like the end of days to her.

Lighted candles in the bar that had burned all night dispelled whatever shadows remained, revealing the havoc caused the night before in violent knife fights. Once again there were overturned tables and smashed, splintered chairs littering the room, and at least two bloodied corpses adorned the bar top. Her angry eyes scanned the room, surveying the carnage. She counted to ten and counted again, her face pale, drawn and anxious. Her unforgiving expression said it all and her pent-up anger smouldered deep within and exploded. She shrieked her protest at the nauseating sight, waking Dardo and Dody with a start. Both men jumped as if slapped.

Dody gasped, bobbing up, banging his head on the table. "Ouch! What the…?"

Dardo fell backwards off his chair with a crash, rolling onto the sawdust-covered floor. "Arghh! What? Who? Where?" He rolled to his knees, pulling himself upright covered in wood shavings and with his wild hair ragged and unkempt he looked like a scarecrow. He stood for a moment, stunned, shook his head and then brushed his clothes with his hands. Dody rolled from beneath the table covered in sawdust too. Climbing to his feet he rummaged amongst the broken furniture for his boots. "Where are they?"

He found them and put them on in haste.

Lira's face was a picture of anger. She screamed. "You will regret this, the pair of you, now you can clean the place up because I'm not going to!" She stormed from the room, slamming the door shut behind her and went back to bed.

Dardo looked hurt. "I'm not the sharpest arrow in the quiver but I'm…"

"No, you're not," interrupted Dody. "But your heart's in the right place and she's just upset. Lira misses

Thomas. We all do." He leaned forward, placing a hand on his friend's shoulder. "She's still in the shock of her abandonment. It's been hard of late for all of us, but Lira's loss is the hardest to bear because Olivia keeps crying for her daddy and asking when he's coming home?"

The tinted windows reflected Dody's brooding demeanour. Hope faded from his eyes as he stared at the door with a pensive glance. "I just keep wishing he'd walk back through the door with that confident swagger of his!"

The whole place was a mess. The friends set about cleaning it, picking up the shards of smashed pottery, splinters of broken chairs and shelves, tidying away anything out of place, including the two corpses from the bar top. Dardo hefted one over his shoulder and Dody carried the other out into the courtyard to await the coming of the undertaker. When they had finished, a great weariness descended upon them.

Dardo collapsed onto a stool at their usual table. "I enjoy the drinking and sometimes even the fighting, but not cleaning up after because it's hard work."

Dody slumped next to Dardo, weariness overcoming him too.

Both men stared at Thomas' empty chair, picturing him sitting there, and both searched their memories for any clue as to his disappearance. Had he mentioned something that might lead them to him? If he had, neither man could recall a word he might have said to guide them to him. Both men sat in silence with jaded expressions.

Upstairs in the darkness, Lira listened to Olivia crying for her daddy. She wasn't a religious woman and had prayed only once in her life but God had not answered her prayer and she and her father had buried her mother as a plague of smallpox swept through the country, causing misery and desolation to the loved ones of the dead. Now she prayed again, but this time she prayed for her husband to come home. This time it was an unselfish prayer. Lira couldn't stand to look into Olivia's grief-stricken eyes any longer and just wanted her daddy to come home safe.

Olivia sobbed. "Mummy, I want to see my daddy again. Can I? I miss him so much."

Lira began to cry. "I know, sweetheart, I miss him too. He'll be home soon, I'm sure."

Olivia didn't want to talk, eat, brush her hair or put on pretty clothes any more with her father gone. Her bedroom no longer overflowed with flowers, homemade toys and straw dolls like it used to, and Lira hated it every time someone mentioned Thomas' disappearance or pitied her for being left with a child to bring up on her own as if her husband had gone off with another woman behind her back. But the worst part was she didn't know if he was dead or alive. This made them both inconsolable.

***

Nearby, Thomas didn't have a care in the world because his memory was as blank as a novice painter's canvas. He still couldn't remember his name, let alone his family and his long history of violence, which had sometimes shadowed his days. But destiny was painting him a new history. He was now rich. So were Mathis and Sanson after finding the Lionheart's treasure and the only downside to recent events was he had all kinds of strange, waking nightmares. Was any of it part of his past, he wondered, pushing them to the back of his mind? Most of them were violent hallucinations and very disturbing.

Thomas had visions of farmers being burned alive in a barn.

A branding iron searing flesh.

An old man having his teeth knocked out.

A whip lashing and flaying skin to the bone.

A jealous husband beating his wife to death.

And so on, ending with an angry mob and a brutal hanging. Then, as usual, the pageant of terror and suffering would stop. Everything would go black.

More days turned into weeks, then one night Thomas relived his past life in a vivid dream. Lira came to him as a lean, shadowy figure, clad in white. She arrived to reclaim him as her own, appearing before him in a dark landscape with bursts of thunder and lightning flashing. Her blue eyes shone like polished sapphires. "Come back to me, my love," she called out with her arms outstretched. Olivia was sobbing somewhere in the background but he couldn't see her even though more bursts of thunder and lightning lit the heavens as a scorching, whining wind burned his face in the chaos of his dream.

Thomas awoke with a start and sat up in bed, wild-eyed with terror, the shutters of the bedroom windows banging in the strong moaning wind. It blew against his face, offering no relief from the stifling heat of the night as it whistled through the hunter's cabin sounding inhuman and mocking.

Outside, the horses whinnied in fear of the sounds of the keening wind, and a door squeaked as it swung back and forth on its hinges. A weather-vane spun on the roof and a tarnished bucket hanging on a rope over the dry well outside clanged as lightning flashed in the heavens overhead and thunder roared.

Again, he made no sense of the wild nightmare, having no conscious memory of his wife and child. And as the morning came, bringing the warm sun, he sat outside relaxing on the porch by the cabin until he noticed men shouting, women screaming and children crying. The tumult filled his ears as the hellish cacophony grew louder and louder with each passing second. It was coming his way with the echoes of speeding hoof beats.

Thomas' new horse whinnied in fear, wanting to bolt from the tethering post. "Steady, boy," he urged, but the awful noise continued its conspiracy to drive the horse out of its mind. The tangy smell of blood, mixed with noxious smoke added to the stallion's alarm. Steam jetted from its flaring nostrils and froth flecked its mouth in its agitated state. Thomas leapt from the porch, gripping the reins, fighting to bring the panicked horse under control while stroking its flanks.

Then the area surrounding the hunter's cabin filled up with farmers and their wives and children, running and screaming, followed by armed warriors on horseback chasing them. An awful noise filled the air around Thomas as it gathered momentum, the ground trembling and rumbling, and once again his sixth sense told him to take cover and find a hiding place until he could gather his thoughts. Thomas ran for the nearest barn. Ignoring the stairs he climbed with haste up into the hayloft and his lightning-fast reflexes served him well as he landed catlike in the hay, where he hid and watched.

The cries of the victims rang out, nearby barns blazed and cattle bellowed in pain as the warriors laid waste to everything in their path. Thomas saw the carnage, death and misery wreaked by the evil men and his eyes were cold and grim. The leader laughed, killing faster, wreaking more desolation and destruction, until there was no one left to kill. Thomas was sick to his stomach but knew there was nothing he could have done to stop the slaughter. He cursed his leaden limbs and for the first time in his new life and knew mindless fear and panic. Sweat dripped from his hands and his lungs felt like they were bursting.

There was the noise of a rusty door hinge squeaking behind him. Thomas rolled onto his back. Too late, one warrior was upon him, stabbing at him with a dagger. He rolled away just in time for his attacker's blade to sink into the floorboards beneath the hay with a heavy thud. He jumped to his feet, cannoning his booted foot into the other's face as he stood back erect with the knife still in his hand. The move caught the man by surprise, launching him from the hayloft, two floors up, and he landed impaled on a wooden fence post and didn't move again. Thomas was fortunate, none of the other warriors saw what happened, and they disappeared back up into the hills after killing every living thing.

When he was sure they had gone, he walked mournfully through the devastation and carnage. Smoke and the smell of brimstone drifted across the land in black trailers obscuring the once beautiful view, which was a now horrendous sight. Bodies of men, women, children and animals lay everywhere in pieces. They had died a horrible, violent death.

Thomas couldn't look at the awful sight any longer; he fixed his gaze on the distant Nottingham road, where a single rider on horseback was heading his way at the gallop, leaving a trail of dust behind him. He recognised the rider as his friend, Mathis, and after a minute he pulled up alongside Thomas, tugging on the reins. The horse reared on hind legs, snorting, shaking its head, its front hooves pawing the air. Steam jetted from its flaring nostrils.

Thomas looked at the man, fear glittering in his eyes.

"Hell, what happened here?" asked Mathis.

Thomas' eyes misted. "A savage slaughter. I watched and couldn't do a damn thing to stop it!" Taking a slow deep breath he knelt over a young boy's body, searching through his pockets. There was a homemade slingshot, a tiny knitted figure and a single copper coin. He held up the items in the palm of his hand. "What's the price of a life?" His eyes filled with tears as somewhere in the back of his subconscious mind he had a vivid vision of his daughter, Olivia. He choked back the tears, swallowing hard.

Both men spent the rest of the day saying prayers, burying the corpses and burning the dead cattle on huge pyres, until at dusk with the onset of night their task ended. In the hunter's cabin afterwards, both men sat eating in silence, staring at each other over the tabletop. "What drives Ozhobar? Cold and merciless he is!" said Mathis.

"Is that the warrior who attacked today?"

"Aye."

"Only two things drive a man like him, greed and pure hate!"

"He has his father's seed within him," said Mathis, "and a great big hole he cannot fill, even with all the misery, suffering and death he causes and he has a passionate taste for that!"

"Can no one stop him? Is there no one skilled enough with a sword or bow to end his reign of terror?"

Mathis shook his head. "There was such a warrior in Nottingham. I never saw the man though. Out here in the wild, I mind my business. His name was Flynn. Passing traders spread rumours he was a formidable and fearsome fighter, skilled with matching short-swords and fast as a lightning bolt. But he went missing. Since then one has heard from him!"

Thomas stood up, yawned, stretched and removed his bloodstained shirt, leggings and boots, and Mathis noticed his scarred body as he marched off to bed without saying another word. Through disbelieving eyes, he stared at the many healed wounds, and that night in bed he had sombre thoughts in his mind and found sleep difficult. But when he succumbed, he dreamt of baron Ozhobar. "I'm coming for you old man, we have a score to settle, you and I," he called to Mathis.

It rained in the night, putting out the fires the marauding warriors had started and Thomas awoke in the early hours, cold and shivering. He rolled from his bed and pushed himself upright, staring out of the window at the night sky. The baron's laughter drifted into his mind and the words, "Kill everyone and everything!" rang clear. He swore and cursed the man-monster.

Thomas closed his eyes and somehow opened an inner pathway, falling back into himself. It was sudden and unexpected and before he realised it, he was reliving his past life. Lira came to him and then Olivia. Dardo and Dody floated before his eyes, then Master Gallus, Nelan and baron Ozhan, and even the hunchback made a sudden appearance, offering another purse of gold coins for a street fight. Now the broken puzzle that was his mind was reforming into a clear coherent picture.

More rain lashed the farmhouse. Thunder drummed out, bringing him back from his thoughts. Lightning flashed nearby illuminating the smouldering landscape, and his blood ran cold remembering every single cry for help, every heart-rending scream and every terrible murder. He swore again and wished the lightning would strike him down for not aiding the helpless and dying, and he felt like a coward, but piece by piece his memory returned.

Taking a deep breath, he sighed as the storm passed and the moon shone in a clear sky. He turned to the full-length polished metal mirror by the bed. "It's me, Thomas Flynn. I'm back. I recognise me!" he said and the raw power of his emotions almost frightened him.

***

That morning the baron awoke and rolled to his feet, striding across his camp, casting his eyes over a stolen black stallion, along the line of its back, the length of its neck, and the shape of its head. Ozhobar looked pleased. "This beautiful creature will bring about two hundred in silver."

"That's a fine animal, over eighteen hands high," said one warrior running his hand over the beast's flanks. "The coat has a healthy sheen and his muscles are supple and strong!"

"The horse has a good front conformation too, the point of its shoulders in line with the knee and hoof," said another.

Ozhobar moved around the horse, stroking its jaw and he looked into its bright, brown eyes and then checked the legs. The horse had strong legs, and the hoofs had been re-shod. He watched the swelling of its rib cage. It was slow and even. He patted the stallion's flanks. "I need a new mount."

A third warrior stared at Ozhobar. "Then this one should be fine, but doesn't it bother you riding a dead man's horse?"

"No!" said Ozhobar. "That's why I cut the man's head off with a blunt knife. I love the horse!"

Forty warriors cheered in unison, throwing their arms into the air. The Baron laughed. "Think yourselves lucky that it wasn't one of your horses I wanted," he said with a good-humoured smile, gesturing cutting his throat with an imaginary knife.

The warriors laughed, cheering again. The campfire was almost dead when a warrior added thin pieces of kindling and blew the flames back to life. He hung a large copper pot filled with beef stew over the flames on a bracket of black iron. Another warrior added the fresh vegetable to the mix, and as it came to the boil, the aroma was inviting. The men ate, drank and made merry and fell asleep around a spreading oak, their bellies full to bursting. But Ozhobar was planning his next raid on the community of Nottingham. He was sitting with his map resting on his knees, trying to figure out his next plan of action.

Eyes wide, his forefinger drifted around the map tracing meadow and field. Ozhobar traced further until his finger stopped at a farm by a wide military road, and then he tapped the location twice. "There," he said in a husky whisper. "Tobin's farm. I *want* that land." Few could understand his way of thinking, and even fewer could follow the twists and turns of his insane mind. Most didn't try, but no one ignored him. If they did, it was at their own peril, and since the farmers and landowners hadn't agreed to sell their land, he fully intended to take back by force what he thought was his birth-right.

***

One day later and ten miles up the military road at Tobin's farm with dusk deepening, the blacksmith was unaware that Ozhobar and his warriors, all armed, were watching. He stood stock-still outside the farmhouse, unblinking, looking at the night sky. It was a beautiful cloudless evening, the warm air still. Tobin stood there for half an hour, eyes searching the heavens, but as the sky darkened the smell of new-mown hay and summer flowers disappeared and he grew tired. Tobin stretched, yawned and went back inside, up to the bedroom, lying down on his bed. Exhausted, he fell into a deep sleep full of hurtful dreams, watching his wife die of the plague.

An hour later, he awoke with a start, eyes wide with terror, his heart beating fast. The baron was standing over him. Tobin fought to focus on the flat, brutal face that was inches from him when Ozhobar grabbed his throat with iron fingers and hauled Tobin upright. "You have no time to sleep," the baron hissed. "In fact, your time's run out!"

Ozhobar's towering figure lifted Tobin from the bed, feet hanging, kicking empty air as he choked. Ozhobar dropped the blacksmith to the floor and swivelled around, ordering Tobin to follow him. "You know why I'm here, don't you?" he said with an icy tone.

"Yes. You will murder me, so just get it done," Tobin replied with fear shining in his eyes, knowing that in this moment of sheer terror his life was at an end.

"We will kill you and take time doing the deed and enjoy seeing you die in agony! Then we will eat your corpse," whispered Ozhobar.

Dread and despair washed the colour from Tobin's face. Stark eyes stared in disbelief and sank deeper into his skull. He seemed frozen. Sick, terrifying feelings burgeoned in his stomach overwhelming him and his legs disobeyed. Tobin couldn't move. His heart pounded in his chest like a hammer. "Death comes to us all one day."

Ozhobar nodded. "You're right, Tobin, but I can be cruel and inventive," he countered. He strode from the cabin, out into the darkness where his warriors were waiting with blazing torches. They wore white masks, hideous caricatures of their own ugly faces and each of them had a hammer in their hand and formed a circle.

Tobin emerged following the baron. Ozhobar's men grabbed his arms and slung a linen bag over his head, tying it around his neck. Tobin struggled, and a man stepped forward and smote him hard on the back of his head, dizzying him. He staggered and fell to his knees. Laughter rang in his ears. Then another man placed a broadsword in his hands and hauled him upright, steadying him.

Ozhobar laughed. "This is my version of Blind Man's Bluff." He nodded to a man who slammed his hammer onto Tobin's toes.

The blacksmith dropped the sword, screaming like an animal as the pain shot up his leg filling his whole body. Another man slammed a hammer onto Tobin's other foot, then another man and another until the surrounding air filled with the sound of screams echoing throughout the night.

Tobin fell to his knees and Ozhobar kicked him in the face with his booted foot, mercifully knocking him unconscious. A man dragged a chair from inside the house, hauled Tobin upright and sat him on it, tying his hands behind his back. The baron filled a bucket with water from the well and poured it over his head, bringing Tobin back to his waking nightmare, and he screamed, the horrific pain of his crushed toes filling his body and mind.

Ozhobar snarled, punching Tobin in the face. "You're alone and will die alone! Then I'll rape Lira, kill and eat your grandchild and no one can stop me! Are you listening, old man? Are you?" The torture began again with hammers beating Tobin's body, striking him from head to toe until he lost consciousness.

A warrior threw more water over the blacksmith, reviving him and he screamed. "No more! No more! Kill me, but don't hurt my daughter and grandchild they mean nothing to you!"

Ozhobar smiled a merciless smile. "But they mean everything to you! And that's why I will rape and kill your daughter, and gut your grandchild like a fish!" He spun on his heel, slamming a dagger into Tobin's chest, driving the blade up to the hilt into his heart. He died screaming.

The baron dragged the blade clear, wiping it on Tobin's shirt. His eyes pulsed with living colour, and his warriors could feel an icy chill emanating from them. Kneeling by the corpse, he whispered, "I will do what I have said, and more!" He forced himself upright, swinging away, climbing into the saddle of his new stallion, bidding his men to do the same, and they rode off into the darkness of the night laughing and cheering their devil-possessed master.

CHAPTER FIFTEEN

Death of a good man

Lira awoke from her dream screaming, wild-eyed with terror, her father's face floating before her eyes, begging for mercy and forgiveness. There was sadness in his eyes. Throwing back the linen sheets she jumped from her bed, staring down at her hands. They trembled. Her eyes were large, dark, and haunted because the dream had been so vivid and clear, and she realised that somehow she had seen Tobin's horrific murder. She screamed again and fainted, falling to the floorboards.

When Lira came back to consciousness, Dardo and Dody were kneeling by her side, holding her. Dardo fanned Lira's face with his hand, trying to get her to breathe. "We heard you scream! What happened?"

"Something terrible has happened to my father!" she said, choking back the tears, but somewhere deep inside she was screaming.

Dody put an arm around her too, cradling her head, letting Lira feel his strength. "It was a bad dream! Tobin's all right, I'm sure of it!"

"No! Something terrible has happened to my father!" Lira snapped back, her face pale and shocked, a look of grief shadowing her eyes. She began to sob against Dody's shoulder. "Tobin's dead. I know it!"

Dody kissed Lira on the forehead, forcing himself upright. "I'm sure you're wrong, but I'll go to Tobin's farm and make certain he's okay."

Lira nodded, wiping the tears from her eyes. "Thank you," she said, trying to find solace in his smile. He reminded her so much of Thomas. Dody cared, as did Dardo, and she couldn't wish for two better friends.

Only five minutes later, Dody had bridled and saddled his stallion and was on his way down the long dusty road in a sustained forced gallop towards the blacksmith's farm. He guided the horse through grasslands and a grove of trees beside a fast-running stream until he came to the long military road that led to the farm. At the end of that road, he climbed the slope, passing under the spreading oak until he came to the farmhouse.

The early morning sun was just clearing the western hills and an eerie white mist drifted above the ground, swirling in murky trailers around a chair with a bloodied body sat on it. Dody's face hardened. Sitting his horse in silence he stared at the corpse, his eyes wide. Heeling the horse forward he dismounted and walked to the chair. Dody touched the corpse. It was stiff. He stared hard at the bloodied linen sack covering the face and knew it was Tobin without even removing it. His whole body was a bloody mess of deep cuts, bruises and broken bones.

Great God in heaven, how can I report this to Lira, he thought? He choked at the gruesome sight. A long sigh escaped from his throat, he swayed forward, almost falling over and he was sick. Then Dody was aware he wasn't alone and a voice he recognised called from behind him. "Don't cry, boy, it won't serve any good purpose. Death is ugly, but Tobin is with his maker now and will never grow old and infirm. Just remember him always with affection as the strong handsome man he was."

Dody spun around, glancing up to see Thomas stepping out from the shadows of the farmhouse doorway. "Oh, thank God. You're back!" He fell to his knees feeling numb.

Both men spent the next few hours praying while burying Tobin's shattered body in a shallow grave, dug in a sea of buttercups beneath the spreading oak. Then at dusk with the onset of night, they sat in Tobin's cabin eating and drinking in silence, staring mournfully at each other, neither wanting to be the one to tell Lira.

"Where have you been? So many people have died of late and we thought you were one," said Dody.

Thomas looked thoughtful. He lifted his tankard of ale, half draining it and wiped his lips with the back of his hand. "I've been so near, yet so very far away."

Dody stared at him. "If that's a riddle I don't understand what it means.

Thomas said nothing more. He just threw his protégé a glance, finishing his drink as Dody rambled on about the troubled people of Nottingham, the kidnappings and murders until Thomas could stand to hear no more. "Bless me, nothing ever changes around here does it? You sound more like Lira every day. Shut up rambling; it does no good! My wife thinks I'm dead. My father-in-law is dead, and Ozhan is back, reincarnated in the form of Ozhobar. That's an information overload without your long-winded tirade!"

Dody looked hurt by the cutting words.

Thomas saw the pain and suffering of Tobin's death shining in Dody's eyes and he took a deep breath. "I'm sorry! I didn't mean to hurt your feelings, but I'll say something now you won't want to know. You look very much like me, but you're not like me in personality. At your age, I was much more aggressive and much more determined. Your father, Cyrano, God bless him, used to say you were like your mother, and you are, and that's not a bad thing. But I have a destiny to fulfil and need the strongest people around me I can find to help me succeed. Are you one of those people?

Dody nodded. "We're both stumbling in the broken pieces of our grief, but we're both aware that our lives will soon change because of the events about to overtake us. I'm strong! You've made me strong and I'll never let you down, no matter what befalls us from this day forward, I so swear it by everything I hold dear."

Thomas nodded looking anxious. "I believe you. Now let's get back and check on our loved ones before anything else happens." And for a single moment, he pictured his wife and child in his mind.

Without another word, he strode out of the cabin to his stallion, followed by Dody. Both men mounted. Then they heeled their horses, riding around the spreading oak and along the hillside, both men giving a backward glance at the makeshift wooden cross marking Tobin's final resting place. Their eyes misted at the loss of a good friend.

Meanwhile, the baron's tyrannical rule was tearing Nottingham apart, bringing about a catastrophe that was robbing the land of hard-working farmers, privateers and nobleman, because smugglers, slavers and cutthroats were replacing them. One man would not allow this to happen any longer. Thomas was back and intended to save the world he loved at any cost, even though doubts of epic proportions beset him. But at least he had solved the riddle of his own identity and intended to bring his own plans to fruition, none of which included Ozhobar and his band of cutthroats.

Thomas knew he had the right mix of magic and mystery to stir his friends into action against the baron, and he would do it without a second thought as soon as he could plan a meeting. Now they rode back along the military road until they came to the fast-running stream and the grove of trees where the territory turned back into grasslands, and both warriors heeled their horses, heading towards home with the greatest of haste.

Later, as they entered the streets of Nottingham after their long ride, it looked deserted except for the usual tramps, down-and-outs and prostitutes plying their trade in the recesses of doorways. A cold wind was blowing from the north as both men, hooded and cloaked, rode through the winding alleyways and passages towards the Dog and Duck. Coming into Gallows Square just as the moon was hiding behind a screen of dark clouds both men paused, gazing at several corpses hanging there. They shook their heads. "Nothing ever changes, does it?" they said in unison.

And even though the moon shone bright and clear, the distant rumble of thunder drummed out and a web of lightning flashed nearby. Thomas held his face to the rain. It sheeted down, and he bared his teeth to the heavens. "Come and strike me if you dare, for I am back!"

Dody smiled at the comforting comment, letting the cold rain wash over his face. Then the storm passed in a minute, leaving a bright moon again. Tired, both men moved on until they came to the inn where they halted, dismounted, and tied their horses to a tethering post. Old memories flared, lifting Thomas' spirits. He just wanted to see Lira and his child again.

The door was open and the candles in the windows lit, so he ran inside calling their names, but there was no one there. He called their names again with no reply. Then he noticed a parchment stabbed to the bar top with a hunting knife. Striding over to it he pulled the knife clear, lifting the scroll and couldn't believe what he was reading. His heart sank like a stone in water. Dody saw him reading the note and asked what it was. Thomas passed it to him to read. Dody gasped. They stared at each other. It said, "You and your kind slaughtered my father and now it's my turn. Tobin squealed like a pig and cried like a baby when we visited him in the night, and now we have his daughter and grandchild. Give yourselves up to me and they go free. If not, they will die. You have until sunset tomorrow to make your decision!"

The note horrified Thomas and Dody.

And where was Dardo they both wondered? Dody had left him protecting Lira when he set off to find Tobin. Now he had vanished too.

Thomas had a glint in his eye now. "The Bible says there's a time to be born, a time to plant seeds, a time to reap the harvest and even a time to die. Well, Ozhobar was born, planted the seeds of his own destruction and is about to reap the whirlwind, for no man takes what's mine and lives!"

***

Later that evening, at the Dog and Duck, Thomas watched for the coming dawn the whole night long, while Dody slept on a table top. Thomas sat in his usual chair with his back to the wall and kept glancing out of the window, waiting for the sunrise. Every now and again he would stand and prowl around the barroom, kicking objects. He snarled and cursed his displeasure, but nothing disturbed Dody's deep sleep. He was so tired that even if a thunderbolt had struck him, he would have carried on snoring. Again Thomas snorted, cursing as old memories of Ozhan and Ozhobar flared, filling his mind with hate. He stewed and fretted for hours, kicking the bar doors open as the first rays of the sun came into view through the windows.

Dody awoke with a start, his heart hammering in his chest. "What?" he said, shaking his head.

Sunshine climbed the walls, turning them gold. Thomas stood calm, savouring the quiet. Then reality struck him. I might die today. It could also be the last day of my wife and child's life and my two good friends. But I will not be a slave to my fears.

He turned around and walked through the bar, exiting the stairwell door and climbed the steps up to his bedroom. Swinging open the door, he plucked his double sword-belt from the back of a chair, strapping it around his waist. With the panic gone, all that remained was the task. He would stab the baron to death today, or the baron would kill him. To Thomas, it was that simple.

He stood and thought of Master Gallus, his trainer, and of the perils they had faced together over the years. More than once they had been alone and friendless on clandestine shores with the enemy baying at their heels, and more than once they had faced the enemy together and overcome them. This gave him the confidence he needed. Ozhobar was a killer of men and there was a time when Thomas had known how many had died under his blade in official duels, but now he was murdering men, women and children and plundering their farms looking for gold. Ozhobar hacked unarmed farmers down without mercy, leaving their blood staining the fields.

Thomas slammed the bedroom door shut, turned and walked back downstairs, across the stairwell and bar and strode out of the double doors with Dody following him. He paused for a moment, watching a flock of wild geese crossing the sun's face. "By sunset, they'll be hundreds of miles away. Ozhobar will wish he were hundreds of miles away too before the sun sets again!" he said with a scowl. He untied his stallion from the hitching post and climbed into the saddle. Dody mounted his horse too. Then, from out of nowhere, Dardo leapt in front of the horses, barring their way. Startled, they reared up on hind legs and whinnied, eyes rolling. Thomas and Dody stilled them, staring down at their friend. "Where the hell have you been Dardo?" asked Thomas.

"Where have you been? We all thought you were dead!" Dardo countered, clutching a lump the size of a duck's egg on the back of his skull. "Ozhobar knocked me cold with a wooden cudgel!"

Thomas shook his head, his face twisted with anguish. "Talk sense, man! I'll explain what happened to me later!"

"The baron came with his band of cutthroats, and when I tried to stop him from taking Lira and the child, he knocked me senseless with a wooden cudgel and left me for dead! I've only just come back to my senses. I was out cold in the stables," said Dardo, his green eyes holding to the warrior's gaze.

Thomas sat his horse in silence for a moment, and in the sunlight, his face looked young, boyish, but it was still the face of a hardened killer. "Four years ago we faced an evil man who we removed from the world by force. He's back in a different guise and once again the blight needs removing, so are you both with me?"

Of all the swordsmen Dardo and Dody had ever known, Thomas was the best. Both men nodded.

Now the three friends rode their horses down the deserted tree-lined streets of Nottingham, and everywhere they looked there were the signs of the baron's oppressive rule. Burned buildings with huge cracks in the walls stood before them, half a dozen corpses were hanging from the gibbet in Gallows Square, and several more chained in the pillory and stocks awaiting the same gruesome fate, their only crime, stealing a loaf of stale bread or a piece of maggoty meat, rather than starve to death. Neither was nourishing, but it was better than having nothing. Thomas shook his head, scowling at the sight.

All three men wore forest greens with their swords strapped to their waists. Dody also carried his lethal slingshot and several black pebbles in a small pouch strung to his sword belt. It was still his favourite weapon and just as effective as any blade. He had proved it years earlier by dispatching Ozhan to his maker with a single shot to the temple.

For fifteen minutes they crossed dozens of roads, avenues and alleys, lines of shops, stalls and workplaces, passing the formidable-looking lion statues on the Nottingham Bridge, until they hit the Great North Road. Then they angled their journey south towards their destination, Ozhobar's almost impregnable fortress mansion. They passed a trickling stream glinting in the sunlight and several landmarks, including a windmill, and there was a farmer working his horses in a nearby field. Then, after crossing several barren fields, Ozhobar's home came into view.

The three friends halted, sitting their horses, awed by the sight. Their unblinking gaze wandered across the great walls of the mansion and the whole place seemed deserted. Thomas turned his head, staring at the neighbouring checkerboard of meadows and fields, dissected by a meandering river and he noticed the distinct absence of farm workers. An odd haze hung over the whole hillside mostly obscuring their vision, but they could see the lie of the land.

The mansion was a mile distant, swathed in mist and shadows, backed by woods. They squinted against the light of the morning sun and the oak and bronze gate caught Thomas' eye.

"What are you thinking?" asked Dardo.

"Ozhobar has set a trap as did his father."

The answer did nothing to reassure Dardo or Dody. Fear shone in their eyes, but Thomas was as stalwart as ever. Leaning forward he stroked his stallion's head. "Listen to me, I would do nothing I didn't think right and you know that but Ozhobar is the living embodiment of evil. And while he casts his shadow over this land, nothing will grow tall and straight, not man, nor beast, nor crop. So, we must remove the blight with swift precision before it spreads further, and that's what I intend to do with your help."

Both men nodded.

Thomas swung from his saddle.
"I can't guarantee we'll survive the day so if either of you has no stomach for what will happen, leave now while you can and I shall say nothing of it!"

Dardo and Dody looked at Thomas, their flinty eyes raking his lean, unshaven face. They shook their heads. "We understand what you're saying," said Dardo, his voice a whisper.

Dody shook his head. "We don't want to leave. We're with you all the way!"

Thomas smiled weakly, tightening his saddle and bridle and then he remounted. "Let's get on with the job. Today is the day of reckoning."

Dody shivered as memories of Tobin's horrendous murder flared within him. His shattered body floated before his eyes and he could hear the baron's laughter echoing in his mind. Thomas hesitated then shook his reins. Heeling the horse forward, Thomas angled it towards the mansion. Dardo and Dody took off after him into the valley of death.

CHAPTER SIXTEEN

The trap

Ozhobar poured a goblet of wine, draining it in a single swallow. It was his favourite, a good full-bodied red wine from the valleys of the river Rhone in France. He poured another, draining it again, staring out of his library window at the riders heading his way. He glanced at Lira. "Look how the three of them hasten to their deaths!" he said with a hiss. "But who is the third rider?"

Olivia ran to the window, staring out at the long dust cloud. She spotted the leader of the three riders. There was hope in her eyes. "Mommy, it's my daddy! It is my daddy! He's back and coming for us!" She choked back tears of joy.

Lira ran to the window to see what was happening. "Oh, thank God!"

"So, Thomas is alive," snapped Ozhobar. "They're brave men, but fools who should surrender to me."

Lira stared at him, tears of joy in her eyes. "That will never happen! Thomas will come for us and will kill you!"

Ozhobar shook his head. "I have a problem now. You have spirit and nerve, but I must kill you and the child for your insolence." His voice was flat and cold.

Lira looked at Ozhobar with venom in her eyes. "Touch a single hair on my child's head and you will die a terrible, violent death!"

He stared at her for a moment and laughed. "I admire your nerve." Pouring a third goblet of wine, Ozhobar sipped at it, but this time the flavour seemed lost on the thought of facing Thomas in combat. He walked over to the polished metal mirror hung on the window wall and stared at his reflection, studying his eyes. Both of them glowed in different colours, just as his fathers had before him. He stared hard at his own flat, brutal face, crisscrossed with deep scars. He was the absolute image of the man who had sired him. "I will grow old and fat with rich living," he announced, "but Thomas will not. Today is the last day he will wake up with his aches and pains. Today is his last day."

Lira shook her head in defiance. "You're a dull-witted, vain man, Ozhobar, and I wouldn't count on that! Thomas is a very resourceful and resilient man!"

Ozhobar shrugged. "I've baited and set the trap. Thomas rides to his death, as do his friends!"

"Thomas isn't stupid. He's a seasoned swordsman with a sharp mind and the reflexes of a cat," she countered.

"Daddy's swords are sharp and he will stick them in you," added Olivia, pantomiming the movement.

"We'll see," said the baron switching his gaze back to the oncoming riders, "but for now it's back to the dungeons where you both belong." Ozhobar clapped his hands and two men appeared in the doorway.

"Yes, master?" said one.

"Take them back to the catacombs."

"Yes, my Lord!" said the other, placing a hand on Lira's shoulder.

Lira shrugged his hand away. "Get off, you great lout."

"Then please follow us," said the man with a stern stare. Lira didn't reply but did as he bid.

The guards led Lira and Olivia away. Ozhobar stood at his high balcony window watching the three riders getting closer and closer. Then his gaze switched to his own horse guards coming up over the crest of a rise in pursuit, and at first, he felt an overpowering sense of relief as his men rounded on Thomas and friends, cutting them off, but his men fell like flies, hacked from their saddles by Thomas' and Dardo's flashing blades and Dody's lethal slingshot. Twenty men fell beneath the warriors' horses' hooves and didn't rise again.

Heat flared inside the baron's head with the onset of terrible fear, watching as Thomas' horse stumbled but righted itself and carried on at the gallop towards the gate of oak and bronze. Thomas heeled his horse harder, faster, lashing the reins from side to side and the stallion's muscles bunched as it surged forward with tremendous power and even greater speed.

More enemy riders cut across the three friends' line of sight, charging at them, and again they hacked them to pieces as they galloped on, outpacing the rest of their pursuers. At the top of a second ridge, Thomas pulled hard on his reins and came to a sudden halt, looking back at the hillside littered with dead bodies and awash with blood. Terrified horses stumbled around the killing fields, whinnying, snorting and tossing their heads.

Thomas turned back around to see the gate swing open and another dozen guards scramble out into a gully, covered in thick chain mail with only their eyes showing. Each had a bow, axe, or blade. A fat warrior was leading the men.

Thomas wondered how to combat the men. Dody answered his quandary when he darted forward from behind Thomas and let fly with his sling, the stone hitting one guard high on the temple, staggering him. The man dropped to his knees and slumped to the floor in an unconscious state. Dody reloaded, methodical in his every action. Then he let fly, again and again, picking off the guards, one by one, until there was only the fat one standing. He turned and tried to run, tripping over his own feet and he fell hitting his head hard, knocking him unconscious too.

Ozhobar saw events unfold and more heat flared inside his head. Fear gripped him. He wondered what to do? Then he fled for the sanctuary of the dungeons in the lower catacombs as Thomas and friends fought their way through anyone that barred their way.

When he reached the dungeons, the gate that stood before him was heavy and he couldn't move it at all. I'll be a lot safer if I can get inside, he thought, wondering how to escape Thomas' wrath. Most who knew him assumed he was fearless, and he had been. In past years the ringmaster had paid him well for his fighting skills in the dungeons against the other warriors, but he now knew Thomas Flynn was even more skilful and deadly.

Outside, the three friends had breached the gate and were scrambling their way through the courtyard to the stables, when another group of twenty men armed with pikes, swords and cudgels rounded on them. Thomas and friends cut their way through each one of them and made their way up the spiral stone staircase leading to Ozhobar's chambers, where Dody's booted foot kicked in the door.

They rushed inside but the room was empty. They ran along hallway after hallway, throwing open every door or kicking them in, until there were no more unopened. Thomas left his two friends searching the upper levels while he went below into the catacombs to search for Lira and Olivia.

Meanwhile, in the dungeons, the baron had found a wooden crossbow with a slim stock and wings of iron, beside a quiver of stiffened buckskin containing thirty short black quarrels. Ozhobar sat in the cloistered shadows waiting, eyes narrowed. He didn't have to wait long. Thomas appeared at the top of the staircase. Outside the wind whipped up and screamed through the catacomb walls, making an eerie whine that seemed to fill the air and a sulphurous odour mixed with coal oil fumes created an awful sickly smell.

Ozhobar loaded the crossbow, waiting as Thomas moved down the staircase with great energy, switching his gaze from side to side. Ozhobar waited until Thomas reached the last step. Then he fired, and the crossbow sang, the bolt hissing through the air, slamming into Thomas' left shoulder. He gave out an animalistic scream as the pain filled his mind.

"If you want to kill me, you'll find it no easy task!" shouted Ozhobar.

Thomas swayed, feeling faint and almost fell, but he stayed upright. Blood flowed inside his tunic, staining it crimson and movement was agony, but he scrambled forward into the shadows as another quarrel flashed past his head with a loud hiss. Pulling the first quarrel from his shoulder, he dropped it to the floor just as the sound of pounding boots came from the top of the stairs. He swore, stumbling further back into the shadows, and only the shimmering glow of the wall lanterns upon his sword blades offered any light.

The catacombs went off in many directions and he could have made a run for it, but he waited, watching the flickering shadows as four of the baron's men descended the stairs with swords drawn.

The first man to reach the bottom step peered around, noticing the glint of polished steel within the shadows and he lunged at Thomas, whose sword swept across his neck slicing through it. Blood sprayed, flecking his face. The second guard swayed away from a slashing cut to his belly, but Thomas reversed the move with his other sword, slamming the blade deep into the man's chest, right up to the hilt. The man groaned, falling to the floor. Thomas pulled his blade clear using his booted foot for leverage as the third guard rounded on him with a blood-curdling scream, his sword held high. Another crossbow bolt hissed past Thomas' head. He hurled himself forward in great pain, his wounded shoulder seeping blood, Thomas sliced through the skull of the guard and swung around to face the last man standing, who stumbled on the bottom step, dropping his sword.

Thomas leapt upon him, using one sword like a dagger, and he drove it down through the man's shoulder into his heart and lungs. Withdrawing the sword he staggered under the sheer weight of the man as he fell to the floor dead, and he stumbled; then hauled himself upright as another crossbow bolt hissed past his head. He swayed away from it. "A pox upon you Ozhobar! I'm not ready to die just yet!" he called out in agony. "I'll spare your life if you let my wife and child go free and leave Nottingham forever!"

The baron laughed, his voice echoing down the tunnels. "When are you going to get it into your thick skull I'm in control? I've got a crossbow. Come on, come and die!"

Of the several tunnels in front of him, Thomas couldn't tell which one the baron was in because of the echoes. He blinked the sweat from his eyes, gazing down at his blood-drenched shoulder. There was no feeling in it now and his vision was swimming. "Where are you, you ugly bastard?" he shouted. "I will kill you if you don't do as I ask. Set my family free now and I'll let you live!"

Ozhobar ignored Thomas, who took three steps backwards with impossible speed as the crossbow sang again and another bolt hissed past him. Then, he was just about to rush forward into the middle tunnel when the sounds of fighting on the upper levels died away, replaced by the sound of pounding boots coming from somewhere overhead. "Oh, no, not more guards," he said, spinning on his heel, only to see Dardo and Dody at the top of the staircase. Lira and Olivia were with them, safe and unharmed. He breathed a sigh of relief. "Thank God," he whispered, trembling. "Don't come down here!" he shouted; his voice deep and resonant as it echoed through the great halls of the catacombs. "I will end this pathetic game by showing Ozhobar the entrance to *Hell*!"

Lira climbed down the staircase. "Thomas, let's get out of here!"

Dardo grabbed Lira by the arm. "It's too late for that. He has to finish it. Now it's personal!"

"I'm coming to kill you, Ozhobar!" Thomas shouted, his voice echoing through the tunnels.

"Please let's get out of here! Please, Thomas!" Lira begged.

Olivia ran down the few steps to her mother, taking her by the hand. She gazed up into her eyes. "Daddy knows what he's doing. The bad man must die before he hurts anyone else."

Lira squeezed Olivia's hand. "I know, darling. I just wish it weren't so."

With a great effort, Thomas staggered forward, his mind empty of all emotion save one – the burning wish to wreak revenge upon his enemy. His forest greens were filthy and blood covered, his dark hair greasy, his face pale and worn, but his resolve didn't waver.

The baron in his arrogance didn't believe his enemy would get so close. Yet such was the power of the hatred that pricked Thomas' soul he wanted to kill Ozhobar and his men.

Black bolts flashed in the air around Thomas. He scrambled forward, panic welling up within him. He saw a bolt flying towards him and hurled his body out of the line of fire as it flashed past him, plunging into the wall by his side.

Ahead of Thomas now was a wide entrance in the catacombs. He knelt, trying to save his strength. Then he hauled himself upright, took a deep breath and began to walk the whole length of the cavernous structure, keeping to the darkness of the shadows. One hundred paces he took to arrive at a huge iron gate barring his way. But Ozhobar hadn't locked it. Now he could hear the high-pitched screams of many men shouting for freedom. And the further inside the catacombs he went, the more the temperature plummeted with ice forming intricate patterns on the walls, bright and white against the freezing rock.

The wailing of human suffering filled the air, and he could sense the pulsing of his own blood like ice through his veins as the tunnels echoed to the dying screams of tortured men. A crossbow bolt struck his left leg just above the knee, and a high-pitched scream tore from his throat. Intense pain filled his body and mind. The bolt hit with such force it staggered him, spinning him from his feet and he dropped his swords.

"Do you feel mortal, Thomas?" came a taunting voice from the darkness of shadows. More of Ozhobar's mad laughter echoed down the tunnel.

Blood seeped from the second wound, staining his leggings as he lay in a crumpled heap on the floor. Thomas pulled the bolt from his leg, screaming, "No. Never!"

Ozhobar threw the crossbow from the shadows to the floor and it landed in front of Thomas, who was at peace with himself, despite his injuries. Stepping out into the dim light, the baron drew his sword. "It's over and time to die!" he said with madness in his eyes. Ozhobar raised his sword above his head and paused, savouring the moment.

Thomas had other ideas flaring in his mind and reached inside his boot, drawing the hidden dagger from its scabbard. Without a moment's hesitation, he pushed himself forward; stabbing the baron deep in the belly several times and then he left the blade there.

Ozhobar pitched backwards without a sound, looking at the blade embedded in his stomach, and a terrible pain exploded in his body. His face was a picture of disbelief and he dropped the sword. His eyes met Thomas' steely gaze. He looked darkly exultant. Ozhobar's knees buckled and a gurgling groan burst from his lips as he slumped to the floor dead.

"Now it's over, and provided your father has no more successors, so is my long history of violence," whispered Thomas, hauling himself upright. He and his companions spent the next hour freeing every prisoner in the dungeons, and every one of them took Thomas' hand and kissed it, blessing his courageous soul.

When Thomas awoke the next morning, the sun was up and the shutters on the bedroom windows open. White linen curtains fluttered in the breeze and it was a beautiful bright day outside with a clear blue sky. He eased his torn, bandaged body out of the pallet bed wearing only his undergarments. Thomas limped across the room, gazed out over the Nottinghamshire landscape and for the first time, everything was peaceful. Will it stay that way, he wondered? He could only hope.

CHAPTER SEVENTEEN

Awful visions

<u>1231 A.D. THE ONSET OF SUMMER</u>

Nottinghamshire's beautiful countryside shimmered in a peaceful haze, bathed in golden light from the high warm sun. Henry III was the ruler of England, spending money building palaces and castles, besides rebuilding Westminster Abbey, and he chose French friends and advisers over his English ones. This annoyed the barons because Simon de Montfort, the king's French brother-in-law led them

Two hundred years earlier, Norman invaders introduced new customs and language, the feudal system, and conquered Saxon England. There were years of violent civil war that saw Magna Carta signed and the birth of Parliament, besides the wars with Scotland and Wales. But, for now, there was peace, even though England was full of castles filled with devils and evil men.

Nottingham Castle was the centre of local power, a law court and a government office where the barons kept official records of villagers who had paid their taxes and fines, and those who had not. It was also the local prison.

All castles had a chapel for prayer, a kitchen for food and drink and a brewery for making beer under the great hall or in the bailey, and within the great hall barons held court, judged land disputes and sentenced criminals. The prison was the Keep and guards stored weapons and armour there. In 1231, Nottingham Castle was no exception, but it held one special prisoner too.

Nottingham Castle stood on the hillside overlooking undulating sweeps of meadowland, with its ancient gates facing down the long Nottingham Road. It stood out on the countryside like a blood-red jewel with its sandstone walls covered in different shades of ivy, which had taken on a fiery hue since the autumn. In its damp dungeons lay Thomas Flynn. His crime was not paying taxes and his imprisonment was driving him mad. He was having insane visions and dreams of horrific murders, with women as the victims. Now he had a visitor who neither knew about visions nor understood his predicament

Father Abbot blinked solemnly at Thomas lying motionless on his iron bed, and his stern expression softened.

"Oh, my son," he said, "what has befallen you? Once you were like a priceless treasure to Nottingham, and now you're like a candle without a flame." Shaking his old grey head, not knowing what to say to comfort Thomas, he stooped, helping him to his feet. Thomas stood, shuffling on the cold stone floor.

The Abbot put his arm around his shoulders, sensing his anxieties, and he smiled at his friend. "We must talk my son. Walk with me and we'll try to sort out your problems."

The two friends made their way at a sedate pace along the length of the dungeon, one clad in the brown habit of the Order and the other garbed in his black and gold tunic, black leggings and boots, and they conversed at length in hushed tones.

"Father Abbot, I have visions and I know not what they mean," said Thomas, his eyes dark and haunted, his skin sallow and chin covered in black stubble. And even as he spoke, a curious Robin perched in an old oak tree outside the window swooped down through the rusted iron bars and landed on his shoulder, pecking at his ear as if it were telling him something. It whistled a merry tune, strolling over his shoulder. It flew back through the bars into the branches whence it came.

The Abbot smiled, studying his friend's worn face. "Maybe the bird can enlighten us both?"

Thomas sighed as they entered the central part of the dungeon where the rack lay silent and unused. "Oh, Father, if only I could make sense of my visions and dreams, but I can't and I'm going mad."

It was cold inside the dungeons, even though sunlight flooded in slanting shafts from the high-arched windows and dust swirled, dancing in the air as the two friends trod the ancient floor.

The Abbot halted in front of a carving hung on the wall. It was a chronicle of Nottingham's early history. He turned to Thomas, sat down on the floor and rested his back against the wall. "What do you see in your visions and dreams, my son?"

Thomas sat down beside him. "A masked man stalking women, but they're more than visions, hallucinations or whatever you want to call them. It's as if I'm seeing through another man's eyes, watching him kill. I think I'm linked to a mass murderer."

Shocked, the Abbot frowned, shook his head and asked a question, the answer to which he was sure he already knew. "How many murders have you seen these past six months?" he asked in a small voice, his gaze stern.

Thomas seemed in a trance. "Six."

The Abbot looked even more shocked. There had been six murder victims, to his knowledge, in the past six months, all women of varying ages, all raped, stabbed and their throats slit. The youngest was seventeen years old and the oldest thirty.

"I'm here to secure your release from this hell-hole, my son. We've paid your taxes with the Abbey funds," said the Abbot, smiling kindly. "You've done much for Nottingham and should not be in prison. Come with me to the Abbey for a rest before you go home and we can converse at length about what you saw in your visions."

The Abbot rolled to his knees, hauling himself upright, holding out his hand to Thomas. He helped him to his feet. Straightening his habit he placed his hands inside the baggy folds of his sleeves, looking out of the iron-grilled window at the cloudless sky. The Abbot blinked, swinging his gaze around to Thomas. "Come, my son," he said in a whisper. "It's time to leave this dreadful place."

Father Abbot led him toward a rusted iron door that squeaked as he opened it, and a guard to his left nodded as they passed through and climbed a flight of spiral stone steps leading to the Great Hall. Abbot Alfred stopped at the top and turned, waiting for his friend to climb the last few steps and he studied the man. The fire that had once raged within Thomas was no longer there and the heroic looking figure with the fearless smile was now a malnourished, ill man.

The Abbot hooked an arm around Thomas' shoulders and they walked the length of the Great Hall together in silence, to where another guard opened an oak door leading into a courtyard and an awaiting horse and cart stationed at a hitching post. From the walls of the castle, several guards jeered Thomas, mocking him. "Look at the great swordsman. Not so tough now is he?" The guards booed and spat on Thomas as they raised the portcullis to its highest point and lowered the drawbridge to its lowest.

Thomas felt the worst he ever had in his life. If he could have crawled under a stone to hide he would have, but he climbed on board the cart and Father Abbot unhitched the horse from the post.

All eyes stared at Thomas. The Abbot climbed on board too, shaking the reins, signalling for the carthorse to make haste. But it took off at a snail's pace, passing under the arches of the thick defensive walls of the Barbican, out under the portcullis with its hooves clip-clopping and the wheels rattling over the drawbridge. And as they came out into the sunlight with heads bowed, town folk greeted them with cheers led by Thomas' wife, Lira.

The Abbot smiled in silent wonder as Lira climbed on board, flinging her arms around Thomas, kissing him as the cart rolled along the road to an even louder hail of cheers.

***

That night, thunder rumbled overhead and rain poured down as a mysterious masked man peered out of the shadows at a lonely young woman making her way home. He rubbed the scar on his left forearm and drew a dagger from his belt, waiting for her to get closer, but at the last moment, she turned a corner and disappeared back into the night. The man cursed.

Then the sound of hooves roused him and in the narrow alleyway, he couldn't tell the direction the sound was coming from as it filled the air, gathering momentum. He slunk back into the shadows as the ground trembled with a rumbling noise, the shiny glint from his razor-sharp dagger the only telltale sign he was there.

The thunder of hooves passed by and faded, replaced by a song that echoed softly through the dark ally. It came from a tall, slim young woman that stepped out of the shadows and approached, and as she came closer, singing, the masked man recognised her as the cook from the Hen and Chicken. When she was within range, the man pitched forward without a sound, dragging her into the shadows, out of sight, and then he raped her, slit her throat and left the woman where she lay.

***

At the Abbey, Thomas, taken by fever, was curled up into a quivering ball, rambling on about another murder. Father Abbot and Lira did their best to calm him, but couldn't. "I saw a murder," Thomas said with a snarl. "And I believe it. I'm not mad. I am not mad!"

Laying there on the bed he was in such a state that he looked devil possessed, so Lira sedated him with the powerful drug, Henbane, and he fell into a deep sleep. But, even as he slept he rambled on about the murders, even down to the clothes the killer and victims were wearing and the triangular scar on killer's left forearm. The Abbot stared at Thomas and began chanting mystical words, placing his hands over him and Thomas calmed and stilled. Now he looked as peaceful as a newborn baby, curled in the foetal position, so the Abbot led Lira to the Great Hall to talk, leaving him sleeping where he lay.

"Has Thomas gone mad, Father Abbot?" she asked as they walked.

The Abbot shook his head and stared out of a window at the sky. He thought for a moment. "I think not, my child. Tobias' visions are all too real! There is a killer of women out there on the loose somewhere, and your husband has a mental link with him, of that I'm sure."

"How can that be, Father?"

"The Lord works in mysterious ways my child and I cannot fathom those ways. Thomas sees his gift as a curse, but I see it as a gift because he may be the one to catch the killer."

The Abbot's words shocked Lira but reassured her that Thomas wasn't mad. "He'll be well soon won't he Father?" she said.

"My child, whatever happens, is God's will, but I'm sure he'll be fine when he's rested and well enough to travel home."

***

That night Lira sat by Thomas' bed keeping vigil over him and he whimpered and moaned in his sleep, his haunted eyes flickering open now and again, gazing around the room. Then he would sigh and ask where he was and she would tell him he was with her at the Abbey under the watchful eye of the Abbot. She stroked his forehead, holding a bowl of water to his cracked, dry lips and he would drink and be still again for another short period and then twitch, scream and whimper, finding himself trapped at the centre of another hellish vision.

Thomas watched a young woman from the shadows.

He stalked her.

Pitching forward he grabbed her, one hand tightening around her neck.

A dagger glinted in the dim light.

He raped her and slit her throat.

Then everything faded to black.

And even as Thomas slept his face contorted into a mask of horror because he had seen another brutal murder.

***

A new day dawned in a haze of soft sunlight and crept over the countryside, bursting forth, as each spider's web became a glittering necklace and each dewdrop a sparkling jewel. Birdsong rang in the air, yet nature's extraordinary extravaganza seemed lost upon the swordsman Thomas Flynn. He was still fast asleep.

Lira had woken early and was helping Friar Hugo prepare the breakfasts for the inhabitants of the Abbey. It was a simple meal of honey cornbread, apple and carrot, but at dinnertime, they would serve salmon, baked to perfection, garnished with cream cheese, cabbage and cauliflower, washed down with their own brew of aged best mead. The Abbots favourite tipple.

Breakfast and dinner came and there was a clattering of chairs in the Great Hall, but nothing woke Thomas, not even the tolling of the Abbey bell. And so, he slept on through the night and into the middle of the next day, before his eyes sprang open and he beamed like the sun on a midsummer morning, greeted by a chorus of ooh's and ah's from several Friars tending his every need. They had shaved him, cut his hair and braided it, bed bathed him and covered his body in oil awaiting his awakening, and now he was stirring. He brushed the Friars aside, stretching and yawning and ran his tongue over his teeth, screwing up his face. "Ugh, my mouth tastes like a dung heap. How long have I been here?"

Several days, my son," said Friar Mortimer. "We thought you would never wake."

Outside the warm sun shone down, but there was grim news of another murder from a young boy runner who had arrived breathless at the Abbey gates, carrying the message. The Friars rebuilding the stone walls were digesting the report as he informed them that someone had found a young woman's body in the middle of a field, on the back of a hay cart. Would they come with him, the boy asked, and help because there was a baby trapped under the cart, crying. The terrible news soon reached Thomas' ears, and he dressed and set off with the Friars as time was of the essence for the baby's sake.

Once again, a dark shadow is casting itself over the whole of Nottingham Thomas told the Friars as they marched over the hillside to the field where the boy had made his grizzly find.

On reaching the field and finding the cart, the scene that greeted their eyes horrified them, and the sight that met one Friar's eyes sickened him so much that he couldn't keep his breakfast in his stomach. The murderer had stripped the girl, raped her and bludgeoned her beyond recognition.

Blood was everywhere, in the cart, on the hay, staining the grass and even in a pool of water yards away. The young woman put up a hell of a struggle, Thomas thought, and then a baby's cries from somewhere beneath the cart startled them all. And the cries were so shrill and sobering that it brought Thomas back from his thoughts and he swung into action, scrambling under the cart. Then he gasped with shock. The baby was only days old.

Picking the child up he cradled it and began to cry, something he had not done since he was a child, and somewhere deep inside he screamed. There was bleakness in his eyes. They sank deeper into his skull. He gazed in despair at the child, not knowing what to do, feeling so bad inside it was as if an unknown force was pulling him through a keyhole and stretching him thin.

Everyone loves their mother, but now this poor wretched child doesn't have one, Thomas thought, sobbing against the baby's shoulder. He cursed God for taking the mother away with such savagery, and the murder reminded him of his own mother's death at the hands of his father.

Now the boy child looked peaceful, his face relaxed. Thomas cuddled him and rolled to his knees, climbing out from under the cart, handing the baby to Friar Hugo, who looked astonished by the size of the tiny child who was not much bigger than his hand. "Why does God allow this to happen?" Hugo asked, questioning his own faith.

Father Abbot shook his head. "Ours is not to reason such things, my son."

Lira came running across the field and spotted the young woman's torn body. She screamed. Her eyes were dark, haunted, and despair washed the colour from her face. Turning, she stared at Thomas with a look of horror and burst into tears. "I knew the girl," she said, a tremor in her voice.

Thomas wrapped his arms around her, cuddling her, looking so sad. He didn't utter a word. Words wouldn't make things better. Worse was the fact he seemed powerless to stop what was happening, even though he had a psychic link with the killer.

***

Days later, after the young woman's funeral, Thomas sat playing with Olivia in the sandbox in their backyard at the Dog and Duck. He filled pails with a small shovel, making her a castle with turrets and windows, a drawbridge and moat while the Sheriff of Nottingham told a gathering crowd outside the yard that the murder victims were women and were all raped. Thomas' friend Dody listened to the Sheriff rant and remembered rumours of a spate of similar murders in London several years earlier. He told Dardo it might be the same murderer. But his friend scoffed at the idea because there had been a ten-year gap. "No killer would wait that long, particularly if he was a crazy man like this one."

"He would if he'd been in incarcerated or at sea for a long time," argued Dody.

***

That evening, just before sunset, a campfire burned low in a cave and a tall man with a mop of dark, curly hair and dark eyes shivered, pushing the hurtful memories of his horrific childhood from his mind. I hate all women just like I hated my whore mother, and I'll kill and keep on killing until someone stops me, he thought. And in that instant, he had a surge of pure hatred and anger. Then he laughed like a maniac, and it echoed throughout the halls of the cavern, dying away like the low rumble of an approaching storm. The man came to his feet.
His experience with the woman in the hay cart and the baby screaming and crying under the cart filtered into his brain and he couldn't shake it loose.

The killer had been a handsome man once, but as a young boy, his mother called him ugly, drumming it into his brain from a very early age, and the only thing that stopped her from saying it was when he slit her throat. Now with the onset of mental illness and self-harm, he was ugly, a bizarre caricature of a man, his face crisscrossed with deep scars.

    The murderer walked to the cave entrance, staring out at the river cutting through meadows and fields. Miles distant, Nottingham Castle, swathed in mist and shadows, seemed a dark forbidding citadel, appearing ghostlike within the swirling haze. He squinted against the light of the setting sun. Now he remembered those long days and nights of torture on the rack, the floggings and the threat of being hanged in that same Castle. He began to cry and dropped to the floor, curling into a quivering ball, huddled against the cold stone wall. "I'm a human being for God's sake, so why has no one ever loved me or treated me like one?" he said. Yet something inhuman shone in his eyes.

CHAPTER EIGHTEEN

A curse or a godsend

Thomas Flynn was also a troubled man, angry inside and unable to rise above it. He walked along a corridor in the Abbey to where it branched and he turned left, humming as he passed each closed door. Then a voice boomed out behind him and he jumped. "Well then, here you are, wandering, so are you looking for me, my son?" said the Abbot.

Thomas turned to see his friend dressed in his familiar brown habit and he smiled, his mind racing. "Can we talk again, Father?"

The Abbot nodded, his shaggy brows lifting. "Yes. Would you mind if we walk while we carry on our conversation, my son?"

"Not at all," said Thomas fighting his emotions to stay calm. Taking a deep breath, he shook his head but could still hear the priest's words at the young woman's funeral in his mind and visualise her torn body. It haunted him. He threw the Abbot a glance as they rambled through the corridors of the Abbey and out into the grey daylight. It was drizzling. Both men were distant and solitary.

"Do you think everyone should love their mother?" asked Thomas.

The Abbot stared at him with a queer expression on his face. "Why do you ask this question, my son?"

"Because the man who climbs inside my head didn't love his."

"I dare say there will be mothers you can't love and fathers, but they don't want you to love them."

Thomas nodded, memories of his own parent's abuse flaring in his mind. "That's so true, and the murderer tries to distract himself from his traumatic memories with silence, but most of all with the company of the dead."

"Then life has been unkind to him, holding many cruel surprises. Sometimes we stumble around in the broken pieces of our lives, wondering why we even exist. But it is Gods will, my son."

Thomas shook his head. "I don't understand why a good God would let terrible things happen?"

"Because God gives us free will and choices, but we're no better than animals. I'm sure the Lord sits somewhere, sad-faced and disappointed by our behaviour, gibbering on in a language that only he understands."

"You talk in riddles, Father, or am I mad? Is this mind linking with a killer a curse or a Godsend that might help me catch him?"

"Only God knows that, my son."

Even as the Abbot spoke pain shot through Thomas' temples and he felt sick. He fell to his knees, his head in his hands.

The Abbot looked shocked. "What's wrong?"

Thomas had a hollow look of terror shadowing his eyes, making them darker. He rocked his head. "Get out of my mind and leave me alone!"

The Abbot realised Thomas was having another vision and watched him shaking his head as if he were trying to rip it off to relieve the pain.

Laughter drifted into Thomas' mind. "Ah, what a tangled web," mocked a voice. "You have no sense of humour man. Do you not find it ironic that I can see and sense what you can, just like you know what I'm doing at this precise moment?"

"Get out of my head, you murdering son-of-a…" Thomas shouted, stopping short of finishing his sentence.

The Abbot took him by the shoulders and shook him. "Come back to me, my son!"

Thomas closed his eyes, opening an inner pathway, falling back into himself. The move was sudden and unexpected, but worked, and the dreadful mocking voice faded away with the words, "bastard, you can't get rid of me that easy. I'll be back!" The murderer's voice had much anger in it and reminded him of his own brother.

Thomas opened his eyes and climbed to his unsteady feet, haunted by his visions. The murderer stepped through rusty gates and a horrible howl rang through the darkness. He carried a bloodied head, talking to it as he cut off the ears, nose and gouged out the eyes with a sharp knife. He fed them to a ghostly-looking hound that raised its head howling as a blood moon shone between the clouds, lighting a ruined manor house. Thomas sensed the people who once lived there had fled years ago, running from the killer, fearing for their lives.

Later that night, Thomas stood on the Abbey wall sniffing the breeze, listening to the sounds of the forest. The evening remained calm and still but he stayed alert, praying that it would pass without consequences for once. And on reflection, he saw the wisdom of the Abbot's words about man's free will and the choice to do good or evil.

And so, long after Thomas had retired for the night, he sat up thinking, but before he fell asleep a thousand mad ideas pounded through his brain on how to catch the killer, each wilder than the last, but he was sure the mind-link was the answer to the problem if he could control it.

***

The next morning dawned in a haze of soft sunlight and crept across the Nottinghamshire countryside. Birdsong filled the air and once again Thomas stood upon the walls of the Abbey peering out across the fields and Meadowlands on a beautiful day.

In the distance through the shimmering heat haze, two riders approached, followed by a long column of dust. Thomas squinted against the light of the sun to recognise the riders' faces. It was Dardo and Piccolo in a mile-eating gallop, heading his way. Thomas waved, and they waved back with an air of urgency. Then they turned, leaving the Old Nottingham Road, taking a shortcut across the fields, the horses' manes streaming out. And having jumped the narrow river, they soared across a large dry ditch and came to a shuddering halt at the gatehouse door. Both horses whinnied, bucking on the verge of exhaustion, their coats lathered in sweat. Thomas stared at his friends. "You rode like the winds to get here, what burden do you bear?"

"A crowd has gathered in Gallows Square, and they're planning to hang three men they believe responsible for the recent murders," said Dardo.

Thomas stared at his friends, the grim news digested in silence.

"They're innocent," said Piccolo. "We know the men; they're half-wits and not guilty of any crime. The angry mob just wants retribution. We've got to do something!"

Thomas' dead father's face floated before him as he considered his friend's remarks. He nodded. "Yes, hanging is a bad way to go if you're innocent. There was a gleam in his eyes. He looked like the fearless swordsman he once was. Turning, he disappeared from the wall. Moments later, there was a loud creak as the Abbot opened the gates and there sat Thomas astride his white stallion. Next moment, the three men thundered along the Old Nottingham Road together.

***

In Gallows Square, Mace, the ringleader of the angry mob scanned their faces. They stared with a look of hatred, fuelled by the wish to kill, and they didn't care whether the three men had committed a crime.

"Hang them!" the crowd chanted in unison as they dragged the men kicking and screaming towards the scaffold steps. And as each man reached them and began to struggle, Mace stepped forward, smiting them hard on the back of their head with an iron bar. Then, one by one, the mob hauled the men up the ten steps and tied their hands behind their backs. The hangman looped a noose over their heads and tightened it around their necks. The terrified men sobbed, whimpered and urinated in their patchwork leggings as they awaited their fate.

"Have you any last words, you sons-of-bitches?" asked the hooded executioner as he grabbed the gibbet release mechanism lever, tightening his grip.

"We didn't do it! We didn't kill anyone!" sobbed one man.

"Please believe us! We murdered no one!" sobbed another.

The third man trembled on the verge of collapsing. "We're innocent! For God's sake don't hang us!"

The hangman tightened his grip on the lever a little more, smiling at the men. "I don't give an owl's hoot whether you did or didn't commit the crime, because I will hang you anyway," he whispered with a sneer. He spat in one man's face and laughed. The mob cheered and yelled. "Hang the lot of them!"

The hangman put his weight on the lever and the three men felt the bolts beneath the trap door loosen. Again they sobbed and whimpered as the whole gibbet shuddered. He added more weight to the lever and laughed, enjoying himself.

The thunder of hooves roused the mob and the hangman's hand froze on the lever. The crowd gasped with shock as three stallions galloped towards them, the riders spurring them on, digging their heels into the horses' flanks. Moments later, they came to a halt beside the scaffold steps and Thomas stared hard at Mace. Thomas' horse bucked, rearing high into the air. "Release the men, Mace, they're innocent of any crime," he said, dismounting.

"What are you talking about we have signed confessions?" countered Mace.

Thomas nodded and snarled. "I'm sure you have and I can see how you got the confessions, by the bruising on the men's faces. Let them go home to their wives and children. You've had your fun!"

"God's teeth, man, they're guilty as hell and this mob wants blood," Mace snapped back.

Dardo and Piccolo sat their horses in silence. The crowd wanted blood, and it didn't seem to matter whose it was.

There was a glint in Thomas' eyes. "I see you for what you are Mace! You were Ozhan's lackey and now you're his son's. Well, Nottingham is our home and we'll defend it against cutthroats like you! You may have the face of a demon, but I have the speed and power of one!"

Mace was a giant of a man with huge muscled arms and a barrel-chest who could crush most men's bones by grabbing them, and Thomas had grated on his nerves for a long, long time. He laughed. "By God man, you think a lot of yourself."

Thomas' eyes were fever-bright as he considered the comment. "And you are a mindless aberration of nature without a conscience, living only to inflict pain upon the weak and innocent. But remember this, you ugly son of a bitch. I'll always be here to protect them."

For a heartbeat, Mace stood stock-still, and then he yanked the lever and the three men fell through the trapdoor of the gibbet, kicking and screaming. "Then let me see you protect this trio before they fade away," he shouted.

Thomas lapsed into silence, staring into Mace's glittering eyes. Then he drew his hunting knife from his boot, throwing it without conscious thought. "Rot in hell you miserable bastard," he snapped, drawing his swords as he vaulted up the scaffold steps.

The knife missed Mace and slammed into the upright of the scaffold by his head. Mace drew his sword and stormed forward. Thomas leaned to the right, his left foot slamming into the giant man's stomach, hurling him from his feet and he slumped to the gibbet howling in pain.

Dardo and Piccolo sat their horses, mesmerised by their friend's speed.

Mace climbed to his feet, slicing the air. "You're a scum-sucking bastard and I will kill you!"

Thomas spun on the spot with both of his blades slicing through the hangman's ropes, cutting the men free. They fell screaming into the shadows beneath the scaffold steps. "Not if I kill you first!"

Mace attacked again, his sword slashing towards Thomas' head. Two short swords flashed up to parry the stroke. But Mace was ready for the move and spun to his right, slamming a fist into Thomas' face. He staggered back, vision blurring. Then Mace aimed a slashing cut at Thomas' head again but Thomas surged upright, his left-hand blade snaking out pricking Mace's stomach, tearing skin and muscle. Mace reeled back in shock. "You better kill me, because I swear I will kill you!"

Thomas grinned. "You're not that good."

Mace launched himself forward and before Thomas could respond a blade slashed down almost decapitating him, missing him by a whisker.

It was then that Piccolo let fly with his sling, striking Mace high on the head, staggering him. He fell from the scaffold in an unconscious state and the mob began to disperse.

Thomas breathed a sigh of relief. "There was a time I fancied his chances."

"You've been in prison for a whole year and your inactivity has slowed you, my friend," said Dardo.

Thomas nodded. "That's true. I must brush up my skills."

Piccolo smiled. "Dardo has been brushing up on his English language."

Thomas laughed. "I'm glad to hear that, his grammar was appalling. The last time he wrote me a letter he doubled a negative, split an infinitive and left out the commas."

Dardo laughed too. "Well, now I can prattle on with perfect punctuation."

The three friends tied Mace up and bundled him into the back of a cart, leaving him there, then the heavens opened, making the mob disperse quicker. It poured with rain and thunder rumbled overhead. Moments later, they huddled under the scaffold tending to the three wretched men Mace tried to hang.

***

At the Dog and Duck the next morning, Thomas awoke early in the faint light of dawn. Rolling to his feet from his bed he left Lira and the children fast asleep and dressed, swinging his sword-belt around his waist, and as the sun rose in the west, the temperature soared. It was a hot day and one never to forget.

For a year, life was unkind. Thomas endured much pain and suffering in prison, and sometimes even the thought of death had a somewhat sweetness to it he could almost taste. Yet his warrior's spirit and stiff resolve brought him back from the brink of madness and was healing his mental scars even though his future remained uncertain. But Master Gallus had raised him on stories of heroes and chivalry, and no hero would ever give up on his cause, no matter what.

Thomas had woken cold and shivering, the murderer's insane laughter drifting into his mind. "I know every move you make," the voice had mocked.

Thomas shrugged at the disembodied voice. "And I know yours and will avenge the dead because I'm a swordsman and not a killer of women." He looked into the flickering flames of his fire, trying to visualise the murderer. But he never saw the murderer's face in dreams or visions because the killer avoided mirrors and windows, which might cast his reflection. And with such sombre thoughts in his mind, he found it difficult to sleep at night and it showed in his face.

Thomas sighed, letting his thoughts drift. "You exist and I'm not insane, although I sometimes wish I were. But one day soon I'll recognise you and then we'll lock you away or hang you for your heinous crimes." There was no reply, only mocking laughter in his mind.

***

Lira woke and with the dawn came pangs of hunger, so she spent an hour in the kitchen preparing dinner for the family, including Dardo and Piccolo, and later at the dining table, she dished out steamed fish with cauliflower, smothered in cheese sauce as the loud voice of the Abbey bell tolled across the land.

Sitting propped on their elbows they sipped barley water as they listened to Lira telling Olivia stories of her father's past exploits. She included Dardo and Piccolo in her stories and her ability to weave such tales enthralled them, but Thomas looked bored. He had heard them a thousand times. Weary, he pondered for a moment, befogged of mind and fatigued in body.

Lira stared at Thomas.

Thomas stared back and shrugged. "Must we listen to this over the dinner table every day?" he snapped his voice so harsh that everyone at the table jumped. Olivia began to cry.

Did you not sleep well last night, my love?" asked Lira.

"I didn't sleep," he snapped back.

"Why not?" she said, trying to calm Olivia.

Thomas sighed, stood up and shuffled towards the kitchen door. Lira stepped in front of him. Thomas' face was resting in his hands. A smile never lit his rugged countenance these days. Austere with himself, he drank gin when alone to mortify the sick images in his mind. He shrank back from her with a hissing intake of breath and they exchanged glances. Lira heaved an irrepressible sigh. "God, I'm at my wit's end and don't know what to do!" she snapped. She began to cry and ran from the room. Their friend's utter despair surprised Dardo and Piccolo. Olivia screamed and began to cry again, and their hearts sank and their hands trembled as they tried to comfort her.

***

In the afternoon of that same day, a warm wind blew in from the west and heavy clouds drifted across the sky. Thomas swung the barroom doors open. He had been drinking gin and looked dreadful. Dardo and Piccolo were tidying up, polishing the pewter goblets ready for the opening time. Startled, both men jumped. "Jesus, Thomas you scared me!" said Dardo.

Piccolo clutched his chest. "And me!"

Thomas looked dazed. "Sorry."

Surprised by his sudden appearance, both men watched him stagger across the room drunk. He sat at his usual table with his back to the wall, appraising his surroundings through reddened, bleary eyes and it saddened his friends that they could do nothing to help him.

For a whole year, life had been uneventful in Nottingham while Thomas rotted in jail, but now things were taking a different course in a bizarre twist of fate. Not only were innocent women being raped and murdered by a crazed killer, but their best friend was suffering insane visions and he was his own worst enemy, having let the demon drink take a firm hold of him. Worn with pain and weak from his prolonged hardship of prison life, he was now leading a meaningless existence, spending such money as he had on gin while his kith and kin had no choice but to let nature and destiny run its own natural course.

"Poor devil," whispered Piccolo.

Dardo noticed Thomas fumble through his pockets with a dreamy, vacant expression in his eyes, searching for his gin bottle.

Then Thomas sprang to his feet with a drunken cry of pleasure when he'd found it. Popping the cork he took a large swallow and slumped back. The chair rocked and almost tipped over dislodging him. "Ha, ha," he cried, slapping the table in front of him. "I could have missed the chair that time!" He closed his eyes and fell into a drunken stupor.

Piccolo sat on a high stool, pushing another one in Dardo's direction with his booted foot. "What are we to do with him?"

Dardo slumped onto the stool looking sad. "We have to leave him alone and hope things come right."

***

The next few days were a blur for Dardo and Piccolo. They cleaned, polished, and repaired everything at the inn. But Thomas lay upon his bed for hours in his room not uttering a word or moving a muscle and he always had the same drunken expression on his face and dreamy, vacant look in his eyes. Then on the fourth day, he rose from his bed and walked to the window. It was a foggy morning. A grey veil hung over the houses reflecting the stark streets beneath them. He stood looking out into the busy road and noticed heavy footsteps ascending the stairs. There was a knock on the door. "Are you awake, Thomas? Are you getting up today?" Dardo sounded impatient.

The colour drained from Thomas' face. He was having his insane visions of murder. Now he no longer looked like the strong, noble hero he had once been, and in his mind, he could still hear the dungeon guards laughing as they tortured him on the rack and with the thumbscrews and it unnerved him.

"Thomas, are you awake? Are you getting up?" Dardo's voice came again.

Thomas grabbed a poker from the fireplace, holding it above his head, ready to strike anyone who came through the door. His hands shook. "No! Go away! Go away or I'll break your head!"

Dardo frowned. "Can I come in and talk?"

"Go away and leave me alone!"

"I just want to help. Can I come in and talk?"

Thomas picked up a pewter goblet and threw it. It slammed into the door. "Don't want to talk and I don't need your help, so go away! I'm alone in here and like it that way!"

Dardo sighed, slumping against the door frame, not knowing what to say or do to help his friend. Inside of him was a mixture of frustration, sympathy and anger, and it seemed as if their thrill-a-minute, fast, fun, adventurous life had taken its toll and ground to a shuddering halt, because of an inexplicable turn of events that neither of them controlled. He turned, head lowered, marching back down the stairs.

Thomas, hands trembling, breathed a sigh of relief and placed the poker back in the fireplace. He slumped back onto the bed and fell asleep. And once again the dreams of powerful faceless enemies, murder and horrific screams of the dying swamped his mind.

CHAPTER NINETEEN

Pure innocence

It was quiet in the Abbey graveyard the next morning. Thomas stood with respect in front of a new headstone looking sombre with grief shadowing his watery eyes. He never expected to feel ashamed, but he did. In past times he had overcome the murderous Baron Ozhan and his illegitimate heir, Ozhobar, but now there was another crazed knife-wielding maniac on the loose and he didn't know how to stop him. Thomas stood in the sunshine trying to find solace and he hesitated before reading the small inscription on the gravestone. Thomas cried while reading it. "It was a game of happy families until father died, heaving with a moan. Now I lay beneath these flowers, leaving my only child alone. God bless her."

The grave was the final resting place of the murderer's latest victim, the young woman found dead in the hay cart. Thomas' wife, Lira, had taken charge of her orphaned child and they were both willing to rear him as their own. A child must have a mother and a father's love, Lira told Thomas. His own violent upbringing in Alnwick Castle with his brother had taught him that much at least. Human beings can endure any deprivation if they know their parents love them, Thomas thought. Yet he himself had survived on the pure hatred of Baron Sedgwick and Lady Ann, their childhood tormenters. Somehow Thomas and Malcolm lived through the sexual depravity and regular beatings they had endured, year after year and it strengthened them and made them less willing to give in to their fears and anxieties. Lesser men might have crumbled and died.

    Thomas came back from his reverent reverie when a soft voice from behind announced, "when I was little, I believed in God and imagined life would be like one everlasting perfect day." Thomas turned. It was Lira, and she too looked saddened; her expression collapsing into forlorn reminiscence. "I imagined I would live in a big fine house one day, be rich, meet and marry my dream man, but nothing could have prepared me for the sad truth. Life isn't perfect! And it's not that I'm ashamed of where I live or bothered because I'm not rich, or disappointed by the man I fell in love with and married. No, it's none of those..." she said.

    Thomas' eyes met hers. He could see she was drowning in the adult world of death and he took her hand, squeezing her fingers in a gentle gesture of reassurance. Lira trembled. Thomas pulled her close, her warm body against his and he smoothed back her golden hair, kissing her full red lips. "I know what troubles you. Life is not the bed of roses or bowl of cherries we expect it to be," he said. "Life is cruel, full of pitfalls and very dangerous and just when you think you're on top of the world it crumbles beneath your feet like dry clay. That happened to me last year when they threw me in jail. My entire world collapsed to the sound of the jail door slamming shut behind me."

    This time Lira squeezed Thomas' hand in a gesture of reassurance.

***

    It was dark and raining when the masked man came to the top of the cliff. He had walked far but wasn't sure how far. Standing on the brink in the darkness, the wind whipped at his cloak and sang through his cold fingers. He could hear the water below and swaying forward with the wind pressing against his back he saw the stars wheeling through the heavens. The hour was just before dawn and the sky was turning blue. Wind tugged at the grass beneath his feet and two gulls flew crying over the rocks, landing on a patch of sand searching for food. The man kicked at the gulls and swore, scuttling hither and thither among the rocks until the two gulls flew up into the wind with a frightened cry and disappeared from sight.

Now he searched amongst the rocks to find a young woman's head he had buried the night before, and picking it up, he clutched it to his chest as if it were a great treasure. The masked man laughed taking out his hunting knife, and he began cutting off the ears and nose and fed them to his ghostly looking hound as the moon slid between screens of dark clouds. The hound howled begging for more, so he gouged out the eyes, ate one himself and gave the other to the dog. Then he stole back to his cave before the rising of the dawn sun.

***

The child's eyes shone with pure innocence. Thomas stared at him. Toys and the smell of roses filled the bedroom. Thomas walked to the window. The sun was up and Lira was in the backyard hanging out the washing, while Olivia sat in the sandbox with her brother, Benjamin, playing with small shovels and pails. They transferred sand from one pail to another and began making a castle with turrets and towers. Thomas watched them playing for a while until Benjamin screamed, throwing his shovel down in an almighty tantrum. Olivia calmed him by giving him her shovel, which was red. He liked the red one better. Benjamin smiled. Olivia smiled back.

Thomas turned again, staring at the baby in the cradle. "We'll call you Elijah. It's a good name, a strong name, and I'll teach you everything you need to know to survive a cruel world I swear it." Thomas walked back across the room, knelt beside the cradle and the child looked up, gurgled, giggled and smiled at him. The child's eyes were fever bright and so were his. "We'll grow old together, you and I, and my family are now your family and we will love you until the end of days. There I've said it," he announced with a happy look.

Thomas' voice was soft and reassuring and in moments the child was fast asleep as if by a magic spell. Thomas walked to the backyard. Lira was still hanging out the washing and the children playing. He hooked an arm around Lira's waist. "I've thought long and hard of late about our future and have decided it's not here. We can't continue to live at the Dog and Duck."

Lira dropped the washing basket, looking stunned, and threw her arms around him, hugging him. "No darling, I agree," she said with a smile.

"Don't you mind? Aren't you angry? Won't you miss this old place?"

Lira sighed. "Put it this way, I won't grieve. This place is hard work." She hugged and kissed him on the verge of tears.

"I always felt sorry for you when customers rushed you. And we've lived beyond our means."

Again, Lira sighed. "I know. We spent money before we had it and the inn is losing money. Dardo and Dody haven't helped either, even though they work hard. They drank the profits while you were in prison." Lira frowned, sat in the sandbox and picked Benjamin up, glancing at Olivia. "We're tired of living this way and the children need more time from us. We should have fun, play games and throw parties."

Thomas nodded. "You're so right, and now there's Elijah to consider too."

Lira looked confused. "Elijah?"

Thomas' eyes sparkled with satisfaction. "Elijah's our third child, and it's a good name. Strong too, and that's why he should have it and bear it proudly." The love that had grown in his heart for the boy was not a sudden fancy, but the wish of a strong man who loves being a father and adores his children.

Now Thomas noticed footsteps behind him, scrunching along their shingle path and he turned to face the newcomer who was a heavy-set, bull-necked, youth with coarse features. Thomas nodded his welcome, and the other nodded back.

"Can I be of service friend?" Thomas asked.

The young man had a troubled look in his eyes, and his strong hands trembled as if a shadowy terror hung over him. "It's my wife," he said, striding up to them. "Someone murdered her." His eyes misted over and his gaunt face looked so sad.

The youth's sombre words shook Thomas' nerves and likewise Lira.

The youth seemed frozen, his hand hovering near his throat and his heart came up darkening his eyes. Something wild and terrifying burgeoned in Lira's heart just from watching him tremble, and his face was so pale it resembled a death mask.

Thomas stared hard at the youth. "Your wife's dead?"

"Yes, murdered," the other whispered back.

Lira shook her head. "God, what's happening to this community?"

The youth's eyes seemed to sink into his skull and he sobbed.

"Sit before you fall over," offered Thomas.

The young man sat on the edge of the sandbox sobbing. "Mary's gone and I'll never see her again," he said in a tight rasping voice. It was pitiful to see the youth crying. "I hate God for taking my wife."

Thomas laid his hand onto the youth's shoulder. "Death is cruel, but we can't blame God if someone murders a loved one. We should only blame the person responsible for the deed, for he has betrayed God's laws and vengeance shall quench the heartbreak that follows in its wake. I will seek this individual and stop him."

Dreadful laughter drifted into Thomas' mind and the murderer's thoughts reared up within him, flaring like a bright torch in his skull. "Just remember, I know who and where you are when you preach to others that you alone will stop me," said the voice. "And you have a bigger family to look after now. Heed my words. I can kill them if I want to, so they might be dead by tomorrow morning!"

Now Thomas was panic-stricken. Within the halls of his own subconscious, he knew the murderer was not just making idle threats. He stood stock-still, shaken and unable to voice a reply. More mad laughter drifted into his mind.

"What, no clever retort? No stern reply?" said the voice.

Thomas closed his eyes, opening the inner psychic gateway, and he fell back into himself once again. The move was sudden, and before the murderer could summon his own defences, Thomas' powerful raw emotions frightened the killer. This time he could hear the swordsman's thoughts and mocking laughter and his mouth was dry, his heart beating fast. "No matter what a dread force you are, I'll rip out your heart and suck your liver dry before I will allow you to touch any of my family," Thomas threatened, and a powerful unseen hand gripped the murderer's throat. He gasped for breath and groaned, terrible pain exploding in his skull.

"Your psychic energy is strong. But not your physical energy."

"And you're a lily-livered, chickenhearted coward who will panic when we cross swords. So prepare yourself, for it will be one day soon," countered Thomas, "and you'll wish that the whore-bitch who spawned you had not!"

Lira's quivering voice dragged him back to reality, breaking the psychic link, and it silenced the murderer. "What are we to do?"

Thomas stared wild-eyed as if in a trance. "I'll probe for my opponent's weaknesses, uncover them and strike. I'm aware of my own weaknesses and can use them against my enemy. In my mind, I'll become him and see what's coming next."

"Can you do that?" she asked.

"Anyone can fight, but it's our wits that make warriors. When I fight, I take strength, courage and the element of surprise with me, and know how to use them to my advantage, and if you're the best at something, you can have anything you wish for in life. I want a reckoning and revenge for those poor murdered women's souls."

Lira's blood froze. She hadn't heard him speak like this in years and from that day forward her sickly husband ceased to drink gin and exercised, running several miles each day, ate good food, climbed trees and swung around like a monkey from morning till night, until his body was back at the peak of fitness. Thomas Flynn the swordsman was back, reborn anew.

***

Two months later, it was quiet at the Dog and Duck. The night was fine and stars twinkled overhead. Thomas stood watching a meteor streak through the heavens and fall to earth in silence. Once again he was a proud, heroic-looking man and his skin glowed instead of looking sallow. His muscles rippled and his speed of hand and foot was as exceptional as it had been before the Sheriff of Nottingham imprisoned him. Even his dreadful nightmares had ceased. But he was still experiencing wild mood swings that he couldn't control and he was dark, stern and menacing sometimes like a monster rather than a man. Even his eyes seemed to glow with a baleful light when a vague, nameless terror came over him. Sometimes he even frightened Lira and the children and hated himself for doing so.

Lira tugged at his arm, interrupting his thoughts. "Only one week and we leave this place for good."

Thomas scratched his head, glancing over his shoulder towards the back door of the inn, "Aye, and I've got a strange feeling I'll miss this place, even though it's been hard work for the both of us."

"Do you think you'll miss it?" Lira asked.

He half-smiled. "It wouldn't surprise me. In fact, after what's happened of late, nothing will ever surprise me again." A terrifying thought entered his mind. *It's been quiet for two months with no murders, but there's still a crazed killer lurking out there somewhere!* And just as he was thinking it, he noticed a big shadow on the stable door, opposite him. An ominous crouching shadow. Butterflies fluttered in his stomach. But before he could react the shadow glided away. Lira hadn't seen it so he didn't mention it in case it frightened her.

Thomas put his arm around her shoulders. "Look, it's getting late, we'd better get inside and open the place or we'll have an angry crowd waiting to get in for their evening meal."

Lira smiled at him. "Well, we can't have that!"

They walked to the door holding hands. Thomas opened it and she stepped inside, but he glanced back at the stable door where the shadow had been. He concentrated, emptying his mind, feeling that someone was close by and trying to pick up his thoughts. His blood froze when he noticed the outline of a shadowy face near the stables. It hovered there a moment and disappeared into the shadows. *Did I see a face or did I imagine it*, he thought? With his nerves jangling he entered the inn, closing the door behind him.

Golden lantern light glowed in the stairwell window and a rush of heat enveloped him when he pushed open the bar-room door. Lira had lit the log fires at either end of the bar and opened the main doors to let the customers in and she greeted each person with her beautiful smile.

Within minutes, the inn filled up with a mixture of privateers and noblemen. Thomas sat at his usual table with his back to the wall, watching everyone enjoying themselves. A short man gazed at him and smiled. Thomas smiled back, nodding his greeting. The man's face was rosy-red and plump, but pleasant. Thomas scanned the room, his gaze stopping at a mirror on a far wall. It was old and cracked and he found himself confronted by his own reflection and liked what he saw. With the demon drink banished from his life, he looked like a different person altogether, strong, handsome and youthful-looking for his age.

Then the lights in the bar dimmed and the surrounding air grew heavy. There was silence for a moment. In the mirror, Thomas' eyes changed to white eyes with no pupils. He blinked, averting his gaze before looking back at his reflection. The mirror seemed to have grown larger and darker and it intrigued him how he looked. It was scary. Thomas had a shock of white hair, his face was corpse grey and his body was a bag of bones. He blinked again, unable to believe what he was seeing and his reflection returned to normal. Thomas breathed a sigh of relief then jumped when a man tugged at his arm. "Are you okay, my friend? You look like you've seen a ghost!"

Thomas shrugged, his mind swimming in confusion. Things were getting weird again. Then Lira's comforting voice sounded and the smell of meat and potato pie with gravy wafted into the bar from the dining room, greeting his nostrils. "Come and get your evening meal sweetheart," she called to him.

Lira's voice sounded soothing, and he ignored what he'd seen in the mirror, shrugging it off as a daydream. But during his meal, he suspected he had somehow seen the murderer, and it was the stuff of nightmares. Thomas always knew he was different, but now he was finding out how different he was. Even worse, his ultimate nightmare was lurking somewhere close in the shadows, threatening to come and kill his family.

Somewhere in the distance, a dog howled. Thomas climbed to his feet and walked to the window, staring out as thunder rumbled overhead and rain lashed the inn. It was dark outside, and the wind howled. He watched the raindrops tapping on the windowpanes. Again, a dog howled. The murderer's coming and is somewhere close, he thought.

The evening started as a clear starry night, but now it was miserable and cold. He walked back to his table and lit the candle at its centre to brighten things up and make him feel better. His spirits were low and dropping lower by the heartbeat when out of the corner of his eye he saw a silhouette through a side window. It was motionless. Lightning flashed illuminating the darkness, and the silhouette disappeared. Moments later, a large stone smashed through the window, covering the customers in shards of glass, and it fell at Thomas' feet. He stared at it and then glanced across at Lira, seeing her scared.

Thomas picked up the stone wrapped in linen clothe and there was a piece of parchment attached to it. Again thunder rolled and a web of lightning flashed illuminating the whole landscape. He stared out of the smashed window, peering through the watery curtain at the black clouds rolling by and could make out a shadowy shape, running near an old iron bridge in the distance. Outside laughter rang in the air. He pealed off the parchment and read the words.

"Blood and more blood everywhere
Thomas, you are a guardian angel in despair,
I am the king of the castle,
and the time is right,
find me if you can
if you want to fight.
This flesh is from the first.
Can you stop me before the last?"

The killer had signed it, "The Mask". Thomas peeled away the bloody linen cloth and to his horror, it was a woman's hand. He could tell by the long slender fingers, one of which wore a diamond engagement ring. Thomas felt light-headed as if he was daydreaming, but someone else's terrifying thoughts drifted into his mind uninvited.

"Where am I? He's stripped me of my clothes and it's cold, dark and frightening. He's taken everything away from me, my home, my warmth, my world. All the things I love and understand have gone and everything looks strange and sinister. I'm a woman alone. I'm lost, and it's scary. What I see repulses me, but I can't go back. I'm trapped. I'm fumbling through the dark. Where am I? No. No! Not you! What are you doing to me? Oh, God, no, not that!" Then the voice was silent, lost forever.

Thomas' mind dizzied, then everything went black, but he knew the severed hand belonged to the woman whose voice had invaded his head. She was dead, but Thomas had homed in on her last seconds of life which had been dreadful and terrifying. No one should suffer as she had, he thought. No one should die like that.

The experience drained Thomas so much he almost collapsed, but somehow he steadied himself and came back to his senses. He made a dash for the main doors, running out into the pouring rain and he ran towards the iron bridge to catch the killer. But when he reached it, there was no one there. Thomas stood catching his breath, his heart hammering and there was no noise other than the falling rain. Lightning flashed illuminating the landscape. The chase over now and the villain gone Thomas looked down at his feet. A grotesque mask lay in the mud. He stared at the corpse grey face and eyes with no pupils.

CHAPTER TWENTY

A force of nature

Later that night, Olivia giggled and climbed into bed, but two rough hewn hands seized her shoulders. "Stop that and go to sleep, it's late," Thomas snapped.

Startled, Olivia stared through tearful, frightened eyes. "Sorry Daddy, did I do something bad?"

Thomas' eyes misted, filling with tears too. "Oh, God, what's happening to me?" he whispered, pulling her close. "No! No! I'm so sorry, sweetheart! You've done nothing bad! I'm wrong for taking my temper out on you. I'm so, so sorry." He kissed her forehead and smiled. "I love you with all my heart and always will."

Olivia smiled back, cuddling him. "Daddy, you're not a bad man. You're just upset because a bad man is out there somewhere. But you must be strong and catch him. Only you can!"

We all have the killer instinct, he thought, but not everyone sees life as a hunting season. And while I'll admit that anyone can do something they shouldn't, they should not repeat it. The killer is a deranged bully of women and a coward in despair, nurturing his bigotry of the opposite sex, besides having no spine or morals. The man must have hated his mother. Thomas' last thought resonated with an uneasy familiarity because his own brother Malcolm had hated their mother with a passion.

Suddenly, Thomas had another vision of a naked woman alone in a field of corn in the dark and his eyes widened with a mad stare that terrified Olivia. A low frightened voice drifted into his head. "I'm alone with him. I can't turn and run because a snarling hound from hell bars my escape. My legs are heavy and I can't breathe. He's behind me. Don't let him take me back. He'll kill me. Please, God, don't let him. No! No! No…" Then everything went black.

Olivia hugged him again. "Please don't stare at me like that, you're scaring me."

Thomas shook his head to rid himself of the dizziness clouding his mind and he tried to think of happier times. "I'm sorry for scaring you, sweetheart." He gave her another big hug.

"Things will get better soon and everything will be alright, I promise Daddy," she reassured, smiling against his chest. It made him feel human again instead of as a lunatic does.

But he knew the shadow of the murderer would spread further, eclipsing his own personal triumphs and tragedies. Thomas wasn't prepared to let that happen, having locked his own terrible secrets away forever. But then the faces of his dead mother, father and brother appeared in his mind, then Master Gallus, Baron Ozhan and his son Ozhobar along with a myriad of others, including the young woman lying dead in the hay cart. The graphic images shook him to his core.

Thomas sat still on the bed, struggling to understand the dreams and visions clouding his life and he hoped tomorrow might be a better day. It would be their last day living at the Dog and Duck. They were moving out of the inn and into rented accommodation.

Climbing to his feet, he kissed her forehead and tucked her into bed, blowing out the candle lighting her room. He said goodnight and went downstairs into the bar to repair the broken window.

***

Lira was up early the next morning, filling their old rickety cart with belongings. Breathless, she rested, gazing up at the blue sky as a light breeze blew in from the north.

The weather was perfect for moving home and it was a glorious day. A good omen, she thought.

Thomas had repaired the cart with new timbers and given it a fresh coat of yellow paint to spruce it up so it was strong enough to move their furniture. But he doubted it and insisted it was too old, even though they were moving less than a mile away. Lira was adamant it could and the Abbot being a sentimental man blessed the cart to make sure it would

"The cart will be our downfall," Thomas had insisted the month before, and they argued for a week, but as usual Lira got her way.

Laden with everything belonging to them, including dozens of straw dolls and most of the children's toys, the cart was ready to roll with Olivia's favourite big doll perched opposite the driver's seat.

Lira sighed, a gentle sadness settling over her. "I will miss this place even though I thought I wouldn't. We've had good times with good memories here," she said to the doll. The sadness deepened into sorrow as she remembered Cyrano, their murdered friend. Her eyes misted and filled as the memories flooded back, the pain of his absence like a dagger in her heart.

Lira came to the inn with Thomas with only a few possessions but was leaving with so much more. Now she was a wife and mother with three lovely children and she loved them all. But it was a sad day because she had found happiness amongst the sweat and toil.

A voice from behind interrupted her daydreams. Lira took a deep breath and spun around seeing a well-built young man grinning at her.

"Can't you fill the cart more?" he said, pointing to the buckling wheels.

Lira smiled and laughed. "You're a cheeky young man. It's full enough. But I could have used those broad shoulders and big muscles of yours two hours ago, seeing as how my lazy husband and his colossal ego are still asleep in bed."

The newcomer shook his head. "What man leaves a beautiful woman to do hard labour on her own?"

"A tired one. My husband didn't get to bed until the early hours of this morning because he was up packing our belongings while I was fast asleep," she said in Thomas' defence.

The young man's face coloured red with embarrassment. "Forgive me milady, I didn't mean to offend you."

Lira smiled again. "There's nothing to forgive, for I'm not offended. I just hope the cart doesn't break and the horses can pull it because otherwise, my husband will never let me forget it."

The young man's eyes sparkled playfully. "Your husband has a forceful nature then?"

Lira studied the young man silhouetted against the rising sun. "No, he is a force of nature."

"I'm saddened," he said, spreading his hands. "I meet the most beautiful woman in the world and you're married and your husband sounds like a dangerous man!"

"Aye," said a husky voice. "I'm highly strung but a thoroughbred – faster than the wind, stronger than a bull and fearless. And that's a fair estimate of my talents!"

Lira chuckled. "Modest too."

The young man spun on his heel, eyes widening to encompass Thomas' well-built frame, also silhouetted against the rising sun and he noticed the harsh tone in the swordsman's voice.

"Where I come from, young men respect women and their elders," said Thomas, anger in his voice.

The young man hesitated. "No need to get your feathers ruffled my friend. I was passing by and saw your wife struggling with her belongings."

Thomas took a deep breath, staring hard at the young man. "Our belongings. And you're not my friend, and I have no feathers to ruffle in case you hadn't noticed. A man should mind his own affairs."

Lira saw that Thomas was angry because she had talked with the young man. "Now, now, boys, no need to get testy, no one's insulted me and there's no harm done," she said, trying to defuse the situation.

Thomas walked to the water barrel beneath their bedroom window and splashed his face. Then he ran his wet fingers through his braided hair, holding his head high, staring harder at the young man, who lowered his head and didn't speak. Thomas studied his swollen face. He had bruises around his eyes and cheeks. Even without the marks, he wouldn't be a pretty sight, he thought.

The young man's face was strong but angular, his brows thick, his nose too wide and it was a stern face, but one that was no stranger to laughter. He twitched in discomfort as Thomas rounded upon him, but there was no expression on his face and no anger showing.

Thomas stepped forward, coming face to face and nose to nose with the young man. "It's not wise to cajole another man's wife if that man is me," he announced in no uncertain terms.

The young man avoided Thomas' steely gaze. "I suppose I'm not a wise man then."

Lira tugged Thomas' arm. "My love, he was doing no harm."

Thomas turned his head to Lira, and she regarded him as if to say the young man was doing nothing wrong. His expression softened and his mood lightened, remembering his own amorous days when young. He was a jealous man but saw no danger from this person, so he forced a smile. The young man smiled back, but beneath the smile was tension and fear. Thomas realised that the young man's interest in Lira was superficial and like many other men, her great beauty fascinated him.

The young man looked into Thomas' eyes, recognising the threat had gone and the tension lifted. He breathed a sigh of relief. "I meant no insult to you sir, or any harm to your beautiful wife, on this you have my oath."

Thomas nodded, his expression softening even more. "What's your name?"

"Ely! And I assure you I am a man of honour."

"The bruises aren't from an incident about another man's wife then?" said Thomas.

Ely looked stunned, and he laughed. "No sir, they're not. I was in the company of men when I received them. We were having a spitting competition to find out who could spit the farthest."

"I assume you lost then?" said Thomas.

"No sir, I won but hit a passer-by in the face and he was the biggest, meanest, son-of-a-bitch ever born."

Lira's expression hardened.

"I apologise for my colourful language, milady," said Ely, looking embarrassed.

Lira forced a smile. "It's not the first time I've heard such language, but it's the spitting that turns my stomach."

"Sorry, I've spent too much time in the company of men and not enough in the company of women," replied Ely.

Thomas considered the reply and laughed. "Maybe it's time that you got in touch with your feminine side."

"There's no fear of that! My comrades would have me doing their washing and I don't even do my own."

Lira nodded. "Yes, your clothes aren't tidy are they?"

Ely's leggings and knee-length boots had cow turds smeared front and back.

"What else were you doing besides spitting?" asked Thomas.

"Well, the truth of the matter is that my friends and I get together once a month to think of several activities we can take part in when we're drunk and boy, were we drunk. This month, it was which one of us could spit the farthest. Then we chased a big round chunk of cheese down the steepest hill imaginable. After that, we competed to see who pissed the highest and whose cock was biggest. I won them all, but my clothes have paid the price." Ely had leaned in close to Thomas and whispered the final activity in his ear.

"I assume there were cow turds at the bottom of the hill?" said Thomas almost wetting himself laughing. The sound rang out rich and merry.

Ely nodded. "Your assumption is correct. The field was full of shite."

Just at that moment, Dardo and Piccolo were staring out of an upstairs window, watching Thomas and Lira talking to the newcomer. Thomas burst into laughter when the young man whispered something in his ear.

"Don't know who that is laughing with Thomas, but his legging and boots are muddy as hell. Must be one of the local farmers," said Dardo.

"He's covered in cow turds, not mud. I can smell it from up here," said Piccolo fanning the air in front of him.

They backed away from the window, closing the wooden shutters and Dardo placed a bunch of crocuses and white lilies in front of the shutters to negate the stench. It didn't work. The awful stink filled their room like a rancid seething mist.

As the morning wore on Thomas and Ely chatted, swapping tales while Lira fed the children a breakfast of porridge, washed down with squeezed orange juice. But her calmness turned to impatience, and she wanted them to be on their way. Lira had loaded the cart; the inn was empty of their belongings and a new life waited. Dardo and Piccolo were going into partnership to run the inn in their stead.

Dinnertime came and Thomas and Ely had talked themselves dry and the latter marched on his way. Lira swore at Thomas with an edge of anger in her voice and she stomped up and down, raising her arms in a gesture of despair. She even threw her treasured Bible at him, hitting him on the forehead, dizzying him. Lira was furious, but life with Lira was never dull. Teatime came, and they set off when the sky was darkening. It rained but the wagons oilskin cover kept them and their belongings dry as they rode down the street to the clip-clop of hooves and iron-shod wheels rattling over the cobbles.

Travelling down Bone street, around Gallows Square and out past a parade of market stalls they went under an old iron bridge and carried on until they reached The Traveller and Merchant shop, where they turned left and kept going with both of them feeling their bones shaking as the cart rattled onward.

The evening was quiet and there wasn't a soul on the streets until they came to a woman weeping over two corpses while her house burned. Children were crying and shrieking in terror, trapped in a second-story bedroom. Bright sparks flew everywhere and huge flames licked at the adjacent buildings, threatening to set them on fire too.

Thomas pulled the cart over to the roadside, yanking back on the reins and he jumped down without hesitation, giving a cautious glance towards the burning house which was an inferno. He closed his eyes, seeing his glory days as a youth when he thought himself immortal. "There's nothing I can't do," he had announced to a gathering crowd, and they had stared at him through disbelieving eyes and laughed. But he climbed to the very top of the tallest tree and ran along the branches as nimbly as any squirrel might.

Now there was a loud scream, and he opened his eyes. Lira pointed upward. Two small children had climbed out of a bedroom window onto a windowsill and were coughing and gasping for air amid the trailers of thick black smoke swirling around them in the rain

There's never a tall tree around when I need one, Thomas thought. His mind raced, trying to think of a solution to the children's plight, for they would die if he didn't act soon.

One of them screamed. "Please help us! Please, we can't breathe and we don't want to die!"

"Child, what's your name?" Thomas shouted to the screaming girl.

"Bethany," she answered with terror in her voice.

"Well, Bethany, I need you to trust me. I want you to stand up and then jump into my arms. I promise to catch you," announced Thomas.

The child looked horrified, fear shining in her innocent eyes. "But it's so far to fall," she whimpered, staring at the stone pavement below them.

"Bethany, the wall of this building will crumble and fall soon." Even as he spoke, huge cracks appeared in the house's side and the brickwork crumbled giving way. A shower of bright sparks rained upon him and he covered his face with his forearms. "Please Bethany, if I'm to save you both, I need you to jump first," pleaded Thomas.

Both children were age five and Thomas couldn't imagine of a more terrifying ordeal for an adult to experience, never mind a small child. Part of the wall gave way and came crashing down in another shower of sparks. The falling debris missed him by inches as he dived for cover behind the cart. Both girls screamed as the flames licked at them. They sprang to their feet on the window ledge, trembling, scared out of their wits.

"Bethany if I could climb up and get you I would, but I can't. You must jump or you'll die," snapped Thomas trying to shock her into action. Then the hand of fate took control. A sickening groan sounded from above him. Debris and sparks tumbled from the widening cracks, striking the street like huge hailstones. There was a thunderous crack and the lintel both girls were standing on sheared away and they fell. The passage of time ceased for Thomas. He watched and knew the girls would die.

CHAPTER TWENTY ONE

A killer on the loose

Thomas, unable to move, never took his eyes off the falling girls. "Come on!" he said to himself, trying to will his limbs to stir.

A strong wind blew in, fanning the flames, turning the house fire into a raging inferno. Then Master Gallus' words rang in his mind. "Act now. Save them both!" He sprang from behind the cart, diving forward with the speed of a god. At that moment, he caught Bethany. A second later he caught the other child. The cracked lintel crashed down only a foot away, gouging a hole in the street. And as he was carrying the girls to the safety of the cart, the whole blazing building collapsed in a shower of sparks and rubble tumbled into the cobbled street with a loud crash.

The children's mother stood up and ran to them. Thomas lowered them onto the pavement with his heart hammering and his mouth dry. "You're safe now," he said, patting their heads. They hugged his legs, and he smiled at them, all weariness and worry vanishing. It was like a shock-wave being lifted and he felt like a hero.

"There will be a story one day about you and your great bravery," said the mother kissing his cheek. "The falling wall could have killed you but you saved my babies despite it. You're a very brave and courageous man and will go to heaven one day and God will bless you as I do now."

Thomas' cheeks coloured red. "I have children of my own and God willing there will be a Guardian Angel looking after them all of their lives."

"You are that Guardian Angel," said the mother.

Thomas rested his hand upon her arm. "No one deserves to die in such a way as this." He stared at the smouldering pile of ashes and rubble lying in the street and then kissed her hand. "Mother, if you ever have need of me, you can find me at the Dog and Duck."

The mother nodded.

Thomas climbed aboard the old cart by Lira's side and shook the reins, beginning their journey again. He waved goodbye as they rolled along the street and around a corner out of sight.

***

That night the sky above Nottingham was heavy with storm clouds and there was a cutting wind blowing in from the west as the masked man walked the streets searching for his next victim. He slipped through the shadows, ghostlike, as thunder rumbled overhead. His hands and feet were freezing, but that wouldn't stop him from satisfying himself. His thoughts took him back to the dark, foreboding time in his life when he had slit his mistress's throat to stop her tormenting him, and in his warped mind that was a good day and the start of his campaign of terror against women.

Rain poured down, thunder rumbled and lightning flashed. He peered out of the shadows at a young woman coming towards him. Superstitiously he rubbed the scar on his forearm and drew a dagger from his belt, waiting for her to get closer. In the narrow alley, he waited, slinking further back into the shadows, and once again the shiny glint of a razor-sharp blade was the only telltale sign he was there. Then as the woman approached, getting within range, he pitched forward and dragged her into the shadows out of sight.

The woman screamed.

Gagging her by clamping his hand over her mouth, he pricked the blade of his knife into the skin of her neck, drawing blood. "Quiet bitch," he whispered, "or you'll join the dead. Do as I say and live."

Terrified, the woman nodded.

He pushed her to her knees, unbuttoning the fly of his leggings exposing his manhood. "Suck on that, bitch," he whispered with a snarl, forcing it into her mouth. She gagged and choked, but did as commanded in fear of her life. But it didn't matter because he would kill her, anyway. The murderer wasn't stupid enough to leave witnesses alive.

***

Next morning, Dardo and Piccolo were up early and were sitting together at Thomas' favourite table with their backs to the wall discussing business for the coming months. The inn wasn't profitable for Thomas and Lira, so things had to change, particularly the aristocratic clientele. It was more profitable when slavers, smugglers and privateers ruled the roost because they came to spend their ill-gotten gains. It had been lucrative though very violent. Both men talked with Thomas and he voiced his displeasure at the idea, but he knew it made sense in the long-term so he agreed to be their doorman and eject any trouble-makers. They would have a night of free ale and wine, putting on good piping-hot food to make the inn a thriving business again.

"We'll do well enough," said Dardo, pride in his voice.

Piccolo rubbed his hands together at the thought of the revenue. "It'll take a while to get the old place back on its feet, but it'll be worth it."

Dardo poured himself a goblet of wine to celebrate.

Anger in his eyes Piccolo stared at him. "You're drinking the profits again."

A loud voice and a heavy knock on the front doors startled both men, and they almost fell off their stools. Thomas pushed the doors open and strode into the bar. Black clouds behind him loomed in the distance threatening rain again. He glanced at his two friends, looking weary but his eyes seemed to blaze red hot. Thomas had a strange feeling, one he had experienced earlier, and it was as if an unseen force was probing him.

"You... you made me jump. What's the matter, you look worried?" stammered Dardo.

Piccolo frowned. "My heart almost stopped!"

Thomas was pale. "The murderer struck again last night, somewhere close by," he announced as the far horizon lit up in a huge web of lightning. And at that moment his friends would have sworn there was something dreadful standing behind him, towering over him like a dark shadow. Both men blinked. It disappeared. Had they seen what they thought they had, they wondered, a shudder running down their spines like so many spiders? Thomas seemed delirious. He babbled on about the killer and victim, and about the murder scene. He turned, closing the main doors. The weather had changed for the worst and the air was cold. It was now sunup. Rain rattled the windows, the wind howled under the doors and there was a clap of thunder that echoed across the land, startling them all.

Piccolo watched the rainwater flood down the street. "We need to build an ark!"

Again the windows lit up with a web of lightning, followed by another tremendous clap of thunder that shook the place right to its foundations. Dardo hauled himself up from his seat and strode to the window just in time to see another searing bolt of lightning flash across the sky. It illuminated him like a Christmas tree, making his blond curly hair even wilder looking than usual. The static electricity in the air made it stand on end and his head looked like a porcupine. Piccolo laughed at the sight.

The storm was getting worse, but it seemed good to Thomas. Nature's raw power was a much-needed distraction. Then his thoughts returned to the murderer. How am I to stop this maniac? Thomas took a breath to steady himself and the pain of his thoughts receded. But then they came rushing back like an incoming tide.

"The murderer struck again last night?" said Piccolo bringing him back from his thoughts.

Thomas took deep breaths to regain his composure. It didn't work. The muscles in his face twitched. He took more deep breaths. His head jerked back and he let out a loud shrill roar. "Oh, God, why is this happening to me?" Once again, dreadful laughter drifted into his mind, the murderer's thoughts rearing up within him, flaring like a flaming torch in his skull.
Thomas dropped to his knees clutching his head, finding himself trapped at the centre of another hellish vision.

He was stalking a young woman, watching her from the shadows.

Listening to her whistling, he waited.

Then he pitched forward, grabbing her, his hand around her throat.

A knife glinted in the dim light.

He forced her to her knees, beasting her, making her suck his manhood and masturbate him and then he raped her and slit her throat.

He drank blood from the cut to her neck and everything went black.

Each new killing was worse than the last, each dreadful murder far more depraved. Laughter drifted into Thomas's mind – dreadful laughter. The words: "I win and you lose," echoed in his head and for a moment, he felt nettled by the irony. He snapped. "I'll drink to your death soon, count on it!" In his mind's eye, there was a blinding flash of white light, an ear-splitting crack and the telepathic doorway slammed shut.

Dazed and half-conscious Thomas climbed to his feet, but as he did so the telepathic doorway reopened and a ghastly rain of flesh and blood-soaked clothing fell around him in glittering shreds. He vomited and his friends jumped from their seats. Dardo reached him first but couldn't see what Thomas could see, and he didn't know what was happening. Thomas seemed stupefied but unharmed. The Abbey bell tolled in the distance heralding breakfast and the bloody vision disappeared from his mind and the doorway closed again. Thomas stood up, screaming, and kicked Dardo's stool, hurling it through the stained-glass window, shattering it into a thousand pieces. Tankards toppled from the shelves behind them, startling them.

Piccolo stared through disbelieving eyes. "What the hell is going on here?"

"The visions are getting stronger and more dreadful by the day," said Thomas, "and they're driving me mad!" He was clutching his head when Lira came bursting through the front doors screaming. All eyes turned to her.

"Horrid! Wicked! Dreadful!" she was saying. "They've found another murder victim with a note left on her naked body." Lira looked as if she might faint.

Another voice broke the silence. A man came rushing in through the open doors clutching a piece of parchment. He stared at the small gathering and turned to face Thomas, handing him the parchment. Thomas stared at the message and read it out loud.

My whole life has been about killing.

I've studied it, learning the lessons well, and I always have an escape route planned.

Neither you nor the sheriff's men can stop me because you're chasing a ghost.

I'll always be one step ahead of you and escape because I can slip through the cracks in the walls.

And when I'm alone after I've killed, I worship the devil and think of murdering you, Thomas. And your whole family.

CHAPTER TWENTY TWO
Seeds of destruction

In the afternoon one day later, panicked by the message, Thomas visited the Abbey in search of the Abbot's wise words.

Father Abbot took Thomas' arm, leading him toward the cloistered halls of the Abbey at a sedate pace. "The truth affrights us, my son," he said, his tone quiet but intense, "it's an indictment against the city that we can't catch this killer. The weak and needy fended for themselves before you came here my son and care for them was never enough. And it's a shame because even now miserable people lay in the streets everywhere, sick and dying. I saw a girl in a doorway yesterday, her hair matted and feet rotted away by the harsh weather. I gave her bread, but it was love and care she needed, and that is why I will canvas for a hospice for the needy and downtrodden. If God's penny is to promise them a better life, it's opportune."

Thomas smiled, nodding to the Abbot. Then his mind flashed back to his own miserable, degrading upbringing in Alnwick Castle with his brother Malcolm. They had endured dreadful beatings and endless sexual abuse at the hands of Baron Sedgwick and Lady Ann, who revelled in every minute. It had been nothing short of torture. "Let's hope for good news then," he said coming back from his painful daydream. Thomas' voice was low and reverent, mindful of his surroundings. "Most people might contribute, seeing as how the poor offend the rich with their stinks and vapours. People may even pay a generous sum to have their streets and alleyways cleared."

The Abbot pressed Thomas' arm. "Aye," he said.

Thomas laid his hand on the Abbot's shoulder. "I'll help, but if anyone can do this task, it's you. Your energy and quick wits will count for much and help you raise the needed subscriptions, I'm sure, even though many people will be hard to persuade. Their purses smart from the king's taxes."

Thomas didn't voice his fears about his temporary madness when he seemed possessed by the evil spirit that was the killer. He was careful with what he said. Thomas didn't want to appear ludicrous in the eyes of his friend even though he thought the Abbot would believe him. Thomas left the Abbey just before midnight. It was a cold but dry evening with no moon showing through the dark clouds, and as he rode his stallion, his mood was not cheerful.

Nottingham was now full of thieves, beggars, and fanatics and many frightened people, any of which might be the murderer, and the only clue he had to the killer's identity was the triangular scar on his left forearm. So, the Abbot's idea to persuade the city folk to part with their hard-earned money to build a hospice might seem an almost impossible task, but he knew that catching the killer was an impossible task.

Thomas arrived back at his lodgings on Bole Street in the early hours of the morning and he stepped from his stallion, tying it to a hitching post. He walked toward his door, but then paused to the sound of quiet footsteps behind him. He turned but saw no one. The street was dark with no lighted windows. "Who goes there? Who is that?" he called.

Somewhere near a dog growled but there was no reply.

Thomas knelt and pulled the hidden dagger from inside his boot. "Come out and show yourself!" Still, there was no reply, but there was the sound of running, so he gave chase following the sound of booted feet.

Suddenly the sound stopped at the end of a narrow alleyway and mad laughter rang in the air. Thomas ran toward the laughter, but as he rounded the corner of a building where the ally ended, there was no one there. He stared up at the twenty-foot-high wall with broken glass, set on top, standing in front of him and then glanced behind him. Thomas looked back at the wall again, staring with incredulity because as agile as he was, he couldn't scale the wall without a rope. But someone had.

More laughter came from behind the wall and a shiver trickled down Thomas' spine like a sliver of ice. Then it went quiet and poured with rain. Thomas ran back the way he came, but by the time he reached his front door, the rain had soaked him. Putting his key in the lock he opened the door, and to his surprise, the fire was still lit and it warmed him. He bolted the door, removed his boots, took off his heavy leather tunic and wet shirt and walked to the fireplace to hang them up to dry. He climbed the stairs to the children's bedroom.

They were asleep in the dark, so he knelt by each of their beds, kissing their foreheads. "Evil will never touch my loved ones, not now or ever, I so swear it before almighty God," he whispered in each of their ears as they slept without a care in the world. "For I am your Guardian Angel and will protect you until the day I die, and I promise that will not be one day soon. For evil carries the seeds of its own destruction and I will find where those seeds lay and how best to use them. Or my name is not Thomas Flynn the Third."

He walked across the landing, lit only by a fat candle that cast a buttery light. He blew it out he walked into his bedroom where he climbed with relief between the linen sheets. Lira was asleep. Thomas kissed her forehead, whispered his love for her, and made the same declaration he had promised the children. Thomas meant every word, and like the true hero he was, he would die before letting any harm befall any of them. He lay on his side watching Lira's eyes flicker, knowing she was dreaming of better days, and then he turned onto his back, focusing his mind toward the tunnel of slumber. Thomas' last action before falling asleep was to snuggle under the bedclothes and cuddle up to his one true love. Then he closed his eyes and his features relapsed into a taciturn mask that seemed cruel as he dreamt of his abusive upbringing.

***

Meanwhile, the serial killer with strange moans and shrieks of laughter was working on a scheme of murder. A final plan of action. The deaths of Thomas' whole family. Killing Thomas Flynn and family would be the culmination to his own long history of violence. Ironically, he'd planned his own death too. His devil-worshipping made him believe he would be the leader of otherworldly creatures in the afterlife and he did not fear death, which made him a more formidable adversary. Could greater evil overcome the greater good? The killer hoped it could.

His cave was dark, lit only by a few candles in iron brackets around the walls and at his side, asleep, lay the hound from hell. Red dye covered the walls of the cave and in a far corner laid the implements of devil worship, discarded and unneeded, for the time had come. His time. The plan was right. All he was waiting for was a blood moon rising, and that was only seven days away.

Now he spent his last hours of life as a phantom, a ghostly figure unseen and unheard. And as he planned those last days and hours his face was expressionless, eyes doll-like, showing neither the pleasure nor the excitement he was experiencing. He lay on his back, stroking the hound to relax and gazed at the cave ceiling, watching the flame-shadows of the candles dance and transform into evil spirits before his eyes. Malevolent, dreadful little creatures, lurking in the dark waiting for life. I'll release them soon, he thought.

***

The next morning, Dardo and Piccolo were up early, tired after an exhausting evening. Neither had slept well, and both men seemed dispirited because their first night of trade in the Dog and Duck had been mayhem and bloody hell, made worse by Thomas' absence. There was no formidable doorman to give them peace of mind because Thomas' employment didn't start for another week, meaning they had to endure another seven days of knife fights and bloodshed.

Dardo was aching all over from carrying the heavy casks of ale and wine and from fighting. His body felt like someone had thrashed him with a wooden cudgel. Piccolo ached just the same and now both men were on their knees, scrubbing the floor, trying to remove the bloodstains. They had watched in disbelief, a single argument between two thieves escalate into a full-blown fight, then escalate further into a bar-room brawl involving every one of their clientele. Even stranger was the fact that the argument started over which of the two thieves were sporting the worst scars and best tattoos. The triviality of it seemed incomprehensible to them.

Dardo stood up and walked to the tavern's mullioned window. Rain was coming down hard, splashing on the panes, distorting his view. "Bad weather again. It's another ill omen!" He frowned and sighed, casting a nervous stare at Piccolo who was now a lively strapping lad. "No disrespect intended to you but we need Thomas' presence here tonight or there won't be much left of this place in a week's time," he said, casting his eyes over the roomful of broken chairs and tables. Dardo felt a flush of anger at the sight of it.

Piccolo nodded with fierce eyes under bushy brows. "It's a sinful world and most people don't believe in the good Lord as we do, and they have no moral code of conduct. The Lord's Commandments mean nothing to thieves, cutthroats, rapists and murderers. Strange though, how they still pray when they're being hanged from the gibbet on their Judgement Day!" He said it with a tone of relish in his voice.

"It's as if God divided the world into the saved and the damned," said Dardo.

Piccolo nodded. "I've thought about it often, and it makes more sense than anything else. God-fearing people know the damned will burn in the fires of Hell one day, and by the dreadful things happening around Nottingham at the moment, I don't imagine Judgement Day will be too far off for us!"

Wild-eyed Dardo nodded, his face bleak, bereft. "Is it not God's way to send doubt to try the spirit of those he loves most?" he asked, lowering his head in reverence as he mentioned the Creator.

Piccolo banged his calloused fist on a table. "But most of God's children have committed every sin. Just look around you and you'll see the evidence you need to convince you of it." He ran his fingers through his hair. "One day, when I'm summoned by Him, I'll dress in rich robes, sit at a great table in a great hall and His angels will invite me to eat, but the wicked will suffer in the fires of Hell with the devil as their gaoler!"

Dardo nodded in agreement. "What will God say to the wicked?"

"Only that they got what they deserved, and that they should have earned an honest crust like the rest of us," said Piccolo. His eyes came up meeting his friend's gaze, and he realised he was the strongest of the two of them. "And whatever happens tonight, it will not be a repeat of last night in this tavern!"

***

By early evening, they had cleaned up the bar and dining room. Fires blazed in both rooms and a new sign hung over the bar announcing: "We will not tolerate violent and rowdy behaviour so take it outside and don't come back!"

There was the smell of steamed vegetables and broiling chicken coming from the kitchen where the cook, Minnie Sykes, was preparing the evening meals. Dardo and Piccolo sat by the fire at the far end of the room awaiting the customer's arrival, but even the warmth of the welcoming hearth couldn't dispel the tension they felt. They exchanged uncomfortable glances as the first customer came through the doors.

He was tall and fat, wearing a food-stained shirt and leather jerkin. A dark stain on his hose showed that he had soiled himself and his deep-set piggy eyes stared at the makeshift sign above the bar as he approached it. "Which one of you pisspots serves tonight?" he asked in a bullying voice.

Piccolo glanced at Dardo. "Do you believe in fate?"

Dardo shrugged. "Fate?"

Piccolo nodded. "Yes. You know, destiny, it doesn't matter what you do because nothing can change your future; it's written already."

Dardo shrugged again. "I – I don't know," he stammered. "I've always imagined the future depends upon the choices we make."

"And you would be right according to my way of thinking," agreed Piccolo. "So what are our choices here?"

Dardo looked confused.

"Choice number one. I can get up off my tired behind and serve this... fat bastard. Choice two. I can let you get up off your tired arse and you serve this... fat bastard. And number three and my favourite choice, I can kick this fat bastard out of here, telling him to take his money and his belligerent self elsewhere. And that's called free-will, which the good Lord gave me an abundance of!" Piccolo hauled himself to his feet, clutching the hilts of his swords. "You can either leave in peace or leave in pieces, spitting blood," he announced with a confident smile and menacing voice.

The big man was dumbstruck. No one dared speak to him thus. "A cocky mongrel you are. But I'm wondering how you will eject me without those blades in your hands?"

Dardo climbed to his feet. "He won't."

"I didn't think so," snarled the fat man.

"But then, he won't have to," Dardo countered.

"Why is that?" the big man asked.

"Because I'll do it, and the pleasure will be mine!"

At that moment, ten men entered the tavern, armed with every conceivable weapon. They were blood-spattered, looking tired. Dardo recognised them as mercenaries. The leader pushed past the big man, smashing his fist on the bar top and roared. "I want mead and mutton, and lots of it!"

Piccolo, clutching the hilts of his swords looked nervous but rounded on the men. "Hard day?" he asked, pushing through them. He vaulted the bar and waited to serve. "Have you been hunting?"

The leader of the pack looked suspicious and coughed, clearing his throat. "Aye, aye, rabbits," he said. "We've been hunting rabbits!"

Piccolo served all of them with a tankard of aged best mead and glanced at the varied array of weaponry the men were sporting. "Were they fierce rabbits of an extraordinary size?" he joked.

The leader considered the question. "Aye, they were huge terrible creatures!"

Piccolo exchanged uncomfortable glances with Dardo.

The leader smiled a gap-toothed smile. "Just kidding. We had a run-in with the Sheriff's men and now they're dead, every one of them in little pieces scattered here and there!" He laughed with gusto. So did his band of followers.

The fat man gave a snort, chuckling to himself.

Dardo and Piccolo stared at each other.

The mercenaries had already tasted blood and had a zest for it, and as good a swordsman as Piccolo was, he was no match for ten seasoned professionals. Even Thomas would struggle to deal with this many thugs, thought Dardo.

The leader stared at the two friends, the whites of his eyes around his scarred irises lending something doll-like to his gaze. "Well, where's the mutton?" he said, slumping to a stool like a sack of cabbages. He was big and ugly and what little hair he had was red. He warmed his hands, the evening being a cold one.

"Is there urgency?" asked Dardo.

The fat man's eyes lit up like candles. "You can serve me mutton too!"

Piccolo rounded upon him, drawing his swords. "The only food you will get is food for thought!" he snapped. "So here's a piece of sound advice. Leave now before I sharpen both of my blades on your oversized arse!"

The other men roared with laughter.

"I don't much like the look of you," announced Piccolo. "You're creepy with a loud mouth and an unpleasant manner. You speak too much but don't listen to sound advice and must have a learning disability. I find you insulting, indecent, coarse, vile; bad-tempered and the worst specimen of a man I have ever had the misfortune to meet in all my days. Did I leave anything out?" He said it all without taking a breath.

The fat man looked flabbergasted.

"Besides that what's wrong with him?" joked the leader of the bunch. "Don't mince your words lad, tell him what you think."

One mercenary laughed out loud, holding his belly. "I think you should have the good sense to leave before the lad butters your head and swallows you whole!"

The fat man marched to the doors. He opened them and disappeared into the darkening night without saying another word.

Now there was the sound of a horse's hooves on the road outside, and within seconds the rider came bursting through the double doors, brushing the dust from his clothes. Thomas was furious. Hopping mad. "I'm not supposed to start work as a doorman for another seven days, so why have you summoned me? Can you not manage without me today? I've urgent business searching for a mindless killer."

Dardo and Piccolo stared at each other dispassionately, while the mercenaries bragged amongst themselves about what they had done to the Sheriff's men. They laughed and shouted, "We're starving here, where's that bloody mutton?" Then one man threw a flagon of mead through the air, hitting Thomas in the face, cutting his chin. Thomas glared at the man. He was arm-wrestling one of his comrades, boasting that no one could win him.

Thomas rounded on the two men, clenching a hand around the two fists locked together, and he slammed them both down onto the table with a crunching thud, glaring into the eyes of the boaster. "I've just beaten both of you with one hand!" he snarled.

Both men jerked their hands away and Thomas noticed a triangular scar on one man's forearm. Thomas' eyes widened encompassing the scar, and he sucked in a deep breath. A hood shadowed the man's face.

Thomas took a step backwards, drawing his swords. "Get up slowly! I've been looking for you! You're a murderer and the manner of your crimes are *monstrous*!"

The man looked for a way out. Then Thomas had a seizure and fell to the floor, dropping his swords. The murderer laughed. Dardo and Piccolo moved to aid him while the mercenaries sneered at the sight of him holding his head, screaming.

"He's the one who looks possessed!" shouted one mercenary.

The killer took his opportunity, rose from his stool and ran for the open doors, and once outside he made a dash towards Nottingham castle a mile away.

Thomas' seizure faded after the killer made a run for it. He climbed to his feet and made a dash for the open doors and saw the back of him disappearing around a bend in the road. He followed and within seconds was close to him. It was dusk; the light fading and pouring with rain. The smell of coal oil lingered in the air from the extinguished wall lanterns of the castle when he arrived. Ahead of him was a wide entrance, blocked by a steel portcullis and now there was no sign of his quarry.

The castle echoed to the high-pitched screams of the howling wind as it blew through the iron grills. Thomas scrambled up the portcullis onto the adjoining wall and leapt onto the battlements. To his surprise, the killer was waiting for him. "For the horror and desolation you've caused, I'm here to show you the entrance to Hell!" Thomas snapped.

    The killer turned and climbed a spiral staircase to the topmost tower. Thomas followed, and his adversary awaited his coming with his sword drawn. Both men heard the city-dwellers rushing from their homes, a huge mob racing to see the action, led by Dardo and Piccolo. Thomas paused on the top step and knelt to check the hidden dagger in his boot. It was there as always. Taking a deep breath, he drew his swords from their scabbards, lunging forward, making a slashing cut. The killer parried the blow, lowering his hood and Thomas couldn't believe his eyes. It was Malcolm, his brother. Yet he had killed him with his own blades five years earlier, he thought. A tiny prickle of regret touched both men's souls. Once they had been inseparable, like light and dark, love and hate, and one could not exist without the other. Memories of their childhoods flared making them feel sad because once upon a time, each would have given their lives for the other. In those far-off days, a brother's love was the most precious thing.

Coming back to the present after reliving his memories, Malcolm in his arrogance didn't think his brother could beat him a second time or even come close. He launched a sudden attack, storming forward, a booted foot slamming into Thomas' stomach, hurling him from his feet. Thomas slumped to the ground groaning and gasping for breath. Malcolm loomed over him, his dark eyes staring. He paused, savouring the moment, watching Thomas roll to his knees and haul himself upright with his limbs trembling. Malcolm looked fierce, his insane gaze holding to his brother's hard stare.

Thomas gasped for breath. "You're more aggressive and much more determined these days, brother."

Malcolm stared at his own hands. They trembled. His eyes were fever bright. "My blood is hot, and I'd say you're right. Are you getting a bad feeling about this fight? Are you ready to die?"

Rain sheeted down and the distant rumble of thunder drummed out. Trailers of mist drifted across the battlements obscuring vision and it was getting darker by the minute. Malcolm hammered his fist into Thomas' chin, spinning him from his feet again, and he tumbled and rolled, gasping for air. Thomas swore, thinking of the perils they had faced together as children, and it tinged his memories with great sadness and regret. They had endured the same terrible upbringing, so why had he turned out to be a heroic man while Malcolm was a deranged, murdering monster.

Thomas wiped the rain from his face and stared at his brother who had many faces, each one as evil as the next. But Malcolm had a love of destruction as a child. "Today you're uncannily fast brother," said Thomas hauling himself upright again, gasping for breath. Malcolm smiled an evil smile, eyes malevolent, and they seemed to glow like white fire. A web of lightning flashed nearby illuminating the battlements and Malcolm bared his teeth. His mocking laughter boomed out, echoing across the castle ramparts. "We're both fast and killing you will be all the sweeter for it!" he said with a snarl.

"What dread force has ripped your soul away brother?" asked Thomas looking miserable.

Malcolm stared at his brother, his sword flashing towards Thomas' chest. "Never had one!" he snapped.

Thomas sidestepped, blocking the thrust, but a fist hit him in the face again as he shifted from one foot to the other. The blow sent him sprawling to the ground. Bright lights shone before his eyes, dizziness swamping him, and through a great buzzing in his ears, he heard his brother's mocking laughter. Thomas' strong face trembled, and he couldn't focus his eyes on Malcolm.

Again Thomas hauled himself upright but was so unsteady he tripped and toppled over the battlements. Pure instinct saved him from falling to his death when his hand shot out grasping the top of the wall. Thomas clung on with his fingertips and glanced back over his shoulder at the long drop beneath him. Panic ripped through his soul.

Malcolm loomed over him. "There's much here to think upon before you die. What would a man's last thoughts be before the eternal blackness engulfs him? And the answer to that question is he leaves his loved one's behind, unprotected and at the mercy of a murdering monster!" Again his laughter boomed out across the battlements.

Thomas' face-hardened. Now the fear gripping him was not of falling. Lira and his children's faces floated before him and his right hand flashed to his boot and back up again, the shiny glint of his razor-sharp knife blade flashing before Malcolm's eyes. It slammed into his neck and blood gouted from the severed jugular, drenching Thomas' face.

Malcolm struggled upright and then slumped to the floor with his back to the wall. More images flashed before Thomas' eyes. His battered mother lying dead in her bed, his father hanging from the gallows, Master Gallus his mentor slumped dead at his feet, and he realised that the sharpness of his sorrows would never fade away. A great sadness touched him then, and he knew he would never recover from it. Thomas sighed, watching Malcolm's warm blood drip through his fingers and then he climbed clear of the wall.

Thomas dropped the knife and rose to his full height to the sound of loud cheers from the crowd below him. Malcolm shuddered, breathing hard. He hauled himself upright from the wall. It stunned Thomas. Blood was pouring from the wound to Malcolm's neck and pooling at his feet. He groaned and sat cross-legged staring at his brother.

Malcolm smiled weakly. "I didn't want to kill you, brother. I wanted you to kill me because I've seen and done things no man should see or do. Horrible things, murderous things.

But I'm mad, driven so by the bite of a rabid wolf."

Thomas looked to his brother, unable to speak.

Malcolm stared at his own trembling hands. "When the disease had taken a hold of me, I began to get bad feelings and hear strange voices in my head, foam at the mouth, get intense pain in my skull and I just wanted it all to stop. And now it has, and it's time to die." His voice echoed. Closing his eyes, he lowered his head until his chin rested on his chest and he looked peaceful, sitting there unmoving. He took his last breath and stopped breathing.

The rain lashed down and mist swirled in murky trailers around his stilled body, making him look ghostlike. Thunder drummed out and a web of lightning flashed nearby, illuminating the castle. Thomas gave a short respectful bow, his eyes fixed on his dead brother. Strangely, there was a peaceful smile etched on Malcolm's face. And for a single heartbeat, before he had closed his eyes, Thomas saw something eminently human beacon from them. Now the rabid, murdering monster that was his brother was no more. Through misted eyes he stared at his brother's lifeless body and sighed, more memories flaring. "You've nothing more to fear brother, I am dead," whispered Malcolm's spirit voice inside Thomas' head and that was the last time the voice ever spoke to him.

EPILOGUE

The following is an extract from Nottingham's archives by Lira, daughter of Tobin the Blacksmith who took over as recorder from her father after his murder.

"It is summer now and my husband is away again, protecting the weak and innocent. Dody, Cyrano's son, went with him. He has grown even taller, stronger and more handsome. Dardo stayed behind to look after their business interests, and though boisterous and untamed he still lives with his beautiful mistress in the Southern Quarter of Nottingham, practising with sword and bow every day. Thomas' mastery of both weapons has rubbed off on him. And because of Thomas' intervention against evil doers, Nottingham has never seemed so tranquil. Every day that passes is a joy, and the poor people have shared in the treasure that Thomas and friends found in the Lionheart's hidden tomb. All of Nottingham blesses my husband's soul for the kindness shown to them. Now we hold festivals and nice folk come from everywhere to take part in the strangest games and events I have ever seen. All belie description and beggar belief, as usual, so come see them with your own eyes.

The inn is busier than ever and still the best place for miles around for decent people to visit. Rowdy, violent customers no longer frequent it since Thomas, Dardo and Dody went into partnership and the food is exquisite and served on time while still hot. The crops are growing well this year too and show much promise. We pray it remains so.

I will finish my entry now and go back to my duties, but please be sure to make time to visit Nottingham if you are passing. The Old Abbey is still one of the most beautiful sights for miles around, and this one thing alone makes the visit worthwhile."

Lira, Daughter of Tobin the Blacksmith (Recorder of the Archive).

THE END

And if you have enjoyed reading this novel please leave a review.

Printed in Dunstable, United Kingdom